FREE RANGE INSTITUTION

A MICK MURPHY KEY WEST MYSTERY

FREE RANGE INSTITUTION

MICHAEL HASKINS

FIVE STAR
A part of Gale, Cengage Learning

Detroit • New York • San Francisco • New Haven, Conn • Waterville, Maine • London

GALE
CENGAGE Learning

Copyright © 2011 by Michael Haskins.

Permission to use Lyrics from the song "Free Range Institution" was granted by Scott Kirby.

Five Star Publishing, a part of Gale, Cengage Learning.

Set in 11 pt. Plantin.

LIBRARY OF CONGRESS CATALOGING-IN-PUBLICATION DATA

Haskins, Michael.
  Free range institution : a Mick Murphy Key West mystery / Michael Haskins. — 1st ed.
    p. cm.
  ISBN-13: 978-1-59414-929-0
  ISBN-10: 1-59414-929-1
  1. Journalists—Fiction. 2. Key West (Fla.)—Fiction. 3. Drug traffic—Fiction. I. Title.
  PS3608.A84F74 2011
  813'.6—dc22   2010043351

First Edition. First Printing: February 2011.

Published in 2011 in conjunction with Tekno Books and Ed Gorman.

Printed in the United States of America
1 2 3 4 5 6 7 15 14 13 12 11

This book is dedicated to the memories of: Norm Cote, the gentlest tough guy there ever was; a better friend you couldn't ask for. Henry Haskins; we were related by mutual choice, not the accident of birth. I miss his tales of old Key West. Marshall Smith, extraordinary bookseller and friend.

As in all things I do, in memory of Sean Michael Haskins.

I miss them.

I especially thank my family, by blood and marriage. Because of their support and love, I have been able to live a life that has often left them wondering about my sanity. I promise I will eventually find it.

ACKNOWLEDGMENTS

Thanks to Jim Linder for reading the many drafts of this book and letting me take advantage of his military experiences and his knowledge of the world of drug cartels. He answered my questions, often more than once, until I understood.

Three good friends—Bob Pierce, who has forgotten more about sailing than I will ever know and he still goes out on the water with me; and Bill Lane, for his friendship and advertising knowledge and letting me take advantage of both; these guys have proven themselves to be good sounding boards when I got stuck in the story. Paul Clarin for letting me pick his brain about handguns and many other things, like pizza, photography, blue money and auto repair. And thanks to Key West troubadours Scott Kirby, www.scottkirby.com, and Michael McCloud, www.michaelmccloud.com, for their songs of Key West; they are inspirational. Last, but not least, I want to thank Bill Hoebee for the air time and his invaluable advice on bar life, rum and weirdness in Key West.

The characters and events in this book are fictitious. Any similarity to real persons, living or dead, is coincidental and not intended by the author.

FREE RANGE INSTITUTION
WRITTEN BY SCOTT KIRBY

I'm living in a free range institution
It's a three-ring circus, with twelve-step programs to choose
    from
An open air asylum, at its best
Your shrink says you need a little sun and rest
Baby, check yourself right in to Key West

We ain't got no bars on our windows
We ain't got no windows on our bars
My doctor, he's a fiend for martinis
He trades me my medication for his brain darts

I'm living in a free range institution
It's a three-ring circus, with twelve-step programs to choose
    from
An open air asylum at its best
Your shrink says you need a little sun and rest
Baby, check yourself right into Key West

And yes, we've got a yacht club
For the criminally insane
PT boats, men in white coats
And the mayor's locked up in chains
I'm living in a free range institution

Jackson, he's running from his ex-wives

9

Jackson's girlfriend's running from the law
I guess we're here all running from our ex-lives
Voluntarily committed, to a flaw

ONE

Tita and I walked the short block from Key West Island Books to Duval Street, wandering between tourists as they window-shopped, drank beer from plastic cups and ignored traffic lights. It was nice to have her back from Boston and talking to me.

The six-story, conch-shell-pink Hotel Key West filled one corner block at Duval and Sweetzer streets, its color faded to a dull white. A yuppie coffee shop took up most of the street side of the hotel's first floor and the Chalice Room, once the hotel's trendy restaurant and bar, had its windows covered with brown wrapping paper. It would reopen soon with a new name and menu. Key West could hold back change for only so long.

Tita stopped to look at the clothing displays in the large windows of Excess. I wanted to get to Jack Flat's, a half block down the street, for a late lunch.

"I love this outfit." She pointed at a mannequin dressed in designer jeans and white blouse.

I turned to look and caught the window reflection of a body falling through the air like a clumsy bird, with only the traffic on a crowded street to stop it. I turned and looked, as the body crashed onto a car's roof.

A wide-brimmed straw hat, with a bright red bandanna wrapped around it, hung high in the air for a moment and then continued its swaying descent toward the street. It was the style of hat that workers along the waterfront wear, because the wide brim offers protection from the sun. I knew a guy who had

11

added a red bandanna to his hat, but I didn't think he was suicidal.

Hotel Key West is one of the tallest buildings in Key West and, historically, has been the spot for jumpers, but that didn't happen too often.

People and traffic stopped, intrigued and shaken, as their minds computed what they had seen. The hat hit the street and skidded across to the curb. Then an impatient driver beeped a horn. As if it were a sign, people began screaming.

The woman driving the lead car in oncoming traffic stepped outside, pointed at the crumpled body and screamed. She had witnessed the deadly collision.

The body's impact bent the car's roof, and the man driving couldn't get either door open. I watched him try. He panicked as blood from the victim began to trickle down the windshield.

Tita turned when the pandemonium started, and she looked for the cause.

"What happened?" She stared at the stalled traffic.

I pointed toward the car stopped by the door of the Chalice Room. She grabbed my arm, squeezed it hard, and looked toward the roof of the hotel. I removed her hand, walked to the curb and picked up the hat.

Jay Bruehl, the guy I knew from the waterfront, kept a fifty-dollar bill pinned inside the red bandanna. I found the bill and a half-smoked roach that I tossed aside, and walked back to Tita. People began to stir on the sidewalk, but traffic was at a standstill.

Then things really turned strange.

Marked and unmarked Key West police cars and Monroe County sheriff's cars came from all directions, lights flashing and sirens wailing. One police car raced down Sweetzer Street the wrong way, two blocked the hotel's driveway entrance, while others stopped wherever they wanted to, encircling the hotel.

An unmarked police van pulled into the middle of the intersection of Duval and Sweetzer, and SWAT officers in black, bulky jumpsuits got out.

This was more than a suicide.

Key West Police Chief Richard Dowley came out of one car next to Fast Buck Freddie's department store, kitty-corner from where I stood.

Richard and I went back ten years. I'm Liam Murphy and when I am not sailing, I'm a freelance journalist. I live on my forty-foot sloop, *Fenian Bastard,* and during the years I've picked up the moniker Mad Mick Murphy. Mad because of the crazy stunts I pulled in college and Mick due to my Boston-Irish heritage; the name has nothing to do with being insane, though if you are insane and live in Key West, it makes many things seem sensible.

Tita Toledo, a green-eyed Puerto Rican and younger sister of my college classmate Paco, practiced law in Key West. We have an on-again, off-again romance that we were in the process of turning on again, when Jay's body tumbled from the roof of the hotel.

Sheriff Chance Wagner, in full uniform, walked from the hotel's driveway. This added to the strangeness, because Monroe County sheriffs do not patrol Key West, the local cops do, and here were both.

The SWAT team waited for Richard and Chance to come to them.

Two men in street clothes, wearing windbreakers with DEA stenciled on the back, walked to the damaged car and stared down at the body, before calling two uniformed officers to help them force open the car's doors. The two cops helped the emotional driver to the sidewalk.

Police closed off Duval at Eaton and Southard streets, which stopped traffic from moving up or down the main street, and

13

then directed vehicles stuck in the traffic to turn onto Sweetzer, to move away. Sweetzer was blocked at Whitehead Street, stopping cross traffic. As the street cleared of vehicles, an ambulance pulled next to the damaged car. There was so much going on, I couldn't take it all in.

Cops began moving people along, clearing the sidewalk. Onlookers snapped quick cell-phone photos of the body. When they arrived home, the photo would fit in with the shots of free-range chickens, dogs wearing sunglasses while riding scooters and drunks painted silver, pretending to be twitching statues; a photo safari of Key Weird.

"Let's go," Tita whispered as a cop approached.

People hurried past us, some turning for one last look at the body, as they told the story on their phones.

"Something's going on." I turned to her. "This isn't because of a jumper."

"You think they're going to tell you?"

"Richard might."

"Isn't that Chance Wagner?"

"Yeah."

"He's not a big fan of yours." She ran her words together.

"Go to Jack Flat's and have Susan put your lunch on my tab." I looked around for Richard. "I'll be there in a little while."

"I've lost my appetite, Mick." She couldn't hide the distress in her words. "But I could use a drink."

"I'll be there as soon as I can."

"I am leaving after one drink." She walked away.

Tita and I were almost on-again, but if I didn't hurry, it would be off-again. People pushed by me, stumbling, not wanting to go, but cops kept yelling at them.

"You, too," the young rookie said.

"I'm with the press."

"Good for you." He smiled, enjoying his moment of control.

"Be a member of the press from behind the police lines."

"Chief Dowley is expecting me," I lied, and looked toward the SWAT team.

"Wait here." He walked across the street while other cops moved the last stragglers across Sweetzer toward Southard.

The rookie held off approaching Richard until the SWAT team began to disperse. After speaking to him, Richard turned in my direction and motioned for me to come over.

"What are you doing here, Mick?" He is a big man, six-four and a good two hundred and fifty pounds. Richard's cop's eyes told me he had enough trouble without me hanging around. "Tell me it's a coincidence that you're standing on the corner."

"Honest to God, Richard."

"Neither of us believes in coincidence." I followed as he walked toward the body. "Do you know him?"

Two medics stood outside their ambulance, smoking. There was no need to verify the person was dead. Jay lay on his back, his arms and legs twisted at unnatural angles; blood caked around his eyes and mouth. It formed a narrow stream that ran off the car's roof and down the front windshield.

"I think it's Jay Bruehl." I waved the hat at him. "This is his hat. It came down after the body hit."

"So you're tampering with evidence?"

"If I hadn't picked it up, it would've been stomped on." I handed it to him. "Jay always kept a fifty-dollar bill pinned inside the bandanna."

Richard turned the bandanna and saw the bill. "You left it."

"Smart ass."

"How'd you know to be here, Mick?" His tone was that of a cop, not a friend.

Jay spent a lot of time working on boats, all kinds of boats. His skin had burned a furrowed reddish-copper long ago and it was quickly fading to a pasty brown while he lay on the car's roof. He didn't smell too good, either. He was also a snitch who liked to play undercover cop and that, I guessed, was how he ended up dead.

"I talked to Jay yesterday." It wasn't a lie: I had run into him at Schooner Wharf Bar.

"And?" Richard held Jay's hat and led me back in front of Excess. The three young employees stared out from behind the large windows and looked like they were giggling.

"He didn't tell me much, but suggested I be here around this time." I kept eye contact, and tried to sound sincere.

"He wanted you to witness his suicide?" He motioned toward the car with Jay's hat.

"He wasn't suicidal," I said without thinking. I looked toward the hotel's roof. "I think it was a drug deal gone bad and he was pushed."

Richard's hard expression told me he was hiding something, so I figured I might as well play for bigger stakes.

"It must have been some kind of drug deal to have you and the sheriff here. Maybe a big shot was involved, or a politician?"

Richard shook his head in disgust or maybe disappointment, I'm not sure, but his expression indicated impatience.

"You're a piece of work." He growled the words, walked to his car, and tossed Jay's hat through the window. He went to Sheriff Wagner, after turning to make sure I was still there.

The sheriff looked in my direction and, while I couldn't hear, it was obvious he was disagreeing with Richard. When Richard signaled, I walked across the street, now filled with Key West cops, DEA agents and Monroe County deputy sheriffs.

"I don't want you here, Murphy." The sheriff greeted me without a smile.

He's a lean man, a little short of six-foot, probably early sixties, with thinning brown hair and hard brown eyes. He wore his Smokey Bear hat. The sheriff still held a grudge because a

16

few years back I covered a corruption trial that involved his deputies, and he thought I reported more than was necessary. The weekly newsmagazine hired me because I could add color and background to the piece, since I lived in Key West. Some things die hard in the Keys.

"He knows what's going on," Richard said, as an explanation.

I wasn't sure what it was he thought I knew, but guessed my bluff had worked. And now I had to keep it up.

"How? Did you tell him, Chief?" Chance stared at Richard.

"The jumper told him."

Chance turned his stare toward me. "What'd he tell you?"

"To be here at this time."

"That it?"

I hesitated, knowing it would anger the sheriff. "Jay always acted like an undercover cop, and most of us knew he wasn't, but we knew he was a snitch."

"Can you speed this fairy tale along—I have things to do," Chance half yelled.

"He told me about a drug deal going down, big shots, a lot of agencies involved." I rushed the words. "I didn't really believe him. That is, until I saw him falling out of the sky."

"You saw him jump?"

"No, I saw him falling. He just tumbled like a bird with no control."

"He screaming?" Now the sheriff seemed interested in what I had to say.

"No."

"You sure?"

"I didn't hear any screaming. Why?"

"Nothin'." He turned to Richard. "You're responsible for him," he said, and he walked toward the hotel.

"We lost touch with our undercover agent." Richard grabbed

17

my shoulder and moved me toward the hotel. "She's one of Chance's."

"Who else is in the hotel?"

"Colombians."

Two

Richard stopped at the hotel's opened fire-exit door on Sweetzer. SWAT team members held assault weapons as they waited on the stairs in the cramped hallway and listened to the squawking sounds from a communications radio. Tension, mixed with excitement, filled the stairwell and hall; I could see it on their anxious faces. An operation like this rarely happened in Key West, though the county sheriff and city police departments practiced for such contingencies with other state and federal agencies. Chances were good that many of the cops had never gone through this type of procedure before. The thought didn't increase my confidence in getting involved.

We stood without talking on the sidewalk; Richard gave me time to stare into the busy fire exit before he spoke.

"You have anything to tell me, before we go in?"

"Tita and I were leaving Island Books when this all came down." I turned and looked at him. "Up 'til now I never gave much thought to the things Jay said. He was always hinting about being an undercover cop, and no one believed him, but he did know what was going on, on the docks."

"He was our snitch." Richard stared back at me. "And the sheriff's, and led us into this. Now, how much did he brag to you about it?"

"The thing is, when he was talking to me, I wasn't paying attention." I needed to round out the lie, to make my story believable. "I thought of Jay when I was leaving the bookstore, because

19

of the time. When I saw him die, I remembered pieces of what he'd told me."

"His pretending probably got him killed."

"You think it was murder?"

"A jumper usually screams, maybe it's a prayer at the end, I don't know, but you said you heard nothing and you were close."

"Why would the Colombians kill him?"

"We don't know yet, Mick. It might have been an accident or he might have already been dead."

"Which means he was helped over the edge."

A loud command came from within the fire exit, and the men inside began running up the stairway. Richard grabbed my arm and kept me on the outside.

"You wait," he said.

A man stood alone at the bottom of the stairs. An earpiece allowed him to listen quietly to whatever commands came over his radio.

"The sheriff has an undercover agent inside." Richard let go of my arm. "Do you know Rebecca?"

"Rebecca Connelly?"

"Yeah, we lost contact with her a few minutes before your buddy came off the roof." He pushed me forward. "Something went wrong."

"Who's in the hotel? This is more than a Key West rock cocaine bust."

"I guess we'll find out," he said, as we entered the hallway.

I recognized Captain Steve Jones from the police department.

"Second floor is secure, Chief." He nodded to me. "You can go on up."

Richard went first and Steve followed me. Two officers stood by the open fire door on the second floor and we walked into a hallway crowded with armed men. All the doors along the corridor were opened inward and anxious officers paced.

A tall African-American man, wearing a stenciled DEA jacket and hat, came up to Richard shaking his head.

"No one in her room, Chief," he mumbled, not happy with what he had to say. His dark-brown eyes were angry. "The room was neat, though, so nothing happened in it."

"Do we know which room the Colombians were in?"

"Yeah, across the hall, and it was clean too."

"We on the roof?"

The man nodded and Richard walked toward the elevator. I followed.

"Now we need to search the entire hotel," he said to himself, as we entered the elevator. He pushed the button for the roof.

The old mirrored elevator was small and jerked along slowly.

"It doesn't look good." I knew he was talking about Rebecca. "Maybe we'll find some answers up here." The elevator stopped and the doors opened onto the large, airy lobby bar, busy with armed officers and a fantastic view of Key West. "Or maybe not."

Three

The view of Key West from the top of the hotel is breathtaking, even on a rainy afternoon, but it wasn't raining and the men and women running around the roof were not interested in the sights. The private banquet room, across from the rooftop bar, held those unfortunate enough to have been enjoying the view when Jay went off the hotel's pinnacle, with or without help. Teams of uniformed police officers and deputy sheriffs interviewed the potential witnesses; those milling around, waiting for their turn to be questioned, gazed out the large windows, but didn't look like they were enjoying themselves or the panorama.

Behind us, the elevator door closed and I heard the straining sound its cables made as it moved down.

"You wait here," Richard ordered, and went outside.

All the seats around the bar were empty, so I sat at the corner stool. The bartender was in the banquet room; I'm sure he was counting the money this was costing him, in his head. A person could sit at the bar, get a hundred-and-eighty-degree view of the island and the waterfront, and still drink away the afternoon, in air-conditioning and safe from the circus crowds below. There was no better view of the famous Key West sunset; at Mallory Square, the popular location to watch, the celebration was all about being in the middle of the circus.

Everyone ignored me. I felt invisible. A walkway circled the roof for spectators to view all sides of the island, but now cops and deputies searched in both directions. I didn't see Richard or Chance.

I took the small notebook I always carry from my cargo shorts' pocket, along with a mechanical pencil, and started making notes of what I had seen earlier and what was happening around me; it's a journalist's trait that's been with me since Wally Walworth and the Gilhooley brothers accepted the challenge to make a newspaperman out of me. It would be years before I became a journalist. That was at the old Hearst paper in Boston; the paper is no longer there, and I think I am the lone survivor of the foursome. But I did learn how to be a newspaperman from them, beginning while I was the weekend office boy in high school; I learned more from the three of them than I ever did in college classes.

Bored, I stood up and was ignored, even by the few cops I knew. Some gave me a nod, others plodded along. I walked to the glass doors, opened them and walked outside, only to run into Richard and Chance.

"Going somewhere?" Richard grasped my shoulder.

"I thought you were lost." I tried a smile, but it was met with a frown. "All right, I watched all the officers circling the rooftop and got to wondering why. Obviously, you haven't found where Jay went off the roof."

"We found the spot." He looked at the sheriff.

"So what is everyone looking for?"

"None of your damn business," Chance hissed and walked away.

Richard pushed me away from the doors and backed me up against one of the bar's large windows.

"Mick, sometimes the less said the better." He ran his hands through his hair. "Rebecca is missing and Chance doesn't have the time or patience to put up with you."

"They searching all the rooms?" I knew there were almost

two hundred rooms in the hotel.

"The idea was to catch them all, Mick," Richard mumbled in frustration.

"So you think they're still in the hotel?" What I was thinking as I said this was how stupid it was of me to leave my cameras in the Jeep. I should have known better.

"I think they threw Jay off the roof as a diversion." He was angry. "We were depending on Rebecca to ID 'em. Without her, they could've walked out the back when we evacuated the hotel."

"If you're right, Rebecca is still somewhere inside."

"Yeah. Maybe they didn't leave and are hiding in one of the rooms with her," he said without much conviction. "We checked the basement, first floor, and all the rooms on the second floor."

It was going to be a long operation, but one of their own was missing and in danger, so it didn't matter how long it took. I looked out across the rooftops of Key West. The springtime sun shone brightly and boats moved across the Gulf of Mexico. Halfway down Fleming, the sign for Fausto's sparkled, and I thought of the Jimmy Buffett song that mentioned the family-owned market. Buffett didn't write about this side of Key West.

"What can I do?" I knew Rebecca and thought there was some way I might help.

"Get the fuck out of here and let me do my job," Richard grumbled. "Chance is already pissed because you're here. When I know something, I'll call you." He opened the glass door and we walked to the elevator.

"Richard. . . ."

"Don't say anything, Mick, just go." He pushed the elevator call button. "This is turning into a shit-storm and I don't need you in the way."

The elevator door opened. Richard hit the button for the first floor, pushed me in and walked away.

FOUR

The elevator doors opened onto the small hallway that contained the back door to Starbucks and a walkway to the hotel's main lobby. The trendy coffee shop was closed to the public, as were the surrounding streets, but it did a brisk business from cops armed with automatic weapons and steaming cups of cappuccinos and lattes. Through the shop's front windows, I could see Jay's body lying on the roof of the car and rookie cops as they patrolled the empty street.

The crowded shop made me uncomfortable. I didn't want to walk through it, so I took the side emergency exit I'd come in earlier with Richard, and it put me back on Sweetzer Street. Captain Steve Jones ran the situation from upstairs now.

Emergency lights flashed from police cars, and armed men stood around the street, anxious for something to happen, while I walked toward Jack Flat's, knowing Tita hadn't waited. Maybe our relationship was off again. I hoped not, but knew whatever the result it was my fault.

The curious filled Jimmy Buffett's Margaritaville bar, hanging out the large open window with drinks in hand, and jammed the sidewalk, staring up the half block toward the hotel; across the street, the entrance of Jack Flat's was crowded, too. I pushed my way through the outdoor collection of the curious and found weekend sports fans crowding the bar, as a dozen TVs played a variety of games. A handful of customers sat at tables, but Tita wasn't anywhere. Padre Thomas Collins sat alone at a back

25

table and waved me over.

Padre Thomas is an Irish-born Jesuit who sees and talks to angels. An angel told him to walk away from his mission church in Guatemala years ago. He is a skinny, five-foot-eight, sunburned man in his late fifties, who chain-smokes Camel cigarettes and volunteers his services to St. Mary Star of the Sea's soup kitchen. His pale-blue eyes are the most intense I have ever seen. And, in the years I've known him, I have come to believe him about the angels.

A half glass of draft beer and an opened package of cigarettes were on the table when I sat down. Hatless, he wore a blue sleeveless buttoned-down-collar dress shirt, extra packages of cigarettes in the pocket, cargo shorts and sandals, his usual attire. He'd cut the sleeves off the shirt himself. A nervous guy by nature, Padre Thomas looked horrible. Dark circles made pouches under his eyes, which were more red than blue.

Alexis Bolter, the waitress, brought me a Sam Adams and a bill.

"Tita said to give this to you." She handed me the bill for a rum and Coke.

Scribbled on the back was one word, *Thanks!* I gave Alexis seven dollars and she walked away.

"Tita didn't stay long." Padre Thomas played with his cigarette package. "Have they found the body yet?"

"Which body?" I took a swallow of beer.

"The one they're lookin' for at the hotel."

No cop would have told him what was going on, even if one knew. My conclusion, as unrealistic as it sounded, was the angels.

"Is that why you're here?"

"In a way," he mumbled, with a mouthful of beer. "I'm looking for you." His somber tone matched his trampled look.

"Well, you found me, what do you need?"

26

"A cigarette." He smiled, and sipped his beer. "Do you believe in evil, Mick? I mean, an evil it seems impossible to stop?" He rubbed his weary eyes.

I thought of Central and South American death squads, but said nothing about them.

"I see it every night on the news, in the Middle East and Africa."

"Could you see it here, in Key West?"

The noise from the sports fans made conversation difficult, but I clearly heard his words and the concern they carried. A lot of people thought Padre Thomas was either a fake or crazy, but for some reason he had chosen me as his confessor, and I've come to believe him to be intelligent and sincere. In his own mind, he is a Jesuit who communicates with angels. He knew things that were unexplainable, unless you accepted the angels.

"No, Padre, I couldn't." I took a long pull from the bottle of beer. "What's concerning you? You look horrible."

"The evil isn't coming, Mick. It's already here." He pulled a cigarette from the package and put it in his mouth. "Jay's dead. I saw his body and there's a dead cop inside the hotel."

"How do you know the cop's dead?"

He stared at me, and his eyes almost came to life. He didn't need to answer.

"Where's her body?" It wouldn't be the first time he helped solve a crime because of his knowledge.

"I don't know." He took his eyes away. "In a dark place that's noisy."

"You wanna take a walk, have a smoke?"

He nodded and picked up his package of cigarettes, the unlit one still dangling from his lips.

"How many beers have you had?" I always seem to pick up his bar tabs.

"Three," he said, and walked toward the exit.

27

I left Alexis twenty dollars under my empty beer bottle and followed Padre Thomas, curious about an evil that couldn't be stopped.

FIVE

Padre Thomas had smoked his cigarette when I came out of the restaurant. Most of the curious were gone and people walked along the sidewalk, ignored by the police, who still had the streets closed. The coroner had removed Jay's body, but the damaged car, pulled over to the curb, waited for a wrecker.

We stopped at the corner of Duval and Sweetzer streets, and Padre Thomas lit another cigarette as he stared across the street at Hotel Key West. Even though most of the cops were elsewhere, the coffee shop was busy. Across the way at Excess, the young girls that had giggled at Jay's death were with customers.

"They haven't found the cop." He dropped the smoldering butt into the street and we crossed.

"That deputy's name is Rebecca Connelly and I know her." I took a cigar from my pocket, cut the end off, and lit it. Padre Thomas was making me nervous.

"I'm sorry." He lit another cigarette and kept walking. "I wish I knew more."

"Me, too."

Police continued to turn traffic off Duval onto Eaton Street, where we stopped. He glanced up at St. Paul's Episcopal Church and slowly shook his head. The old church's stained-glass windows were open for the afternoon breeze, and tourists walked in and out. Key West's free-range chickens, two roosters, a half dozen hens and too many chicks pecked at the manicured lawn and tossed up the flowerbeds.

"I need a favor." We crossed with the light. "You know Captain Maybe, right?"

Captain Maybe had to be in his eighties and spent most of his life on the water, the last forty years in Key West. When asked a direct question, especially one that required a yes-or-no answer, he always replied *maybe, maybe.* He was Captain Maybe when I arrived more than twelve years ago and that is how most people knew him.

"Yeah, I know him. What's the problem?"

"You remember the kid's story about the little train that thought it could? 'I think I can, I think I can,' it responded when asked if it could make it over the hill." For a brief moment, he smiled. "That's Captain Maybe's story. He was never sure of what he could do, so he always replied, maybe, and now it's kind of his trademark. Some people think it's a joke because he's an old man."

"A sick old man, I hear." We were close to the two-hundred block of Duval, and the tourists were everywhere. It was a chamber-of-commerce spring afternoon, with warm sun shining and a clear sky above. Hints of honeysuckle wafted in the breeze.

"Yes, a very sick old man."

We stopped at the intersection of Duval and Greene streets, in front of Sloppy Joe's where the crowd inside yelled and laughed as the two comic-musicians on stage strummed their guitars and told off-color jokes. Padre Thomas lit his last cigarette and tossed the empty, wrinkled package into a trash container.

"Do we have a destination, Padre?" I enjoyed my cigar, but the honeysuckle was gone, replaced by the stench of spilt beer, sweat, marijuana and restless excitement.

"Hog's Breath Saloon." He crossed Duval Street toward Rick's Bar and then crossed Greene Street, and we continued along Duval toward the saloon.

"Do we have a purpose?" It was rhetorical, because Padre Thomas always had a purpose.

"Yes, I have to remove a burden from me and give it to you." He stopped and opened a new pack of Camels. "Captain Maybe has very little time to live and he doesn't want to die in a hospital. He wants to die at sea."

"Is it cancer?" I heard months ago that he had gone to Miami for treatment.

"Yes." He lit the cigarette. "And he has decided against treatment. He feels there is no hope and the treatments will only take away what quality of life he has left."

"Cancer does that, Padre. I remember my father dying in Boston." A flash of anger shot through me. "The shitty doctor at the Catholic hospital was about as sympathetic as a Nazi at the death camps. He told my father, in front of all of us, that he was gonna die and could give him something for the pain, but not enough so he could kill himself. I wanted to punch the son of a bitch."

"I'm sorry, Mick." He inhaled deeply and let the smoke come out his thin nose. "But the Church wouldn't allow him to help your father kill himself."

"My father would never have killed himself." I bit down on the stub of my cigar. "It was the cold, careless way he said it, the way he treated my father."

"I'll pray for your father's soul." He looked at me, his eyes too red to show their true color. "And for your forgiveness for the doctor."

I said nothing, letting the long-ago hate rush through me. We had stopped in front of a T-shirt shop.

"I tried to convince Captain Maybe to go for the treatments." He dropped the butt onto the sidewalk and stepped on it. "But he has a strange story to tell and I can't deal with it, not with

31

everything else that is coming down."

"You lost me there, Padre. What is coming down?"

He took a cigarette from the new package and lit it. I had never seen him chain-smoke like this. Something was eating away at him, and it made me nervous thinking about it.

"The evil, Mick, the evil." His eyes bulged as he hissed the words. "What is happening at the hotel is part of it."

We were only yards away from Hog's Breath Saloon, so I grabbed his arm and we moved on. "Let's deal with Captain Maybe and then you can tell me about the evil."

Six

The Hog's Breath Saloon is one of my favorite bars. It's open to the elements, has live entertainment, friendly bartenders, and doesn't pretend to be what it isn't. A jury-rigged canopy protects the small outdoor bandstand from sun and rain; the concrete floor is cracked and uneven from foot traffic, and two large trees grow in at different areas of the outdoor section, offering shade during the setting sun and a place for free-range roosters to crow.

I followed Padre Thomas through the crowded, outdoor bar into the interior restaurant and found Captain Maybe, the old pirate, sitting at a corner table by the T-shirt shop entrance. He didn't look sick, he looked old. His bushy white hair and close-cropped beard framed his leathery face, and a large smile showed stained teeth. He would never be mistaken for a Disney pirate, but I heard stories that suggested he had been one when he was a smuggler.

Lively brown eyes betrayed the imp hidden inside Captain Maybe. His long, bony fingers held a cup of soda and he stood as we approached. We shook hands and his grip was firm, but he looked thinner than the last time I'd seen him. Like Padre Thomas, Captain Maybe wore an old, faded-yellow sleeveless dress shirt, cargo shorts and sandals. The popularity of wearing Oxford-collared dress shirts, minus the sleeves, instead of T-shirts was growing. His arms and legs were muscular from his years on the water. Unless you've lived on a sailboat, you can't

33

appreciate the work it takes to keep her shipshape, and sailing is great for building upper-body strength.

"Can I buy you a drink?" he asked as we sat down.

We ordered two beers from Kris and waited quietly for them to be delivered.

"Thank you for coming, Mick," Captain Maybe crunched a piece of ice from his cup of soda. "I need to ask a favor."

"No, first you've got to tell him your story." Padre Thomas took a cigarette from his pocket.

Captain Maybe stared at me and smiled. "Once a priest, always a priest," he laughed. "Here I am telling the good padre why I believe in God, and he doesn't like my reasoning."

"You are on your own, you stubborn old coot, but you gave me your word," he said, with a fondness that indicated a long-term friendship.

"I did, Padre, I did, and I am a man of my word."

"So tell Mick." Padre Thomas turned to me. "You won't believe this."

Captain Maybe smiled. "I believe it, and that's what's important."

"I'm not sure what I'm doing here, guys," I said, to help speed it along.

"Mick, you don't know much about me," Captain Maybe began. "A long time ago I was married, with a son, two daughters and a lot of money." He scratched his nose. "I still have the daughters and most of the money. When my son died, my wife left me, and I went to sea. If the truth be told, one of the reasons she left was I wanted us all to go to sea."

He made eye contact as he talked, but never seemed to find a comfortable position in his chair. "It seems like a long time ago now, so, whenever it was, my oldest daughter became ill with what the doctors thought was a neurological problem. For no reason she'd lose feeling in her legs or arms for a while and she began to have horrible migraines." His face tightened with pain as he remembered. "She went to the best specialists in Boston and New York. They all had opinions, but not answers. The frustration was killing her . . . and me." He paused and took a sip of his soda.

"I need a cigarette." Padre Thomas walked to the outdoor bar.

"I guess he gets upset at this part," Captain Maybe mumbled, as if it confused him that he could upset Padre Thomas. "Anyway, Mick, I don't know how, but I ended up in a church after taking my daughter home from a doctor's visit. I hadn't been in a church in a long time and I ain't sure I was even a believer. But there I was, on my knees praying. . . ." He stopped and I could see his expression change. "No, it wasn't praying. I was trying to make a deal with God." His eyes watered and he rubbed the tears away with a paper napkin.

"Did you make a deal?"

"Yeah." He blew his nose in the napkin. "I told God . . . maybe I asked Him . . . that if He needed to take someone, He should take me. I told Him I already knew how cruel it was to have a parent bury a child, especially one so young and beautiful and talented." The tears came again and he wiped them away, unembarrassed. "I made an agreement with Him, me for her, and I walked out of the church feeling it was a done deal."

He wiped his eyes again and finished his soda. "My daughter got better," he said with a smile. "And today she's healthy and happy and married. A few months ago I found out I have cancer. I guess that's no secret on the rock. Is it?"

"Rumor has it." I sipped the final drops of my beer.

"Well, I got it and I got it good." He smiled again, as if it was a reason to be happy. "I went to Miami six weeks ago and the specialists told me what to expect and what they could do for me. When I walked around the hospital I saw men and women

35

of all ages, walking the halls with IVs attached to poles. Others were in wheelchairs, IVs hung above 'em. The living dead, that's what I saw." He frowned, remembering. "I forgot all about my deal with God, and then the doctors were telling me about treatments and hope and how no one knew what cures might be found overnight, and it was like then that God slapped me upside the head." He laughed softly. "He was calling in my marker! I got up and walked out of the hospital and flew to my daughters." His smile widened. "I didn't want my life to end in a hospital, one of the living dead."

He signaled for another soda, and Kris brought us both drinks.

"I looked back on my life, after that experience, and concluded that I'm pretty satisfied with it. There are things I didn't do and a few things I shouldn't a done, even a few I would probably do differently, if I could do 'em again, but overall I've had a good life. I couldn't really ask for more. Want, yeah, sure, but deserve, I don't know.

"I left Miami and spent a month with my daughters. It was nice. We had videos taken of me and the grandkids and photos, so later, when I'm gone, they'll have something to remember me by. I like that." He nodded to me.

"That's nice," I said. "It'll be something they'll always cherish."

"Yeah, they will," he said. "Anyway, now I believe in God. I ain't afraid to die because I have proof He exists."

"Because you have cancer?"

"Because He's calling in my marker, yeah, I'm dying. I never welched on a bet in my life, Mick, and I ain't about to begin. My daughter lived and the doctors had no explanation for it, but I do. That's when I knew there was a God. I just kind of lost track after I didn't die that first year or two. Hell, He gave me more than twenty years to enjoy and I sure did enjoy 'em."

Arguing with Captain Maybe about his deal with God would have been like arguing with Padre Thomas about his angels. I couldn't fault him, if the memory helped him find peace with his own death. He had a month with those he loved, and that's more than a lot of us get before we die.

"Do your daughters know?"

"Hell, no!" He laughed. "They'd think I was crazy and want me to take the treatments. Damn, Mick, I don't want them to see me at the end, remember me that way, an old man kept alive by an IV drip. No, they got the video and photos of Pops, that's what they call me, and that's how they'll remember me."

"Sounds like you got it all worked out, Captain." I finished my second beer and didn't want another.

"He telling you he's got his deal with God?" Padre Thomas sat down. "You believe him?"

"Why not," I said. "You have your angels, why can't he have a deal with God?"

"And God waited almost twenty years to take him?"

"Aren't you the one who lectures me on how our idea of time isn't God's? What is it you told me once, a thousand years is but a blink of the eye to God. If that's true, twenty years is probably less time to God than what it took you to smoke your cigarette." I enjoyed tossing some of his words back at him.

"I'm eighty-five," Captain Maybe said. "I've done all I can do about death. I've eluded it for years by exercising and watching my diet and being moderate with alcohol. I don't have a complaint about dying now. I just wanna do it on my own terms and that means not being a burden to my family or anyone else."

"It sounds like you're giving up." Padre Thomas signaled for a beer. "There is always hope, a miracle."

"Well, Padre, hope, in my case, doesn't exist because the cancer has spread throughout my body. I could delay dying and

37

die something I ain't; or I could go sailing and die on the water. Miracles, I would rather have them saved for my girls, if they ever need 'em."

We sat quietly listening to the mixed conversations from within the restaurant and the live music that wafted in from the outdoor stage. I didn't need the two beers I'd had and I certainly didn't want another one.

"Captain Maybe, I respect your decision." I drained my beer. "Is there something you need me to do?"

"Yeah, there is." He pulled two manila envelopes from the seat next to him. "I have a small home on William Street, close to the cemetery." It embarrassed him to admit owning property. "And I got some rental properties in other parts of Old Town. Padre Thomas and I talked and agreed you were the best man to handle this." He pulled some papers from one of the envelopes and handed them to me.

I looked at power-of-attorney forms, all filled out, and signed by everyone, including a notary, but lacking my signature. "I don't understand." I scanned the papers.

"A couple of those give you direction to sell all my property and distribute the money between my daughters. All but my house on William Street," Captain Maybe said. "The kids are cosigners on my other bank accounts and investments, but not on anything in Key West." He opened the other envelope and pulled out a book. "I have a library you will appreciate. Lots of first editions and many signed. In payment for doing this for me, I'll give you this book. I'm told it's one of your favorites."

I took the book and was shocked to see a first edition of Hemingway's *The Sun Also Rises*. The dust cover was well preserved and in plastic. I opened the book; it was signed. Its value was in the thousands.

"I can't accept this." I closed the book and offered it back. "This is valuable."

"I know, but you're the only person I trust to see my library is sold at its real value." He smiled and pushed the book back into my hands. "Your friend Mitch at Island Books can do most of the work and you can see that the money reaches my daughters."

"Captain, I'll be happy to do this for you without payment. Do you know this book is worth more than ten thousand bucks?"

"I'm a big Hemingway fan. I bought most all his works, signed, right after his suicide." Captain Maybe thought back years; I could see it in his expression. "I think that edition cost me less than a grand."

"How many books do you have?"

"More than a thousand."

I whistled. "What about your house on William Street, what happens to that?"

"Padre Thomas lives there and it's his for as long as he wants it." He smiled. "When he doesn't want it, my daughters can figure out what to do with it."

I scanned all the papers. There were rental properties that he wanted offered to the renters at below market value, but that still showed a profit for his daughters. His instructions for the properties and books were clear.

"Okay, Captain." I signed the papers, all three copies, and handed them back. "It instructs me to begin this in ninety days."

"I'm told I have less than three months to live." He stood up and put the papers in an envelope. "My attorney will send you your copy of these. Mick, thank you, it helps to know you will take care of this for me."

"You're my friend, Captain, I'm glad to help. I only wish the circumstances were different."

"I don't." He almost laughed. "I saved my daughter's life and believe in God. I have no regrets." He walked out through the T-shirt shop, whistling.

39

"Thank you, Mick." Padre Thomas picked up the Hemingway book. "God forgive me, but he's probably doing the right thing."

"He's braver than I would be." I took the book, looked at Hemingway's signature, and then put it back into the manila envelope.

"Maybe his faith is stronger than yours."

"I'm sure it is." I went to stand up. "I need to get something to eat."

"But I still need your help." He reached out, grabbed my wrist and squeezed.

"With what?"

"The evil, Mick." He let go of my wrist. "What are we gonna do about the evil that's here? Jay is dead and the deputy is dead, and if we don't do something, it's only the beginning."

SEVEN

I wanted to call Tita, explain what happened, take her to dinner and avoid Padre Thomas's discussion on evil, but it didn't look like I'd be successful. I could have eaten at Hog's Breath, but I thought getting up to leave would be a hint that I wanted to be on my own. Padre Thomas didn't get it. Or more likely, he ignored it.

"You should call Tita." He lit a cigarette as we walked through the parking lot to Duval Street.

"Yeah, I need to," I mumbled, and thought maybe he could read minds, too. "Where you off to?"

"We can eat wherever you want." He exhaled smoke through his nose. "My bike's locked up across from your Jeep."

Traffic filled Duval Street; it was a mixture of worn, tinny-sounding scooters that belched smoke, loud motorcycles, cars and trucks in a variety of makes, colors and conditions, and those god-awful snail-paced electric cars tourists pack into to crawl along the streets. Like walking around the island wouldn't be a health benefit to them.

The extended daylight that came with spring kept the late afternoon sun warming the sidewalks, as groups of men and women window-shopped along Lower Duval. Padre Thomas and I became part of the gaudy parade as we walked toward Hotel Key West, dodging crowds that held drinks in plastic cups and stopped in the middle of the sidewalk to talk or gawk.

Two Key West police cars remained parked outside the hotel,

41

but the deputy sheriffs' cruisers and unmarked cars were gone. Starbucks had a line waiting to order, and traffic rushed along Duval, to stop only when the signal light turned red. Everything seemed normal; there were no signs of the violence from only a few hours ago.

"The chief didn't call you," Padre Thomas said, as if he was reading my thoughts.

"Nothing to tell me, I guess." We crossed to the other side of the street and stopped outside Jack Flat's. "You coming in?"

"We need to talk." He inhaled deeply and tossed the smoldering cigarette into the street.

Basketball fans watched the NBA playoff games on a selection of TV screens that hung above the bar, and baseball fanatics watched a variety of games on the bar's other TVs. The sound was off, but the crowd made up for it with their applause, mixed with cries of "Foul!" and loud explanations of what should have been.

It's often pointed out to me that I'm one of very few American males that do not follow sports. My father was a big baseball and hockey fan, but it didn't rub off on me. He often spent evenings and weekends in front of the TV watching sports and sipping his highball. Once or twice a year he would take us to Fenway Park to watch a Red Sox game, and the only thing I remember about those pilgrimages were the large, delicious hot dogs and wondering why my mother couldn't get the same ones at the Stop and Shop. When I was growing up, they were frankfurters, a word not heard often in Key West.

Padre Thomas led me to a table at the far end of the cavernous bar, where the screams and cries of sports fans echoed off the wall. Alexis brought me a Sam Adams and a draught for Padre Thomas.

"Are you eating?" She smiled the whitest smile in the Keys.

"Cheeseburger, well done." My smile paled in comparison.

"Dolphin sandwich," Padre Thomas said, while he stared at me, his blue eyes circled in red.

"Be right back." And she left.

We sipped our beers. I was curious as to what could turn this usually upbeat-but-hyper priest into a neurotic paranoid. I put my cell phone on the table and willed Tita to call. She didn't and neither did Richard. A beautiful day had turned sour when Jay fell through the sky and died in front of me. I'd lost any progress made in my relationship with Tita, and the chief of police and county sheriff lied to me. And, of course, I had lied to them first.

Padre Thomas fumbled with his pack of Camels.

"You can't smoke here," I said, and wished I could light a cigar.

"I know." He picked up the package and then put it back on the table. "I need to talk to you, Mick, because this is too much for me alone."

When he first came to Key West, Padre Thomas got in trouble because he went to the local authorities with information on violent, unsolved crimes. It would have been obvious to anyone else that bringing this knowledge to the police would make them a suspect, but he came forward and it resulted in his being detained.

You couldn't blame the cops. Here was a stranger to the island, a skinny, homeless-looking man spouting off about being a Jesuit missionary who talked to angels, while he rode a rusty bike around town. Sanity was never an issue. As hard as they tried, they couldn't connect him to the crimes, but they closed cases because of him.

The police, he found out the hard way, were not big believers in angels. Now he keeps his insider information to himself, but often confides in me.

Alexis brought our food, smiled brightly, gave me a split-second callous stare, and walked away without saying anything. It made me think of Tita, and I wondered what they had talked about while I was with Richard at the hotel.

"I'm a captive audience." I splashed hot sauce and salt across the burger and fries, and then added ketchup.

"I'm not sure where to begin." He added salt to everything on his plate, removed the lettuce and tomato, left the raw onion, and placed the bun on top of his fish sandwich. "I haven't been this concerned since Guatemala."

Padre Thomas had his missionary church in Guatemala, before the angels told him to walk away. While there, he stood up to government soldiers and brutal death squads, defending the villagers who scraped a living from the land. He didn't consider himself brave, just a man of faith.

"Begin at the beginning," I said between bites. I added a few fries as I chewed the burger. "What's the beginning?"

"Early April, the angels warned me about what was to come." He finger-fed fries into his mouth. "First, I thought it was another drug deal and I didn't pay it too much attention." He sipped his beer. "Then they told me. . . ." He paused. "I had a vision while they were with me. Evil men were coming to meet with men here . . . and they were bringing a new evil with them . . . ," he mumbled, while he searched for the words, his food all but forgotten. "It would all begin with two deaths . . . murders . . . and it would only get worse . . . unless. . . ." He stopped and the sadness in his eyes reminded me of the stare of madmen I have known.

EIGHT

Padre Thomas picked at his fries. He sometimes went a day without eating and at other times he ate enough for two, but I have never seen him waste food. He looked up at me; his red-rimmed eyes looked frightened. I thought he might have lost that thin thread of sanity some of us hold onto while we live at the end of the road.

"Unless what?" I bit into my burger and tried to act natural.

"I don't know," he moaned, with a teeth-grinding frown. "I don't know, and that's what's driving me crazy. I can't think of anything to do."

Two days ago, we'd shared lunch and beers at Schooner Wharf Bar and he was his old self: talkative, curious and playful. Now he seemed defeated.

"What do you think I can do?"

He looked up at me, pushed his fries around the plate and sighed. "You've always been a good sounding board, Mick. You hate drug dealers; I thought maybe there was something you could do. I mean, use your contacts."

"You said two deaths."

"Murders."

"You think Jay is one of them?"

"Yes." He fumbled with the cigarette package. "And the deputy is the other."

"But we don't know she's dead. She may have left the hotel with the Colombians."

"She's dead," he said flatly, like you would tell someone the time of day. "And the men that did it got away."

"Why couldn't all the cops searching the hotel find her?"

"Because she's at the bottom of the elevator shaft." His expression turned to surprise as he said the words, as mine must have.

"What?" I yelled, but it was lost in the cheers of sports fans.

"It just came to me, dark and loud. I kept seeing the darkness, but now I know where she is. Tell Richard to look there."

"Padre, are you willing to pay that price again? If I tell him, and you're right, they're going to be all over me," I warned him. "And then you."

"There must be a way to make them look there."

"The hotel is back to normal, they've finished looking, and for me to call. . . ." I left the words unfinished. We both knew I would do something.

My beer tasted flat and the burger had lost its flavor. I poured more salt and hot sauce on the fries and fingered a few into my mouth.

"Go home, Padre Thomas." I licked salt off my fingers. "Don't go to the Schooner or the Hog. Go home and stay there."

"What are you going to do?" He sat straight up in the booth, and his eyes opened wide.

Did he expect me to solve his problem? I couldn't straighten out my love life with Tita, and that should have been simple. I learned a long time ago that few things are as simple as they appear. Usually it's the other way around. Computers, for example. They were supposed to make our lives simpler, give us more free time. The flaw with computers is the same flaw that exists in horseracing: human beings. The computer has been my lifesaver and just as often the cause of outrageous angst in my life. I can say the same about horseracing.

"I'm gonna do something radical." I ate my last fry. "I'm

46

gonna tell the truth."

Padre Thomas's expression went from excited to puzzled. "What are you going to tell them?"

"I'm going to tell them to check the elevator shaft." I took a French fry off his plate and ate it. "And, if you're right, and she's there, I'll tell them you told me."

"What will happen then?" His eyes came back into focus.

"They'll come looking for you, Padre Thomas, and you've been down that road."

"Yes," he mumbled. "They won't believe me, will they?"

"About the angels, no."

"About the evil?"

"They're more likely to believe in evil than angels. But I still don't know what has you spooked. Jay's murder or even Rebecca's murder, that's evil, but there's more to it and you're not telling me."

"Drugs, Mick, they are bringing a new drug with them." He looked tired again. "It's cheap and addictive and it kills. This town hasn't seen anything like it."

Alexis came by our table and took my empty plate. She hesitated when she saw Padre Thomas's untouched food.

"You want this to go, Padre?"

"Do that, will you Alexis?" I answered for him. "He's not himself this afternoon."

She smiled a silent reply and took both plates.

Padre Thomas's nervous hands fumbled with the cigarette package. He left the glass of beer untouched.

I dialed Richard on my cell phone. When he answered, I put a finger in my other ear to block the noise.

"Richard, did anyone check the elevator shaft at the hotel?"

"What bar are you in?" I could barely hear him over the noise.

"Did you?"

"Ten minutes ago."

"And?"

"Where are you, Mick? We need to talk."

"I'm a little busy right now, Chief. Can we do it tomorrow?"

"I want to talk now and I want to know how you knew where Rebecca's body was, or is this another coincidence?"

I looked at Padre Thomas and slowly nodded my head. He closed his eyes, and tears began to run out of them.

I closed my cell phone.

"Padre Thomas, go home and stay there." I put the phone in my pocket as it rang. I didn't answer. "Rebecca was one of theirs and they're not gonna be nice."

"They weren't nice last time." He opened his eyes and wiped them with the napkin. "Richard will come looking for you." He took the packaged leftovers from Alexis as he stood up.

"And eventually, I'll tell them the truth and they'll come for you."

NINE

There is an advantage in knowing the chief of police and most of the cops in a small town like Key West, but there's a downside, too, especially if they're looking for you. It wouldn't take Richard long to have a car at the marina, checking my boat, even though from the noise on the phone he knew I was at a bar. Dispatch had probably already put out a BOLO for me.

Be on the lookout for Mick Murphy, the dispatcher would radio the officers, *and bring him into the station for questioning.*

The cops knew what I looked like, what I drove, where I lived, and where I hung out; I had little chance of avoiding them for long. There was no place to run and hide.

It wouldn't mean much that the cops knew me or that the chief and I were friends. I wouldn't be able to talk my way out of being brought in. They might not handcuff me, but then again, they might. For sure, they wouldn't let me ride in the front.

My only hope of keeping out of jail, I guessed as I left Jack Flat's, was if Richard hadn't told Chance about my call. I knew he probably would, eventually, but expected he would talk to me first. I was counting a lot on friendship.

It was a short walk to Key West Island Books, so I headed there. Mitch Dexter, the owner, was an old friend. We shared a love of books. The shop takes up two narrow storefronts on Fleming Street. The shelves are packed from floor to ceiling

49

with books and dusty, unopened boxes of books lay in stacks on the floor.

The sun had almost set, so the busy street was in shadows, and the air was cooling off. The sidewalk was more crowded than earlier in the afternoon. Off in the distance, I heard a siren and wondered if it had anything to do with me. I doubted it. I didn't require a siren. Unless, of course, Chance was after me, and then I'd need a bulletproof vest.

"Twice in one day," Mitch yelled from his backroom office as I walked in. "To what do I owe this?"

I made my way down the maze of books until I stood in the doorway of his office. The back door was open; I had an escape route.

"Can I use your phone?" I smiled, but knew I looked guilty of something.

"Sure." Mitch stood up so I could sit down.

The office is full of collectible books and had little space for more than one person. The phone is next to the computer. I sat down and dialed Tita. I had a feeling she wouldn't answer my cell call, because my name would appear on her caller ID.

She picked it up before the message ended.

"Hello."

"Tita, don't hang up, please." My pleading tone was obvious to Mitch, who raised his bushy eyebrows, smiled and left me alone.

"Why would I do that?"

"I thought you might be mad at me."

"And why would I be mad, Mick."

"It's a long story, but the punch line is, I need your legal help." I rushed the words out, because I still feared she'd hang up. I knew how stubborn she could be.

I took a deep breath and rattled off the events of the afternoon. She didn't interrupt me.

"Why is it when you put two Irishmen in the same room, trouble soon follows?"

That's how she responded to my situation, and I didn't have a clue if it was a good response or not. It wasn't what I expected from her.

"Is one of them Protestant and the other Catholic?" I decided to go along with her attempt at humor. She often made fun of the Irish; she'd been doing it since she was a teenager, when her brother and I were in college together.

"No, they're both Catholic."

"Is there enough to drink for both of 'em?"

"The Irish never have enough to drink." Her tone became warm. "Where are you?"

"Mitch's."

"Can you stay inside until I get there?"

"Yeah, I think so."

"Do I hear sirens?"

"Yeah, they seem to be getting closer."

"Mick, don't go melodramatic on me," she laughed. "Richard isn't going to use sirens to find you, he's going to call me."

I closed my eyes and suppressed a laugh. "You've been waiting for my call?"

"I just got off the phone with Richard. Let me call him back and see if we can meet at his office. Okay?"

"I'll wait for you inside the shop." I looked at the opened back door. "Use the back parking lot."

"I'll see you in fifteen minutes." She hung up.

"Love-life problems," Mitch said from behind a bookcase, his glasses hanging around his neck.

51

TEN

Tita drove her scooter into the back parking lot. Mitch and I heard her before we saw her. She took long enough that I was able to give him a quick rundown of my situation. I showed Mitch the autographed copy of *The Sun Also Rises* and asked him to hold it for me.

"If the rest of his library is as well preserved as this, I won't have a problem finding collectors for it," Mitch said as he examined the book.

The wait for Tita was worth it. Her midnight-black hair was pulled back into a long ponytail. She wore one of my old Hawaiian print shirts, the one with colorful hibiscus flowers, faded jeans that were not too tight, but tight enough they helped show off her hourglass figure that the shirt half hid, and flip-flops.

"Do you think he'll ever grow up?" She removed her sunglasses, and her green eyes sparkled as she walked through the back door.

"I hope not." Mitch smiled. "I live vicariously through his misadventures."

"Misadventures is right." She gave me her tough-attorney stare.

Once, after she moved to Key West and we began seeing each other as more than old friends, she won a jury trial. While we were celebrating, she showed me her collection of attorney looks. She was an actress, the courtroom her stage, and the jury her audience, she explained. She showed me her "help me" plea, her "tough" scowl, her "sincere" smile and a half dozen others.

"Hey," I protested, "all I was doing was looking for you. If you had waited a half hour, I would've had lunch with you, instead of drinks with Padre Thomas."

"Sure," she sneered, "if I had waited a half hour you and the good padre would have put me, an officer of the court, in the middle of this conspiracy."

"You know, Mitch." I turned to him; he was almost laughing. "I stop while she window-shops, and I see a guy I know fall to his death, probably murdered, and somehow she holds me responsible. If she hadn't stopped, I wouldn't be involved in any of this."

"Now it's my fault?" She pouted to get Mitch's sympathy.

"As much as it's mine." I tried to match her pout, but I don't think it came close.

She kissed me high on the cheek, to avoid my beard, and squeezed my hand.

"The problem is, there's a murdered sheriff's deputy, and you knew where the body was." I was getting her down-to-business look and speech. "No one thinks you did it, but taking into consideration some of the people you associate with, the cops want to talk."

"The sheriff, too?"

"Right now, it's only Richard and a DEA agent—who, by the way, seems to like you."

"And you find that strange?"

"Do you know any DEA agents?"

"I saw two today." I shook my head. "But I wasn't introduced to them. I knew a couple in Central America, but that's more than ten years ago."

She smiled. "Well, maybe your dumb Irish luck is holding."

I don't know what it is about scooter drivers in Key West, but

53

if you are not a few bricks short of a load when you buy the scooter, it isn't long before you've definitely lost a brick or two. Tita, usually a rational person, drove through Old Town streets like a kamikaze pilot. I was hugging her waist and not enjoying it.

After her brief speech in Mitch's office, I thought we'd take my Jeep, but she was concerned that the police might be keeping an eye on it.

"If you come in on your own, it looks better," she said in the parking lot.

"Better for what?" I asked, from the back of the scooter.

"If you're arrested and we have to go for bail."

I smacked the back of her head. "I thought you said—"

She didn't let me finish. "Mick, the cops are going to say whatever it takes to get you to the station. The smartest thing you did was calling me."

"Richard's my friend."

"Mine, too." She sped down Fleming Street. "But he's also the chief of police and working with Chance, who, I don't need to remind you, has not forgiven you for that story on his deputies. And there's the DEA."

"They like me."

"Yeah, and I'm a virgin. Get real, Mick. How have you survived this long?"

I finished the ride by concentrating on her words instead of her driving. Bottom line was, if Richard wanted to play hardball, I could deny telling him to look in the elevator shaft. After all, it was on the phone between us, not in front of people. If I gave up Padre Thomas as my source, he would be picked up and questioned. They might Baker Act him because of his angels, but they couldn't pin a murder on him. Even Chance knew I didn't do it, but that didn't mean he wouldn't enjoy making life tough on me for as long as possible.

"Now comes the hard part." Tita parked outside the police station across from Garrison Bight.

It was dark already. Whatever reprieve spring had brought was over; each day it would get better, longer sunshine, but now it was gone.

"You think they're going to arrest me?" I ran my fingers through my hair to untangle it.

"Mick, you have to go in there." She straightened her ponytail and smiled. "You think you know what's happening because Richard is your friend, but I am telling you first and foremost, he's a cop and this is about a fellow officer's murder. All bets are off, remember that. And"—she shook her finger at my nose—"listen to me and do what I say or I will leave you on your own."

I was seeing this side of Tita for the first time and was glad she was with me. I assumed she dressed the way she did to put Richard at ease. We were there as friends who knew and trusted him. If he went with that, it was going to be okay. If not, she had a bag of tricks, and one of them, I feared, was to go for his jugular. I smiled as I picked up the wall phone to announce our arrival, because she was on my side.

ELEVEN

We met Richard in the lobby and he walked us to his second-floor office. His bifocals were wedged on his prominent nose, and he wore loafers, brown slacks, and a dark-blue pullover shirt with a badge insignia on the breast pocket. He looked more relaxed and less official out of his dress-blue uniform with its gold stars, buttons and badge. Susan was working late and smiled as we walked by her desk and into the chief's office. He pointed to chairs around the small conference table, and we sat.

"Tita, thank you for finding Mick." He took the seat at the head of the table.

She smiled back. "He wasn't lost."

"He wasn't answering his phone."

"Probably couldn't hear it in the bar."

"Probably."

"Hey, guys, I'm here." I pointed to myself. "And, why am I here?"

They both turned to me.

"I have a couple of questions about your phone call and there's a DEA agent that wants to meet you," Richard said.

"Richard," Tita said, continuing her smile, "I need to know if this is official. I am Mick's attorney."

He looked hurt as he stared at her and then at me, with sad gray eyes.

"I'm a cop in the middle of a double homicide." He let out a deep breath. "Mick shows up at an undercover stakeout where

56

two murders occur. One happens in front of him and then he calls me and tells me where the other victim is." He pushed himself away from the table. The chair squeaked as it rolled. "I don't think he murdered anyone, but I'd be a bad cop if I wasn't curious."

"I never said where Rebecca's body was," I answered him.

"Mick!" Tita's look chastised me. "Chief, what did he say on the phone?"

Richard smiled and rolled back to the table. "Counselor, he said 'did you check the elevator shaft?' "

"And?"

"And that's where we found Rebecca's body." He turned to me. "Mick, you knew her. If you have anything that can help us, we need it."

"We need it badly," came from behind us.

Tita and I turned to see the large African-American DEA agent I had seen talking to Richard at the hotel. He was a big man, the size I pictured a football player would be. Big framed, not fat, and he moved smoothly, showing he controlled the size, not the other way around. He still wore the DEA ball cap and T-shirt.

"Mr. Murphy." He extended his large hand as he walked to the table. "Reed Fitcher, DEA."

His hand swallowed mine and he shook it firmly.

Richard introduced Tita. "Mick's attorney."

"A pleasure, miss." He sat down to Richard's right and looked at me. "The sheriff doesn't like you."

"He used to," I said.

"Yeah, well, he should be more careful about the men he puts on the street." Fitcher rubbed his big hands together. "They got caught and you did your job."

"Thank you."

"You knew the jumper, right?"

57

Tita and I both looked at Richard.

"I don't think he jumped." I turned to Fitcher.

"That's the story we put out"—he smirked—"but you're probably right. Tell me about him."

"I told Agent Fitcher that Jay talked to you yesterday about what was going on, but I didn't have the time to get all the details," Richard said.

"I am concerned about your possible misinterpretation of my client's conversations with the victim." Tita spoke up. "This isn't being taped, is it?"

"No, Tita, no tape."

"Mr. Murphy is not a suspect in any aspect of this case," Fitcher said. He brought his large arms up behind his head and locked fingers. "We are at a loss right now. And, I mean more than the loss of an undercover officer. Our slate has been wiped clean, and some real bad guys are on your streets and we want them!"

Tita pushed toward me and whispered, "Did you talk with Jay yesterday?"

I turned and whispered back, "Yes."

It wasn't a lie, I had talked with Jay, but everything I said afterward to Richard at the hotel had been a lie, and it looked like the lie was beginning to spin a web of its own. If I told Tita the truth, she'd skin me alive and that was the upside of it.

"Did he say anything you don't want to admit to knowing?" Her head pressed against mine.

"No."

Tita pushed away and nodded to me, but her green eyes held a warning, and I knew if she told me to stop, I would.

"I was at Schooner Wharf yesterday afternoon having a beer." I began with the truth. "I saw Jay, but he wasn't the reason I was there. We were sitting at a table in the patio, Bob Lynds, Burt Carroll, Doug Bean, Padre Thomas."

"What time was this?" Fitcher asked.

"I got there around two and left a little after three." I had to keep the timeline honest, since I had no idea what Jay was doing before or after I had seen him. "We were there to discuss the Minimal Regatta."

Fitcher got a puzzled look on his face. "What's a Minimal Regatta?"

"A silly, homemade-boat race held on Memorial Day weekend. We were thinking of participating."

"So Jay talked about today with everyone at the table?"

"No," I said, quickly. There was no need to involve my friends in this, especially because it was a lie I couldn't control. "He wasn't at the table. He said hi, but kept moving and when I left he came up to me on the dock by the Sebago catamarans."

"So it was a little after three?" Fitcher listened but didn't write anything down.

"Yeah. I was walking to my Jeep parked at the Conch Farm, and he told me there was something going down tomorrow that might make a good story for me. He said, 'Be at Hotel Key West around three.' Jay was like a sponge, he soaked up all kinds of things from along the waterfront. Most of it was crap, but he knew what was going on around the island. You know he liked to pretend he was an undercover cop?"

"Yes, I've been told that."

"Probably what got him killed," Richard said.

"It's a two-minute walk, so to be polite I asked him what was going down. He said, 'It's drugs, with high rollers,' or something along those lines. Like I told Richard earlier." I turned to Richard. "I didn't pay much attention to what Jay was saying. I didn't think of it again until Tita and I left the bookstore on Fleming. It was around three and then all the shit began to happen."

"You didn't see him come off the roof?" Fitcher had his

59

elbows on the table and rested his broad chin on his large hands.

"No, I watched his reflection in the store window, but didn't know it was Jay until I saw his hat in the air. Even when I turned and saw where he landed on the car's roof, I didn't recognize him."

No one said anything. Fitcher sighed loudly and Richard pushed himself away from the table again. Tita took a quick glance at the two men, trying to size up the situation, and gave me a blank look. Fitcher nervously drummed his fingers on the table.

"When Rebecca and Jay were murdered, the knowledge of who they were dealing with locally died, too." Richard pushed himself back to the table. "They had met with the Colombians and were supposed to meet with the local buyers in the next day or two."

"You ever hear of *paco?*" Fitcher sighed. "Not the Spanish nickname for Francisco. Or maybe you've heard it called *basuco?*"

"If it's not the name Paco, no."

"We think this group has smuggled *paco* into Key West, or is about to. *Paco* is a residue left over in the processing of cocaine. We always know where the drugs are being processed because *paco* becomes the locals' drug of choice. It's cheap, mixes easily with cigarettes, and is addictive as hell." Fitcher sat back in his chair and made it moan. He balled his hands around each other. "If this shit hits the streets in Key West, hell, anywhere in the States, it'll go for less than a buck a pop. School kids will be able to afford it, and they'll be hooked before they've spent a week's lunch money."

"We have names of the Colombians and an Englishman," Richard mumbled, "but their faces died with Rebecca and Jay. We can't ID 'em, so they're walking our streets—"

"And preparing to distribute the *paco.*" Fitcher finished Richard's sentence. "If you've got anything, if you are holding back any information, this isn't the time. If you've got a name, if Jay said anything that might make you suspect someone, we need that, Mr. Murphy."

Both men stared at me, their hard looks, their unbelieving cop's eyes, hoping for a change in what I had said.

"I've told you everything I know," I lied, realizing the web I'd created had snared me.

TWELVE

Richard opened a large manila envelope and shook its contents of newspaper clippings onto the table. Agent Fitcher reached and pulled a clipping from the pile.

"Let me read something from a newspaper account on *paco*," he said. "It's from Argentina. '*Paco* is highly addictive because its effect is so short and intense that many users resort to smoking twenty to fifty cigarettes a day to make its effects linger.'" He looked up and continued. "'*Paco* is even more toxic than crack cocaine because it is made mostly of solvents and chemicals, with just a dab of cocaine.'

"These are for you." Fitcher pushed the clippings toward us. "Read them. *Paco* can kill addicts within six months to a year. It's cheaper than grass and addictive as hell. If you know something that will help us get these bad guys off the street, you better tell me now." He looked very unfriendly as he stared. "Otherwise, by this time next year, you will be responsible for the deaths of local kids."

"Agent Fitcher." Tita used her hands to straighten the pile of papers. "I knew Jay, too. And what Mick says about not paying attention to him is what most of us did, especially when he began bragging. I can assure you that being in the vicinity of your crime scene was my responsibility, not Mick's. I wanted to go to Excess and Banana Republic to shop and he agreed to come along, if we'd eat first."

Richard and Fitcher turned their cold eyes to me. I nodded

62

in agreement.

"I'll tell you again, not until I saw what was happening, and that it was Jay's body on the car's roof, did I think about what we'd talked about," I said, in support of my lie. I should've kept my mouth shut.

Richard rolled his chair away from the table and stretched his legs. Fitcher's chair squeaked as he turned to face Richard. The office seemed deathly quiet. I turned to Tita, but her expression told me nothing. I hunched my shoulders and she smiled.

"Is that all?" She collected the clippings and put them back into the envelope.

"Chief." Fitcher had his back to us. "What do you think? Is he telling the truth?"

Richard stared at me, before answering. "I can't see a reason for him to lie."

"Is there a story in this for you?" Fitcher turned to me. "I would think this is kind of juicy. Drugs, murder, make a name for yourself."

"The story would be in the arrest—it needs an ending. And I don't need to make a name for myself."

"The daily paper will go wild if the two deaths are connected," Fitcher said.

"You reported Jay was a jumper. Without a photo or more information, it might only make page three," I said. "If it's a slow news day, maybe someone will write about the history of jumpers from the hotel."

"And if they find out about the undercover officer's murder?" Fitcher's tone was hard; he delivered the words with cold detachment.

"If you release the truth, all the details, you can expect Miami media to cover it, and more likely than not, cable news."

"And we can expect the bad guys to run." Fitcher sighed, letting a deep breath escape. "And two people died for nothing."

"Mick, can we keep this under wraps?" Richard looked at Tita. "For a while?"

I scratched my bearded chin, hoping it made me look thoughtful. As a journalist, I have a problem working with the police, even when I know them, but in this case, I felt I had little choice, since it was built around my lie. "Yeah, I think so. I have no desire to see this exposed in the local press right now; both Jay and Rebecca were friends of mine, and I'd like to see you catch their killers."

"And keep the *paco* off the streets," Fitcher added.

"Yeah, of course."

"That's all I've got for now." Fitcher stood. "Chief, you know how to reach him?"

"I have his number and I know where he lives."

"Richard, if you need to talk with Mick, you call me." Tita stood and picked up the envelope.

"Of course, Counselor," Fitcher said. "Do you have a business card?"

Tita took one from her purse and wrote her cell number on its back. "I'm reachable any time of day or night."

"Can I ask a personal question?" Fitcher took Tita's business card, but was talking to me. "I checked you out and know more than I need to, but there's no explanation of why you're called Mad Mick Murphy when your name is Liam." He smiled. "I'm just a curious cop."

I wondered who he'd checked me out with, was it Richard or some DEA computer in Washington? It didn't matter, because I knew years ago that my life was well documented in government computers. Too many Americans' lives are.

"It's left over from college." I pushed away from the table. "Mad as in crazy from the stunts we pulled around campus, and Mick because of my Irish heritage. It stuck with me all these years."

64

"Must have been some stunts." Fitcher held his smile.

I didn't tell him it was Tita, as a teenager, who coined the moniker and her brother Paco's offbeat sense of humor that helped it stick.

Richard and I stood. He nodded to Tita and me, and we began to leave.

"Thank you for your cooperation," Fitcher said before we got to the door, his grin still locked on his broad, black face. "Most journalists would run with this and not look back."

"This isn't a story I want to write."

"But you might have to," he said, as if he understood.

"If it turns out right. Then maybe Chance will speak to me again."

Tita and I walked through Susan's empty office and took the elevator to the first floor.

Tita handed me the envelope as she started her scooter. "You told the truth up there, right?" she asked, as I got on back and we sped off.

"The whole truth and nothing but the truth." I tried to joke about my lie.

She dodged the scooter between cars and trucks and took me to city hall, where I had parked my Jeep.

"You want to get a drink?" I got off the scooter and was surprised I hadn't dropped the envelope.

"I've known you a long time, Mick." She straightened her ponytail while straddling the scooter. "And one thing you always forget is that I can tell when you're lying."

I said nothing and tried to look hurt, but I don't think it worked.

"You can look Richard square in the eye and lie as coldly as you want." She revved the tinny engine. "But not to me. This DEA guy is serious trouble. He'll throw your ass in a federal jail and leave it there."

"But you'll get me out." I tried to joke, but it went over like a stink bomb in church.

"It's getting out of my league, Mick." She frowned, maybe disappointed in me. "You know what makes me a good attorney?"

"Because of the college you went to?" I should've quit while I was ahead.

"No, Mick. Knowing when I am in over my head, that makes me good. Tonight was a social." She forced a smile. "Between the sheriff and the DEA, your life could become a living hell real shortly." Her Boston accent came out strong on the word *shortly*. "And I'll tell you something else: Fitcher doesn't believe you."

"What do you mean, he doesn't believe me?"

"He's playing you, Mick, and you're playing along." She wasn't smiling. "Don't trust him. And I'll give you one last piece of free advice."

"Over a drink?"

"It's not a joke, Mick." She revved the engine again. "When Fitcher comes after you, you'll want someone like Nathan Eden defending you, not me. Give him a call," she said, and sped off.

THIRTEEN

I lit the cigar stub I'd left in the Jeep's ashtray and wondered how such a promising day turned into a shit-storm so quickly. Of course, it began with the lie I told Richard at the scene of Jay's death. But that was me; that's how I thought on the run, as a journalist, and got stories I wouldn't have if I'd depended on others to come forward with the facts.

Before I came to Key West, when I worked full-time, I was on the go twelve months a year, living out of a suitcase and camera bag, sleeping in airports, jungles, third-world shanties and low-cost hotel rooms, and the ability to bluff my way into and out of trouble helped me get award-winning exclusives. Even in minor scrapes with the law at home, or in foreign countries and with drug cartels, I managed okay.

The problem now was, if I decided to write this story, I couldn't hightail it out of town after I'd written it as I normally did. I would still be in Key West, it's my home, and I have regular contact with Richard. There was time, after the story hit the newsstands, for Richard to find out I lied, and that was a downside, since we were friends.

Would I lose his friendship because of a lie? Would he understand it was what I did to make a living? I understood his reluctance to involve me in the situation at Hotel Key West, so maybe he would understand why I did what I had to do, to get the story. Or, maybe he wouldn't; he's a cop before anything else.

67

I started the Jeep, drove up Simonton and turned on Caroline, looking for somewhere to park near Schooner Wharf Bar.

Was it my fault that a news story unfolded in front of me? If I hadn't told a lie to the rookie cop, Richard would have had nothing to do with me. That was his side of the coin. I don't believe he would do anything I'd consider a cover-up of the incident, but until he, the sheriff and the DEA were ready, he wouldn't be calling me or anyone else in the media. The bigger this *paco* drug situation became, the further involvement of federal agencies, the more Richard would want to control how, and when, the story came out.

Tita was a problem all on her own. She knew I was lying to Richard and Fitcher and held that against me. It had more to do with my lifestyle than missing lunch and shopping with her. I guess, to her, it had to do with trust. To me, it had to do with distancing her from possible trouble. Hell, I was damned if I did, damned if I didn't, with Tita.

I parked outside B.O.'s Fish Wagon on Caroline and William streets and decided to have a sandwich. Buddy Owens, the owner, served the freshest fish, usually because he caught it on an early morning fishing trip. If he wasn't fishing, he knew the fishermen he bought from.

I ordered a fish sandwich special from the trailer-like kitchen—which got me a free half-order of fries—and sat down at one of the old cable-spool tables under the slapped-together roof. Nailed to the driftwood walls were a variety of bent and bruised out-of-state license plates and faded Key West business signs. B.O. knew what he was doing. The décor was Key-West-rustic—mismatched waterlogged planks and tin roofing—the food was top notch, and the joint was often mentioned in national magazines as offering the best fish sandwich in Key West. The magazines were right.

Padre Thomas walked by as I was finishing my sandwich. I

whistled and he turned and saw me through the shrubs that served as a wall between the open-air restaurant and William Street.

"I thought you were gonna stay home tonight." I couldn't help but be taken aback at how disheveled he looked.

"I figured by this time you fixed the problem," he mumbled. "If not, there was no place I could hide, anyway."

"It's fixed temporarily." I wiped my mouth to make sure the catsup was off and walked with him up the street. "So, where are you going?"

He checked his wristwatch and didn't bother to ask how I'd fixed the problem. "At eight, we're going to talk about participating in the Minimal Regatta. I thought you were joining the team?"

"Yeah, well, things got a little out of hand this afternoon," I said, and we walked into Schooner Wharf. "I forgot."

Fourteen

Schooner Wharf Bar is open on all sides, and what structure there is to it is made of shipwrecked gnarled wood, covered with worn fishing nets and colorful lobster trap buoys. The old center building had been an icehouse when the waterfront held working shrimp boats, and now it is home to a second-story deck bar that offers a postcard-view of the harbor's yachts, a first floor TV-poolroom and a marina library of used paperback books for the taking. Across from the bar is a P-rock patio area with tables and a stage and a kitchen that fronts two restrooms. A few of the larger tables have their own thatched roofs; the picnic tables have umbrellas.

Night had almost blanketed the harbor, but the soft rustling of waves as they broke against the sides of moored boats overcame the anxious cries of tourists and drunks. The Sebago, Fury and Sunny Days catamarans were coming in from their sunset sail, filled with excited tourists who would soon file into Schooner Wharf or the Conch Farm for a drink. The pungent aroma of marijuana smoke mixed with the salt and seaweed tastes of the harbor and spilt beer.

Bob Lynds, six-foot with silver hair he wore in a ponytail, sat under a thatched-hut table drinking with Burt Carroll, a lanky six-footer with bushy sandy-colored hair and mustache, and Doug Bean, the shorter of the gang, who was burned brown from working as the dock master at Conch Marina. They are three of my sailing cohorts and friends, and waited for Padre

70

Thomas and me.

The bar and patio were crowded. I ordered another round. Tara, the California surfer-blonde server, knew us well enough to know our drinks. Bob, Doug and I got a Kalik, Padre Thomas had his Budweiser, and Burt his scotch and water.

"What the hell's the story with Jay jumpin' from Hotel Key West?" Bob got up as he spoke and came back with cigars from the bar's Cuban roller. "Didn't we see him here yesterday?"

"Yeah." I cut the end of my cigar and passed the cutter to Bob. "What are you hearing?" I lit my cigar with the fancy wind-resistant propane lighter Tita gave me as a birthday gift.

Padre Thomas lit a Camel, cupping a match in his hand, and looked at me strangely, waiting for me to lie.

"Some say he was pushed." Doug cut his cigar. "I guess he was braggin' about an undercover deal he was on." He reached for my lighter.

"Did anyone ever believe him?" Burt took the cutter. "He didn't seem like a jumper. He was always excited about whatever he was doing—why would he jump?"

"If I see the chief, I'll ask him." I blew thick smoke into the warm night.

They seemed to accept what I said and we drank and smoked before Burt brought up the Minimal Regatta.

"Are we going to build the boat?" Burt asked.

"What's the cost?" Padre Thomas crushed out his cigarette and lit another one.

"A sheet of quarter-inch plywood, a roll of duct tape, two eight-foot two-by-fours and a pound of nails." Bob drummed his fingers on the table. "I think that's all you're allowed to use. Maybe some paint. I'll get it and we'll split the costs later."

"We using my design?" Burt lit his cigar.

"Yeah," Doug said.

No one objected as we looked around the table. Burt's design

71

seemed an awful lot like a kayak.

"Who do we get to paddle it?" Padre Thomas was on his third cigarette and second beer.

"I think we need to get that skinny kid with the rainbow hair that hangs around your marina." Bob looked at me, the cigar stuck in the corner of his mouth.

"Alex Fierro?"

"Yeah," Burt agreed. "He's got those long skinny legs for balance and the arm strength for the paddle."

Schooner Wharf Bar puts the "Minimal Regatta" on every Memorial Day weekend. It consists of a bunch of homemade boats racing a short course in the harbor competing against each other and the clock. There are about thirty entries each year.

Ten years ago, only locals filled the seawall next to the bar as spectators, watching other local crazies compete in boats that usually sank before finishing. It was a fun event and a reason to drink just before hurricane season—as if we needed one. Today, contestants come from all around the state to participate for bragging rights and a variety of gift certificates. The bragging rights are what's important.

The seawall circling the harbor fills with tourists and locals, watching and cheering the regatta contestants as the sun beats down, and even the Conch Farm Restaurant and Bar joins in, and that's across the harbor. There are small satellite bars set up in the roadway—which the city closes for pedestrian safety, because of the crowds—and the hot sun encourages the consumption of cold beer. It's a Key West event and it looked like we were going to be in it.

"Another round," Bob yelled at Tara, and she nodded.

Larry Baeder, Bubba No-Tunes, Norm Cote, Ken Fradley, Joel Nelson, Texas Rich and a collection of long-haired local

72

musicians were setting up on stage as Tara delivered our drink order.

"Mick." A hand touched my shoulder as someone whispered my name from behind.

I turned to see Jake Thomas. I put my beer down and took the cigar from my mouth. Jake is the young protégé of billionaire realtor Carl Dey. As usual, he dressed casually in an expensive sport shirt, creased linen pants and Italian loafers. He contrasted greatly with the sunburned, wrinkled-clothing crowd at the bar.

"Jake, what a surprise." I shook his hand. He had a firm handshake. "Can I buy you a drink?"

"Mr. Dey and I are having dinner at the Marquesa in a half hour." He checked his wristwatch. "He would like you to join us for dessert, at ten."

"Did he say why?" I tried to smile and not sound piqued.

"His grandson is back." For the first time I saw Jake frown, something he rarely does. "It's important he talk to you."

"Save me a piece of key-lime pie." I reached for my beer. Jake forced a smile and walked away.

FIFTEEN

Carl Dey came to Key West sixty years ago, in his early twenties, when the island really was a one-horse, wide-open town. He married a local girl and stayed. Carl told me once, during an interview on Florida Keys real estate, that he fell in love with his wife, Carolina Smith, and she wouldn't consider leaving Key West even if—and he said it was a big IF—she'd marry him.

"There wasn't much to do here, back then," he said, as we relaxed with Cuban rum on the second-floor balcony of his secluded estate, "and I wasn't a fisherman and didn't know much about bars, except to drink in 'em, so I went into real estate."

Long story, short, he earned his real-estate license, sold real estate and then, as times got better, he bought real estate. He struggled during the bad times, but in the end, he made the right decisions. He expanded to the Upper Keys and today has an interest in most of the major hotels in the Keys, especially in Key West. He and Carolina have two boys and three grandchildren. Two of the grandchildren are very successful businessmen in Florida. The third, Johnny Dey, is the black sheep of the family, and that's putting it politely.

Like many people in the Keys, I owe Carl Dey a favor or two, so if he wanted to talk, I was going to listen. I knew Johnny before he left for college. He was a handful, but he loved his grandfather and vice versa. I heard what everyone else did; Johnny got himself thrown out of Florida International

University because of drugs. Since then, he'd been in and out of trouble with the law, skirting jail time. He also traveled to Peru and Colombia, often.

Parking is a problem in Key West, so I walked the couple of blocks to Simonton and Fleming streets, where the Marquesa Hotel and Restaurant is. Carl Dey's real-estate office is across the street. The hotel is a first-class place that almost goes unnoticed from the outside.

The restaurant is intimate: tables with white-linen tablecloths, candles and crystal glassware for the wine and water. The food is amazing.

Large lace-curtained windows allow guests to look out onto both Fleming and Simonton streets and, of course, those walking the streets get to look in. Servers are always busy seeing to customers' wishes, refilling crystal wine goblets and taking away dishes.

There were a few empty tables as I walked in. The maître d' greeted me and asked what I would be drinking. I settled for a Corona and found my way to Carl Dey's table. Jake Thomas got up and politely excused himself.

"Mr. Dey," I said as he stood.

We shook hands and sat. For a man in his eighties, he has a full head of white, wavy hair and dark-blue eyes that have faded little since I've known him. The server brought my beer and two slices of key-lime pie.

"Thank you for coming on such short notice." He sipped wine; I thought he'd be drinking coffee after dinner. "I have a big favor to ask." He looked into my eyes, trying to find something.

"About Johnny?" I took a bite of the key-lime pie.

"Yes." He ate a small piece of pie. "I need you to find him and let me know where he is."

"He hasn't called you?" I was surprised.

75

"No." He seemed embarrassed and ate another piece of pie. He looked up at me. "I need to trust you, Mick."

"Mr. Dey, I think we've both trusted each other before."

"Yes, we have. But this time, what I tell you might put you up against the law, and I know you and the chief are friends." He sipped wine without taking his stare from me.

"I won't rob a bank for you." I smiled and took a drink.

He laughed. "Fortunately, I don't need you to do that."

"I can always say no."

"Yes, you can." He cut a piece of key-lime pie and left it on his plate. He leaned toward me. "This mess at Hotel Key West. . . ." He hesitated. "I have a bad feeling Johnny could be involved. I know it's drug related."

That Carl Dey knew about what happened at the hotel didn't surprise me. I wasn't the only one in the Keys that owed him, or watched out for his interests.

"Why do you think Johnny's involved?" I wasn't sure I wanted to hear the answer.

"People I know have seen him in town." He frowned. "He wouldn't be here without calling me unless . . ."—again, he hesitated—"unless he didn't want me to know he was here and the only reason for that is, he's up to no good." He sat back in his chair, took a deep breath and pushed forward again. "I have a couple of professionals ready to fly him to Colorado for drug treatment. I just need to find out where he is, so they can get him."

I hadn't expected that. He was a desperate old man and I wasn't going to judge him.

"Mr. Dey, if Johnny has a drug problem, he has to *want* to kick it, or rehab won't work," I said, softly. "It's not cough medicine you can make a kid swallow to feel better."

"I'll pay you." His eyes pleaded.

"No, you won't." I swallowed some beer.

76

His lips trembled and I saw a side of him that must have hurt. He glanced around the room, looking for someone, or avoiding me.

"I need to try, Mick." His voice quivered. "I've got to get him away from Key West."

"Away from the law?"

"Yes." He stared coldly at me. "This may be the last chance I have to help him, and I will pay whatever it takes, name a figure."

"I won't take your money."

"If the police find him, I'll lose him." His cold eyes weakened.

"Let's go to your office, so we can talk." I finished my beer.

He nodded and we got up. He walked slowly; Johnny rested heavy on his shoulders, as we headed across the street to his office.

Sixteen

Simonton Street traffic was Saturday-night busy and we had to wait for the light at the corner to cross. Carl Dey had transformed the first floor of an old, three-story brick apartment building into his elegant but simple real-estate office. He rarely sold property any longer, but he kept the desk he had used for years and came to the office most days. Large windows looked onto Simonton and showed poster-size display photos of property for sale, and also allowed a nice view of the open-spaced office. His name was prominently displayed over the door. The office was dark wood and bright lights, with plenty of local art on the walls.

When Carl Dey sat at his desk, he looked like a tired old man. I sat in the client's chair, and his silent stare pleaded for understanding.

"You surprised I think Johnny's involved?" He spoke the words as if people still surrounded us. "I'm not senile yet." He tried for a smile, but it failed.

"Mr. Dey, if I found out you didn't know something that was going on in Key West, I'd be surprised." I kept his stare. "What I don't understand is how you connect Johnny to the two deaths at Hotel Key West."

He cleared his throat, and his thin frame seemed to relax into the old padded chair. "I have enough money to keep track of him." He looked away, maybe ashamed for spying on his grandson. "To Johnny's credit, he has never asked me for money

78

or help. Legal help, I mean."

"So you've kept track of your wayward grandson, is that it?"

"Yes." His chair squeaked. "And in doing so, I am aware of his troubles, his problems with drugs and alcohol."

"Have you tried to talk to him about these troubles?"

"Yes." He coughed. "He promised me that he would move back to Key West next year, settle down. He promised me that," he repeated, more to himself than me.

"Maybe he's here early to surprise you." I didn't believe it as I said it.

"I hoped." His frown told me he'd lost that hope. "But he has been here almost five days and not a word. Then, this afternoon, the two deaths at the hotel. I am told they were locals who were dealing with Colombian drug peddlers, maybe even top-echelon cartel people."

"You know more than I do," I said.

He stayed quiet. His expression grew sadder in the silence, and then I got it.

"You think Johnny spotted the locals as undercover cops?" I almost shouted.

He didn't move for a long moment, and then he nodded, and tears came to his eyes.

"You don't know it for sure," I said more calmly, wanting to believe my words. "I mean, it doesn't sound like the Johnny I knew."

"It doesn't sound like the Johnny I know, either," he mumbled. "He wanted to be a cop, go to college and come back and join the Key West PD." He pulled a handkerchief from his pants pocket and wiped his eyes. "I've consulted with experts and have to accept he is not the Johnny I love, not with the drugs in his system." He turned in his chair and stared hard at me. "Do you have any idea how difficult that is to say? God, I hope you never do."

We sat silently in the empty office. I thought of the mischievous young man I knew, who laughed and winked when he pulled his pranks. He might have been wild for Key West, but he never hurt anyone, and wasn't any more crazy than others blowing off steam on a two-by-four island. He sailed, dived and loved being on the water. He was no crazier than I was at his age.

"If I can find him. . . ."

"I know you can," he said, with more excitement that he'd had all night. "My plane is ready to fly him to Colorado and the drug-treatment center. I can get him back, Mick. It might take six months, but it can be done." He turned his stare to the street. "You can find him, I know you can. Please do it, before the police do, before he does something stupid, again."

"I'll try, Mr. Dey, but I can't promise anything." I stood up. "Does Johnny know what you think?"

"Not about the hotel, no." He looked up at me and smiled. "Money is no problem."

"Yes, sir, it is." I shook his hand and left his office.

SEVENTEEN

Some days just seem to begin right, to hold promise. Sunday morning began that way. The horrors of yesterday seemed distant and that was okay with me. Tita and I planned to meet for breakfast, and maybe, I hoped, get our relationship back on track. During the Sunday barhopping we did, I planned to let people know I was looking for Johnny Dey, and possibly I'd get lucky there, too. Yeah, the day held promise as only beautiful mornings do.

I stood barefoot, shirtless, wearing cutoff shorts on the deck of the *Fenian Bastard*. I had a cup of fresh-brewed coffee and the daily *Citizen*. The morning sun began to inch its way over Key West, and the breeze carried scents of tropical flora and almost tasted salty. Cotton ball–like clouds moved across the dark-blue sky. The temperature had to be in the mid-eighties. I loved it. It looked like another perfect day in Paradise.

Sunday morning held promise, that is, until I saw a naked body floating face down less than ten feet from the *Fenian Bastard* and then all promises quickly faded.

Key West has more than its share of quirky characters, so seeing a naked person in the bight wasn't shocking. I stared, expecting to see movement, but instead I saw a head angled strangely in the water.

"Hey," I yelled, but received nothing back.

I jumped down to the finger dock, still hoping to see movement. When I didn't, I dove in and swam to the body. Long

81

dark hair danced in the warm current around the half-submerged head. I reached out and touched an arm. It was cold, even in seventy-six-degree water. I grabbed a hand, its fingers wrinkled white from being in the water, and swam back toward the dock.

I turned the body face up and saw it was a young Latina, maybe early thirties. She had been attractive, but in the last few hours, death had stolen her beauty. Her mouth was slightly ajar, as if she was ready to scream. Her large brown eyes were fogged and swollen. They stared into a dimension I couldn't see, and wasn't sure I ever wanted to. She had contusions around her neck, not a good sign.

There were no fish-nibbling discolorations or marine life visible on her body, so she hadn't been in the water long. I pulled myself onto the dock and wondered what to do. I couldn't pull her out of the water without doing more injury to the body. As a journalist, I had covered murder trials and knew moving a body often tainted evidence, and I didn't think this was an accidental drowning.

I rushed to the deck of the *Fenian Bastard,* took my cell phone from the cockpit and grabbed a pole hook. She began to float away as I jumped to the dock, so I entangled her hair in the hook and mumbled a prayer of apology. I dialed nine-one-one, told them where the floater was, and hung up as they asked me to stay on the line.

I called Richard Dowley next and he told me not to let her float away. Gallows humor from Richard, I guessed. It was an eerie feeling as the incoming current tugged at the body. I didn't want to hurt her, even though I realized it was too late for that.

Sirens wailed outside the marina. First the fire truck, then a police car and finally the paramedics. The main fire and police stations were only a long block away, but as I stood holding her body in place, it seemed to be forever before anyone arrived.

Two firefighters, Craig Davila and Jerry Karash, in jeans and gray Key West Fire Department T-shirts, ran down the dock. I whistled to get their attention. They looked at the body. One mumbled in surprise, while the other used a two-way radio to talk to Pat Wardlow in the truck. I knew Pat; he was part of the fire department's dive team.

Firefighter Billy Fraga arrived, mumbled when he saw the body and asked for the pole hook. I gave it willingly. Two Key West police officers walked down the dock with Pat, who was carrying a small scuba tank and dive bag. Another firefighter, Harry Sawyer, came down behind them with a rolled-up SKED, a collapsible hard-orange-plastic backboard with straps. Its main use is for removing an injured person or body from the water.

Pat nodded and looked down into the water. "She float face up?"

"No, I turned her."

He put the tank and dive bag on the dock. "Why?"

"To see if she was alive."

He knelt down and touched her arm. "She's already cold."

"Yeah, but the body's clean. She hasn't been in the water long."

"You after my job?" The voice came from behind me. "Or are you watching too many CSI shows?"

Sherlock Corcoran, the police department's crime-scene investigator, stood there with an impatient expression etched on his face. The nickname came with the job. He set his crime-scene box on the dock, opened it and removed a camera. He took photos of the body in the water, adjusting the lens from wide angle to close up, without looking at me.

"Get her out, Pat, before she becomes bait." Sherlock bent down with the camera hanging from his neck to check the bruises.

Pat slipped into the water from the other side of the dock. He

83

opened the SKED, loosened the straps and slipped it under the body. Then Billy unwound the hook from her hair and caught the SKED, while Pat strapped the body in place.

Sherlock and another firefighter, David Fahey, grabbed the SKED and pulled it onto the dock as Pat pushed from the water. It moved easily, splashing water as it came to rest. Pat lifted himself onto the crowded dock.

"Does anyone know her?" Richard asked from a gathering of police officers and firefighters. He moved forward and bent down to examine her. "Sherlock, what are these?"

"It looks like rope burns on her neck, Chief."

"Like in a hanging?"

"Be my guess right now."

"How'd she get into the water? You don't hang yourself and then walk into the bight."

Sherlock took close-up photos of her throat but didn't answer the chief's rhetorical question.

Paramedics rolled a gurney down to the finger dock; an opened body bag lay on it. Wearing latex gloves, Billy and David, and two paramedics, unstrapped the body from the SKED and moved it into the body bag. They lifted the unzipped bag and strapped it to the gurney.

"Pat, dive the dock," Sherlock said, "and figure out where Mick found her?"

"Sure."

"Look for anything interesting, clothing, rope. . . ."

"Mick, I need to talk to you." Richard straightened his sunglasses as he stood up.

"I need him first." Pat slid the small air tank on. "Tide's comin' in, right?"

"Yeah." I was still dripping water from my short swim.

"About where was she, when you first saw her?"

"No more than ten feet off the bow."

84

"Current bring her in?"

"She was floating with it."

"Did you hear anything, before you saw her?" Richard moved toward us.

"No, it was quiet. I walked up and bought the paper, came back, poured a cup of coffee, and was on deck when I spotted her."

Richard looked off toward the forty-foot-wide cut, which allowed access to Garrison Bight from the Gulf of Mexico. To the right of the cut was Hilton Haven, an area of million-dollar homes, and to the left was Navy housing. On the other side of the cut was Rat Island, home to vagrant boaters and close to the city's mooring field, where live-aboard boaters occupied most of the moorings.

"Could she have come from the moorings or Rat Island?" Richard continued to stare.

"I don't think so." While keeping her from floating away, I had thought about where she could have come from, instead of what I was doing. "The charter boats leave early, and one of them would've seen the body."

Pat dropped into the water and swam to where the body had been. "Here?" he yelled.

"Close enough."

Pat went under to begin his search.

"I want you to come to the station." Richard put his hand on my shoulder. "Go change."

"All I did was find her, I didn't. . . ."

"I have something to show you." Richard's expression became serious. "It involves her, the floater, and the Colombians." He turned away. "Don't be long." He walked toward the parking lot without turning back.

EIGHTEEN

After a quick shower, I put on dry cargo shorts, a T-shirt, my faded pre–World Series Red Sox ball cap and flip-flops, and rode my bike to the police station.

"Do you recognize her?" I was seated in Richard's office when he handed me a fax sheet with four photos of the floater. One could have been a driver's license photo; the other three were more spontaneous. No information appeared on the page.

"She was pretty." I gave him back the fax, and realized that someone had stolen more than her beauty; they stole her future. "Where's the cover sheet with her name and rap sheet?"

"No rap sheet." Richard hesitated before picking up a few sheets of paper from his desk.

"Someone's princess trying to find excitement in Paradise?" If she had a scandalous background, maybe I would get past being upset.

"You're an unsympathetic son of a bitch," Reed Fitcher said from the doorway.

Richard slid papers toward me that were in English and Spanish and had the seal of the Colombian government's *Departmento Administrativo de Seguridad*, its secret police. Another sheet was from the DEA. I read the English first and then scanned the Spanish to see if it translated correctly.

Her name was Gabriela Isabella Yanez, a thirty-one-year-old Colombian.

"How'd she go missing?"

86

"She was an undercover agent for the Colombians," Fitcher said. "Our DEA down there knew and trusted her, she gave them a lead that brought her from Colombia to Miami, and that's where they lost her. She was the last link we had to the bad guys."

"And you are telling me this because?"

"You're involved." Richard sipped from a cup of coffee.

"With her?" The accusation surprised me. "You don't believe that."

"No." Richard smiled and walked out of the office, and when he came back he put a cup of coffee in front of me. "By noon, I'll have more Feds converging on my office than I care to."

"DEA?"

"Yeah," Fitcher said, "and Colombian DEA and they'll want to know what happened. They confided in the chief, they expect something in return."

"What's her story?" The coffee was horrible, even with two sugars. "Why was she in Miami?"

Fitcher told me.

Years ago, right-wing Colombian militias hired foreign mercenaries to train them, so they could protect certain haciendas from the leftist guerillas. As the militias became successful, they began to work with the Colombian drug cartels, which then used the protected haciendas as transportation centers. One of the mercenaries was a Brit, Neville Cluny, who soon realized there was more money in drugs than in war. He befriended the drug lords and became their security chief for the cocaine's trek from Colombia to Miami.

Gabriela met the mercenaries, because of her contacts with the cartels. She recognized Neville's plan to distribute *paco* and wormed her way into his trust. Being bright and pretty didn't hurt, either.

87

"How does all this lead to Key West?" I left the coffee untouched.

Fitcher frowned. "It led here because you found her body. It's all wrapped around the group we're after. She was the last person on our side that could identify the bad guys. And the Colombians don't like that they lost a deep-cover agent here."

"And the Limey? Can't someone ID him?"

"He's vanished."

"Maybe he's dead, too."

"Possible, but you didn't find him, so maybe he killed her."

"I was thinking of how she died." I had spent too much time thinking about her. "If looks are right, and Sherlock's right, she was hanged. You saw the marks on her neck."

Richard nodded halfheartedly.

"Or maybe she was strangled with a rope." Fitcher just stared at me.

"Sherlock said hanging," I said. "How do you hang someone around here without being noticed? If you wanted to hang a person on a tree in Bayview Park, to set an example, you'd leave the body. I can see that—a drug gang making an example of someone." I picked up the fax sheet with her photos. Unlike the dead eyes I had seen in the morning, her large brown eyes in the photos seemed to sparkle, imp-like, and there was even a sprinkling of freckles across her nose. Was she a victim of Padre Thomas's prediction of evil?

NINETEEN

I rode my bike by Schooner Wharf Bar, at the Historic Seaport, on my way to meet Tita at Harpoon Harry's for a late breakfast. The traffic was mid-morning light and the sun had risen halfway to its noon high. The temperature was climbing, too. Young girls with ponytails, bronze tans and bikinis laughed as they washed down the Sebago catamaran, spraying each other in the process, while preparing for an afternoon sail and snorkeling trip full of tourists.

Seagulls and pelicans rested on pilings, waiting for the afternoon arrival of the seaport's few remaining charter boats and their free meal. Six-foot tarpon skimmed the surface, looking for handouts in competition with the seabirds. Small groups of tourists wandered along the wooden pier, stopping to gawk at the tarpon and the classic ships that rested in their slips.

"Mick." Someone called my name as I rode by the bar.

The tables in the dirt and pebble courtyard of the driftwood-built Schooner Wharf Bar were mostly empty, because the open-air bar would be closed until noon. Padre Thomas sat at one of the tall, thatched-rooftop tables in the sunny courtyard with someone I didn't know. He waved me over.

A tall, lanky guy with bushy sun-streaked hair that would have been an Afro if he had been African-American sat with him. They had Styrofoam cups of coffee.

"Mick, this is an old friend from Guatemala." Padre Thomas stood and slapped the man's shoulder; his demeanor had

89

improved overnight. "Coco Joe, meet my friend Mick Murphy."

Coco Joe stood—he had to be six-foot-six—and smiled as we shook hands.

"Visiting?" I sat down with them.

"No," Padre Thomas answered. "He's playing the Hog's Breath."

Hog's Breath is one of my hangouts. "You're with the California band?"

"Yeah, we just drove down from Atlanta, from another gig." Coco Joe kept a smile on his boyish face.

"You don't sound Guatemalan."

He laughed. "No, I worked with Padre Thomas as a Peace Corps volunteer, years ago." Coco Joe turned to Thomas and his smile got larger. "He actually saved my life."

Padre Thomas looked embarrassed and slowly shook his head. "No," he mumbled.

"Yes, you did," Coco Joe protested with a smile. "He's the bravest man I've ever known."

"How brave?" I had to ask. Padre Thomas never looked like the heroic kind to me.

"When a group of the junta's goons came into the village," Coco Joe said with a frown that turned to a grin, "he confronted them with only his Jesuit clothing and a rosary."

"The rosary has always been a shield to the Irish." Padre Thomas tried to explain, but Coco Joe kept on.

"He stood his ground, quoted Scripture and demanded they leave the village." He touched Thomas's shoulder. "They meekly retreated. It was a couple of days later I thought they had come back and disappeared him." The smile evaporated. "I came with the villagers looking for him and he was gone. A few nights later, the death squads came back and massacred the villagers." His words came out angrily. "I was away, or I would have died that time, for sure."

"If I had stayed, maybe things would have been different," Padre Thomas said softly. "I live with that shame, but the angels made me leave."

"And I am glad they did." Coco Joe smiled again. "Otherwise you wouldn't be here, Padre."

"How'd you know he was in Key West?"

"Rob O'Neil, a man I was in the Peace Corps with, came to the Keys shooting photos of what he called 'Key West characters' for a book." Coco Joe touched Padre Thomas gently. "When he saw the photo of Thomas riding that old bike of his, he thought he looked familiar and sent me a copy. 'Doesn't this guy look like that priest they murdered in Guatemala?' He wrote and sent me the photo. That's all it took."

"That's some story," I said. "The angels took care of you, Padre."

"I live with the guilt," he mumbled again. "Not my proudest moment."

"Hey, dudes, I need to check in at the club and then get some sleep. It was nice meetin' you," Joe said.

He picked up his bulky backpack as we shook hands; he and Thomas hugged like brothers—*abrazo* it's called in Spanish countries—and he headed toward Duval Street, a distinct limp to his right leg.

"Looks awful young to have been in the Peace Corps when you were in Guatemala." I sat down.

"Yes, his boyish looks can fool you." Padre Thomas smiled. "He was a good kid down there, a lot of help to the villagers." He sipped his coffee.

"Where'd he get the limp?"

"He was shot by a soldier for helping villagers sell their produce, but he doesn't like to talk about it."

"Why Coco Joe?" When the time was right, Padre Thomas would tell me the story of the shooting, because I didn't believe

91

Peace Corps volunteers got shot. "At least you can't say his name without smiling."

"I don't know. He was Coco Joe when I met him. Once I overheard him say an uncle called him that and it stuck. I guess it's a California thing." He hunched his shoulders with a who-knows expression on his face.

I went to stand, but he held up his hand and motioned me to sit.

"Something I can do for you, Padre?"

"I know about this morning." He pulled a wrinkled package of Camels from his shirt pocket, took a cigarette out and lit it.

"What about this morning?" I returned his roguish smile.

"Not a believer today?" He exhaled smoke.

"I believe in a lot of things this morning, Padre. What do you believe in?"

"I believe you care about the young woman." He took a long drag on the cigarette and crushed out the stub. "I believe you feel a responsibility to someone you never knew. I believe it is part of the evil I told you about yesterday."

"If I plead ignorance. . . ."

"Ah," he shook his head slowly and forced a soft brogue and smile, "would a nice Irish Catholic *boyo* lie to a man of the cloth?"

We both laughed, but it was with sadness, not humor.

"You wanna know what I know?"

"Of course." He lit another cigarette.

"I know her name was Gabriela and that she was an undercover agent for the Colombian DEA." I wished I had a cigar. "She disappeared from Miami and I found her floating just before seven this morning."

"You didn't mention she'd been murdered, hanged to be exact." Padre Thomas inhaled, left the cigarette dangling from his lips and exhaled smoke through his nose.

I looked at him and wanted to be surprised by what he said, but I wasn't. He didn't get his information from officials, but I thought he might have overheard someone talking. Otherwise, he'd have me believing in angels again. I now understood why he believed in them, but they hadn't saved my life.

"Thomas, I need to know how you know this. It could be important."

He sipped from a Styrofoam cup of *café con leche* as he stubbed out the cigarette. "You know how I know it, Mick."

I pulled closer to him. "If you overheard someone talking, I need to know."

I had a feeling I didn't want to hear his answer.

"I overheard no one, Mick." He pulled the cigarette package out of his pocket, but didn't take a cigarette. "At five-thirty this morning, my vision came."

"The angels?"

He nodded, his face lost all expression, and his pale-blue eyes widened. "I saw the girl gagging for breath, her hands scratching at the rope around her neck as she hung from a tree. I saw two men toss her into the water. I saw you on your boat." He held onto the table so fiercely his knuckles turned white. "I know you care and don't understand why."

"Wait a minute, Padre." I moved closer. "You said a tree, what tree? Where?"

"I don't know, somewhere close." Finally, he let the table go, pulled a cigarette from the package and lit it. "Close to the water." He inhaled deeply. "Close to your boat."

"Padre, if I take this information to the cops they're gonna come looking for you," I said out of frustration. "And we both know they aren't big believers in angels."

"But you believe me, right?"

"I know you didn't kill her, Padre. That's all I know."

93

TWENTY

Before I ran into Padre Thomas, I'd had enough sense to call Tita from outside the police station, to change our normal Sunday breakfast to late morning. I had to promise her answers to why, over our *café con leches*. I rode my bike from Schooner Wharf through the Waterfront Market's parking lot, to Caroline Street and Harpoon Harry's Restaurant. Thomas seemed happy to have Coco Joe in town, but he hadn't let go of his "evil is here" theory and it was beginning to look like he might be onto something, again.

People waited outside for seating, as I locked my bike, but Tita was already inside at a table, waiting. Ron, the owner, pointed her out as he sat four tourists at a window seat. I kissed her on the cheek before sitting and was glad to see her smile.

The waitress brought my *con leche* and I ordered eggs over easy, with home fries and wheat toast. Tita ordered French toast with a side of fruit, her *con leche* almost gone.

"Okay, what happened?" She looked at her wristwatch.

I told her about finding the floater, the trip to the KWPD office and the meeting with Richard and Reed Fitcher, and the connection to the two deaths at Hotel Key West—Colombians, drugs and mercenaries. I spoke softly, trying not to scare the couples sitting on either side of us. A few times, Tita asked me to repeat myself and moved closer. Our breakfast came before I finished the story. Tita spread jam on my toast as I came to the end. I ordered refills of the *con leches* for us.

94

"You shouldn't have gone without me." She chided me and put butter and syrup on her French toast. "Legally speaking, the only thing connecting the three people is death."

"Hotel Key West," I reminded her.

"One outside, one inside." She ate a strawberry.

"We know they're connected because of the DEA."

"The newspaper is full of speculation about yesterday and part of that is the history of suicides at the hotel." She sliced her French toast into small bites as it sopped up syrup. "But they don't know what we know. There's no mention of Rebecca."

"I didn't think there would be. You heard 'em, they want to keep it under wraps for a while."

She smiled a little and after a moment asked, "Was she pretty?"

"Yeah." And, as I answered, I realized that one of the things that bothered me about finding Gabriela was how much she and Tita had in common: the bronze skin, the petite body, long hair and their age. "She could've been your sister."

"That's not funny, Mick." Tita stared at me and drank her *con leche.*

"It wasn't meant to be." I splashed hot sauce over my eggs and potatoes. "It was frightening and I realized, right now, that what bothered me most when I found her were the similarities to you." I mixed the eggs and potatoes and added salt. "She wasn't the first dead person I'd seen, so I couldn't figure out why it bothered me. Now I know."

"Thank you, I think." She played with her food, but didn't eat. "Are Thomas's premonitions coming true?"

"I think all his premonitions come true."

"But you believe in his angels." She bit a grape in half. "I don't have that kind of faith."

"I don't either." I ate some eggs and potatoes.

95

"You believe he sees angels, you go to church." She let her words run together.

"Yeah, I believe he sees angels and I believe Captain Maybe made a deal with God." She hadn't heard about that, so I went into another explanation while we finished our breakfast.

"You have to have faith to believe those things." She drank from a glass of water.

"No, you need to believe that Padre Thomas and Captain Maybe believe. If Captain Maybe accepts his death more easily because he believes he made a deal with God, more power to him. I am scared to death of dying, because I lack that faith you seem to think I have."

"What about Thomas? How does he know the things he knows?"

"No logical explanation, unless you believe in his angels."

"And you believe in angels? You believe him?"

"When it's the only explanation, yeah, I do." I sipped the last of my *con leche*. "But I have my doubts."

Tita ordered more *con leches* from Ron when he came over to our table to say hi. The caffeine and sugar would keep us moving like Mexican jumping beans all afternoon.

"And here I thought you were one of those devout Irish Catholics boys from Boston I grew up with," she smiled, making her usual ethnic joke about my heritage.

In Boston, Tita had to learn to live with degrading, racist spic jokes growing up, and when she discovered there were sayings that belittled the Irish, she never let me forget it. For a long time, when she first came to Key West and we dated, she referred to us as *Spic and Mick*.

"I've known you all these years and I'm just finding out you question your own faith, how surprising. You have secrets, but I somehow find out about them."

"Tita." I sipped *con leche* and smiled at her. "I have no secrets from you."

"Liar," she pouted.

"Religion causes enough problems in the world without me adding my questions." I tried to explain to her. "My search for faith is personal. I am not very happy with the Church and its years of scandals, but it's my Church."

"Well, I thank God you are not a Bible thumper," she laughed, and got up to go.

TWENTY-ONE

Of course, I've lied to Tita. But, they were lies of omission, not what I would call lying about something like being somewhere or doing something that I wasn't. A lie was what I'd told Richard and the DEA. My mother used to call omission a "little white lie," so, if I forgot to mention it in confession on Saturday afternoon, I could still go to communion at Sunday Mass. I know better now, but I always support the white-lie argument, because it helps my conscience. Plus, my white lies were said to protect Tita.

Sunday in Key West, if I wasn't sailing, is a social time. I would meet Tita at Harpoon Harry's, if we hadn't spent the night together. Of course, if we hadn't spent the weekend together it was my fault, or so she always pointed out. Anyone and everyone might show up at Harpoon's for breakfast, or a *café con leche* and Cuban bread.

Sunday mornings are slow in Key West, because the island has Sunday Blue Laws. Yeah, no alcohol sales before noon, so there were no bloody Marys or screwdrivers to help get the blood flowing the morning after. At noon, the gloves came off and Key West got back to normal concerning alcohol, the first cold one of the day always being the best one.

Tita looked at my bike, shook her head with a smile and took my arm. "I walked," she said, as we headed to Schooner Wharf for that first cold one.

"I didn't think I was going to be so late." I tried to explain why I had the bike and not the Jeep. "It's not the best Sunday morning of my life."

"Maybe I can make the afternoon memorable," she laughed, and pulled me along Caroline Street.

Jimmy Buffett wrote a song, I think it was called "Woman Going Crazy on Caroline Street," and the change in Tita since last evening when she dropped me at the Jeep made me believe she'd gone a little crazy herself. But, her mood held promise for my afternoon delight.

Buddy Owens was in the trailer-kitchen at his B.O.'s Fish Wagon shack, prepping for lunch. "Fresh mahi-mahi," B.O. yelled, as we walked by. "Mick, be gone by five." He knew mahi was my favorite fish.

The bar at Schooner Wharf was full; it was only a few minutes past noon, and empty beer bottles were already waiting to be picked up.

Bill and Karen, from Fastlane Advertising, were sitting on the waterside at one of the tables for two, their mimosas almost gone. "Are you going to enter a boat in the Minimal Regatta?" Bill offered me a cigar and cut the end off one for himself.

"That's the plan."

Tita and Karen spoke softly, their voices lost in the din of the bar.

"If you need a sponsor." Bill lit his cigar.

I used his cutter to remove the end of his gift as he extended his lighter to me. "What do you want?" I pointed the cigar into the flame and puffed it to life. Bill only smoked good cigars and this was no exception.

"I'll pay for the materials and you put my dot-com address and name on each side of the boat." He blew thick white smoke toward the boardwalk and tourists.

"Sounds like a deal. Let me tell the others."

"It's going to float, right?" he laughed as Tita and I walked toward the courtyard.

"For a few minutes," I yelled back, not sure he heard me.

I used getting our beers as an excuse to talk to Bob the bartender. He got my two Kaliks, with lime, and then I asked him about Johnny Dey.

"Hell, Mick, I ain't seen Johnny in more than a year." He took my money.

"He's back, so if you do see him, tell him to call me. It's important." He gave me my change and I left a two-dollar tip.

"Sure thing." He picked up the tip.

Tita doesn't usually drink in the afternoons, but recently she'd begun to nurse a cold Kalik or draft on Sunday afternoons. We found Bob and Doug at one of the patio's larger thatched-roof tables and joined them. I told them about Fastlane Advertising, and Bob said he'd bring the receipt to Bill in the morning.

I had a second Kalik, while Tita sipped hers. Then we said our good-byes and walked to the Conch Farm, across the bay. The Sebago, Fury and Sunny Days catamarans were gone on their snorkeling trips, filled with tourists looking for the sights around the reef, and most of them wouldn't be wearing sunscreen, so they'd be red as lobsters at four P.M.

The afternoon would take us to many of the bars along Duval Street, next stop being the Rum Barrel, then the Hog's Breath Saloon. Before we got to Tita's there would be stops at the Conch Farm, Sloppy Joe's and Rick's. By mid-afternoon Tita and I had also grabbed a drink at Margaritaville, because the bar was not overpacked with Parrot Heads; then we crossed the street to Jack Flat's, and finally we made it to the Green Parrot to see Scotty Griffiths, the day manager. At each bar, I left word that I was looking for Johnny Dey. I hadn't told Tita about meeting with Carl Dey, but it was only a little white lie of omission, or so I thought.

TWENTY-TWO

I like to think that all the walking Tita and I do on Sundays burns off the alcohol I consume during the afternoon. It is always a slow walk down Duval, but we got to see all the sights and, believe me, there are sights to see between the tourists and the characters on the street.

Tita usually leaves her drink half filled when we move on. Me, I prefer a Bahamian Kalik, but if it's not available, I'll drink a Jamaican Red Stripe or Mexican Dos Equis or Corona. We eventually meet most of our friends on the island on these jaunts, and even make some new ones. The conversations are as quirky as the characters we run into. A lot of it concerns city politics, sailing and the waterfront.

The Minimal Regatta was the topic at most bars, because many of the patrons were representing their favorite watering hole in the holiday event. It seemed everyone had a secret that would keep their makeshift boat afloat this year. I knew Bob and Burt thought they had one, but I kept it to myself. I let the others brag and hoped I remembered their secrets.

It was a beautiful afternoon, the sidewalks were filled with tourists and the streets busy with cars and scooters. There were no obvious signs on the street of what had happened to Jay outside Hotel Key West. His death had reverted to a page-three story, and Tita and I were probably the only ones that looked up and remembered as we passed the hotel. Well, maybe the young salesgirls at Excess across the street still giggled when they talked about it.

"Do you have any more secrets I should know about?" Tita and I walked holding hands along Southard Street, toward her home.

Yeah, I should have told her, *I killed the woman I loved when a bomb I placed exploded in a drug dealer's car in Tijuana, Mexico,* but I didn't. I didn't tell anyone. It's the secret I'm running from, that is chasing me, and it's the reason I left Southern California more than twelve years ago, and the reason caring for Tita scares the hell out of me.

"I suppose there are a few things in my life we haven't discussed, but I'm not sure you'd call 'em secrets," I said instead, knowing I might be pushing the envelope on omission. "Lots of things happened in Central America. I wrote about most of them, but some were. . . ." I wasn't sure how to explain what they were.

"Unbelievable?"

"For a Puerto Rican girl from Lares." I tried to make the words sound light.

"And for a tough Irish Catholic boy from Boston?" she joked.

"You ever have anything happen in court that you just couldn't believe? Something so outrageous you didn't want to accept it?"

The topic had turned counterpoint to the beautiful spring afternoon. As we moved away from Duval Street, the aroma of blooming jasmine and honeysuckle wafted by, and scents of grilling steaks and chicken and pork, from backyard barbecues, filled the narrow, old streets. The sky was picture-perfect blue and it was almost eighty degrees. Plants and trees with colorful flowers were beginning to spring to life.

"I was part of a prosecution team on a child-abuse case in Boston," Tita finally said. "The photos taken at the hospital made me sick, I mean literally. I threw up."

"What happened?"

"The mother and her boyfriend went to jail." She squeezed my hand, not wanting to give a full explanation. "The baby went to foster care. No one knew who the father was. After that, I came to find you." She let her words end softly. "What happened in Central America? I read your news stories, some of them were horrible."

"Thanks." I pulled her to me.

"Not the writing." She bumped me off the sidewalk. "The subject matter."

We were playing, but the topic had lost its playfulness.

"That's a relief." And I was quiet.

"You're not going to tell me?"

She held my hand again. We passed over Solares Hill, the highest spot in Key West, and were close to Frances Street, where we'd turn toward the cemetery and her Conch house. The air smelled like spring flowers.

"I think the worst thing I witnessed was what one human being can do to another and not understand the barbarity of it." I saw the images again in my head, a defect I have when it comes to recall—I see it over and over. "You and I were brought up on the sanctity of life. Imagine the kind of person it takes to kill a child or a pregnant woman, just because they're different. Age, gender, it doesn't matter; people become roaches to be extinguished. Then you find the killers socializing with your diplomats, like normal people. Governments are still unearthing mass graves in Central America, but those responsible go unpunished."

"You know the serenity prayer. Apply it."

"Yeah, but there were places I thought I could do something, but failed."

"Oh, I think your stories reached a lot of people." Tita pulled closer to me. "I came to find you, after all, and if I hadn't been captivated by your writing I wouldn't have remembered what a crush I had on you when I was young."

"And now that you're older, how's that crush?" I put my arm around her, wondering how much alcohol played a part in our conversation.

She laughed. "Oh, I am planning on showing you as soon as we get home."

TWENTY-THREE

Tita stood naked, brushing her hair while looking into the bureau's large mirror. The bedroom was very feminine: print curtains on the windows, a frilly bedspread, throw pillows, cut flowers in a vase and a framed photo of her and Paco. She was beautiful and I fought to keep images of Gabriela floating offside the *Fenian Bastard* from spoiling my view.

"Do you think the paper knows about the woman in the bight?" She continued to run the brush through her long, raven hair.

"Too many witnesses on the dock to keep it a secret." I stared at her breasts, as they moved with the motion of her brush strokes. "Richard can hold off a while, calling it an ongoing investigation."

"Will they connect the deaths?" She turned briefly and smiled at me, aware of her teasing movements.

"Depends on if they find out about Rebecca," I said. "I don't know how long they can keep that quiet. If she has family here, it might become difficult real soon."

She continued to brush her hair and smile into the mirror.

"You like what you see, Mick?" She almost whispered the words.

"You are beautiful." I stared and added, "Dressed or undressed. Like the old country song, 'Nothin' Looks Good on You.' "

"I've filled out since I was a teenager." She touched her

105

smooth stomach. "I've put a little weight on."

I laughed. "And you filled out wonderfully."

"You should have seen me fifteen years ago."

"I did."

"Not like this." She turned to me. "Not when I had a mad crush on you."

"Paco would've killed me." I sat up. "Or I would have gone to jail."

"You will never know what you missed." She put the brush down and sat on the bed. "I think I still have a crush on you."

"A mad crush?" I pulled her to me.

"A little more realistic than mad." She kissed me softly. "I was so in love with you." She leaned her head against my chest. "And you broke my heart, when you left after graduation."

I squeezed her tight and remembered the raven-haired teen that pranced around her Roxbury apartment braless, teasing me.

"You were a confused teenager," I said softly into her ear. "I was very tempted, but you were too young."

"I'm still young." She sat up and smiled. "I will always be younger than you."

"And smarter."

"I'm glad you realize that." She gave me one of her romantic stares; something the jury didn't get to see. "Paco got me to go to college, because he said you'd never fall in love with someone that wasn't at least as smart as you."

"Paco knew how you felt?"

She nodded and continued her grin. "And he knew you were tempted. Anyway, that's what he told me to get me into college."

"And law school?"

"That was my decision and had nothing to do with you." She stood up and slipped on an oversized T-shirt. "I wanted to lose

106

my virginity to you. Your loss."

"I thought you said yesterday you were a virgin." I tried acting surprised. "You lied to me?'

"Well, whatever, I'm not a virgin now." She laughed, and walked out of the room.

I started to get dressed when my cell phone rang.

"Hello." I slipped my cargo shorts on.

"Mick?" Came across quietly.

"Yeah." I got my flip-flops on.

"Know who this is?"

In the background, I heard music and loud voices. The call came from a bar, and the readout only indicated it was a private call—something I knew without needing to read the small screen. There was no phone number.

"No, I don't." I didn't want a long conversation with a drunk, friend or not.

"You asked me to call." The voice almost giggled.

"Johnny? Johnny Dey?" I said, surprised.

"One and the same, Mick. What can I do you for?" Johnny spoke clearly, now that the game was over. "I've almost run into you a couple of times today."

"Wish you had." I sat on the bed.

"I wish I had, too."

"Can we get together? I heard you're in town and thought we'd get a drink or something."

"Why?"

His reply caught me by surprise. It was a good question; I would've wanted to know, in his place.

"Catch up on old times," I lied. "Your grandfather told me you were moving back."

"Next year," he said, after a brief silence. "Look, I'm here on business. I don't have a lot of time and then I'm going back to Miami."

107

"I never knew you to turn down a free drink." I tried to put some levity in my voice.

"Well, a man's gotta drink, doesn't he?"

"In Key West, yeah. How about tonight?"

"How about midnight," he mimicked. "At the Hog? You still hang there?"

"Midnight," I said.

"Mick, if something comes up and you can't make it, I'll catch you next time, okay?"

"I'll be there, Johnny."

He hung up.

"Who was that?" Tita stood in the doorway. She was wearing jeans.

"Johnny Dey. I'm meeting him for drinks later." I put on my shirt. "What smells so good?"

"Guess."

Tita was, without doubt, the best cook of *arroz con pollo* in the world. In Boston, all Paco had to say was she was cooking it for dinner and I'd invite myself over. Now I realized she did it on purpose back then, to get me to come by. A teenage trickster.

"Arroz con pollo?" I laughed and hugged her. It was almost nine. "I need to meet Johnny around midnight."

"Plenty of time for dinner and dessert." She put my hand on her breast.

108

Twenty-Four

I arrived at the Hog's Breath a little before midnight, while the crowd in the patio listened to Tim and Danny Carter and their band from Nashville. The Carter brothers are a regular attraction at the bar, sometimes playing the mid-shift gig from five to nine P.M. as a duo, but as a four-man band for the late-night gig, and they keep the club jumping with lively country-rock music. Tim plays a mean fiddle, and Danny is the rocker.

I pushed my way in off the Duval Street parking lot, past the small stage, and looked around the bar for Johnny Dey. I didn't see him. Randy and Kevin were behind the raw bar, and Frank and Brian tended the crowd seated at the main bar. The music was loud and people were singing and clapping, standing room only on the worn concrete dance floor.

I checked the indoor restaurant bar, but it was midnight empty. Alon, the inside bartender, waved and I waved back.

Art, the night manager, and Kris, an assistant manager who fills in as a bartender and sometimes server, worked on the night's receipts at a table in the restaurant, and said hi when I looked in.

"A little late for you, isn't it?" Art said, and went back to discussing the night's business with Kris.

Johnny walked in from the Front Street entrance a little past midnight. He wore a wrinkled denim shirt over a black T, faded jeans and scruffy tennis shoes. His hair was stylishly messy and he looked like he hadn't shaved in two or three days. I guess the

109

scruffy look is popular. Me, I grew my beard when I was twenty, trim it bi-monthly and have a friend cut my red hair every two months, whether it needs it or not. It's a habit left over from my early journalist's days, when time for a barbershop haircut didn't exist, but there was always a pair of scissors and a friend hanging around.

We met by the stairs to the second-floor office and shook hands. Johnny looked tired. His dark-brown eyes were dull and nervous, unable to focus clearly on me, and his once elfin smile looked a lot like a sneer.

"You still like this shit-kicker stuff?" His laugh seemed forced as he led me to the bar. "I bet you still drink Jameson."

Frank brought my double Jameson on the rocks and took Johnny's order, a rum and Coke.

"Too much time on South Beach, Johnny." I toasted him after his drink came.

"Beaches and babes, man, don't knock it." He raised his glass and took a long swallow. "You ever been to South Beach? String bikinis, tans, tall blondes and salsa."

"You know me, Johnny, I don't go to Miami." I sipped the Jameson. "Probably for those reasons."

"Jesus," he sighed. "I was born here and you're more of a damn Conch than I am. Still sailing south?"

He meant Cuba.

"Not in the last few years. What have you been up to?"

"This and that." He lit a cigarette. "I'm workin' a deal now that will let me move back, maybe retire."

"Tell me about it." I tried to say it in a friendly tone.

"Can't do that, Mick," he said, too quickly. "You workin' on somethin' local?"

"I don't work local," I said. "I'm sailing as much as I can before the summer doldrums arrive."

"I guess I like airplanes, like you like boats."

"I didn't know you flew."

"Been doin' a lot of things since I left college, Mick. Might surprise you." He laughed again.

"You ain't flying out tonight, are you?"

"No." He sipped his drink. "I wouldn't drink and fly." He smiled, briefly.

"I was thinking you looked tired, Johnny." I put my drink on the bar and lit a cigar. "You're up in the air, you fall asleep, I can't see it as good thing."

"Thanks for worrying about me." He took another drink. "This business deal I'm working on, it's a pain in the ass. There are others involved, so it's compromise here, compromise there, until the concept is watered down and I ain't sure all the effort is worth it."

The Carter Brothers Band was loud, and people by the stage sang along. We moved back from the bar and sat on the stairs that went to the office. Johnny nervously looked around as he talked, and his words came slowly. Every so often, he stared out onto Front Street.

"Some people say life is a compromise." I chewed on the end of the cigar.

He looked at me with a blank expression.

"Is that a good thing?" He took a long swallow and finished his drink. "Do you make compromises as a journalist?"

"I get a lot of 'off the record' comments and I can't use what's said. That's kind of a compromise." I blew smoke into the evening. "I get told stuff that could make or break a story, but I need to find another source. Sometimes I can, sometimes I can't."

"Yeah, well, I got a dilemma, see," he mumbled, and looked away. "The deal is ready to happen, but things I can't control have come up." He lit a cigarette. "If I walk away, I lose everything and I'm back to bein' a workin' stiff. Maybe literally.

111

If I stay, it's kinda like I condone their actions, and I don't. I keep tellin' myself, 'the end result, the end result.' Do you believe that?" Johnny smoked the cigarette to its filtered stub.

"The end justifies the means?" I rotated my cigar as I blew smoke out.

"Yeah." He played with his empty cup. "Does it?"

"Who knows?" I sipped my drink. "I guess it depends on how badly you want the end result. Politicians seem to think so, the Church doesn't."

"Hell, I don't wanna be a politician, and I ain't no priest." He slouched against the step. "Christ, could you see me and R.L. Beaumont working together on the city commission?"

"R.L. is greedy. Are you greedy?"

"Not R.L. greedy." He almost smiled for real. "To him it's about power, always has been. He preaches taking care of the city, but the result of what he does fucks the residents and benefits his friends. And he's still in the closet."

"Life's a bitch, and then you die," I said, not believing it but feeling the negative vibes he gave off. "Johnny, your grand-father's worried about you. Why don't you go see him, talk to him?"

He looked toward the bar, as if he wanted another drink, and then he watched the traffic on Front Street again. He looked at his wristwatch. "I'll work things out with Gramps real soon. Tell him that for me, will you?"

"What are you up to, Johnny?" I leaned back, held my cigar and sipped my drink. The Jameson had melted most of the ice, and the chilled whiskey tasted good.

"I've got to do things that are gonna appear real bad to you, but they need to be done so I can achieve the end result. And it's hard." He put his empty cup on the step above. "People may not want to forgive me, especially you, and it's clouding my judgment. For the time being, all I can say is, I'm sorry."

Johnny was acting bizarre. His words concerning me seemed to be without reason. I wasn't his grandfather, I had nothing to forgive him for—or so I thought at the moment.

Johnny stood up and leaned in, like he was going to hug me, but he pushed me against the steps to keep me down, pressed something against my side, and then he shot me. I barely heard the pop of the gun over the noise of the bar, but I felt the burning and I think I heard him whisper, *I'm sorry, Mick,* before he fired the small-caliber automatic three more times into the wooden steps beside me. I dropped my cigar.

Twenty-Five

I sat on the steps, dazed, lost in a fog of music and the loud mixture of people singing and talking, all trying to be heard. Blood seeped out of my side. I watched Johnny walk up to Frank behind the bar, point at me, and then walk away. No one sitting or standing around heard him shoot me or saw his three wild shots into the steps. Johnny never looked back, just walked to Front Street and got into a waiting car.

Frank hurried over and brought Andy, a daytime manager who must have been hanging around for the band. They looked down at me. I pulled my hand away from the wound, and it was covered with blood. I couldn't hear what Frank or Andy were saying, I wasn't even sure they were talking to me, so I leaned against the stairwell and tried to smile. I laughed, maybe only inside, because I had been through civil wars in Central America without getting a scratch and here I was, in my hometown favorite bar, and got shot by someone I knew.

Andy handed me a couple of bar towels, I don't remember where they came from or who got them, and he said something to me I couldn't understand. He gave up talking, sat down and pressed the towels against my wound. I was surprised it didn't hurt. I looked down at the towels, and they were turning blood red. Sounds were a mishmash of music and talk, and I thought to myself, *it takes a lot of blood to do that to white towels.*

I remember thinking, why did Johnny shoot me? Then a Key West firefighter was staring at me. The KWFD are usually the

114

first responders on nine-one-one calls. I knew the fireman; it was Harry Sawyer again.

The band had stopped playing, probably couldn't compete with the fire engine's siren.

"What happened, Mick?" Harry pressed clean bandages to my side.

"I think someone shot me," I said slowly.

"Do you know who it was?" He put another bandage over the first one.

"No," I mumbled.

Donny Barroso and Alfredo Vaca, two KWPD officers, looked down and asked me the same question, but two paramedics showed up and moved everyone away while they worked on me. They cut my shirt off and yanked off the bandages Harry had put on, checked the wound and applied new bandages. The gurney was low to the ground and they helped me move from the steps to it. My legs didn't want me to stand, but with their help I stumbled to the gurney. They strapped me in, raised it up and pushed me to the ambulance. Donny and Alfredo were close behind.

The siren bothered the hell out of me, because I wanted to sleep. Why did Johnny shoot me? I also thought about Carl Dey and how his plan to help his grandson would go up in smoke if the cops knew who shot me. By the time I got into the ER, my side was hurting and I missed the fog that had surrounded me on the steps at the Saloon.

Twenty-Six

The medical center on Stock Island is about five miles from downtown, and I've spent too much time there, usually with a friend in need of its ER. Though it was very early Monday morning, the ER was Sunday-night light and I had most of the staff looking after me as I came awake. I didn't remember the end of the ambulance ride. My hat, shorts and flip-flops were gone and someone was swabbing my side. It stung, but a nurse was inserting a needle into the top of my hand, above my knuckles—she smiled warmly—and then hooked it to an IV line. The swabbing was uncomfortable, so I tried to focus on the friendly nurse. There were a lot of people moving around and talking over one another; it was almost as confusing as the Hog's Breath.

"How am I doin'?" I turned to the guy at my side and had to force the words.

"Stay still," he said. "I'm Dr. Quirk and you're very lucky."

"Of course you are." I looked at the dull ceiling and tried not to move. "And yes, I am."

"You've got more of a gash than a bullet wound." Quirk poked my side; I felt the pressure, but not any pain, as he ignored my attempted humor. "There's a lot of debris in the wound. I have to clean it out."

"It doesn't hurt." I choked the words out.

"I hope not," he said, still poking around, "you've had a local to numb the area, but I promise it will hurt later."

"Thanks, Doc."

The next thing I remember is being awakened and asked how I felt. It was still dark outside and I was in a two-bed hospital room. An IV hung above me, and its line ran into the top of my hand. A large piece of tape held the needle in place. Light from the hallway filtered into the room.

"Do you have any pain?" the nurse asked, from the shadows.

I shook my head no. My mouth was dry and I looked for something to drink.

"Can I have water?" The words seemed to drag out.

She brought a plastic cup with a straw in it and I sucked up a mouthful of water. She pulled it away before I finished. I went back to sleep.

Sunlight filtered into the room and woke me. Donny and Alfredo stood at the end of the bed. They didn't look like they'd had any sleep.

"How you feeling, Mick?" Donny looked at some papers he held.

"Okay, I guess." I fumbled around until I found the control for raising the bed. It came up slowly and I stopped when I was in a comfortable sitting position. I reached for the cup of water and emptied the glass.

"You remember anything about last night?" Alfredo asked.

"Yeah, someone shot me."

"The guy you were drinking with?" Donny looked at the note in his hands. "Frank said you were sitting with someone, and he told Frank you'd been shot."

I was a little groggy from the drugs dripping into my veins, but I knew I had to keep Johnny Dey out of this, for his grandfather.

"Frank's mistaken," I mumbled.

"Who was with you?"

"Earlier, I had one drink with a friend."

117

"Got a name?"

"Yeah, Johnny. Johnny Dey."

"And Johnny told Frank you'd been shot and left you there?" Alfredo asked.

"No," I shook my head. "Johnny left before that."

"Who shot you, then?" Donny asked, again.

"I don't know. I was sittin' there, finishing my drink and got shot."

"A man, a woman? Can you give us a description?"

"Why would Frank say it was Johnny Dey?" Alfredo moved closer to the side of the bed.

"The bar was crowded. The guy could've been Johnny's size or wearing a denim shirt and had messy hair, I don't know."

"Can you describe the shooter?" Donny asked, for the third time. "Did you know him?"

"I was sitting there, finishing my drink. There were no seats at the bar, the band was playing, and then I felt a burning in my side." I took a deep breath. Talking seemed to be making me tired. "I touched it, and my hand came away with blood."

I stopped, and they said nothing in reply for a moment.

"You didn't see who did it? No one walked up to you and pointed a gun and shot you?" Alfredo's words were a challenge.

"No," I said, and closed my eyes. They didn't leave.

One of them turned the light on over the bed. I opened my eyes.

"You want to read the doctor's report? It was a gunshot wound; he had to file a report," Donny said, and held his pad out.

"You tell me what it says."

"It says there were powder burns on your shirt and skin," he said. "Which means the gun was real close."

"Why would I lie to you, Donny? You think I want to protect someone that shot me?"

118

Twenty-Seven

Donny and Alfredo kept rewording the same questions for almost a half hour, trying to get me to say what they wanted to hear, and then left. They said they'd be back. But not before telling me how lucky I was, a couple of times over.

I heard the rattling of carts and trays as people moved in the hallway. It was a lonely sound and I wanted to get out of there. It was a typical hospital room, a TV mounted to the beige wall in front of each bed, a privacy curtain, and two small rolling tables. A blood-pressure monitor was wrapped around my arm, and every few minutes it inflated, sending its information to a machine mounted behind the bed.

I pulled my hospital gown up and looked at the large bandage on my left side. At least there wasn't any blood seeping through it.

A nurse brought me a gelatin cup and a small glass of juice. I gulped the juice and ate the red gelatin.

"Has someone called Dr. Morris?" Jack Morris is my physician and friend.

"Yes, he was here last night when you were brought into the room." She took away the empty cups. "Dr. Boros, too."

I didn't remember Jack or Lee Boros being there. Whatever drug they had me on sure did its job.

My side felt weird, like I was stretching stitches when I tried to lift my left arm, so I stopped. Jack and Lee would have admonished me and then said something like, *don't do it, if it*

119

hurts. The thought made me smile. I poured lukewarm water into the plastic cup and drank it.

"You look none the worse for wear," Richard Dowley said from the doorway.

"I'm feeling fine," I lied. "Ready to go home."

"What happened?" He moved next to the bed. "I'm told you don't remember."

"I didn't see who did it; I remember otherwise."

"How does someone get close enough to shoot you and you don't see 'em?" Reed Fitcher came in. I guess he'd read the doctor's report too. "You're one lucky guy."

"So I've been told."

They stood over me, staring down, but they weren't smiling.

"What are the chances this has something to do with what went down at Hotel Key West?" Fitcher asked.

"That would be a stretch of the imagination." I moved around in the bed, looking for a comfortable position. I couldn't find one.

"Think so," Fitcher said.

"You don't?"

"Two things come to mind."

Richard nodded. "Yeah, Mick. Listen to him."

"One"—he held up a finger—"maybe someone was tailing Jay and sees him talking with you outside Schooner Wharf. Two"—his other finger popped up—"maybe that same guy sees you with the SWAT team outside the hotel. Then he sees you leave alone, follows you. Where to?" Fitcher made a fist and rotated his shoulders like they were stiff. "Some bar?"

"Jack Flat's."

He smiled. "You wouldn't be hard to follow. How many redheaded guys with beards you got running around Key West, Chief?"

"Not many."

"So the guy follows you into Jack Flat's and asks the bartender, 'Who's the guy with the red beard, I think I've seen him somewhere before,' and the bartender says, 'Oh, that's Mick Murphy.' "

It wasn't hard to pretend I was concerned, because that guy would have been Johnny Dey, and he didn't have to ask who I was. "Sure, it's possible," I finally said. "Do you think that's what happened?"

"I think it's something we gotta consider." Richard frowned.

"What you need to remember is that the Colombians are killing everyone that might know who their local contacts are," Fitcher said sternly and rolled his shoulders. "Why? Because they're protecting the locals' ID. You know how they work?"

"Yeah, you betray 'em and they kill you and your whole family."

"They don't believe in loose ends." Fitcher kept the stern voice. I guess he thought I could be a loose end.

"If they think Jay confided something to you. . . ." Fitcher's expression grew serious. "You don't stand a chance, and I don't care how tough you are."

"I'm not tough," I admitted. "If he'd told me something, I would tell you and then go sailing, so I'd be safe."

"You wouldn't be," he said, and looked at Richard.

"Someone shot at you four times," Richard needlessly reminded me. "They were trying to kill you, Mick. Did you see who did it?"

"Why does everyone think I wouldn't say if I knew?" I wiggled around the bed, but remained uncomfortable. Where was the nurse who woke me to ask how I felt, now that I could tell her something?

"We're concerned about you." Richard's tone softened. "And sometimes you do stupid things for stupid reasons, and I'm afraid you're acting like a journalist looking at a story and not a

121

sailor wanting to chase the wind."

I think Richard was sincere and, maybe because of the drugs in my system, his sincerity surprised me. It also concerned me a little that he seemed to know me so well. And I wanted to ask him: what stupid things?

Before I could ask, Jack Morris walked into the room holding a clipboard. He shook hands with Richard, who introduced Fitcher.

"Would you wait outside, please?" He smiled at Richard. "He won't escape."

They walked out of the room, and Jack pulled the privacy curtain to separate us from the empty bed.

"You remember me coming in last night?"

"No." I tried to sit up straight. "Did I say anything?"

"You asked me a couple of times about getting out of here, but I think the drugs were talking." He pulled at my hospital gown and removed the bandage. "The bleeding has stopped."

"That's a good thing, right?"

"Yeah." He took a clean bandage off the rolling table, along with some ointment, and bandaged me back up. "You want to go home?"

I looked at the IV tube attached to my hand. "Can I take this?"

"No, but I'll give you some medicine almost as good." He pulled my gown back in place and stood up. "What happened?"

"Someone shot me."

"Mick, someone shot you up close and I heard you denying it to the cops." He moved around the bed.

"Jack, I want to stick to that story for a while."

"Okay." But he didn't look happy. "You're not fooling the cops: they know you're lying."

"For a while, Jack."

"Take the extra bandages and ointment home and have Tita

change it in the morning." He showed me the bandages and ointment on the table. "And come into my office before noon on Wednesday. If you start to bleed, get into the ER and call me."

"Is it going to be painful?"

"Keep your arm in the sling they give you and just take it easy." He wrote out two prescriptions. "Follow the instructions for these, and, yes, it's going to hurt like hell for a week or so, longer if you do anything besides rest."

TWENTY-EIGHT

"I talked to Tita," Jack said as he removed the IV needle from my hand. "I told her you should stay off the boat for at least a week."

"Why?" I watched him unhook the needle from the IV line and place it in the hazardous waste container by the door.

"The cramped quarters, climbing in and out of the cabin, will hurt." He sat on the bed. "And aggravate the wound. At least until I see you Wednesday, okay?"

"If it's okay with her."

He sat there quietly, turned, and looked past the curtain toward the hall. "Was the guy a bad shot?"

"Huh?" The question caught me unprepared.

"Four shots, point-blank range, and only one grazed you." He was serious. "It was either a lucky shot by someone who didn't know what he was doing, or it was a well placed shot by a pro."

"Give it a rest, Jack," I said, as he removed the blood-pressure wrap from my arm. "Maybe we'll talk Wednesday. Believe me, it's no big deal."

"I need to dust off my old psych books; there was a chapter or two on people like you."

"Like me?"

"Yeah, people who laugh at everything, take nothing serious, and I forget the reasoning behind it, but I want to find out." He left the blood-pressure wrap hanging down from the machine.

124

"Jack, I'm just a guy with an easy sense of humor." I tried to smile like Alexis and Tara. "Who would rather laugh than cry. No one wants to be around a whiner."

"I have a good sense of humor, Mick, but I can tell the difference between funny and serious." He straightened up the bandages and ointment on the table. "You're getting too old to take these chances."

"Is he decent?" Tita called from behind the curtain.

I lost my chance to ask him what psychology had to do with my sense of humor, and what he meant about *getting too old,* because it wasn't a subject I wanted Tita around for.

"Has he ever been?" Jack pulled the curtain open. "Will you keep him for a week?"

"I've nursed him through hangovers worse than this." She kissed my cheek. "How are you feeling?"

Tita sounded a little too jovial, considering we were in a hospital and she never lost an opportunity to lecture me on my lifestyle.

Richard and Fitcher walked in behind her. "Is he going home?" Richard asked.

"Unless you want to take him to the station and beat him into submission," Jack said with a laugh, showing me his sense of humor. "Yeah, he's okay to go home."

"Not a bad idea, by the way." Richard placed his hand on Jack's shoulder and they laughed together.

I didn't think it was funny.

Tita handed me a cloth bag decorated with the logo from SleuthFest in Miami, an annual long-weekend seminar of mystery writers put on by the Florida chapter of the Mystery Writers of America. She'd taken me there last year. The bag held my clothes for the trip home.

"I got your phone, hat and sandals from the ER," she said, and left, closing the curtain behind her.

"Thank you," I called after her.

My red, pre–World Series Red Sox hat had been a gift she'd brought from Boston when she first came to the island. Though we didn't talk about it, the hat meant a lot to me.

"I'll see him in my office. Right, Tita?" Jack called to her. He nodded to Richard and Fitcher and left to talk with her.

"You think it's a good idea you stay with Tita?" Richard moved closer to the bed and spoke softly.

I dressed slowly, putting on a pair of shorts before I stood on the cold floor. I slipped my left arm carefully into the shirt first, then my right. "Why wouldn't it be?" I got half the buttons done using just my right hand.

"Your life's still in jeopardy," Fitcher said as he finished buttoning my shirt for me. "You could be putting hers at risk."

I looked over at Richard and he nodded in agreement. "You're not telling us something, for whatever reason, so I have to agree with the DEA about the Colombians."

"You mean, you think they're trying to kill me because Jay told me who the local contacts are for this *paco* shit?" I couldn't do anything about the bitterness in my tone.

"Yeah, that's exactly what we're saying," Fitcher said, with a dark stare.

"They're wasting their time: he told me nothing." I almost moaned out of aggravation, but the looks on their faces told me they thought it was pain. My lie to Richard outside Hotel Key West had taken on a life of its own. "If that's the case, then I ain't safe anywhere. Not on my boat, not at Tita's, what about a hotel?"

"You don't understand how serious this is." Fitcher's stern voice returned. "They don't care, at this point, if you do or don't know anything. They're covering their asses and that means they have to kill you. I can put you in protective custody in Miami if you tell us what you know."

126

Here I was, telling them the truth—I didn't know anything because Jay never told me anything—and they refused to believe me. I fought the idea of creating another lie to get them off my back. I slid my flip-flops on as a nurse pulled the curtain open.

She had papers for me to sign and helped me arrange the sling on my left arm. She put the extra bandages and ointment in a bag, and said Jack had released me. I had to wait for a wheelchair to take me downstairs.

"Tita." Richard called her back into the room. "We don't think it's a good idea for Mick to stay with you." He spoke quietly. "We don't know what he's got himself into and we're concerned for your safety."

"My feeling," Fitcher spoke up, "is Mick's getting shot has something to do with Saturday at Hotel Key West and he is withholding information. You should talk to him like a client, not a boyfriend."

"Your safety could be in jeopardy. Please consider that." Richard touched her shoulder and then pulled his hand away.

"I will talk to Mick at my house," she said in her attorney's voice, and looked Richard in the eyes. "I assure you, my advice to clients is to always cooperate with the police." She turned to Fitcher. "Though I've never advised anyone on how to deal with the DEA."

The nurse brought in the wheelchair. I sat, and she pushed me out of the room.

"Call me when you get home, Tita." Richard walked with us into the hall. "I'll have a police car go by hourly for the next few days. Turn your porch light on, if you need an officer."

127

Twenty-Nine

Tita drove her white SUV and made me sit in the backseat where, she said, I would have room to stretch out. I was more nervous about her quiet disposition than I was about my wound. I waited, not patiently, for the questions I knew would come.

"I told Jack I would bring you to his office Wednesday morning." She drove more sanely in the SUV than she did on the scooter. I swear a scooter turns a sensible person into a careless daredevil.

"Thank you, I appreciate it." I didn't know what else to say. She reminded me of a Fourth of July firecracker you've thrown and there is no explosion after the fuse burns down. Common sense makes you afraid to pick it up, because you know it's going to go off eventually.

She drove over the Cow Key Channel Bridge and headed toward Flagler Avenue, not the direction home. "Where are we going?"

"I thought you'd be hungry." She looked at her wristwatch. "El Siboney will be open in a few minutes."

"A good idea, but I was thinking of *arroz con pollo*," I said with a smile, because I saw her staring at me in the rearview mirror.

"We finished all of it last night," she said as she smiled back into the mirror. "So, the pantry at Casa Toledo is empty. After you settle in, I'll go pick up your prescriptions and shop."

I relaxed in the backseat as Flagler went from four lanes to

128

two. Traffic was light. Maybe the drugs were still in my system and made me little paranoid. Tita had been trying for a year or so to get me to spend more overnight time at her place, and now I was doing it. She was tired of the cramped quarters on my sailboat, she said. Her deal with Dr. Jack could explain her mood. Was she quietly celebrating a victory over my elusiveness?

El Siboney is my favorite Cuban restaurant and owned by an old friend, Julio Bustillo, from Havana. The food was authentic, good and inexpensive.

"You don't have to park out front," I said as she pulled the SUV into one of the restaurant's narrow parking spots. "Walking will be good for me."

She always parked under a tree a block down Catherine Street, because the narrow spots out front were an invitation for a ding to her SUV.

"Get out, old man," she laughed when the door opened. "I get a scratch on this car and I'll give you the bill."

I usually have the garlic chicken with *morros,* a rice-and-red-bean mixture cooked together, and a side order of *tostones,* a thick-sliced green plantain that is fried on one side, crushed gently to flatten it, and then fried on the other side. While not Tita's *arroz con pollo,* the food at El Siboney is delicious. However, with my arm in a sling I wasn't sure it was the right dish for me.

"The chicken falls off the bone," Tita said. "I'll cut it for you, if it comes to that."

Tita had pork chunks with yellow rice and black beans, and we shared the *tostones.* She cringes whenever I salt them down and add hot sauce, so she quickly moved hers to an extra plate she asked for. A basket of cut-up, hot-buttered Cuban bread was mostly gone by the time we finished lunch.

I stuffed myself, more out of frustration and anxiety than

hunger. My appetite was gone before I had half finished, but I ate, picking slowly from my plate. I knew I needed to focus on what was going on with Johnny, why he hadn't put a shot into my head and how it all connected to the Colombians and the deaths of Jay and Rebecca, but it would wait until the afternoon. Maybe Richard and Fitcher were right and I was putting Tita in harm's way.

Tita helped me back into the SUV before checking for dings. Thank God there were none, because a small one might have set her off. She drove down Simonton Street to Fleming and turned toward her house across from the Key West Cemetery on Frances Street. I expected something from her when we got on Fleming, because it gave her the opportunity to bring up what happened Saturday when we walked from Island Books to Duval. She didn't.

There was a residential parking spot three houses up from hers, so she took it. Parking close to your destination, especially your home, is a luxury in Key West. Tita turned in her seat and looked at me with what I would have to call her attorney smile, because I knew it was masking her feelings.

"You okay?"

I nodded, waiting for the firecracker to explode.

"Before we go in, we need to get something straight." Her smile stayed, but I didn't believe it.

"Okay." The fewer words said, the safer it was for me.

"Listen to me, Mick, and don't, please don't give me one of your smart-aleck answers." She lost the smile.

"Talk to me." What I wanted to say is, please wait until I'm medicated, but I shut up. Dr. Jack accused me of making everything a joke and now Tita accused me of the same thing.

"I don't know what's going on. I don't know if you know, but if you cut me out of your life again, like you did when Tom was killed, and treat me like the teenager I was in Boston, I will

130

walk out of your life forever." She smiled for a brief second, then her eyes watered, while her expression told me she was serious. "It's not a threat, it's a promise. I need the truth. If you can't give me the truth, if you don't care enough to be honest with me, say so, so I can get on with my life." She wiped her eyes, but didn't look away. "I will back you up one hundred percent, even if it's against Colombians, but I need to know you care and that you trust me. No more lies. I need to be a part of your life."

"Wow," I gasped.

Her eyes hardened. "No wow, Mick. Answer me."

"I left Boston because you were young and Paco's kid sister." I sat back and drew a breath. "When you showed up in Key West, older and an attorney, I couldn't have been happier. You have to know that."

She nodded and gave me another brief smile. "This is going someplace, right?"

"I don't know what you want, not really." I stared back at her.

She pointed at my side.

"You want to know who shot me?"

"Yes, and why you are not saying who did it, and what it has to do with Jay's murder. Are Richard and Fitcher right about it being connected?" She sounded different; maybe it was the voice she used in court.

"Can we go inside and I'll tell you everything."

"But will you tell me the truth?"

"I don't know what that means. I can only tell you what I know."

She sighed. "I've seen you in action. You tell the truth, but it's often wrapped in a lie of omission, like our recent trip to the police station. I don't want any omission in our relationship. I want the truth and the facts, all the facts, because things are go-

131

ing to change when we get in the house." She looked at her wristwatch. "Am I part of your life, or am I a nursemaid looking for a ticket off the island?"

"I don't want you to leave. I'll tell you what I know and if you feel I'm leaving something out, say so and I'll try again. Sometimes I use omission because I don't want to jeopardize your legal position." I took a deep breath, because this was more than a firecracker exploding in my life. "Things don't have to change, Tita, not when we go in the house, not tomorrow—"

"Things will change when we go in." She cut me off and got out of the SUV. "Hopefully, for the better." She opened the door for me and smiled. "But my life is going to change for sure."

I wasn't prepared for what waited for me and where it would lead. If she had given me ten guesses, I wouldn't have come close, probably because I was trying to reason with our hurricane-like relationship, and the good possibility that Richard and Fitcher were telling the truth, and our lives were in danger. I wouldn't put Tita's life up against a story, and if it meant getting the hell out of Key West, I was ready to make that commitment.

THIRTY

It seems my little white lie was so believable, people wanted me dead. Was there a lie I could tell that would fix the madness? This thought was running through my head, and the hospital's medication was slowly leaving my system, as I walked into the house, unprepared.

Norm Burke, my friendly nemesis from Los Angeles, was asleep on the couch. His long legs, fitted in cowboy boots, hung off the end. At first I thought I was hallucinating, but when Tita gently put her hand on my shoulder, I knew I wasn't.

"He was up all night getting here," she whispered into my ear, and led me to the kitchen.

"Why?" I pointed behind me. I was speechless and that doesn't happen too often.

Tita made it clear to me, after Norm's last visit, that she didn't like him. Half the time I've known the guy, he and I have argued, because there is little we agree on. I am not sure how to explain our friendship. Maybe, because we have such different philosophies and beliefs on everything from politics to books, we can be honest with each other. More important, when we are not honest with each other, we don't hide it. A good example of that honest-dishonesty is that Norm denies being a government black-ops agent. I haven't any idea what agency he works for, but I know he does.

I met him in Central America while researching a drug smuggling story that got me into deep shit a lot quicker than I expected. Norm and his team were tailing me because they were interested in the smugglers, too—though obviously for different reasons. Though I've asked, he has never explained how he knew where I was going. When it looked like the smugglers wanted to talk to me in more private quarters in Colombia, and wouldn't allow me to leave, Norm's team came in and saved me. Not without a lot of gunfire and risk to their own lives.

Right after that, I discovered he lived by the Los Angeles International Airport, in a complex that was also a gym for boxers he trained and managed. That's his cover and it allows him to travel throughout Central and South America, checking out fighters and attending boxing matches. Back then, I lived in Redondo Beach, only a few miles away. He denies the government agent accusation, but we both understand that it's part of his job to do so.

"Why is Norm here?" I finally blurted out and sat down. My side was smarting.

"I called and told him what happened." She kept her voice low.

"Why?" I didn't understand how she was able to call him. "You don't even like him, if I recall you said—"

"In my line of work," she cut me off, "you sometimes have to deal with the devil to win a case. I appreciate Norm's *special abilities.*" The words came with a sour expression. "And I am afraid of losing you. What's going on is beyond my understanding, so that means it's within his *expertise.*" The sour look again, and then she sat down and suddenly looked tired. "I kept his cell number because I feared this day would come."

"You did?"

"This is the part of your life I don't want to be cut out of, Mick." She slumped in the chair and looked at her wristwatch. "He told me to wake him at two, so in a few minutes you can tell us both what happened."

"Now's as good a time as any, hoss." Norm's drawl came from the door.

His gray eyes smiled as he walked to me and we shook hands. He's a little over six feet and has his brown hair cut military style. I noticed flecks of gray along the sides.

"How'd you get here so soon?" I went to stand, but he used his palm to push me back into the chair.

"I flew. No direct flights to Key West from LA." He pulled out a chair and sat down.

Tita offered to make Puerto Rican *café con leches* and we both nodded our approval. She stayed within earshot; she wasn't going to miss anything we said, especially from me.

He grinned. "I had an associate fly me in his Lear. I didn't have much time to check into what's going on, so why don't you fill me in."

"Us," Tita said from the espresso maker as she steamed the milk for our *con leches.*

"Us," Norm mimicked. "Make the devil's strong." He turned and smiled at her.

Tita stared at him, as she realized he must have been standing at the kitchen door since we walked in. I wasn't surprised. Nothing Norm did or knew surprised me.

"So." He stretched his large frame in the chair and turned to me. "Why'd someone shoot you and why ain't you dead? Four shots at close range and only a scratch. Gotta be a story behind that."

I protested. "Hey, it's a nasty wound."

"No stitches," Tita said.

"You goin' to answer me?"

"Us." Tita brought three cups of *con leche* and sat down.

"I thought this was Cuban coffee." Norm sipped from his cup.

"I'm Puerto Rican; this is how we make coffee. You want

Cuban coffee, go to the Cuban café." She may have needed him, but she wasn't happy about it, and her tone made that clear to both of us.

"I stand corrected, Counselor." Norm took another sip. "Damn good Puerto Rican coffee." He smiled sheepishly. "Now, back to *our* patient." He stressed our, to let Tita know he understood she was part of whatever it was they were doing.

"I'm not used to being on this end of the interview." I drank the coffee. It was strong and had lots of sugar in it.

"Get used to it," Tita said, "because the DEA doesn't believe you about anything concerning the case, neither does Richard, and I, for sure, don't. So you can expect, when they want the truth, they'll bring you in for a real interrogation." She turned to Norm. "Fitcher, the DEA agent, had him in the police station Saturday night and Mick lied himself blue, and he thinks that's that, but it's not."

"Reed Fitcher, big black guy, quick to smile?"

"Yeah, do you know him?"

"I've heard the name," he mumbled and looked like he was trying to remember why he recalled it.

"Can you get my prescriptions filled?" I turned to Tita, and the pain in my side sent spasms into my shoulder. "I think the hospital's medication is wearing off."

She shot me a look of disgust. "I am not leaving you two alone. I want to believe we're all in this together, but until I see your actions, words are meaningless. We're hooked at the hip."

Norm laughed. "You know, Counselor, I bet you're an act to watch in court." His laugh tapered off. "How about you drop me at the Mango Tree Inn while you do his medical run?"

"You're not staying here?" There was concern in her voice.

"No." He was serious again. "And if what I hear from Mick is what I think, neither are you two."

The Mango Tree Inn is on Southard at Simonton Street,

about a dozen blocks from Tita's. "Why there and not the Pier House?" I stood up to get some motion in my side and took my arm out of the sling.

"Jack told you to keep the arm in that," Tita chided me.

"It's stiff, I need to move it." It hurt my side when I moved my arm around, so I put it back in the sling. "Why not the Pier House?"

"The inn is in a residential neighborhood and on two busy streets." He stood up and we followed him into the small living room. For the short time he'd been in Key West, he had a good awareness of the inn's location. "Strangers aren't walking around the grounds, and if a carload of Colombian hit men stops, they'll be noticed." He smirked. "Also, keeping it under surveillance without being noticed would be difficult. The rooms are big and it's quiet. I also like the owners, Peggy and Johnny."

"Are you ready to go?" Tita tossed her SUV's keys in the air.

"Yeah, you should go by the *Fenian Bastard* and pick up some things for Mick." Norm looked out the window and then opened the door.

"I don't know where he hides his gun, so we'll go there first, and you can get it, while I pack his clothes," she said, before Norm closed the door.

She was full of surprises.

Thirty-One

I found over-the-counter extra-strength pain reliever in the medicine cabinet, took three, and tried to sleep on the bed in Tita's room. My side hurt like hell, but it didn't stop my mind from racing with thoughts about the past few days. Tita says my curiosity is a disease, but editors tell me it's my genius. She's told me that getting the story is my search for the Holy Grail, that it is my god. Sometimes, though, I just can't help myself.

A guy I know comes off the roof of Hotel Key West and dies in front of me, and then cars from multiple local and federal law-enforcement agencies converge on the Duval Street scene, while a SWAT van unloads men in black jumpsuits preparing to raid the oldest hotel in Key West, and my curiosity automatically goes into overdrive. The situation was journalistic catnip. So, I tell a lie, because I need to find out what happened.

The thought of putting Tita's life in harm's way kept popping into my head, as my heartbeat pulsed in my ears like it was on a cross-country run, and sleep eluded me.

I couldn't make sense out of Johnny Dey's shooting me, either. It would've been easy for him to put one quiet shot into my head, killing me, and then walk to the car waiting for him on Front Street. But, he didn't. He gave me a flesh wound, said he was sorry, and shot the steps. What had the steps ever done to make him shoot them three times? For that matter, what the hell had I done to make him shoot me, besides befriending him?

138

His grandfather thought he was involved with the deaths at the hotel. If that was true, did his shooting me have some off-the-wall connection that I was missing? Agent Fitcher thought so. If true, it brought my little white lie full circle, and back to me. I didn't want to believe it, but in an odd way, it made sense. Someone thought Jay had confided in me. What did he know that brought fear to drug dealers? What could he possibly have known that was worth killing him for?

I opened the room's two windows and turned on the ceiling fan, hoping the breeze would help me sleep. I lay back down and pulled the visor of my Red Sox hat over my eyes.

Killing isn't something I would do for a story, but I have killed to defend myself. It isn't something I am proud of, and I'm not sure God distinguishes the difference, but the bottom line is, afterward I was alive and that made all the difference.

A sane person cannot take a human life without some remorse, some guilt, no matter what the reason. Granted, Norm's remorse and mine are not alike, but I know he doesn't gloat about lives he's taken. Walking away alive from a situation that's caused people to die violently is an adrenaline rush, because life is precious, especially when you come within a hair's width of losing it. Maybe, you rationalize, the other person was a psychopath, leaving you no choice, but after a while you realize you've lost a little something of yourself because of it and hope you are not turning into that demented person.

I fell asleep with these thoughts and woke up with the aroma of *arroz con pollo* coming from the kitchen. The house was quiet when I got up and went to see what was going on.

Norm sat hunched over his laptop at the table, a bottle of Anchor Steam beer next to the computer, as Tita stared over his shoulder, holding a glass of wine, watching as the computer's printer spat out documents.

"Thanks for not waking me." I looked over Norm's other

shoulder. "What are we doing?"

They both looked toward me and then returned to staring at the computer screen.

"You meds are on the sink," Tita said, captivated by the laptop's screen.

"Thanks." I got a bottle of water from the fridge and took the pills.

"It's amazing." Tita turned to me as I got behind Norm. "Do you have any idea of what he can get copies of?" She picked up papers from the table. "He has reports about what happened at Hotel Key West, including one about the sheriff's undercover agent. There's one on the Colombian DEA agent you found by your boat, and even one about your being shot." She said all this with a wrinkled expression, finding it hard to believe. "Even the media doesn't have this information."

"Sometimes it's better the media can't get information." Norm watched as the computer screen went blank. "That's it." The last paper slid from the printer.

"They don't believe you, and Fitcher thinks the murders at the hotel are connected to the attempt on your life." Norm pushed away from the table and gave me a conspirator's smile. "But they have no idea who shot you. Fitcher believes you know."

They looked at me, and then Norm spoke for them both.

"Why didn't you tell them?"

"Because I lied."

"You lied?" He tried to sound serious, but couldn't. "Can you believe that?" He turned to Tita.

"Oh, yeah, I believe it because lying is a full-time profession for Mick."

I knew she was serious.

"I had my reasons."

They both looked at me quietly, waiting to hear the reasons.

Because they already knew what happened at the hotel, I began with my meeting Carl Dey at the restaurant, and his concerns about Johnny, and explained how, on my Sunday stroll with Tita, I had left messages for Johnny to contact me. If looks could kill, Tita's expression would have done me in.

I explained everything that happened Sunday night at the Hog's Breath and how I couldn't make sense of it. Why hadn't Johnny put a shot in my head and been done with it? Why did he take the three shots at the steps, inches from my head?

"Let's see what we can find out about Johnny Dey. And you know what you have to wonder about?" Norm pushed back to the table and began to type. "Who was waiting for him in the car?"

I didn't missed Norm's use of the word *we*, so I guess Tita had her conversation with him while I slept. It seemed to be okay for her and Norm to be alone without me. My curiosity, that evil genius of mine, was beginning to wonder about them.

"Hadn't thought about that," I said.

"It's frightening what he can do." Tita picked up the papers again and shoved them at me. "If he can do this, imagine what Big Brother is doing."

I took the papers, without telling her Norm was a cog of Big Brother's machinery. Before I could read them, Norm pushed back from the table.

"If I am frightening," he drawled, "this should scare the hell out of you."

Across the computer screen, *Access Denied* flashed in big letters.

"I know what access denied means." Tita put her hand on Norm's shoulder so he couldn't turn away. "But what does that mean?"

"It means spooky stuff is happening." Norm leaned back and looked at me.

141

Spook is what I call Norm, meaning he's a government spy, like with the CIA, something he always denies. I guessed this was his way of talking to me without Tita understanding.

"You think so?"

"Be my guess."

"What's it mean?"

"I need to call a friend at JIATF." He stood up and walked to the front porch as he punched numbers into his cell phone.

"What's JIATF?"

Tita was right; this was way out of her understanding.

THIRTY-TWO

Tita looked at me for an answer.

"JIATF is the acronym for Joint InterAgency Task Force," I said. "It's a drug-interdiction agency within the military. I think it's under Homeland Security rule, because the commander is a Coast Guard admiral."

"They chase drug smugglers?"

"Yeah, something like that, and they have the best intelligence on smugglers and cartels, and probably terrorist suspects. Most of what they do is secret."

"Is it here in Key West?" She was getting a touch of my curiosity bug.

"They have offices on the Navy base, but the group is low key."

"And Norm knows people there. Why does that surprise me?" She sipped her wine.

"I told you before, I think Norm's an intelligence officer, so he would know people in JIATF. They probably exchange information, have a lot of the same training, things like that."

"I keep trying to remind myself that he's one of the good guys." She looked toward the window and watched Norm pacing. "But he is so far out of my comprehension of legal procedure that I find it hard."

I didn't have an answer she'd accept, so I said nothing. Norm, I knew from experience, does the off-the-record dirty work that it takes to chase down cartel members and, these days, terror-

143

ists, all the bad guys. Federal law enforcement has a dismal record for stopping crime before it happens, but Norm goes after it in its nest, and does what it takes to destroy it before it reaches our shores. Hell, he could be working for JIATF, for all I knew.

"If you're in a jam, he's a good guy to have on your side," I finally said.

"I know that." She finished her wine and smiled. "That's why I called him. Do you want a beer and *arroz con pollo?*"

She poured wine into her glass and brought one of Norm's beers from the refrigerator for me. Smiling, she moved the printer and Norm's laptop from the table.

"You need to ask?" I knew I had to be smiling as she filled our plates. "When are you going to tell me about calling Norm? I wouldn't have expected that." I took the beer, sat down at the kitchen table, and began reading the papers Norm had printed.

"Maybe when we're alone," she teased as she sipped wine. She put three plates of dinner on the table.

It amazed me that Fitcher was able to get his reports written and sent to Washington as fast as he did. Someone at the KWPD had also sent reports to the DEA, and I wondered if Richard was aware of it.

Norm came back into the house with Padre Thomas tailing behind him. Tita got up and filled another plate.

"Look who I found." He motioned Padre Thomas forward, with a comical sweep of his arm, but the look in his eyes asked me what was going on.

"You didn't find me." Padre Thomas looked beaten down. "I was coming here."

Tita gave them each a beer, and Padre Thomas didn't complain it wasn't a Budweiser.

I could tell Norm was hesitant to talk because of our guest, and Tita's expression went along with him.

"Padre Thomas, what brings you here?" I put the papers on the counter.

"Let's eat while we talk." Tita sat down.

"A couple of things." Padre Thomas sat, took a drink of the beer, and then read the label. "I wanted to see how you were, but it looks like you're fine, thank God."

"A little sore, but otherwise fine." I had a mouthful of rice and chicken.

"And I wanted to let you know that Captain Maybe left this afternoon." He closed his eyes and frowned. "I have misgivings. . . ."

"He's doing the right thing." I stopped him before he could get on a roll. "We both know that."

I gave Norm and Tita a brief account of Captain Maybe's predicament and my involvement. I don't think Norm understood why the captain got his name.

We ate quietly for a moment. I could see that Padre Thomas was also hesitant to open up in front of Tita and Norm, so I figured I'd do it for him, before he tried to light a cigarette.

"Padre Thomas brought the situation with the *paco* to my attention, right after Jay's death," I explained. "He is concerned."

"It's more than concern." He got up, his food barely touched, and paced in the tiny kitchen. "I told Mick, there is an evil coming, and the murders at the hotel and the young woman he found are all part of it. And so is your being shot." He turned to me and stopped pacing. "I am confused, though, because Johnny Dey is not a bad guy, so why did he shoot you?"

His comment about Johnny caught me off guard. Norm and Tita looked at me, and I shook my head to let them know I hadn't said a word to him.

"Padre, how do you know Johnny shot me?" Before I finished, I knew what he would answer.

Padre Thomas gave a quick glance at Norm and Tita. "You

145

have to ask?" He turned to me. "Everything I see, everything I am aware of now, has to do with the evil, Mick." He glanced back at Tita and Norm, and flashed a tired smile. "You need to do something. I can't find a solution; I can't fight this. It's way over my head."

"Maybe we can help." Norm pulled a chair out, and Padre Thomas sat back down. "Tell me exactly what you know, Padre, and maybe we can come up with a plan. I'm especially interested in what you know about Johnny Dey."

THIRTY-THREE

Padre Thomas didn't seem to know where to start. He rubbed his bloodshot eyes and took a long swallow of beer, but said nothing.

"Padre, what have you seen?" I tried to lead him.

"A couple of weeks ago the angels showed me the evil," he said quietly, almost as if he was afraid of his own words. He took a forkful of food and ate slowly. "If it isn't stopped, more people will die. Lots more, eventually."

"Why don't they do something?" Norm got up and leaned against the wall.

"The angels?" Padre Thomas looked at Norm.

"Yeah, the angels." Norm got a cold beer for himself. "They know it's comin'. They know the who and the how. Tell us and I guarantee the right people will get the information and stop it before it begins. This can all go away."

"I don't know." Padre Thomas's words came out angrily. "I have tried to understand, but I'm tired and afraid of losing them. I know things, like where the body of the sheriff's deputy was, but it took time with Mick for me to realize it. Maybe I know more and that's what's tormenting me. Am I doing all I can?" The anger was replaced with self-doubt.

"You saw Gabriela die." I finished my beer. "What else have you seen?"

"You saw that?" Norm jumped in.

"In a vision with the angels," Padre Thomas mumbled, his

147

body squirreled into the chair. "I wasn't there."

Norm looked at me. "This is about dreams?"

"It's how the angels communicate with him," I said. "Sometimes at night when he's sleeping; other times, images come to him in the daytime."

"They come clearly, like I'm a ghost and can see what is happening without being seen." Padre Thomas sighed and toyed with his empty beer bottle. "And the angels are with me."

Norm shook his head, but he had heard it all before, when he was here last year and we were tracking the Cuban army deserters. He sat between the priest and me. Tita remained standing quietly, forgetting about her dinner, and I am not sure she believed what she heard. It wouldn't work in a court of law and that was how she judged things.

"Okay, let me get this straight. Sometimes the angels show you things. In a dream?"

"I think it's a dream." He looked at me. "It has to be a dream, right?"

"What's different between when they talk to you and you see things?" Norm didn't allow me to answer Padre Thomas.

"I am at home, reading or praying, and they appear," he answered. "When I see things, I can be sleeping or sitting, like here, and suddenly the angels are with me and I am someplace else, watching as something happens."

"Like you would disappear from right here?"

"I guess, I don't know," he mumbled, and bent his head. "I can't disappear, can I?"

"When you saw the woman die, what were you doing?" Norm seemed interested, like he believed. He wanted to keep Padre Thomas talking.

"Sleeping, but I woke up and it was like I was there and watched the two men hang her and then throw her in the water." His words came serenely, the angry tone gone, but sadness etched itself across his face.

"Okay, that's the past, like where the deputy's body was." Norm moved in his chair. "What about the future, what's coming? Tell me about tonight and tomorrow."

Padre Thomas sighed and tried to sit straight, but the weight on his skinny shoulders shrunk him into the chair. He closed his eyes, and his lips moved silently, as if in prayer. Norm and I looked at each other and I hunched my shoulders, to say I didn't know what was happening. Tita moved closer, still holding her empty wine glass.

"What are you seeing, Padre?" Norm said, quietly but firmly. "Tell me."

"A seaplane landing by a cluster of deserted islands." He gasped the words, his eyes closed. His voice seemed strange, lower than normal, and the words stretched as he said them. "A fishing boat, like at the marina where Mick lives, and two smaller boats. I think they're waiting for the plane. There are ruins on one island."

"Nighttime?" Norm's voice stayed firm.

"Yes, a lot of stars and a moon." Padre Thomas sat back in the chair and opened his eyes.

"Are the angels here?" Norm stared at him.

"Yes."

THIRTY-FOUR

"What are they telling you, Padre?" Norm leaned in close. "Where are they?"

"By the back door."

"How many angels can fit on the head of a pin?" Norm walked to the door, leaving his comment to puzzle us.

Padre Thomas stared at Norm, his confused expression turned into a smile. "In this case, Norm, none."

"I thought according to the Bible—"

"They are as big as you," Padre Thomas said, before Norm could finish. "And they don't have wings or flaming swords. That's how they appear to me. They are God's warriors. Maybe, if they appeared to you, they would have wings and swords. It is symbolism, Norm."

"Big as me, without wings, but still warriors." He smiled, put his arms in a boxer's stance, and punched at the empty space where he thought the angels should be. "Here?"

"No," Padre Thomas mumbled. "They're gone. They do not tolerate fools."

Norm frowned and sat down. "Did anyone else see them?" He looked at Tita and me.

We said nothing. Our dinner was getting cold, and Tita looked puzzled.

"Padre, I am beginning to doubt you." Norm stretched back in the chair, a large grin spread across his face. "If the angels have the answers that will save lives, many lives you said, why

150

don't they?"

"Angels cannot affect the course man sets for himself." Padre Thomas closed his eyes and brought his hands to his head, the smile gone from his weary face.

"Why do they tell you some things and not others?" Norm's voice was harsh.

"The things I know, like the body in the elevator and the seaplane." Padre Thomas sounded as if he was ready to cry. "I see them in visions. The angels are not allowed to tell me about them."

"They can show you the future, but not talk about it?" he said, sarcastically. "I don't understand."

"You think I understand?" Padre Thomas yelled. "This is killing me, driving me mad." He sat back in the chair. "Maybe I am mad?" he mumbled. "We talk theory. We talk about religion, how man has moved away from Christ, exploited Him. We talk about good and evil and how easy it is to be evil. Angels"—his tone seemed to relax—"watch over people, listen to their prayers, no matter their religion or what country they are in, but they cannot contact the living, especially in a way that would affect what is ahead for them."

"So if something horrific is about to happen to a person, a very good person, they allow it to happen?" Norm's tone had softened, too, as he shook his head in disbelief. "I don't know if I like that. It sounds like the angels are losing the war on evil."

"Not really." He forced a short smile. "Evil has a better press agent. You know the old maxim, good news doesn't sell newspapers. Right?" He looked at me.

"Padre Thomas." Tita broke into the conversation. "You're alive, and they have contacted you."

He looked up at Tita and hunched his skinny shoulders. "You're looking for answers I don't have, Tita. You all are. I don't know if it is a gift or a curse, maybe I am being tested, but I have learned to live with my visions, with the angels. I have learned from them and been confused by them, but I believe there is a reason; I just don't understand it. Not yet, maybe never." He held out his empty bottle, and Tita brought him a cold beer. He took a long swallow.

"Once I asked the angels why the dead don't come back, just to say they're okay, to prove there is an afterlife." He sipped more beer. "They told me to think back to the things that seemed important to me once, things I thought I couldn't live without, but in time I understood better and didn't need them. Things that were important became irrelevant, as time passed." He finished his beer.

"The angels told me the life we hold so precious is irrelevant to the dead; once our soul crosses death's threshold there is no need to come back, there's no desire to return." He squirmed in the chair. "Life, as we understand it, loses its importance, its hold on us, after death."

"If that's true," Norm stretched, "why should taking a life bother anyone? Why is life so precious to all of us? According to your interpretation, killing someone is helping them to move forward in their journey."

"It's more precious to some than others." Padre Thomas grinned at Norm. "But life is a gift, and man does not have the right to take it away."

"To take one life to save another? That's wrong?"

"It's not an easy question to answer, Norm." The smile came back. "I believe it's a question we must ask ourselves when, and if, we take a life. And, maybe there are no wrong answers in God's eyes, as long as the questions are asked honestly."

"Where's that leave us, Padre?" Norm stood and paced. "I've flown into the Keys, and there are a lot of small islands out there. How does this help us?"

"I don't know." He looked at his wristwatch. "Can I go?"

"Of course, Padre Thomas." Tita took his empty beer bottle.

I could tell from her expression that she was bothered by the whole conversation, maybe because what was happening was something not covered in her textbooks.

"Where are you off to?" I looked at the kitchen clock and it was almost eight.

"I promised Coco Joe I would stop by and hear him play." He stood.

"Coco Joe?" Norm seemed surprised. "The California singer?"

"Yes, do you know him?"

"I've never met him, but I've heard him play in Redondo Beach."

"They're playing at the Hog's Breath, but their set is over at nine."

"Have you ever heard him?" Norm looked at me.

"I met him the other day, but I've never heard the band."

"Do you want to catch the last set?" Tita seemed a little confused that the conversation had changed so quickly from angels to rock 'n' roll. "I can drive."

"Can I leave my bike here?" Padre Thomas seemed to get a little life back in his voice.

"Of course."

We followed Tita into the living room, where she picked up her purse. Our food cooled on the kitchen table, mostly uneaten.

"You want this, or should I hold onto it?" She opened her purse and showed me my Glock.

"I'm not dressed right; you keep it for me." I kissed her on the cheek as Norm laughed.

153

THIRTY-FIVE

Tita parked at the courthouse on Whitehead Street and we walked the few blocks to the Hog's Breath. She berated me for trying to be macho by taking off my sling and reminded me that I had taken a strong pain pill and should not drink more. Norm laughed in the backseat while Padre Thomas told him stories about Coco Joe in Guatemala. I wondered who'd made him laugh, Tita or Padre Thomas.

Streetlights cast twilight's wind-driven shadows from the large trees and bushes along the jasmine-scented street. As we passed Greene Street, the breeze from the harbor behind the Custom House added a salty humidity to the air. Tourists mingled on the sidewalk, drinks in plastic cups, some stopping to visit T-shirt shops.

We went into the Key West Sunset Cigar Company on Front Street and bought cigars from Steve, and then we walked through the Hog's busy T-shirt shop and indoor restaurant to the outdoor bar where Julie, Nickie and Kris bartended and business was good. Alon waved from inside; he was busy filling drink orders. Bob, Burt and Texas Rich sat listening to the band on the parking-lot side of the club. We slipped past the large tree that grows into the property at the bar, to join them.

"Mick's girlfriends are behind the bar." Tita pulled Norm's arm.

"Good lookin' blondes and Mick?" he joked. "Naw, he likes you exotic types, like the brunette."

Tita smiled and pinched my right arm. "He'd better not."

Julie had my Jameson on the rocks waiting. Norm ordered the same, Padre Thomas ordered a Bud and Tita asked for a key-lime cocktail, a mixture of clear liquors and cream that somehow tastes like a key-lime pie, not liquor. The bartenders stared at me and smiled. The looks had more to do with their curiosity about my being shot on the steps last night than what Tita thought.

"How the hell are you?" Bob, surprised to see me, got off his stool and accepted a cigar.

"When did you get out of the hospital?" Burt saw Norm and they shook hands.

"I'm fine." I sipped my Jameson and kept my back to the steps.

"One cannot believe rumors," Texas Rich drawled.

The bar was full and a sing-along crowd swayed with the music.

"What happened?" Bob greeted Norm and Tita, and gave a small smile to Padre Thomas. He didn't think much of Thomas.

"Someone mistook me for Burt; isn't that the rumor, Texas?" I cut the end of my cigar and lit it. I gave one to Burt.

Texas Rich laughed. "I hadn't heard that one."

"What about me?" Norm stretched out his arm and I gave him and Rich cigars.

"You could've bought one." I handed him my cutter and lighter.

"I spent enough money getting here." He cut and lit his cigar. "Pretty good," he said, and blew thick white smoke into the breeze.

"What happened, really." Burt sipped his scotch.

Texas Rich was the last to light his cigar.

"Some nut came in and started shooting." I took Bob's stool and leaned against the bar. "It's only a scratch."

155

"You okay?" Julie asked, with Nickie and Kris next to her.

"The doctor prescribed Jameson and pain pills."

"Yeah." Nickie shook her head and walked to a customer.

"Will he ever grow up?" Kris asked Tita and went to a customer.

"Is that what the paper's reporting in the morning?" Bob lit his cigar.

"If they report anything," Texas Rich answered for me.

Padre Thomas moved to the side of the stage and made sure Coco Joe knew he was there. The music was classic rock 'n' roll, with a little country-folk mixed in. It wasn't what I expected from a California band. It wasn't beach melodies or guitar twang. Maybe I expected surfer music, but we were all pleasantly surprised with the band's talent and showmanship.

"The nut knows that guy?" Bob puffed on his cigar as he stared at Padre Thomas.

"Old friends." I enjoyed the taste of my Trilogy *madoro* cigar.

"And to think I like the band." Bob sipped from his Red Stripe. "They are pretty good, especially for Yankees."

"California doesn't make 'em Yankees," Norm said with a laugh. "How you guys been?"

Bob, Burt and Texas Rich went into stories with Norm, while Tita and I leaned against the bar.

"You shouldn't drink."

"One is okay, right?"

"Like it matters." She sighed and looked worried.

"What's the matter?"

"Padre Thomas scared me." She took a drink of her key-lime cocktail and smiled. "Norm scares me all the time. What happened at my house?"

"I don't understand the question."

She gave me her evil-eye stare. "What happened, Mick? Does Norm believe Thomas or does he think he's crazy? All that talk

156

about angels. I've heard Bob's comments on Thomas, but this is the first time I really got to hear Thomas express himself and it concerns me." She took another drink. "I don't understand any of it. Do you? I wouldn't put him on the stand."

"Do I believe he sees angels?" I wasn't sure what an honest answer to my own question was.

"That's a good beginning."

"I believe he believes it."

"That's not an answer."

"Well, in the past Padre Thomas has known things he couldn't possibly know. If you believe angels told him, then it's understandable." I sipped my drink and then sucked on a piece of ice from the cup.

"And if you don't?"

"Then there is no answer."

"Do you think he was in a trance when he talked about the seaplane and islands?"

"Did you see the angels?"

"No." She frowned. "But he said they can't be seen by the living. How does he see them, then? He doesn't make sense."

"Remember him telling you, you were looking for the wrong answers?"

"Yeah, kind of."

"Sometimes a person needs to be a believer and that's the answer." I chewed on my cigar. "If I had to choose, I would say I believe him. I believe in the angels."

The stunned look on her face surprised me. I surprised myself.

"Why? Is it an Irish Catholic thing?"

"I don't know, maybe. You weren't there at Jack Flat's when the image of where Rebecca's body was came to him." I stretched my right arm and tried to hunch the stiffness from my left shoulder. "Other times, he's told me things he couldn't pos-

157

sibly have known about me."

It was about as close as I'd come to telling her about Mel and how a briefcase-bomb I delivered to a drug lord's henchman had blown up and killed her, along with the drug trafficker in Tijuana. Mel was a woman I dated from Redondo Beach, California, a CPA, and she had joined us in a scheme to bilk the Mexican drug lord of millions of dollars, so he would come across the border after us in California. Once across the border, Norm had assured our team, the authorities would arrest him. It didn't work out the way we planned.

I probably went a little insane afterward, and my Mexican friend Alfonso Ruiz and Norm got me back to Redondo Beach. After a while, Norm sailed with me as far as the Caribbean side of Panama. I made it by myself along the Antilles and finally to Key West.

"A penny for your thoughts." Tita ordered another key-lime cocktail. "You do that sometimes, you know."

"Do what?"

"You leave." She took a drink from her new cocktail. "Maybe you're like Padre Thomas and go off with your angels?"

"More like devils, Tita." I finished my drink and put the empty cup on the bar for Nickie to refill.

Thirty-Six

Julie brought me a fresh drink, and Tita frowned as I took a sip. We sat quietly, listening to the music. Padre Thomas stood next to the raw bar, directly across from the stage, and seemed entranced by the band. Norm, Bob, Texas Rich and Burt moved toward the tree that grew into the bar, to talk.

"You don't need to say things like that." Tita waited for the band to end its set and say good night to the applauding crowd.

"Like what?" I turned to her, my drink in hand.

"That you have devils chasing you." She turned to face me. "Sometimes, Mick, you can get real dark and that scares me."

"You wanted to be part of my life," I said with a grin. "You get the good with the bad."

"Can I beat the devil?" Her expression was almost sad.

"I have to, not you."

"Will you let me help?"

What could I say to that? I let out a deep sigh and smiled. "I can't think of anything I'd like more."

Andy and Art, two of the bar's managers, made their way to where we were and asked how I was. Both had been there last night when I was shot.

Andy told Kris our next round of drinks was on the house. "What the hell happened?"

I tried to assure them. "Some nut."

They looked doubtfully at me and said they were glad I was okay.

159

"Try not to get shot tonight." Art told Julie and Nickie the next two rounds were on the house. "We don't like our customers to be taken out on a stretcher. You make a habit of it, I may eighty-six you," he joked, and walked away.

Tita frowned. "Just what you need, two more drinks."

"We can cut him off," Nickie offered.

"I wish." Tita stood up as Norm came over for his drink.

"No wonder you like this bar." He smiled and took a long swallow of the Jameson. "If we run out of money, I'll shoot you."

"Thanks." I went to punch his arm, but pain shot through my side and I winced.

"You wouldn't have done that if you had the sling on," Tita said.

Fortunately, as the band began to take equipment offstage, people I knew came by to say they'd heard about what happened, and most said they were surprised to see me. I assured them it was nothing but a scratch.

Padre Thomas waited for the well-wishers to leave before coming over. "Mick." He saw the cold bottle of Bud on the bar and left his empty in its place. "Coco Joe's band is going to Duval Street, but he wanted to know what we were doing."

I looked at Tita. "We staying or going?"

"Who plays next?"

"Tim and Danny Carter?"

Tita decided for me. "We'll finish our drinks and leave after their first set. Padre, I think Norm would like to meet Coco Joe." When she said the name, Tita smiled. "What kind of name is that?"

"Californian." I sipped my Jameson and puffed on what was left of my cigar.

"That's your explanation?"

"You've never been to LA," I said. "In LA, people have

strange names. For all I know, his parents called him that."

"Isn't there a song called Coco Joe?"

"No, ma'am," Coco Joe said, as Padre Thomas led him to us. "Mick, nice seeing you again. You look good for someone that's supposed to be dead."

"Dead? Me?"

"That's what most everyone was saying when we got here this afternoon." He took a Bud from Kris. "Someone came in and shot you. Actually, I think the story went, someone emptied an Uzi on you."

"I guess they missed," I said. Norm walked over and I introduced them.

"Mick is bulletproof," Norm said.

"Well, dude, I guess that's a good thing."

"I've seen you play at Starboard Attitude."

"Redondo Beach."

"Yeah, I live toward the airport. You're good."

"Thank you, I can never hear enough of that."

"I'm Tita." She stuck her hand out toward Coco Joe. "These gentlemen seem to have forgotten their manners."

"A pleasure." He grinned as they shook hands. "Padre Thomas has told me all about you. By the way, the song is Kokomo, not Coco Joe. It was the first number-one song by the Beach Boys that wasn't written or produced by Brian Wilson. It was written for the nineteen-eighty-eight film *Cocktail.*"

"So, how did you get the name?" The trivia sailed right over her head.

"A crazy uncle called me Coco Joe when I was a kid and for some reason it stuck." He smiled and took a long pull on his beer. "The whole family eventually accepted it."

Most of us laughed politely and assured him we all had an uncle like his. Norm talked to him about clubs in southern California, while Bob went to the Sunset Cigar Company to

161

buy cigars and Texas Rich joined a group of locals at the raw bar. The Carter Brothers Band set up on the small outdoor stage.

Tita pulled my right arm and pointed toward the parking lot entrance between the raw bar and the stage. Snooper Scooper, an alcoholic wannabe newspaper publisher, fumbled through the crowd. His newspaper appropriately displayed a yellow banner across the top with the proclamation: *what others fear to print!*

The writing in that rag wouldn't be called journalism anywhere outside of Key West. It attacks city officials, mostly, and Snooper rides the coattails of some well-intentioned locals and claims a leadership role when their projects succeed. Those attacked in the rag are public figures, so there is a fine line about what they can do when their character is impugned.

Once, Snooper assured me he only printed the truth, and used the fact that he had never been sued as proof. I laughed and reminded him he lived hand-to-mouth, so there was no gain in suing him. Most of his food and beverage advertisers paid in-kind, which means they paid half cash for the ad and he ate and drank the balance.

If the local daily ran one of Snooper's ridiculous articles, it would be sued, because they had deep pockets. Now he lives off a businesswoman. He is an overweight, balding man with a greasy rat's tail popping out of the back of his sweaty head. His large ears stick out and when he goes hatless, he looks a lot like a hairless caricature of a famous mouse from California.

"Brother Mick." He slurred the words as he shuffled around the crowded bandstand. He stopped just short of where we stood and tried to focus on who was with me. "It is good to see you looking so well, after all the rumors." He moved forward, taking my silence as permission. "I need a drink," he yelled to Kris.

I waved her off and she smiled a thank-you. "Snooper, I've told you before: I am not your brother."

Tita squeezed my leg, warning me to keep control of my temper.

"In the spirit of journalism." He looked at the bar and seemed confused that there was no drink waiting for him. "We are brothers."

"Snooper, you're as much a journalist as Stalin is a saint." I sipped my drink. "Just leave."

"I want to write something about your being shot." He looked from Tita to Nickie, who was serving a customer. "My drink," he bellowed.

"No one's giving you a drink, Snooper," I said harshly. "You're not welcomed here, especially in my group."

"Who shot you?" He ignored everything I said. "I want to report the story."

"Why don't you go home and make it up, like you do with your other stories." I watched as Norm walked toward us. "You can start with the fact that I was shot and then spin your lies."

"This deadbeat still in town?" Norm's words came out hard.

Snooper tried to focus on Norm, to see if he knew him. "I am interviewing Mick," he mumbled, trying to put some force in his slurred speech.

"Interview this." Norm pulled his Glock and pushed it against Snooper's fat belly.

"The press isn't intimidated by violence," Snooper said, before he knew it was a gun.

Norm pushed Snooper against the bar, hiding his gun hand from the patrons, and then placed his sinister-looking Glock against Snooper's nose. Snooper stammered for a response, and when he went to raise his hand to remove the gun, Norm slapped his face hard enough for it to turn another shade of alcoholic red.

163

"You want to know firsthand how it feels to be shot?" Norm whispered, bringing his sneering face inches away from Snooper. "For the sake of research?"

"I protest," he said meekly.

Norm moved back, laughed and pointed at Snooper's stained crotch. He had wet himself.

"A proud day for journalism." Norm reached for his drink and put the Glock away.

Snooper turned and pushed his way out of the bar.

"Why does the town tolerate an asshole like that?" Norm walked back toward the tree and Coco Joe.

"That was uncalled for." Tita finished her drink.

"Let me tell you." I couldn't help but laugh. "There are a lot of people in town who wished they could do that."

Tita shook her head in disbelief. "Let's go home."

THIRTY-SEVEN

Tim and Danny Carter were getting on stage as we followed Tita out of the bar to Front Street. Bob walked into the Hog's Breath Saloon with a handful of cigars and gave Norm, Coco Joe and me one. I like to think he didn't give one to Padre Thomas because he knew Thomas didn't smoke cigars, but that probably wasn't the reason. Before we reached Whitehead Street, we had cut and lit the cigars.

"You don't like him." I was talking about Snooper and trying to discover what it was that made Tita upset with Norm's scaring the piss out of him, literally.

"It was not called for." Tita kept her voice low.

"You can't be looking at him as the underdog." I heard the surprise in my voice as I said it. "He's a manipulator. He exploits the First Amendment, and what he does has nothing to do with truth or journalism. As long as he attacks the city and its officials, he knows half the kooks on the rock will read him."

"He's still a human being."

I laughed, maybe a little too loud. "Tita, you attorneys would defend the devil, but not God."

"And what does that mean?"

Norm moved up, just in time. "Counselor, are we gonna be able to smoke in the car?"

I wondered if he was aware of what we were arguing about.

"No!" She pushed away and walked on her own.

165

Norm arched his eyebrows and smiled. "Puerto Rican temper."

"I can't believe it. She's defending that scum bucket." I chewed on my cigar.

"You should know by now, you can't separate an attorney from the person she is." He laughed. "You got yourself a handful there. She know about Mel?"

Norm and Alfonso in Mexico are the only two people who could broach the subject of Mel without my going ballistic. They had been with me when it all came down. My hope was that no one would ever bring it up, since I had regular nightmares without outside reminders.

"No, only you and I know. And let's keep it that way." I turned to look at him.

"You're the boss."

Tita had the van's engine running and the windows open when we got to the courthouse. We cut the burning ends off the cigars and got in. I went in the front and she squeezed my knee and smiled, so I guessed the argument was over. I assumed I had lost it.

As the SUV pulled out onto Whitehead Street we could hear music coming from the Green Parrot, a half block away. Traffic was light on Fleming, but crowds filled the corner at Duval Street, ignoring traffic signals as they came from or went to Buffett's Margaritaville club.

"Norm, do you want me to drop you off at the Mango Tree Inn?" Tita asked as we approached Simonton Street.

"Naw," he drawled, "I wanna finish that *arroz con pollo.*"

I think she sighed quietly, but kept driving and turned onto Frances Street. The Key West Cemetery, on our right, was a shadowy image of itself, as moonlight reflected off the white crypts that took up most of the grounds. She slowed down, looking for the valuable empty parking spot.

Norm leaned forward and quietly spoke to Tita. "Keep going to the next block."

"What?" She slowed and turned to Norm.

"Four guys just went into your house." He kept his voice low, but there was urgency in it. "Go to the next block and stop."

Tita drove past her house and began to slow down.

"Don't slow down," Norm ordered.

Tita passed Olivia Street and pulled over. She shut the engine off. "What the hell is going on?"

THIRTY-EIGHT

Norm moved Padre Thomas into the front seat. "Go around the block, park on the cross street and wait for us." He closed the car door; he wasn't waiting for an argument from Tita. She sped off without looking back.

Coco Joe walked with me into the shadows of a decrepit two-story building on the corner. Norm pushed us further back into the darkness.

"Shit," he mumbled, and got his Glock. "Friends of yours?"

"I didn't see them. Four?"

"Yeah, I caught it just as they hesitated in front of the house." He looked up the poorly lit street. "It didn't look right."

"Tita must have agreed with you." I tried to see past him, but he pushed me back.

"Is there a cemetery gate we can go through?"

"Halfway down Olivia, but it's locked."

"Joe, stay here, keep an eye on the van." Norm didn't care about the lock. He looked again at Tita's house. "If they leave, call me."

He pushed me out onto the sidewalk, and we turned left onto Olivia and were soon lost in the shadows. I mistakenly thought he took me instead of Coco Joe because he knew I could handle myself in a fight.

"Why don't we climb the fence?"

"With your side?" Norm laughed. "Great idea."

I was so caught up in the moment, I had forgotten about my wound.

"It's kind of weird going into the cemetery without rain," Norm whispered as we crossed the narrow street and walked next to the fence.

Last year, Norm had saved Tita and me as we avoided two Cuban hit men by hiding in the sloppy-wet cemetery during a thunderstorm. This time the air was warm and aromatic, and the moon was almost full. A lack of streetlights darkened the neighborhood around the cemetery, and the moonlight helped the swaying branches of old trees cast horror-movie shadows across the old compound.

Norm stopped at the gate, took a set of lock picks from his wallet, and had it opened in less than a minute. We walked along the fence, between crypts, small headstones, trees and sunken impressions of old graves. It took longer to get to where we could see Frances Street than it did to get to the gate.

Norm stopped next to a small crypt. He knelt down and looked toward Tita's house.

"There's a van outside with its engine running." He spoke softly without looking at me. "Get down here and look. Do you know who owns it?"

I knelt down and looked over his shoulder. "I can't even tell what color it is."

"Dark blue, probably." He pushed me back.

"You think it's the Colombians?" I leaned against the crypt as a car drove past.

"Anyone else trying to kill you I should know about?" He handed me my Glock. "You might need this."

"Tita gave you this?" I took the Glock, surprised he had it.

"No," he whispered, "I took it from her bag when I put Padre Thomas in front."

I didn't see him smile, but I would bet a round at Finnegan's that he did.

Norm surprised me when he called Coco Joe from his cell phone. I racked a bullet into the chamber of my Glock and stuck it into my waistband.

"Stay there. If you can get a plate number, it would help," he said, and then listened, nodding his head. "They're headed away from you, so when they leave, walk up Olivia and get into the backyard, and wait for my call."

I thought it was strange that his conversation with Coco Joe seemed casual, as if it was something they'd done before, but wrote it off as Norm using whoever was available. He did it last year, taking into his confidence Bob, Burt, Doug and even Padre Thomas.

"What's up?" I hunched my shoulders to get the stiffness out of them.

"Hurry up and wait." He sat against the crypt and watched the house.

The van was parked in a no-parking zone. Its engine ran with no one in it. The porch light was off, but muted light came through the porch windows. When we left for the Hog's Breath, the lights were off. We knew someone was inside, but we didn't know who.

"Should we ask Padre Thomas if he knows anything?" I said, mostly to hear something besides a passing car.

Norm looked at me and shook his head. "No, Mick. I don't need the shaman right now."

"You gotta admit he has something."

"I ain't knockin' him." He talked, but kept his sight on Tita's house. "He believes he sees 'em, so maybe he does. It ain't my place to doubt him."

"You, not doubt something? Come on." It was hard for me to keep from shouting. "You're the most Doubting Thomas I know."

He turned briefly and smiled at me. "That's why I've lived to be this old." He turned his stare back toward the house. "Plus, people lie all the time." He laughed, and I guessed that was meant for me and my lie that got us into this mess. "If I didn't doubt, I couldn't separate the bullshitters from the honest folk. Now, you wouldn't want that, would you?"

"Tita asked me what happened at her place, when Thomas had his vision." I wanted to change the topic, because the silence was spookier than the cemetery. "What's your take on it?"

"He has a gift." Norm leaned back against the crypt and stretched his legs out. "I don't know what it is. You, with your Irish Catholic upbringing, you believe in the angels easier than I do. With what I've seen in life, I gotta wonder if God is worth knowing. I never had much religion in my life. With the shit you got yourself into in Central America, I don't know why you ain't dead or in a third-world jail." He laughed quietly and turned to me. "Hell, Mick, maybe you got your own guardian angel. Now *that* I could believe, because sure as shit, I've never known anyone with the dumb luck you have when it comes to survival."

My mind flashed back to times I'd sat in Central American jungles, waiting for an interview, or to return from one, often with fighting going on around me. Somehow, I survived. I remembered the time in a banana plantation with government soldiers on one side, guerrillas on the other, and a battle going on over my head as I lay in the sodden ground praying for my life.

Scarier than the guerrilla wars were the dealings I had with drug smugglers. You could never trust them or know if men in uniform who were supposed to protect you were soldiers on the take, or hit men in disguise—not that it made a difference, if they were going to kill you. The obscene wealth in the illegal-drug business allows anyone's price to be met, and everyone

171

has a price. The cruelty in that business is unimaginable to most Americans. An honest cop that can't be bought will be shown a photo of his family and asked, would it be better to have the money and a family or to have neither. If that doesn't work, the oldest child shows up dead, usually tortured. Yeah, everyone has a price and it ain't always money.

"Maybe you're my guardian angel," I said seriously, trying to escape my frightening memories. "Hell, Norm, how many times have you pulled my ass out of the fire?"

"Countin' this one?" He kept his stare on the idling van.

"This isn't over yet."

"Glad you realize that, hoss," he drawled. "And I can't be your angel."

"Why's that?" A whispered conversation was better than sitting quietly.

"Too many people can see me." He got a chuckle out of that. "Hold on." He reached out and touched me. "I think they're comin' out."

He grabbed his cell phone and called Coco Joe. "They're leaving," he said and hung up.

I looked over, saw the windows were dark again, and watched three people get into the van. The driver checked the road and pulled away.

"Where's the fourth guy?" Norm was speaking more to himself than to me. He called Coco Joe. "They left someone behind. Be careful, but get into the backyard." He didn't wait for an answer.

"Did he get the plate number?" We both stood up.

Norm looked at me and shook his head. "Of course he did, I told him to."

To keep from being seen, we walked two crypts in from the fence to the Frances Street gate, where Norm picked the lock and we came out on the sidewalk.

"I only saw three leave the house."

"That's all I counted," I assured him. "Do you think he's waiting inside?"

The thought that I had somehow put Tita's life in danger sent nausea through me. I wasn't finished running away from Tijuana; I didn't want to add Key West to the nightmare.

"They were in there a long time." We walked across the street and stopped in the shadows of a large Poinciana tree. "They could've been searching it, but for what, if their job is to eliminate you?"

"You tell me."

Norm's cell-phone screen lit up. "Yeah." He nodded. "Okay, stay there." He closed the phone. "Well, I got one answer: I know what they were doing in there."

"Are you going to tell me?" Anxious, I was no longer whispering.

"Pouring gasoline." He frowned. "Looks like they want to burn it down, but where's the fourth guy?"

THIRTY-NINE

"How do they set off the gasoline?" I took a deep breath and felt for the Glock. It was still in my waistband. Then I exhaled. "That why they left someone?"

"Beats me," Norm answered, with furrowed eyebrows.

The eyebrow thing, I learned after first meeting him, indicated he was thinking, so I shut up and stayed in the shadows of the tree.

A car drove up Frances from Truman Avenue, and as it passed Olivia, I saw Tita and Padre Thomas crossing the street. I pointed them out to Norm.

"Shit." He moved out of the shadows toward them and I followed.

Tita and Padre Thomas walked toward us. I thought for sure she was going home.

"I told you to wait," Norm grumbled when we all came together, two houses away from Tita's.

"I saw them leave," she said. "Padre Thomas said it was safe."

"Well, maybe the good padre didn't realize they left someone behind," he bitched aloud. "We don't know where he is."

"It's okay," Padre Thomas said, his normal voice surprising me.

"It's not okay. They've poured gas in the house, and my guess is they plan to burn it down with us in it," Norm argued. "To me, that's not okay."

174

Concern showed on Tita's face, though she did her best to hide it.

"I didn't mean to say it was safe." Padre Thomas tried to explain himself. "But they are gone, Norm. I just wouldn't go in the front door."

"I was going in, but he stopped me." Tita grabbed Padre Thomas's arm.

"Please go across the street and wait for us to check this out," Norm said politely, but it wasn't a request.

He called Coco Joe as Padre Thomas walked across the street with Tita still holding his arm. "We're out front. Any lights in back?" He waited. "Can you look in any windows? I'll hold." He started walking slowly, the cell phone in one hand and his Glock in the other.

I looked back to make sure Tita stayed put and then I got my Glock. You would think that this was the time for me to get overly nervous, but I wasn't. I took deep breaths and was calm to the point of forgetting my injured side.

Norm put his phone away. "He can't see anything in the bedrooms or kitchen, but the smell of gas is strong."

"That leaves the living room and bathroom."

"It doesn't make sense." We stopped at the steps to Tita's. "Pour the gas and set the blaze, but pour the gas and leave someone behind to do what? Shoot you and then set the fire?"

"Why not?"

"Gas fumes are building up inside the house." Norm thought aloud. "Electric stove, right? So, no natural gas, no pilot light, right?"

"Yeah."

"Gas fumes build up, you go in and light a cigarette and the place blows, so how's the fourth guy gonna do it? Why not pour the gas after he's killed you?"

"Maybe a timer?"

"You stay here, let me check the windows." Norm rubbed his forehead. He gave a quick glance toward Tita, to make sure she was at a safe distance.

The old stairs creaked under Norm's weight, even though he walked slowly. He kept his back to the side of the house and looked through the top of the living-room window. He moved to the other side of the window and looked in again. With hand signals, he indicated I should join him at the other window. I climbed the few steps, Glock in hand, finger on the trigger, and looked into the house.

Tita's living room was dark, but slowly my eyes adjusted. The stink of gas seeped from the walls, or maybe came under the door, but the fumes were strong. Something was out of place in the room. As I squinted, I saw a chair and it looked like someone was sitting in it. I looked toward Norm and used my raised arms as a question. He motioned me over.

I looked through the other window and could almost make out the person.

"It doesn't seem right. Why isn't he hiding?"

"Because he's tied to the chair." Norm sighed. "This keeps getting stranger and stranger." He tapped on the window, and the person in the chair slowly raised his head.

"Jesus, that's Johnny Dey," I yelled when I recognized him.

"The guy who shot you?"

"Yeah. What's going on?"

FORTY

"I'm going around back." Norm looked toward Tita and Padre Thomas. "Do not"—he stressed the two words—"touch anything, especially the door or windows, and don't let them get any closer." With a nod toward Tita, he walked around to the back of the house.

The odor of gasoline oozed from inside. I tried to get a better look at Johnny Dey as he sat tied to the chair, but he was covered in darkness. He appeared to lift his head once to stare at me, but I couldn't be sure he did it or if he was even conscious.

Tita and Padre Thomas stayed back. I knew her curiosity, and she's not always the most self-controlled person, so I wondered how she was able to stay away. Frances Street was quiet, almost as quiet as the cemetery. A dog barked up toward Eaton Street and I heard the muted sound of a TV show, but wasn't sure where it came from. Windows were open in the neighborhood, to catch the spring breeze, and the aromas of fried, spicy meats wafted from them as I thought of the ruined *arroz con pollo* left on the table.

A light flashed through the window, and my attention was drawn back inside. Norm stood in the kitchen doorway with a flashlight and indicated for me to come around back. I used my raised hands to warn Tita to stay where she was, and then I rushed around back.

Coco Joe stood at the back door with a flashlight. Because of

177

the constant loss of electricity during windy rainstorms in the Keys, I had made Tita buy a flashlight for each room. They came in handy many summer evenings.

"Don't touch the light switches." He led me through the dark room to Norm.

"Glad she had the flashlights." He handed me one and shone his toward the front door. "See the wire?"

I turned the flashlight on and followed the light beam from Norm's. A thin wire ran against the door and was attached to two gas cans, one at each end of the room.

"See that?" His light caught a small box on the gas can. "Think of it as a match. When the door pushes the wire, the match strikes and ignites in the box, which is full of more matches. Within a few seconds, poof, up goes the room."

His light's beam lit up a pile of rags around the can.

"It's full of matches?"

"Shit no, Mick." He sighed. "I said think of it as a box of matches. It's an igniter."

I walked toward Johnny, my flashlight beam aimed at his back.

"Don't touch him." Norm quickly grabbed my arm. "He could be wired, too."

"Damn it, Norm, we can't just leave him there."

"Stay back here," he ordered, and searched the floor around Johnny with a beam of light.

Coco Joe used his flashlight to search the floor, too. There were two more gas cans lying on their sides by the bathroom and two more outside the kitchen. My eyes were beginning to sting from the fumes.

"Can we open a window?"

"No!" Both Norm and Coco Joe answered at the same time.

"We don't know what else could be wired," Norm explained, as he and Coco Joe used hand signals to communicate.

I recognized some of the signs, but wondered how Coco Joe did and why he, instead of me, was working so closely with Norm. Coco Joe pulled duct tape from Johnny's mouth. I heard a tearing as he did, and then a loud moan.

"Quiet, buddy, you're okay now." With his pocketknife, Coco Joe cut the ropes holding Johnny in the chair.

"Open some windows," Tita yelled from the kitchen.

Norm turned quickly and held up his hand to stop her from coming into the room.

"Tita, wait outside," he said firmly, but in a low voice. "We don't know what might set the gas off."

"Norm, this is my house, so don't tell me to get out." Tita lowered her voice. "I need to pack things if we can't stay here. Why can't we open the windows?" A picture of what she had stepped into was forming in her analytical head. It couldn't have seemed real.

Norm didn't answer her. He wasn't used to anyone questioning his orders. I knew there were good reasons for that, but Tita . . . what can I say? Her life was built around the regimen of law, and everything we were doing was frenzied and lacked any organization.

"Let me check the front ones." Coco Joe sat Johnny back down and went to the closest window. He ran his fingers along its side, looking for a tripwire. "I'll open it." He slowly unlocked the hasp and moved the window up an inch at a time. He did the same to the opposite window, avoiding the wire and gas cans on the floor.

"Tita, stay still, don't touch the light switches or anything." Norm walked to her. "I'm sorry, but your house is rigged to explode. The opened windows will help get the fumes out, but the place is soaked in gas and I'm not sure what else they've rigged to ignite."

"I can smell the gas, Norm." She looked toward the wall.

"The light switches?"

"Put a little fuel into a light bulb with a hypodermic needle and when the switch turns on, it explodes and drops fire onto the floor," he explained. "You'd never have a chance. Where's Thomas?"

"Outside, the fumes were making him sick."

"Norm, we'd better get Johnny out of here." Coco Joe lifted Johnny from the chair. "He can't make it on his own."

"Pack something, Tita." Norm aimed his flashlight beam toward the bedroom. "And get out."

"I have Mick's stuff too."

"Help her," Norm said to me. He walked toward Johnny. "Get the van and meet us out front. And, Mick, they could be waiting outside."

I nodded my head and followed Tita into the bedroom.

FORTY-ONE

My eyes watered from the fumes, and my throat hurt with each short breath I took. The windows I'd opened earlier in the bedroom were closed. The arsonists were thorough. Tita took the flashlight off her bureau and found an overnight bag in the closet. I opened the windows, not thinking about checking to see if they were wired. Luckily, the arsonists weren't that thorough.

"You okay?" I picked up my gym bag from the floor. "I think I'm crying." I tried to say it with a smile, to make Tita smile back, maybe even admit her own discomfort.

"I hate them," she mumbled, without a smile, as she yanked clothes from the bureau drawers. She filled the bag without much thought and went back to the closet. "This is my hurricane-escape box." She held a large lidded plastic container.

I bought her the container when she first moved here and suggested she store her priceless mementoes and important papers in it, so that on a short notice to evacuate she wouldn't have to go searching for them. Of course, I was thinking of hurricanes at the time, not arsonists. But, the idea worked for both.

I went to take it from her, and the pain in my side made me wince. It wasn't heavy, but it required stretching both arms to pick it up.

"Sorry," she said, and took it back.

I reached for her overnight bag and lifted it to my right shoulder with my bag. "Let's go."

"Am I going to lose it all?" She looked around the small bedroom and I was glad I couldn't see what had to be her confused and sad expression, and maybe anger.

"I don't think so." I took her hand, but wasn't sure I believed what I said.

"I didn't realize it meant so much to me." She squeezed my hand. "It's the most expensive thing I've ever owned and . . . and. . . ." Her voice began to falter. "Damn, I hate them, Mick."

It was my turn to squeeze her hand as we walked slowly through the house, not knowing what good, if any, it did. Tita looked carefully at the darkened rooms, seeing in her mind everything that was hiding in the night from my eyes, until we reached the back porch.

"Why didn't Norm do something about the gas in the living room?"

We stopped outside and took deep breaths. The cool night air smelled tropical and was a welcome relief, but the taste of gas remained in my mouth.

Norm, Coco Joe and Padre Thomas sat at the picnic table in the backyard, leaning over Johnny Dey.

"Why didn't they go for the van?" She put the container down on the lawn. "What are we supposed to do if there are people out there?"

Tita's life was preparing to unravel and she feared losing control; her fate was in the hands of others. I knew the feeling well, but she was used to being in charge and performing for a jury. This wasn't a performance, it was life and death. I kept hold of her hand and led her toward the table, to confront Norm and see Johnny.

Coco Joe picked up the container from where Tita left it and had her sit in his seat. I walked around until I was looking at Johnny. His face was a mess. Swelling had closed one eye and enlarged an ear; his bottom lip was puffy and split, and covered with dried blood. He had received a brutal beating.

A cool breeze blew through the backyard, and there was no smell of gas, but I could still taste it. "Johnny, you look like shit." I leaned onto the table.

He looked at me with his one good eye and I could see a smile try to form on his damaged lips.

"How's the side?" He spat the words out one at a time.

"What the hell is going on?" I yelled at him.

"This ain't the time," Norm answered for him.

"Yeah, well, if you think they could be watching the house, why the hell send Tita with me for the van?" I rushed the words out, knowing this wasn't the time to second-guess him.

Norm stared up at me as I remained leaning in front of Johnny. "Tita, give Joe the keys." He spoke a tad over a whisper.

He had also stopped calling Coco Joe, Coco. It didn't seem important at the time, or set off any warning bells, which, if I had been at my best, it would have.

Coco Joe took the keys and walked out of the yard.

"What do we do about the gas bomb?" I turned to Norm, but remained standing. "Tita's a little concerned about her house."

"I would be, too," he mumbled, in his lazy drawl. "I just ain't a bomb type of guy. You bein' Irish, maybe you learned some of those IRA tricks when you were in Belfast. Aren't the Irish supposed to be good with bombs?"

I ignored his slam against the Irish. It wasn't like what Tita said to tease my heritage, it was cold.

"So what should we do?" I said calmly, reminding him I was asking for help.

"Call Richard and tell him what you found." He looked between Tita and me. "Make sure he doesn't come through the front door and make sure he brings the bomb squad."

"The city uses the sheriff's bomb squad." I didn't know what difference it made to our situation.

"It's past midnight." He stared up at me and smiled. "If it were me, I'd call the guy that hated me least and, if I ain't mistaken, the sheriff isn't that guy."

I let his words drift into the night and said nothing.

"Mick," he finally said, "call Richard and don't tell him where we're going, because he's gonna want to talk to you, and so is Fitcher. But stress it's a bomb-squad situation."

"And not to come through the front door."

"Right. Now, you're back on track." Norm helped Johnny get up, and without speaking we followed him to Frances Street.

"I don't understand." Tita carried the plastic container.

"Norm didn't think he could defuse the gasoline igniter," I whispered. "He didn't want to chance burning your house down, so I'm calling in the bomb squad."

"Just when I'm sure I don't like him, he goes and does that." She turned to look at the front of the house and then got into the back of the SUV.

Forty-Two

No one spoke on the short ride to the Mango Tree Inn. There was little traffic on Southard at one A.M., as Coco Joe stopped the SUV in the red zone; a few feet away the cars and scooters hummed along Simonton Street, only stopping for the light on the corner when it turned red.

Norm helped Johnny through the gate and up the long stairway to the second-floor guest rooms, while I called Richard and explained what happened to a very-pissed-off cop. He got madder the less I cooperated.

Streetlight reflected off the pool, and the breeze filled the yard with fragrance from the surrounding tropical plants and trees, helping to clear my head of the gas stench and my eyes to stop watering. Coco Joe took Tita's plastic container. She held tightly onto my hand as we climbed the stairway, followed by Padre Thomas, as he hurriedly inhaled his first cigarette in hours.

I hadn't thought of what torture it must have been for him to be at the house and not be able to smoke. I laughed to myself because I realized how lucky we were that he was able to fight his habit of lighting up and chain-smoking throughout the day. Or maybe Norm threatened him when he saw Padre Thomas reach for his pack of Camels?

There were three bedrooms upstairs. Norm helped Johnny get on the bed in the first room. "You and Tita in the end room." He pointed down the hall.

185

How had he arranged all three rooms at the popular bed-and-breakfast?

Coco Joe opened the door to our room and put the container on the bed. "See you in a minute," he said.

Tita looked around the large room. "He's coming back?" She stuck her head in the bathroom. "Big rooms."

"No, I think we're expected in Norm's room." I tried to talk calmly, but I'm not sure how well I hid the stress I felt, because Tita had become involved.

"I am so damned worried about the house." She went into the bathroom and I heard water running. "Hell, Mick, it's only a material thing, I can buy another, I have insurance, we're safe, we're alive, that's the important thing, right?" She rushed the words and then the water stopped and she stood in the doorway drying her face. "How safe are we?" she asked, in a much stronger voice than I heard from her in the last few hours.

"Probably safer than riding a scooter down Duval at one A.M."

"Ah, Mick." She tossed the towel into the bathroom and hugged me. "Always my white knight. Save me with a lie. I got into this willingly; it was my call that brought Norm here." She kissed me gently on the lips. "So let's go see if he'll tell me the truth." She pushed away and walked down the hallway, stopping once to make sure I followed.

Johnny sat up in the bed, all the pillows behind him. Whatever they were talking about stopped when Tita entered the room. She waited for me in the doorway.

"What can I do?" She took my hand. "What can we do?"

"I need you, Thomas and Joe to find an all-night drugstore and buy these things." Norm handed Tita a piece of paper. "Mick's the main target; he's gotta stay close."

"There's one on North Roosevelt." Tita took the list and surprised me with her willingness to go. She read the list and looked at Johnny. "Shouldn't he be at the ER?" she whispered to me.

"Ours is not to reason why," I whispered back.

"And, Tita." Norm walked to her. "We need to lose your van. Not near here, or your place, maybe leave it somewhere like the movie theater. Can you do that after you bring these items back?"

"Yes." She smiled at him. "I'm safe on the street?"

"Safer than Mick," he replied coolly, "but not safe enough to be running around in the daytime."

"What's going to happen, Norm?" She let go of my hand. "He won't tell me the truth, will you?"

Norm walked out into the hall and then onto the balcony overlooking the pool. We followed.

"I don't know how safe any of us are, until I can get some intel from Johnny." His words came slowly. "First, they're after Mick; second, they don't care who else they gotta take out to get him." Norm turned to make sure she was listening. "And right now that's all of us."

"Are they watching the house?"

"Joe doesn't think so."

"Will the house blow up?'

"It could catch fire, if the bomb squad screws up," he told her honestly. "But they should have a fire engine standing by. The house needs to be aired out before they try anything, so the explosive fumes will be gone."

"Best-case scenario?"

"Yup."

"Worst case?"

"There's another bomb hidden in the house, and the bomb squad misses it."

"I hate these fuckers." Tita held in the scream and walked down the stairs. She stopped and looked up at us. "I'm ready to

187

go, where are the other two?" She walked to her SUV.

"Feisty." Norm walked back inside.

Padre Thomas and Coco Joe passed us in the hall, headed outside.

Norm stood by my room, talking on his cell phone. "You know where it is, Jim?"

He listened, and then said, "Use the stairs by the pool. Beat up pretty bad, but he can walk and talk."

"Who's that?" I opened the unlocked door to my room.

"Jim Ashe from JIATF. He has some medical background."

"I didn't think you knew anyone down here in intelligence."

"After my last jaunt through this paradise of yours, I thought it was good idea to make some contacts."

"How honest were you with Tita?" I put my Glock on the bed.

"More than you were."

"Why send her out if you have this Ashe coming?"

"She doesn't need to hear what Johnny has to say . . . and you do." He drawled the words and smiled.

FORTY-THREE

I unpacked my carry-on, while Norm went back to his room. Tita had thrown in extra magazines for the Glock 29, along with my five-pack carrying case of cigars. Or, did Norm do that? I stuck the Glock in my waistband and found Norm standing at the outside door.

"What's Johnny gonna say?" I stood next to him.

"I don't know."

"Should he be in the hospital?"

"Jim will tell us that."

"Will he be safe in the hospital?"

"No."

His briefness bothered me, because it meant he really didn't have the answer I was hoping for. Norm is rarely without answers, or at least ideas that turned into answers.

"Is Tita safe?"

"For the next few hours." He turned to me. "Don't think about Tijuana, Mick. Second-guess me again, or even yourself, and it could cost someone's life."

Three men got out of a sedan parked in the red zone and I went for my Glock. Norm stopped me.

"Jim Ashe," he said quietly.

Two men stayed in the darkness. One of them moved across the street into deeper shadows as Ashe climbed the stairs, a large bag hung over his shoulder.

Jim was about five-ten and carried himself like a military

189

man. If that didn't give him away, his haircut did.

"Inside." Norm nodded to Jim as he got near the top, and walked to his room.

Jim smiled as he passed, but said nothing. The bag looked heavy, even on his strong shoulders.

Norm turned on the light by the double bed and got out of Jim's way as he pulled smaller bags from the large one.

"He in a lot of pain?" He put two small bags on the bed.

"I think so, but I don't want him knocked out with meds right now."

"You wash him up?"

"I did my best."

With the light on, I was able to see that most of the crusted blood from Johnny's face was gone, especially around his eye and lip.

"How you feeling, buddy?" Jim spoke softly, as Johnny moaned an answer I couldn't hear. "Can you tell me what they hit you with?"

Johnny stirred on the bed and opened his one good eye. "Fists."

"Did they break any ribs?"

"Maybe. You got somethin' for the pain?" He mumbled the words, slowly.

"Yeah, in a minute." Jim looked at Norm. "Make it quick."

Norm moved next to the bed. "Johnny, who are we lookin' for and where are they?"

"Colombians and locals." He garbled the words. "Don't know where they are now."

"Cluny?" Jim asked.

"Yeah."

"Who are the locals?"

"Beaumont."

"DEA?"

"Yeah, I don't know him," he moaned, and moved slightly. "Never met him. I think he's local."

"Name Reed Fitcher mean anything to you?" Norm leaned forward as Johnny's replies got weaker.

"I've heard the name."

"How'd they catch on to you?"

"They didn't."

"Why'd they do this?"

"Because I didn't kill Mick." He looked toward me. "My head is killing me. Got that pain shot?"

Norm nodded to Jim, who opened a bag and took out a case with a hypodermic needle, tested it and put a shot into Johnny's arm.

"Thanks." Johnny almost smiled. "Talk to you later, Norm."

Jim took some meds from another bag and applied them to Johnny's lips and eye. He took the pillows away and laid him flat on the bed.

"If they only used their fists, he probably looks and feels worse than it could've been." Jim put the med bags on the dresser. "I can find some clothes for him."

"Thanks." Norm looked out the window. "Who's downstairs?"

"Paul Carpino and Bryan Papaccioli." Jim moved the heavy bag and sat down.

"What are you doing, importing muscle from Italy?" Norm laughed.

"You know we ain't supposed to be here." Jim ignored Norm's laugh.

"Yeah, thanks for coming." Norm finally stopped laughing. "How long will he sleep?"

"Give or take, about four hours."

"Let's go downstairs by the pool and talk."

"You want your shot first?" Jim pulled another needle from

191

one of the bags.

"Got one for Mick?"

"Got enough for everyone." Jim opened a small container of needles he had taken from the bag.

Norm, because of his long sleepless hours of work, often gets by with self-injections of what I call doctor-feel-good shots. He swears it's agency approved, though he always denies working for an agency, but I think it's a vitamin shot laced with amphetamines, to keep him going. We both dropped our pants and let Jim inject us in our butts.

It was almost two A.M., and Johnny had just implicated R.L. Beaumont, self-appointed king of the city commission, in the scheme to smuggle drugs into Key West and commit murder. R.L. was powerful and I doubted he was working alone. I had some questions about Johnny, too. How'd he know Norm?

FORTY-FOUR

We smoked cigars in the shadows, sitting on the lounges by the pool. I looked into the darkness of the neighborhood, but couldn't see the two men from JIATF hiding in the night. Security, I guessed. Doctor-feel-good vitamins rushed through my veins.

The underwater pool lights reflected off the breeze-driven ripples on the water and sent shadows dancing around the landscaped yard.

"Norm, we can't help you." Jim blew smoke from the cigar into the night. "We're not even supposed to be here—it's illegal."

"Illegal?" I tried to keep my voice down.

"They're not supposed to work within the country," Norm explained.

"That's what we've got the FBI, DEA and some other agencies assigned to our command for," Jim went on. "We're interdiction outside. We gather intel and report back."

Norm laughed. "Yeah, that's what they're supposed to do."

"I want to stick around and find out what he knows about Cluny, the slimy-Limey son of a bitch." Jim spat the words out.

"And that's illegal?" I enjoyed the breeze and the taste of the good cigar.

"Yeah, because Johnny's—"

"He doesn't know." Norm cut Jim off.

"Know what?" My voice carried in the night.

They said nothing. I could hear traffic rushing by, probably from Duval Street two blocks away.

"When this is over, he's done, anyway." Norm chewed on his cigar. "He's leaving the agency."

"It's your call." Jim was noncommittal. "Does anyone really leave?"

"Johnny's been deep undercover since he attended FIU. One of the few 'need to know' DEA agents they have." Norm spoke as if the garden had ears. "He roomed with a Colombian kid whose family was in the drug business and found himself a close friend."

"Yeah, close because he took a drug bust for him." Jim hissed the words.

"He wanted to work with us, offered us a deal when we went to interrogate him." Norm picked up the tale. "He said that's why he took the fall. Long story short, he passed a lie-detector test, and we did some background on him. He got on the team. The rest you know."

"What concerns me is, we have a dirty agent out there, and he's getting people killed." Jim changed the subject back to the DEA agent.

"And a city commissioner," I reminded them. "A powerful city commissioner."

"You know how he became so powerful?" Jim couldn't hold back a laugh. "In college he had his own condo and got booze, drugs and girls—or boys—for the other Conchs at FIU, and he kept good records of who, what, when and where. Rumor is, he even has photos."

"College shit, how'd that make him powerful?" It didn't sound right.

"Well, eventually, some of these people went places in the city and the state, even in Washington," Jim recalled. "When old R.L. was in need of a favor, he'd ask for it by reminding the person how much fun college was. It probably wasn't said that nicely."

"So he gets appointed to all these boards, elected to the city commission?"

"And never had an honest candidate run against him. And along the way he continued to take care of his old college friends."

"And you know all this because?"

"We've known for a long time that he's dirty. We just haven't been able to prove it. People who have bad business dealings with him leave town bought off, or they disappear. Getting rid of witnesses isn't something he learned from the Colombians."

Holy shit, I thought. I came to Key West to get away from this and here it was, festering all around me.

"How can the DEA know he's dirty and not get him?" I knew better, had seen it happen in other countries, but had to ask.

"I don't know, it ain't my bailiwick, but maybe he's smart or lucky." Jim checked his wristwatch. "How long before they're back?"

"I told Joe to keep 'em gone for at least an hour."

"You know Coco Joe, too?" I sat on the edge of the lounge and faced Norm. "Is everyone here an agent but me?"

"Who's to say you're not an agent?" Jim laughed. "I've seen your jacket, and it could be interpreted that way."

"I hope he's shittin' me." I stood up.

"You got a jacket, Mick." Norm didn't move. "You've helped me. You did recon, intel, and I had to report it."

"I never got a dime—"

"You got your ass saved." Norm cut me off. "But I never put you down as cooperative, did I, Jim?"

"No, that he didn't." Jim backed Norm up. "A few times he clearly pointed out your ideological support of the leftists and

195

your uncooperativeness."

At least he said leftists and not communists.

"How much help can you be?" Norm brought the subject back to its serious side.

"I can't." Jim repeated himself.

"Yeah, I know that, but what kind of support can I count on?"

"Whatever I can get away with." Jim sat up. "Carpino and Papaccioli are off duty, so you've got those two for backup. Me, I am on duty, so it's touchy, but I am here for you, especially because I want that Limey. By the way"—he leaned in toward Norm—"Joe was sweet on Gabriela Isabel, the Colombian operative Mick found floating, so keep him away from Cluny until I get there."

Norm laughed. This time it was deep. "You know, I just realized what this fuckin' town reminds me of." He stood up. "Key West is an asylum being run by the inmates. Jesus, I need the sanity of Los Angeles. Give me Latin street gangs, punk drug dealers. I want chickens runnin' around the streets, I'll go back to Central America."

"Norm, the island has always been a free range institution," Jim said with a laugh. "We have a local singer named Scott Kirby who wrote a song about it, I'll send you the CD."

"No, thanks, I don't want to think about Key West after this is over." He put his cigar out in a planter. "You need to come back to LA, Mick. At least you can ID the crazies and they ain't running the government."

FORTY-FIVE

We stood by the gate, watching the quiet street. I saw one guard off to the corner of the inn's small, off-street parking lot, but it was still too dark to see clearly across the street where the other sentry was. Southard is one-way, so our attention focused in the direction Tita would drive from.

"You know R.L. is a fag?" Norm's voice was low and I barely heard him.

"You mean gay?" I looked toward him, wondering why he used the offensive term. In Irish, a fag is a cigarette, but that's not what he meant. "He's married with three kids."

"Yeah." Jim got a chuckle out of that. "An arranged marriage years ago to a woman with three small kids and he treats them as if they were his, but he's as fruity as they come."

"That's no big thing here." I looked to Jim, who was smiling.

"Back then, before he left for college, it was," Norm said. "He had expectations in the political arena, and Florida wasn't gonna vote some backwater fruit into office, especially not in Tallahassee or DC."

"I wouldn't have guessed," was all I could think to say in reply. I was as surprised by his anti-gay sentiments as I was about hearing that the father-like figure of the city commission lived a secret second life. "I never even heard a rumor, and around here those kinds of rumors are everywhere."

"According to his file, he spends a lot of time in Kentucky," Jim added quietly. "You might be surprised what old-time college buddies he meets up there. Boy's day out, kind of."

I didn't like R.L., but it was his phony attempt at frugalness when it came to the city coffers that angered me. His outbursts against departmental expenditures during the yearly city budget hearings were feisty, legendary. They always made the front page of the paper and got a sound bite on news director Bill Becker's Morning Magazine show, on US-1 Radio. I knew enough from the behind-the-scenes people in city government to know he, or friends, often benefited from his votes and budget decisions, something that didn't make it into the paper. Becker told me once he had suspicions, but without proof, he couldn't report it. R.L.'s sexual preference, if it was true, was unimportant to me.

Coco Joe drove the SUV into the parking lot. Tita sat in front. Norm met them, so they wouldn't panic when they saw Jim and the sentry. Jim and I stayed by the fence. Padre Thomas jumped out of the backseat and lit a cigarette. Tita carried a shopping bag when she got out, while Norm talked with Coco Joe.

I took the bag and she gave me a tired smile.

"Why are you down here?" She frowned. "Is Johnny okay?'

"He's sleeping. A friend of Norm's showed up with some medication."

"JIATF?"

"Jim." I nodded and led Tita in his direction. "This is Tita."

They shook hands in the darkness.

"Do you need any of these things?" She pointed to the shopping bag.

I wondered if she was aware that her errand had been a ruse to get her out of the inn. Some things are best left unsaid.

"Probably be able to use 'em," Jim lied, with a smile.

"Tita." Norm called her to the parking lot.

Jim took the bag of pharmacy medication from me and

walked upstairs. I went over to the SUV.

"It's almost five." Norm leaned against the vehicle. "We've got to put this somewhere. If these guys know where you live, they know what you drive."

"The airport?"

"No." He shook his head. "By now someone will be watching it. What about the Albertson's parking lot? There are a lot of shops there, or by the movie theater."

"Okay." Her voice was tired.

"Joe will go with you." Norm opened the door for her. "Look like you're a couple getting a cab after a late night."

Her weary, green eyes stared up at me, and a short smile formed on her lips. I wondered what she thought about being a part of my life now.

"Be back soon," she said, yawning.

Coco Joe caught a green light at the corner and turned left. Padre Thomas waited by the gate, probably on his third smoke.

"We are doing something about this, right?" He crushed the butt under his foot, but hadn't forgotten the evil that tortured him, and followed us upstairs.

Forty-Six

Jim had the shopping bag's contents on a chair and smiled at Norm. "You thought this would help?"

"It bought us time." He hadn't wanted Tita around when he questioned Johnny. "We need to eat, Mick, anything open?"

"Harpoon Harry's opens in half an hour."

"Up by the waterfront?" Norm looked out the window. "Get it to go and eat here?"

"I'm just tired." Padre Thomas yawned. "Do I have a room or should I walk home?"

"Next room on the right," Norm directed him. "And no smoking."

"God bless you," he mumbled, and left.

"Let Carpino drive." Jim picked up some of the medicine packets he had brought. "We'll eat anything you bring back. Coffee would be good."

"Cuban or American?"

"How's their *con leches?*"

"Good and sweet."

"Maybe some extras for the microwave."

"You plan on hanging around?" Norm looked suspiciously at him.

"You'll have me or someone," Jim said. "He'll wake up in a couple of hours and may need a real medic."

"I have to get more from him," Norm complained. "I need an idea of where to look for the Colombians, because we can't

200

stay hiding here."

"What do you have in mind?" For someone who shouldn't have been with us, Jim was getting involved very quickly.

"It has to be ready to go down, whatever it is." Norm thought aloud. "Something's scaring 'em. Maybe it's time to grab the goods and run?"

"You think they've had enough of Key West and the locals?"

"I have," Norm complained. "But I ain't waiting on a payload. Do you think this R.L. would double-cross the Colombians and try to get away with one big score?"

"Be stupid, but. . . ." Jim hunched his shoulders. "No, not unless it was the only choice he had left. He's too old for that, these days."

"Think about it," Norm said, "while we pick up breakfast. Maybe we can make him think it's his only choice."

When we got downstairs, Carpino was in the government sedan, ready to pull out.

"You know where Harpoon Harry's is?" Norm sat in the front and I got in back.

"Yes, sir, Caroline and Margaret streets." Carpino turned right onto Simonton and drove slowly up the deserted street.

"You always carry this?" Norm touched something on the seat.

"Yes, sir." Carpino kept his eyes forward. "Thirty-round clip."

"You good with it?"

"Everyone with Captain Ashe is good at what they do, sir."

The "sir" with each answer bothered me, maybe because of my lack of military training, but it didn't seem to affect Norm's attitude at all. I had never seen him real big on command protocol. Of course, I'd never seen anyone give him orders, either.

Simonton Street was quiet. A few people rode bicycles to early jobs, and one scooter sped past us illegally before we

201

turned right onto Caroline. I looked for Jimmy Buffett's woman going crazy, but didn't see her. I saw a few people walking, but how could I tell if they were crazy?

B.O.'s restaurant was lit up, its stools resting upside down on the railing counter, but the eatery was closed. The city's parking lot had two RVs inside; otherwise, the large lot was empty. Carpino pulled over and let us off in front of an empty Harpoon Harry's.

"I'll park across the street, sir," he said, and turned left onto Margaret.

Before we opened the door to the restaurant, he had parked in the darkness of the trolley stop turned art gallery across the street. The corner market hadn't opened yet and the Key West Electrical Supply building sat dark on Margaret Street. Light came through the glass doors of the restaurant, showing empty booths and the lunch counter with its colorful stools. Ron was behind the counter, working alone.

"Going fishing?" he asked, as we walked in.

"Late night, Ron." I introduced Norm. "Can we get twelve *con leches*, two sugars—"

"Make it four sugars, Ron," Norm said. "It's going to be an early morning."

"And we need eight Denver omelets, six with home fries, two with grits and whole-wheat toast." The aromas of coffee, potatoes and bacon coming from behind the kitchen's closed doors made me hungry.

"Where's everyone else?" He wrote the order down and brought it to the kitchen.

Norm looked out onto the empty streets. "Quiet at this hour."

A taxi crept by, looking for a customer, its headlights splashing light through the restaurant.

"Six o'clock and people will start coming in, hung over or hungry." Ron began to fill the espresso machine. "Would one of you open a couple of those doors while I make the *con leches*, please?"

Norm and I leaned into different booths, opened the glass doors toward the sidewalk, and then secured them to the wall.

"Two enough?"

"All of them, if you don't mind." The espresso machine hissed as Ron heated the milk for our *con leches*.

We opened two more doors, making sure they were secure. A city bus drove down Caroline Street, and a couple of cars pulled into the city's parking lot on the corner. The boating community was waking and people moved around the Margaret Street Pier and docks across the street.

I saw John Kitritch load the daily paper into the vending machine, and I went out to buy a copy.

"Hey, John, anything worth reading?" I tossed him two quarters.

He looked up, his black eye patch in place, caught the quarters, and handed me a copy of the paper. "Something on every page," he laughed, and went back to his van.

A car drove down Caroline as I scanned the front page, and I heard brakes squeal before I entered the restaurant. The car stopped in the intersection. Two men got out and started walking toward the restaurant. Each carried an Israeli Galil.

"Norm," I yelled, dropped the newspaper and pulled my Glock.

"See 'em," he shouted, and fired from the back booth's open doorway.

The quiet morning shattered like a bar mirror hit with a bottle of booze, as the two men fired wildly at the outside glass doors of the restaurant, hoping to hit someone. Between them, they shattered most of the doors and windows. I squeezed into a small section of the inside wall at the corner and fired toward the shooters. The Galils' bullets pockmarked the restaurant's trivia-decorated walls, breaking coffee cups, liquor bottles and the espresso machine.

I saw the car begin to back up and then the government sedan shot out of the darkness and rammed the driver's side, pushing it sideways toward the two cocaine cowboys shooting at us. One shooter ran toward the closed market, sliding past a group of newspaper vending machines; the other shooter wasn't as lucky and went down hard as the car smashed him to the ground.

Broken glass sparkled like diamonds along the sidewalk and booths inside the restaurant. The diner's counter was speckled with bullet holes, and the liquor shelf above the coffee machines held shattered bottles that spilled booze oozing down the wall and into the shot-up espresso machine.

Carpino got out of the government car and fired a long burst from his M4, a short-barreled version of the M16, point-blank into the driver's side of the disabled car. At about the same time the surviving Colombian cowboy began shooting at us again, spraying the street from the car to the restaurant and back, before changing magazines. The shooter had his back to the closed convenience store, when Carpino fired six quick shots from his M4 that knocked the cowboy against the wall and shattered the store's window. The Galil fell to the pavement as the man slid to a sitting position on the sidewalk, his head resting against a vending machine.

The sound of gunfire echoed in my ears, even after everything stopped.

Norm looked behind the counter and helped Ron up. "You okay?"

Ron stared big-eyed at the damaged doors. "Holy Christ," he mumbled. "What was that?"

"Looked like a drug deal gone bad," Norm suggested. "We'll be back later."

"I need to call the cops."

"I'm pretty sure they're on the way." Norm pointed toward the gathering of boaters across Margaret Street.

FORTY-SEVEN

Paul Carpino slipped the damaged government car into a parking space a half block from the Mango Tree Inn as an early-morning gray dawn began to usher in the day.

"You need to take this upstairs." Carpino popped the trunk and handed Norm a large duffel bag.

"Where are you going?" Norm took the heavy bag.

"Change cars at the base." He got in the car and drove off.

Bryan Papaccioli opened the gate for us, an M4 held in his free hand. "Sir," he said, as we walked by. I almost expected him to salute.

"Are you alone?" Norm stopped next to the fence.

"Yes, sir." Papaccioli closed the gate. "I expect a couple of men will come back with Paul."

"Thank you." Norm hefted the duffel bag and climbed the stairs.

"I don't suppose that's breakfast and *con leches.*" Jim took the bag from Norm as we walked into the hallway. "Everyone okay?"

"Luck on our part," Norm said. "Where's Tita?"

"Sleeping." Jim put the duffel bag on the floor and opened it. He pulled out six M4s and stacks of ammo magazines. "I have a couple of men joining us. What happened?" He handed Norm and me a weapon.

The M4 is a short-barreled, .223-caliber version of the better-known M16 and comes with a thirty-round clip. The weapon is popular with some branches of the military because of its size,

206

but it felt uncomfortable in my hands.

Norm quickly told Jim about the shoot-out at Harpoon Harry's.

"Where's Joe?" Norm took the M4. "Shit, I hope it doesn't come to this."

"I was a Boy Scout." Jim put the other M4s and clips on a chair. "Be prepared. I told Joe to get some rest, so at least one of us won't be tired later."

"How long before I can talk with Johnny?"

"A couple more hours. What are you hoping to get?"

"I don't know." Norm looked out the window. "I think they trusted him because of his contacts in Colombia—"

"They were going to kill him." I cut Norm off.

"That was a poor judgment call from someone here." Norm turned from the window. "It's why I think there's something scaring them. If I had a hint of what it was, maybe I could use it to our advantage."

"You think he knows where the Colombians are?" Jim's interest perked.

"I know he knows about the Colombians. The guys we ran into were cowboys and acting like they were in Cali, not Key West." Norm paced the room. "They were looking for you and must have had shoot-on-sight orders"—he turned to me—"because they don't act without orders. But they do act without concern for the law. What I need to know about are the locals; R.L. and whoever else is involved. Are they depending on the Colombians for muscle?"

"The Mexican narcos are just as crazy," Jim said. "But you're probably right. What's the interest in R.L.?"

"This *paco* shit is for local consumption." Norm stopped pacing. "I'm wondering if it's a joint venture or are they doing him a favor? If the Colombians are his security, this Limey Cluny, then we can expect them to play hardball. This'll get hairy."

"My guess is that R.L. was scared shitless when he discovered one of the local dealers was an undercover cop, and panicked." Jim slapped Norm on the shoulder.

"The cops probably used Jay to get Rebecca in," I said.

"That would explain why he went off the roof." Norm looked at Johnny, then at his wristwatch. "Two hours?"

"Could be a little less, could be a little more." Jim searched through the medical supplies he had laid out. "Nothing here to wake him up with."

"I'm gonna check on Tita." I quietly walked down the hallway and into the end room.

Tita was under the covers, hugging the large pillow. She breathed slowly. Doctor-feel-good juice rushed through me and I knew that even if I lay down, I wouldn't sleep. I also knew we would need another jolt of the elixir in about four hours or we'd become tired and irritable. The way things were going, I wasn't sure when I would sleep again.

Norm and Jim were at the head of the outdoor steps when I closed the door to the room.

"What happens next?" I walked outside and saw the sky, as it turned from a purple to a clean dark blue. A light breeze kept the morning cool.

"What do you know about this R.L.?" Norm kept his eyes on the one-way street.

"I've met him socially a few times." I thought back to see if there was anything memorable about our meetings. "I only know what I hear from city-hall insiders about his control of the commission. I'm not sure what Jim said about using his college experiences to influence people would work with this commission."

"Why not?"

"In most cases, it's a younger commission," I said. "Hell, R.L. has to be in his late sixties and most of the commissioners are at least twenty or thirty years younger than him. Of course, that doesn't make them smarter."

"What's his hold?" Norm looked at Jim.

"They're Conchs, there's a family hold," Jim said. "They stick together and they probably grew up with R.L. being the *patrón* and have a respect for him. He may have even helped out a family member or friend."

"It's almost a quality," Norm smirked. "Will he be forgiven for this *paco?*"

"Let me tell you about Key Westers," Jim scoffed, quietly. "Back in the square-grouper days, Customs sent a bunch of investigators down here and the operation concluded with about half the police force, and most of the shrimpers, being arrested for marijuana smuggling. They literally had tons of evidence, when they went into court." He laughed. "But they didn't get one conviction."

"Things have changed in the thirty years since that happened," I reminded them.

"Yeah, but I bet the remaining Conch families still stick together. But this shit is for local consumption, and it kills."

"There is that to add to the mix."

"We need someone who knows this guy today. What he's about."

"I know someone who might be able to help," I said, and watched the first clouds skirt across the sky.

FORTY-EIGHT

Norm turned to me. "A friendly?"

"A local journalist."

"Shit." Jim sighed. "A journalist isn't exactly what I'd be looking for."

"Tell me about him." Norm leaned against the railing and continued to watch the street. He trusted me, and I was a journalist, so he wasn't as cynical as Jim.

"An English guy named Kram Rocket. He works for a local weekly, writes about the city commission."

Both men looked strangely at me as I said Kram's name. I could see hesitation in Norm's expression, but we both knew this wasn't the time for practical jokes.

"English?" Norm stared hard, and then smiled, as if that explained the odd name. "I thought you hated the English."

"The government, I hate the government." I smiled my reply. "I hate the Churchills, but I have nothing against the English people. If they support making the Royal Family the ultimate welfare recipients, more power to 'em."

"You hate Winston Churchill?" Jim's curiosity was piqued.

"Jesus, don't get him started on the Irish problem."

"Yeah," I said. "Winston's father chose to feed cattle being raised in Ireland, for export to England, instead of the Irish people during the potato famine in the eighteen hundreds. 'Let them eat grass,' he's quoted as saying about the starving Irish, and his son Winston was no better. During World War I he used the Irish volunteers as cannon fodder against the Kaiser, and he wasn't any different in the next war." The subject made my blood boil. "The Churchill family supported genocide against the Irish, but they've rewritten history, because of being on the winning side of the war. Churchill is quoted as saying history would be good to him because he would write it."

"Enough history," Norm grumbled. "What makes you think this Kram can help us?"

"Like I said, he covers local government for the weekly and has written in-depth profiles on commissioners." I tried to remember some of the things he'd written about R.L., but couldn't. "We've talked at lunch about what the new commission is doing and he sees them in the pockets of big developers. Kram is a longtime resident and doesn't like the developers taking over."

"I ask again," Norm said, "why's he going to help us?"

"If anyone on the island knows R.L.'s inner workings, it's Kram. Even if it's an outrageous rumor, he's got it locked away in his head. If he smells a story in this, he'll deal with us."

"Maybe we don't want a story." Jim let us know how he felt.

"It's already too big to avoid coverage." Norm looked at his wristwatch. "How do we meet this Kram?"

"I don't suppose we have much time?" As I asked, I thought of John Prine's song about a question not being a question if you already know the answer.

He shook his head. "After I'm done with Johnny, we need to have a plan and be working on it."

"Well, he used to eat breakfast at Harpoon Harry's, but I know he won't today."

"But he's a journalist." Norm smiled. "His routine takes him there, he'll go, and when he sees what happened, his curiosity will get the better of him."

"He'll stick around, bother the cops, try to get something

211

from Ron." I saw where Norm was coming from.

"You guys are predicable," Norm laughed. "Speaking of predictable, do you have a story ready for Richard when he calls?"

"Hadn't thought of that."

"Well, you'd better, because he'll want you to come in and explain three dead Colombians." Norm turned to stare at Southard Street as cars drove by and then turned to Jim. "When do you expect them?"

"Any moment, and we should be checking on Johnny." He walked into the hallway. "Bryan can handle the street."

Jim sat on the bed and shook Johnny's shoulder. He moaned and Jim lightened up on the shaking. "Johnny, wake up, we gotta talk."

"Aw, shit," Johnny cried. "Christ, I need another shot." He reached out and grabbed Jim's arm.

"Where does it hurt?"

"Everywhere." Johnny rubbed the sleep from his eyes. "You still here?"

I wasn't sure if he was talking to Norm or me.

"Need to ask you some questions, Johnny." Norm moved Jim aside and sat down. "Then we're getting you to a real doctor."

"Hell, no." He moved uncomfortably on the bed. "I'll be okay after a little more sleep. I wanna help take down the bastard."

"Who's the bastard?" Jim asked.

Johnny grimaced as he forced himself to sit up. "Cluny. He killed Gabby."

"We know. Mick found her in the marina." Jim spoke quietly.

"We need R.L. What can you tell us about him?" Norm spoke firmly; he didn't have time to waste.

"He panicked, because he knew who Rebecca was," Johnny said through clenched teeth. "He went crazy. I'd never seen anything like it. Cluny and the Colombians killed Jay and then Rebecca."

"Jay was a decoy?" Norm asked.

"Yeah, and then we all got out of the hotel in the evacuation."

"Why didn't they kill you?"

"Because I'm tight with the *jefe*. I was one of them."

"Why didn't you do something to help Jay and Rebecca?" I asked.

"They separated us, to keep the suspicion down," Johnny mumbled. He looked hard at me, winced in pain as he moved himself up onto the pillows. "It was ten to one against me, Mick, and I wasn't gonna die for nothing."

"It's a decision call, and a hard one," Norm said. "Why'd you end up like this? What happened?"

"I told you, R.L. lost it," he moaned. "I didn't kill Mick, and he didn't trust me after that."

"What about the *jefe?*"

"R.L. was calling the shots and assured Cluny that he would see the Feds got the credit for my death, if they survived." He coughed and his face filled with pain. "I could really use that shot."

"Where can we find R.L.?" Norm ignored Johnny's plea.

"Jesus, guys, this hurts."

"Where's R.L.?" Norm stood up.

"On his boat or at the warehouse."

"And they are where?"

"Boat is at Conch Marina, and the warehouse is somewhere on Stock Island. Maybe on Shrimp Road." Johnny's words came out forced and slow. "Point me toward the head." He forced his legs off the side of the bed and almost fell as he tried to stand up.

Norm grabbed his arm and helped him to the bathroom.

213

My cell phone rang and startled me. I looked at the readout screen and saw Richard's name. I hate it when Norm's right. "Good morning, Richard. What are you doing up at this hour?"

Jim shook his head and went to tell Norm I'd received the call.

"Where are you, Mick?" There was tension in Richard's words.

I could hear all the commotion in the background. I knew where he was.

"I'm still in Islamorada."

"Stop being an asshole," he shouted. "Ron said you and your buddy showed up here ordering enough food for an army, and then all hell broke loose."

"It's not what it looks like, Richard."

"Why don't you and Tita come into my office and explain what three dead Latin males in the middle of a main street looks like, and maybe you can tell me how they got there."

"They're Colombians, and I need a little time."

Norm stood at the bathroom door and shook his head.

"I'll give you a little time," Richard screamed, again. "In half an hour, if you aren't in my office, I will put a vice grip around your ass so tight you won't ever shit again. You understand?" He hung up before I could answer.

"How much time did he give you?" Norm asked.

"I got a half hour."

"You should have seen that coming."

My cell phone rang again. I looked at the readout and saw Richard's name again. "It's Richard."

"Answer it, maybe the half hour's gone."

"We got disconnected," I said, and saw Norm's whimsical grin as he shook his head.

"Shut the fuck up and listen to me." Richard words were rushed but his voice was low. "Don't go to my office. I doubt you were, but don't. Your life ain't worth shit right now, and I can't protect you."

"What's going on, Richard?"

"I don't know if it's one of my men or the DEA, but we've got a dirty one somewhere." He was quiet for a moment. "Are you there?"

"Yeah."

"Did you hear me?"

"Yeah. Richard, it ain't a cop, it's the DEA agent."

"How do you know that?" His voice came across anxious.

"You know I have contacts."

"I gotta go," he mumbled. "When I get free I'll call back. Watch yourself." The phone went dead.

"He knows there's a dirty agent," I said, as Johnny limped his way to the bed.

"At least one," Johnny winced and lay back down. "This Cluny spreads money like it's sugar for *con leches.* I know he's got a DEA agent in his pocket, so I figure he's probably got local cops too."

FORTY-NINE

"Whatever you're up to"—Johnny made himself as comfortable as possible on the edge of the bed—"I want in. I don't want to be left out."

Norm told him about the shoot-out at Harpoon Harry's.

"Cluny's got a dozen *cholos* here," Johnny said. "All cowboys, you're right there. They ain't the brightest guys in the world, but you couldn't find anyone more loyal."

"Aren't they worried about being caught in the States?" I asked.

Johnny half smiled at me. "You've written about these clowns before." He shifted his weight, still looking for that comfortable spot. "If they get busted, someone posts bail, usually in cash, and they're on their way back to Colombia in a matter of hours."

"Not always," Jim said. "We've kept a couple from making bail, but then someone killed them in jail. Money rules."

"I want something for the pain," he said to Jim, "but I don't want to be knocked out. I want to be part of whatever you're doing."

"Tell us about what's going down." Norm walked to the window and looked outside. "What's the reason behind the two murders?"

"R.L. and some friends heard about this *paco* drug from Cluny." Johnny winced. "They put local money together and arranged to have some *paco* delivered with the next coke shipment. It's off the cartel's books."

216

"We know about the *paco.*" Norm continued to look out the window. "What's happening now and how close is it to going down?"

"What's today?"

"Tuesday," Jim answered.

"They're waiting on a call from Mexico, but it should go down this week." He winced the words out.

"There are three four-door green Jeeps pulling in," Norm said, turning toward Jim and cutting Johnny off.

"Mine." Jim walked to the window. "Nothing says military like Hummers."

"So you use Jeeps?" Norm walked out of the room, followed by Jim.

"The island's full of Jeeps, they don't stand out and the soft top comes down. Probably got Mississippi and Alabama license plates."

"Are they armored?"

"No," Jim laughed. "But they get good gas mileage."

"Help me outside." Johnny stood slowly. "You okay?"

"I've been better," I said, and let him take hold of my elbow. "Thanks for not killing me." I tried to put a little levity in my tone. It was a topic I had a lot of questions about, but they would hold until this was over.

"You're gonna have to do better than that, Mick," he mumbled as we met the others on the porch. "I could be doing my job now, if I had."

Each Jeep carried two men, all six dressed in shorts and T-shirts. Papaccioli greeted Carpino as he got out and then greeted the others. Some carried boxes, others had duffel bags slung over their shoulders. Norm and Jim went to meet them and I watched as they directed the men to the first floor. Jim signaled me to join them. The sun was up; traffic flowed along Simonton and Southard as people began the workday. There

217

were no shadows to hide in.

"You be okay standing here?"

"I'm not going anywhere." Johnny tried a thin smile.

When I got to the Jeeps, Jim was talking on his cell. Norm introduced me to Dave Grizzle.

"Paul, Bryan and Dave are going to pick up Kram," Norm said. "What can they say that will make him come along without a problem?"

"Do you know him?"

Papaccioli stepped forward. "I can recognize him from his mug shot in the paper."

"Tell him I sent you and that I have an exclusive that connects the shooting with Hotel Key West." I knew Kram's curiosity would take over; mine would have. "If he has doubts, have him call; he's got my cell." I turned to Norm. "Maybe I should call him?"

"No," he said quickly. "We don't want anyone to know what we're doing."

Jim met the three men at the Jeep, talked to them briefly and then joined us.

"Hungry?" he said, smiling.

"What do you have?" Norm asked.

"Finnegan's Wake will open for us in half an hour and we should be eating breakfast within an hour."

Norm looked at his wristwatch. "It's almost eight, what time do they usually open?"

"Eleven." Jim greeted one of the men walking out from the first floor. "If we have to, we can close off the dining room. No matter, it's ours for as long as we need it. I know the owner."

"We're set up, sir." The young man from the first floor almost saluted Jim.

Carpino drove one Jeep out of the lot, while the rest of us

walked to the inn's downstairs living quarters. I was curious to see what was set up.

FIFTY

I knew it had been a living room once, because there were family photos on the walls, framed proclamations from the city and the Innkeepers Association, bright curtains and a large grand piano off to one side. The last time the room had been this active was probably at a party, but this was not a party and the conversation wasn't casual. There was nothing casual in the room now; it was all deadly serious.

An opened laptop computer sat on a small desk; two others sat opened on opposite ends of the piano and a fourth atop a large coffee table, along with a compact printer. A satellite phone lay next to each computer.

"Jesus," I mumbled. "What is all this?"

"Our communications room," Jim answered.

"I thought you weren't getting involved."

"I'm not." He grinned. "This is a training exercise and I thought the current situation would add a . . . ah . . . sense of realism and urgency to the training."

I shook my head and looked at Norm, who smiled and raised his eyebrows.

"What do we have, gentlemen?" Jim bellowed.

"We're locating Beaumont's financial records," the man at the desk said, "checking property in his name and the names of his wife and children."

"Checking for recent intel on drug shipments," the man at the coffee table replied, "and DEA reports."

"Searching state and federal surveillance records, sir," a man yelled from the piano. "We are also trying to tap into his cell phone."

"How long?" Jim yelled in reply.

"Damn soon, sir," the men answered in unison.

We followed Jim onto the outside wraparound porch. Tita and Coco Joe were helping Johnny walk up the steps as Jim leaned against the railing.

"We'll find him for you," he said to Norm. "We tap into his cell, he can run, but he can't hide."

I walked over to Tita as she helped Johnny sit down. Coco Joe nodded and continued to walk toward Norm and Jim.

"Jesus, that hurt," Johnny said, about coming down the steps from the second floor. "I hope there's a bathroom around here."

"I'm sure there is." I almost laughed and turned to Tita. "You get some sleep?"

"Yeah, a little, but I'm feeling better." She smiled. "And you?"

I told her about Harpoon Harry's and Richard's warning on the phone, and watched her expression change from improbable to fearful.

"How is this happening?" She stared hard at me, needing an answer.

"Blame R.L." I tried to explain. "From what Johnny said, he recognized Rebecca and panicked. His world is unraveling and he's trying to hold it together."

"By killing people?"

"By doing whatever it takes to hold onto what he has," I said. "It's the attitude that keeps dictators in power. Corrupt politicians and successful thieves, too. R.L.'s been at this so long he looks at everything he has as owed him, and that gives him the right to do whatever it takes to keep it. I doubt it's the first time he's had people killed."

"I thought things like this only happened in the big cities," she moaned, as if uncertain of what to think. "How can it be happening here in Key West? How could it go this far?"

"Remember how I would go to the South End and Roxbury years ago, when they were black and Puerto Rican neighborhoods?" I pulled her next to me and leaned against the railing. "I loved your parents, and Paco, and never felt threatened on those streets. The Irish were stoning school buses with black and Puerto Rican kids on them, because they didn't want those kids in white South Boston schools; meanwhile, I'm waiting at a bus stop for a ride to Field's Corner. Go figure, a white Irishman in the heart of the ghetto without a problem, while kids who never did anything to the people of South Boston were getting pelted with stones, and people like Louie Hicks got elected to city office because of hatred."

Tita looked at me, confusion and fear in her expression. "I don't understand."

"That's my point." I kissed her cheek. "You look for the rhyme and reason of why things happen, or don't, and it's not always there. It just is and has to be dealt with. Right now we're focused on R.L and his people, but this island is full of good people who give selflessly of themselves."

"You know, Mick"—Johnny sighed and took a deep breath—"at heart you're a damn romantic. I always knew that." He almost laughed, but it turned into a cough and I could see the pain on his face. "R.L.'s a greedy bastard who doesn't care for anyone but himself. He'd have you killed, or me, hell, he'll have Tita killed and then go have dinner to celebrate. That's what you need to understand, that's the real answer to your question, Tita." He coughed again. "R.L.'s a son of a bitch who needs killing."

"You want that shot now?" Jim came over, followed by Norm and Coco Joe.

He winced. "I want something that won't knock me out."

"We're going to Finnegan's, maybe a few shots of whiskey?"

"Maybe a shot of doctor-feel-good?" He smiled toward Norm.

Norm looked at his wristwatch. "I think it's about time we all had one."

"I'm not walking back upstairs," Johnny complained. "Bring me something for the pain, too."

"What's going on?" Tita turned to me as Jim walked toward the stairs.

"I guess we're going to Finnegan's for breakfast."

"I figured that," she snapped. "You guys on speed? Norm's doctor-feel-good crap?"

Tita had seen too many childhood friends go to jail, or the graveyard, from drugs and had no tolerance for them. Her belief was, there is no reason for drug use, none.

"Lighten up, lady." Johnny sighed. "Sometimes even bad things are for the best."

She looked at him and pulled away from me. "And boys will always be boys," Tita sulked and walked to the pool.

"She's a handful." Johnny tried to smile. "She mad 'cause I shot you?"

"No." I watched her walk away. "She's mad at me for getting shot."

"She shouldn't be here." He moved around on the hard patio chair. "You shouldn't be here. You're civilians."

"I put this in motion."

"No, you didn't," he said slowly. "R.L. put this in play long before you arrived in Key West."

223

FIFTY-ONE

Tita stood by the pool with Padre Thomas. The sun was beginning to brighten the sky, and the morning breeze rustled tree branches and filled the air with the aromas of honeysuckle and jasmine.

Coco Joe helped Jerry Blankenship and Dan Arthur, two of Jim's JIATF men, load duffel bags into the Jeeps. The other man, Matt Pierce, was staying behind to monitor the communications equipment; the rest of us were going to Finnegan's for breakfast and to talk with journalist Kram Rocket.

After getting our shot from Jim, we climbed into the Jeeps. Johnny's expression indicated he was still in pain as he hoisted himself into the backseat with Padre Thomas and Tita. I got in the front with Blankenship, who followed the Jeep driven by Arthur.

Finnegan's Wake is a short block from Harpoon Harry's and there was still police action in the vicinity. Cops had Grinnell and Eaton streets closed to through traffic, but let us pass when Blankenship showed his military ID and explained we were on our way to Finnegan's.

The back gate to the restaurant's outdoor Paddy O's Pub was unlocked. When we entered the dinning room from Paddy's, Kram Rocket was sitting with Carpino and Papaccioli. His coffee cup was full and his plate held crumbs and a wrinkled napkin. He looked up and smiled at me. Carpino and Papaccioli excused themselves and went to sit with Grizzle.

A buffet breakfast waited for us on a large table, along with an oversized urn of coffee. Jim pulled me aside, "Grab some coffee and let's talk to this guy."

"Go do what you have to do." Tita added two sugars to a mug of black coffee and handed it to me. "I'm afraid of getting used to this," she mumbled and began filling a plate for herself. "It's exciting and it scares me that I feel this way."

I took the mug, kissed her cheek. "It'll be okay," I said and walked away.

"Finnegan's should open for breakfast more often." Kram smiled as we sat down. "You know something about that fiasco?"

Kram talks as if he's getting ready to run out the door, quick and with flailing arms. He is known around the island as an eccentric and still has a hint of his English accent, but it sometimes gets lost in his hurried speech. His toothy smile hides an amazing memory and an analytical mind.

The dinning room was all dark wood with large poster-size photos of famous Irishmen hanging on the wall, men who were probably not recognized by the majority of guests usually in the room.

Kram looked at the posters over the booths. "Eamon de Valera"—he pointed at one of the posters—"was an ugly politician. He and Brendan Behan, faces only a mother could love. William Butler, on the other hand," he went on, pointing at a poster of the monocle-wearing poet, W.B. Yeats, "was good-looking and a ladies' man. We didn't get a good education on the Irish problem when I was in school in England." He continued to stare at the posters. "I read everything I could when I arrived in the States and it took me a long time to decide the Irish Catholics are some talented men and women. Murphy being the exception, of course."

"What did they say we wanted, when they picked you up?" Norm spoke up as soon as Kram stopped to take a breath.

Kram looked toward Carpino, Papaccioli and Grizzle. "They were polite, but I had the feeling that while they offered me a choice, I didn't really have one." He sipped his coffee. "But they did use the word exclusive and assured me that what happened one block up was connected to the suicide at the Hotel Key West." He smiled at me. "I, of course, didn't believe the suicide story. I knew there was more to it." He rushed the words together and then sipped his coffee.

"There are conditions and we want something in return." Norm leaned toward Kram. "Until we set the rules and conditions, everything is off the record. Clear?"

"Of course. The coffee is good, so I will listen." Kram got up and refilled his coffee.

Norm and Jim gave me a look that indicated they were not sure this was a good idea. I said nothing, but drank my coffee, and it was good.

"We need to know everything you know about R.L.," I began when Kram sat down. "Rumors as well as facts."

"And in return?" Kram pushed his chair back from the table.

"We'll tell you how R.L. is involved in all this shit," Norm said. "We'll keep you up on how we're gonna bring the son of a bitch down and that will be your exclusive."

"That you can't tell anyone, and that includes the editor or anyone else on the news staff, is part of the deal," Jim said, before Kram could respond to Norm. "Anyone, news staff or drinking buddies."

"I don't drink." Kram turned toward Jim. "I used to, but I have too much to do these days to waste hours sitting in bars thinking I am accomplishing something."

"Will you help?" I asked.

"Are these men for real?" he asked me.

"Yes."

"Then why aren't you getting the exclusive?" He smiled.

It was a good question and I should have expected it. "You know I was shot the other night, right?"

"Yes, of course, but you look well. Were you really shot?"

I realized, as I watched his smile widen, that he was having fun. A conspiracy theorist at heart, his abduction and this covert meeting were right out of his fantasies.

"Oh, yeah. And my being shot involves R.L. and drugs."

"Drugs?" His smile expanded. "I knew it." Kram stood up and refilled his coffee mug again, and ate a piece of bacon off the buffet tray. "For years, there have been rumors about R.L. and drugs. And I don't mean back in the square grouper days when everyone on the island was making a living being a pirate or smuggler." He walked around holding the coffee mug, sipping a little and staring at some of the smaller framed photos of Irishmen. "When the serious shit began to arrive, R.L. used his influence to get a piece of it. He sold protection; he even bought into some of the shipments." He was excited and his speech sped up, while his free hand swept hair from his forehead. "And he didn't do this on his own.

"Synge, the playwright, he's another ugly mother's son," Kram continued as he stopped by the black-and-white portrait of John Millington Synge. "Hell of a playwright. Today, we don't understand why there were riots over his *The Playboy of the Western World.*" He stopped talking and looked at the wall of portraits.

"I watched his warehouse once for more than a month, knowing it was being used for storage of drugs." He kept his back to us. "There's no proof. I've spent years looking for it. I've witnessed a rare collection of city officials meeting him there."

"We have proof," I assured him.

"Where is the warehouse?" Norm asked.

"On Stock Island, near the marina." He began to pace again. "It has some shops out front, but the whole backside is empty.

227

And it has some state-of-the-art locks on its doors."

"You tried to break in?" I laughed.

"I didn't say that." He stopped in front of me.

"Do we have a deal?" Jim asked.

"Do I stay with you?" There was concern in his voice.

"You can go anytime you want." Jim got up to freshen his coffee. "But we expect this to be going down real soon."

"It might be better if we put you up, keep you informed as things happen, but we can't let you come with us," Norm explained.

"Are we talking days or weeks?" He sipped coffee, but I saw his eyes focus on Norm.

"Honestly?" Norm pulled closer to Kram. "We're waiting for some intel on the drug shipment. But, I believe it will be within a day or two."

"I will need my laptop."

"We need your files."

"My files?" Kram's voice hesitated for a moment. "My files are personal. I'd go to jail before I would give my notes to the authorities."

"If you're with us, and we need something that's in your notes, an address or name, you can't be running back and forth," Norm said quietly. "Your notes are for your memory."

"Where are you taking me?"

"I can't tell you that, until you're there."

"Mick, what am I getting myself into?" He grinned as he shook his head. "Would you bring your files into a situation you knew little about?"

"Kram," I said, trying to put as much sincerity into my words as I was capable of, "what you've been told here is all true and these men agreed to deal with you because I gave 'em my word you were a man of your word. You can get up and leave right now, or you can have a ride to wherever your files are and be in the safe house in less than an hour. The choice is yours."

FIFTY-TWO

Kram thought over his decision as he helped himself to a second order of breakfast. Norm, Jim and I filled plates with eggs and sausage and went off to a booth to eat. The food was as good as the coffee, and I hadn't realized how hungry I was. We ate impatiently, but watched Kram, who seemed to be holding a one-sided argument with himself. Tita sat with Padre Thomas, their plates gone.

"You trust this guy?" Jim mumbled with his mouth full of eggs.

"He's got what we need squirreled away in his head." I chewed my food.

"What do you think he'll do?" Jim watched Kram.

"He'll go along," Norm answered for me. "One thing I learned about journalists is that curiosity drives 'em more than common sense." He laughed. "I have Mick to thank for that."

"Curiosity killed the journalist and the cat." Jim joined the laughter.

Blankenship's satellite phone rang. The room became quiet as a morgue, because the call meant something was happening. Blankenship nodded as he listened and wrote into a notebook. He hung up and walked to our table.

"What do we have?" Jim barked.

"Seaplane loaded and ready at Chetumal, Mexico, sir." Blankenship read from his notes. "Intel expects it will leave late tonight for the Bahamas. We are also tracking Cluny's cell."

"Chetumal?" Johnny called from a few tables away. He stood slowly and walked to us. "That's the transport point. There's a warehouse in Belize and then the drugs are moved across the border to *Bahia de Chetumal* and flown out."

"So, tomorrow morning, early," Jim said. "Before sunrise."

"Yeah," Johnny agreed. "But it's not coming here. They'll land in Cay Sal."

"What's Cay Sal?" Norm asked.

"A popular Bahamian dive spot with underwater caves." Jim pushed his plate away. "It's about one hundred miles southeast of Key West and rarely patrolled. Kind of a no-man's land."

"It's an Albatross seaplane, right?" Johnny was getting excited. Blankenship looked at his notes. "Yes."

"It's a big shipment. Maybe a thousand kilos and R.L.'s *paco* as a side deal."

Norm and Jim whistled.

"At a street price of twenty grand per kilo, that's a lot of money," Jim said.

"Would they bring twenty million worth of coke through the Keys?" Kram was standing next to our table.

"R.L. convinced the cartel that he can move the product to Miami with fewer problems and cost than the Bahamian connection," Johnny said. "This is his big moment. He gets a cut of the pie for delivery and the *paco* as a side benefit."

"How's he going to get that much coke into Key West?" Norm pushed out from the table to get another cup of coffee.

"Fishing boats was the last I heard." Johnny sat at our table. "Unload the coke onto them and then move the boats into different marinas by late afternoon, load the product onto vans and be on US-1 by early evening. The keep-moving philosophy."

"Could work," Jim mumbled. "Two or three charter boats, with the kilos and a couple of fishermen on board, coming in after three P.M. mixed in with about twenty returning charter

231

boats. A normal charter-boat day."

"How's the seaplane getting past Fat Albert?" Norm knew about the military radar blimp flying high above the Lower Keys.

"It flies low over the west end of Cuba, and Fat Albert thinks it's a boat," Johnny explained. "Then it stays in Cuban airspace and looks like a plane leaving Havana for the Bahamas. They've done it a few times I know about and I was trying to work my way onto the trip."

"You can kiss that idea good-bye." I had to say something.

"Thanks to you." Johnny stared at me. "Probably one of the stupidest things I've done, not killing you."

I couldn't tell from his tone, and painful expression, if he was kidding or if it was a Freudian slip.

"If you had, we wouldn't be here." Norm grinned. "And this shit would make port."

"Would it?" Johnny asked, his stare locked on me. "JIATF knows it's leaving tonight. The Coast Guard could've intercepted it."

"Unlikely," Jim chimed in. "Our assumption would have been the Bahamas, not Cay Sal. They could have landed, unloaded and been gone before we realized our mistake."

"Okay, I'm glad I didn't kill Mick." Johnny smirked and pointed at me "But you owe me."

"No argument," I said.

Jim turned to Blankenship. "What about the cell?"

"Got it, and can track its location, no voice."

"Where is he?"

"Up the street at Conch Marina." He laughed. "Probably been there all night."

"He's gotta be shittin' bricks, because he knows the house didn't blow." Norm finished his coffee. "And the dead Colombians were probably on their way to him and he knows they ain't coming."

"And my being alive," Johnny added. "He's a thinker. He'll figure since I'm one of the bad guys, I'll talk and implicate him, to cut a deal."

"Yeah, but the cops don't have you," Jim smiled. "We do. Will he figure it out?"

"I can tell you," Kram spoke up. "He will make a number of assumptions and come to the conclusion that no matter what, his game is over. He would already have checked with his police contacts and know that Johnny isn't under arrest. And he has an exit plan and by now, he plans to use it. I don't know what it is, but he's too cautious not to."

"He's still got the dirty DEA agent," I said. "Won't he try to milk that for all it's worth?"

"The local agent?" Kram asked.

"There are only two here," Jim answered. "Do you know him?"

"Joel Martin," Kram said. "He was here years ago. Left for another assignment and was reassigned back to Key West about two years ago. He gives good quotes to the media."

"Could he be dirty?"

Kram laughed. "Christ, with the money these guys throw around, we could all be."

FIFTY-THREE

We looked at Kram and knew he was right. The amount of drug money being spread around in cities like Miami, New York and Los Angeles could change a lot of lives, and in some instances all that was asked for was a head turning away. Other times, the money meant escape from a mundane life. What would that kind of money buy in Key West, where people worked two or more jobs to survive?

"Look it," Kram said, after he received no response. "I know R.L. is corrupt. I've spent ten years or more trying to prove it, and I haven't been able to. Sometimes I've even thought I was wrong. Now you guys come along and offer me hope," he spoke quickly, using his hands like an Italian politician to point and jab his words at us. "I like Joel, he's always been available for the media, and I'd hate to say he is bad, but at this point in my career it would not surprise me."

"It's him or Reed Fitcher," I said. "They're the only two DEA agents here."

"That we know about," Norm added to the discussion. "They don't all run around with stenciled ball caps and jackets."

"I've decided to accept your offer of the exclusive." Kram leaned on the table. "If you let me use my cell phone, maybe I can find out who is and who isn't DEA."

"Give us a minute." Jim said, as he and Norm stood and walked to the patio bar.

I left Johnny and Kram and walked over to where Tita and

234

Padre Thomas sat. "How was the breakfast?"

"Bangers, what kind of breakfast is that?" Tita smiled. "The coffee is wonderful."

"What did you want, *bacalao fritos* and *tostones?*" I sat down next to her.

"I would have enjoyed them." She kissed my cheek. She liked Irish food as much as I savored her Puerto Rican cooking, but refused to admit it. It was a game and I often wondered if she knew she was playing.

"How you doin', Padre?"

"Praying a lot." He smiled and sipped his coffee. "I wish they had *con leches.*"

"What's going on?" Tita whispered.

"They know where the drugs are in Mexico, and it looks like the delivery is planned for early tomorrow morning at Cay Sal." I brought them up to date with what I knew. "From what I understand, the seaplane and islands Padre Thomas saw in your kitchen pretty much describe what's happening."

"Cay Sal is a lot of islands?" Padre Thomas asked.

"One hundred miles from Key West. A popular dive spot because of the underwater caves."

"What are they doing out there?" Tita pointed toward the patio bar where Norm and Jim were huddled together.

"Plotting something, I'm sure."

I learned a long time ago in Central America to let Norm do what he did best and try not to interfere. Of course, it didn't always work that way. Sometimes I was too inflexible to go along. Our politics, in these instances, didn't mesh and that sometimes drove my decision. But after the disaster in Tijuana, I decided to let Norm be Norm. And me, I never wanted to find myself in a situation like this again, so I didn't care what Norm did. Now, almost ten years of my peaceful life in Key West had been erased and I was in the middle of another crapshoot, and my life and Tita's were in the hands of others. My only peace of mind came from knowing Norm was one of them. The anxiety I dealt with, because Tita was with me, was almost too much. If I could have come up with an excuse that would have sent her to Boston I would have used it, even if it meant the end of our relationship. Sleeping, I knew, would only return my nightmares of Tijuana. I hoped Norm had something in his plan that would keep me busy.

"Padre, do you know what's going on?" Tita asked.

He returned her smile and shook his head. "I'm as much in the dark as you." He looked around the room. "There are no angels in this group."

"Blankenship," Jim yelled as he and Norm came into the restaurant. "Get on that phone and see if you can find us a reliable weather forecast from eighteen hundred to zero six hundred."

"Yes, sir," Blankenship answered and walked outside with the satellite phone against his ear.

For the first time, I noticed Arthur sitting in a corner booth talking on his phone, nodding and writing.

"R.L.'s on the move," Arthur said as he hung up.

"You should get him," Kram yelled across the quiet room.

"He'll not be moving on his own," Jim replied. "Bryan, you and Paul take Kram with you and stake out that warehouse. Give me a call in a couple of hours, or when he shows up."

Papaccioli and Carpino went with Kram out through the patio bar without saying a word.

Norm came over and sat down. "Curious?" He smiled.

"I am," Tita answered.

I was too, but my curiosity was directed toward Jim, who called his remaining JIATF crew, Grizzle, Blankenship and Arthur over to a corner booth. Jim talked and the crew listened.

"If I want your attention I could slap your left side," Norm said as he put his hand on my right shoulder. "We're going back to the Mango Tree Inn and get some rest."

I had been so preoccupied that my gunshot wound had slipped my mind. That, and the doctor-feel-good shot was still running wildly through me. I knew I wouldn't be able to rest or sleep for hours. Norm, too, but I left it unsaid, because he must have had something in mind.

"Jim and his men have to go after the shipment," Norm went on. "But we're going to try and let the *paco* get to Key West."

"How?" I asked.

"Our guess is R.L. will use a go-fast to meet the plane, pick up his shipment, and get back to the island," Norm said. "What Johnny said about the fishing boats makes sense for the coke, because the shipment's so big. Also, security on the water will be by go-fasts, so there'll be at least two there anyway."

"R.L. will be there?"

"Probably not. We think Cluny will do security and bring back the *paco*. He and R.L. are in some kind of cahoots. Who knows, maybe Cluny gets paid off upon delivery and then he follows the shipment to Miami."

"R.L. is dangerous." Padre Thomas broke into our conversation. "You should deal with him carefully."

"A vision, Padre?" Norm smiled.

"Just thinking of him and his scheme frightens me," Padre Thomas mumbled. "He is evil."

"Whole bunch of evil here right now," Norm agreed.

Padre Thomas looked sternly at me. "I warned you days ago, but you wouldn't listen."

"I always listen, Padre." I grinned back. "It's just sometimes there's nothing that can be done until the shit hits the fan and then you need to react."

"We're going to stop the drugs from getting here," Norm added. "And your vision wasn't too far off."

"I think it was damn right on the mark." I tossed my two cents into the conversation.

"Probably close to the mark." Norm nodded. "We'll find out before sunrise."

"What do you mean we, white man?" Tita tried to put a little levity in her comments, but I heard the stress in her voice.

"Jim has two *Eduardoño* go-fasts and we're going out to observe the operation," Norm said.

"And those boats make it safe?"

"They're the boats the Colombian smugglers use, so we'll be less obtrusive if we're spotted from the air or from the charter boats," Norm explained patiently.

"Is he going?" She pointed to me, without a smile.

FIFTY-FOUR

"You ever seen him on a speedboat?" Norm stifled a laugh. "He gets seasick."

Tita and Padre Thomas stared at me. "Mick?" they said in unison.

"Yeah, our seafaring friend here." Norm pointed at me. "He's a sailor, he's not a fisherman or a motorboat person. I know this from personal experiences."

Tita was quiet for a moment while she looked hard at Norm and then me. He had almost fooled her by answering her question with a question, but her legal mind was humming. "You get sick on speedboats?"

"Yeah," I admitted. "Kind of. I don't have the stomach for all that bouncing around in the rough surf."

"But you sail everywhere," Padre Thomas said.

"Sailboats cut through the surf, Padre, they don't bounce over it," I tried to explain. "Unless it's a storm."

"You didn't answer my question." Tita turned to Norm. "It was a good try, Norm, but I still want to know, is he going?"

Norm looked at me and almost suppressed a what-can-I-do smirk. "If he wants to, I guess."

"It would help if I knew what the hell you were talking about," I answered both of them.

"As I said, Jim's group has two *Eduardoños*." Norm sat back in the booth and stretched. "They're open boats with a capacity to hold seven-thousand-plus pounds and, with two two-fifty

239

engines, they can almost fly."

"How many can the boat hold?" Tita looked from Norm to me.

"Three or four each, the way we're planning it."

"Are you going to tell us the plan?"

"Sure, why not?" Norm shook his head and gave me one of his raised-eyebrows looks. "What Jim wants to do is keep the delivery under surveillance at Cay Sal. Get out there around midnight and hide between the dive boats and islands. Once we see the go-fasts leave for Key West, we'll know the *paco* is on its way and then the Coast Guard can be notified that the coke delivery was made in Cay Sal and is headed toward Key West. JIATF is expecting that delivery."

"Where are they expecting the plane to land?" Tita's curiosity was getting the best of her and I heard a hint of excitement in her voice.

"More toward the main islands," Norm said. "The Coast Guard can get planes in the air and the cutters heading back to Key West immediately. The planes will follow the charter boats and report what marinas they go to. Before they're unloaded the marinas will be raided by DEA."

"What's to keep the dirty agent from warning them?" I was trying to follow the scenario.

"Timing," Norm said. "Coast Guard gunboats will be in place by the time the word gets to the DEA and there'll be Miami agents here, too. The JIATF plan is already in motion; they just don't know what we know—yet."

"Jim's following the smugglers' go-fast," I said aloud, trying to figure out where all this was going. "Then he contacts us when he knows where the smugglers are going with the *paco?*"

"Basically." Norm nodded. "The whole plan is to catch R.L. with the drugs. Jim wants to put him away and it has to be a righteous bust. The Coast Guard and DEA get credit for the big bust."

"Who busts R.L.?" I wanted in on that.

"It would be good if the local cops helped, but. . . ." Norm waited for me to say something.

"I need to talk to Richard."

Norm nodded toward Jim. "That's one of the things being discussed. What if Richard's right and there's a dirty cop?"

"It's not Richard."

"We need to meet him alone and without him trying to arrest us."

"We can do that." I didn't have a clue how I planned to pull it off.

"First things, first." Norm nodded toward Jim as he walked to our table.

"We've got to go back to the inn," Jim said and sat down. "Dan and Jerry will take you back and stay there."

"The inn is safe," Norm said. "You should be okay."

"But you need to be alert." Jim looked sternly at me. "We've got a lot of downtime until we move and so do they. If I were them, I'd still be looking for you."

"Where are you going?" Tita asked.

"We have things to check on for tonight." Jim turned to Norm. "You tell them the plan?"

"Yeah, but we still need to talk about the local cops."

"Richard is the question."

"Richard's an honest cop," I said.

"I agree." Jim nodded. "But we can't be sure of those around him, or Fitcher."

"I can talk to him, get him to meet with us."

Jim looked toward Norm. "Is it worth the risk?"

"He's protecting Mick, we know that from the last phone call."

241

"Okay, get back to the inn and call, but don't tell him where you are. Meet him someplace in the afternoon."

"How about at Kyushu? They've got those private dining rooms in the back."

"Keep Jerry and Dan with you." Jim stood up. "You comfortable with the M4?"

"Yes." I nodded.

"What about you, Padre?"

Padre Thomas looked surprised at hearing his name. "I know nothing about firearms. I couldn't use one."

"Not even to protect yourself?"

Padre Thomas avoided eye contact with Jim, but shook his head. "No, I will pray. It's what I do and we will be safe."

"From your lips to God's ears, Padre." Jim turned to leave.

"What about me?" Tita's words stopped him.

"You good with firearms?" Jim turned back and smiled at Tita, then looked at Norm.

"I'm good with a handgun and I used to shoot an M1 up in the mountains in Lares, Puerto Rico."

"Well, there are enough M4s at the inn for you to have one, just in case God isn't answering the good padre's prayers."

"God always answers my prayers." Padre Thomas looked at Jim. "But sometimes the answer is no."

"Then if God says no and Norm is wrong, we'll be prepared to defend ourselves at the inn," Jim said.

"God may say no, but He is never wrong." Padre Thomas sat up. "He is often misunderstood."

"Let's get out of here before the lunch crowd begins to wander in." Jim slapped Norm on the shoulder and laughed, as the JIATF crew walked out through the patio bar.

Blankenship stayed with us while Arthur went for the Jeep, shouldering the duffel bag I assumed held M4s. The outside patio, with its tin roof and ceiling fans, was cool but I could tell the late morning sun had brought a little humidity with it. When the Jeep stopped outside the gate on Grinnell, we ran and got in.

The streets were open and the cop car was gone when Arthur drove across Eaton Street, following it to Southard, where he turned right. Blankenship checked the side yard of the inn, an M4 hanging from his shoulder. Mat Pierce called a welcome from the porch and we rushed into the yard. Johnny moved slowly, Tita walking along next to him.

"What do we do now?" Tita stopped by the pool.

Padre Thomas lit a cigarette.

"Hurry up and wait." I hunched my shoulders.

"Do you think they can do it? I mean, catch R.L.?" There was more excitement in her voice than fear. "This whole thing is amazing."

"It's what these people do, Tita." I walked toward the inn. "Most of the time it's routine and boring, but when all the routine and boring gets put together right, the chase is on."

"Aren't you excited?" She followed me onto the porch, leaving Johnny with Padre Thomas. "You've done stuff like this before. Doesn't it become an adrenaline rush?"

"More so when the bullets start flying," I lied.

FIFTY-FIVE

It was hot for May. The scent of spring flowers eddied through the yard and hung in the humidity. The sky was a beautiful robin's-egg blue, a color I remembered from growing up in Massachusetts where robins foretold of summer. There were no rain clouds visible that could promise a cooling off.

Growing up, I remember the robust fragrance of my father's flower garden, especially after a shower, but the scents that accosted me on my first trip to Key West were mostly tropical and new to my senses. I was accustomed to them now, but could only name a few of the plants and flowers that brought the aromas. I wanted to know where they all came from, as I walked along residential streets blanketed in the spring bouquet, but when the scents were gone, I forgot and never remembered to ask anyone that could have helped me.

Coco Joe had been mostly silent during our time at Finnegan's, almost as if he was as much of an outsider as we were. He was inside the communications room with the others when we arrived. I thought about what Jim had said earlier, that Joe wanted to get to Cluny because of his relationship with Gabriela, and wondered if it caused a rift between him and the others.

We watched as Johnny slowly made his way to the second floor. There must have been something upstairs that he really needed, to be willing to torture himself with this climb.

I followed Tita into the small kitchen. She took two bottles of water from the refrigerator and handed one to me. Through the open door, we could see Norm, Jim and the others going over charts on the top of the piano.

"What are they doing?" She sipped from the water bottle.

"Planning."

"That's it?"

"I guess they're estimating the route to Cay Sal, maybe tidal and weather conditions. Let's go in and find out." I took her and she reluctantly came along.

Norm looked up, but said nothing and then returned his attention to the charts.

"Blankenship, you update the weather again at seventeen hundred and every hour after that," Jim said without taking his eyes off the chart. "The Albatross won't risk landing in rough seas—too expensive a cargo."

"You assume their weather forecasts are good?" Norm asked.

Jim and a couple of the JIATF guys laughed.

"Yeah." Jim looked up. "They probably got the forecast from a military contact in Mexico, who probably got it from JIATF or the Cubans."

"Cuban forecasters are good?" Tita spoke up, surprised at hearing Cuba mentioned.

"Cooperative with us and good, especially with predicting and tracking hurricanes," Blankenship said.

"It's actually easier to get the info from the States than from Cuba." Jim rolled up the charts. "Norm and I are going to be gone for a while," he said quietly. "Jerry, Dan and Matt are staying around. You're as safe here as you are anywhere."

"When will you be back?" Tita asked.

"As soon as we can, Tita," Norm answered. He knew Jim wasn't used to being questioned. "Johnny's upstairs, so you might want to keep an eye on him."

"I'll be gone, too," Coco Joe said.

245

"You be careful. Don't be foolish." Norm turned to him. "And get back here as soon as you can."

"Yeah," he mumbled and walked out of the room.

Through the window, I watched Coco Joe walk to Padre Thomas, who sat by the pool.

"There a problem?" I was nosey, because as a team they had to be coordinated. They didn't need someone with a separate agenda screwing things up.

"No." Jim handed the charts to Dan. "He's here on one assignment, we're after something else, and it intermingles in some places."

"Like Cluny?" I watched for a change in Jim's facial expression, but got none.

"Cluny's where we connect." Jim looked at the screen of the computer on the piano. "He's not our target, R.L. is."

"If he murdered Gabriela?"

"That's Richard's problem. After this goes down, feel free to tell him all about Cluny."

"It's all connected."

Jim looked at Norm.

"Mick." Norm tapped my shoulder. "We don't have much say in this, right now. We needed help, and the help is in charge."

"I don't have a side in this," I answered Norm. "Coco Joe, JIATF, Richard or you, it makes no difference to me, just so it comes to an end. I got caught up in all this by mistake."

"Mick," Norm smirked. "You lied to get yourself involved in this. You could've walked away."

"Could you have?" I challenged him.

"I get paid for this shit, Mick. I'm not sure why you do it."

"It's my job."

"Yeah, well, when you're on an assignment, it's your job. Not when you need to lie and make yourself a target."

"We've got to go." Jim tossed his words in between Norm's

and my argument. "Right now, we all need to be together to get R.L. And Mick," he turned to me, "we get him, we get as many people around him as possible and that includes Cluny. We don't get him here, we have to chase him in Colombia."

When I looked out the kitchen window, Padre Thomas sat alone.

I needed to talk to Norm about tonight, but I wanted it to be away from Tita. She was caught up in the moment and I didn't want her anywhere near Cay Sal.

"I'm going to set up that meeting with Richard. Will you be there?" I walked with Norm onto the porch.

"Call me, but don't tell Richard too much."

"And don't get trusting and tell him where we are." Jim reminded me of what he had said earlier. "The only people to trust are the ones with you right now. That way you're safe. You can apologize later."

"Safe and alive," Norm said, as he walked to the Jeep.

"Do you know where R.L. has gone?" I asked Pierce, as I returned to the inn's living room.

"No, sir," he replied. "He turned his cell off and it has to be on to track him."

"Do you think he knows we're looking for him?"

"If he's been running around all night, he might not have charged his cell, so maybe he shut it off to save the battery or to charge it," Pierce explained patiently. "He'll have to turn it on eventually, to see if he has any messages."

"Thank you." I walked to the pool where Tita was talking with Padre Thomas. "How you holding up, Padre?"

He rubbed his tired eyes. "Okay, Mick. I liked the breakfast."

"It could have been a little more relaxed."

"Will this be over, tomorrow afternoon?" There was a hint of hope in his voice.

"These guys do this for a living and they seem to think so."

"I wonder how many more will die before then?"

"Not us, Padre, we're staying here until this is all over," I lied with a smile. "Tita, you, me, even Johnny, we're out of it."

"What about meeting Richard?" Tita asked. "Are we doing that?"

"Oh, yeah." I gave her a half-grin and looked at my wristwatch. "After Kyushu's lunch rush. I just have to reach him and hope he can talk freely."

"I told you about this evil." Padre Thomas wheezed the words and lit a cigarette. "It has affected so many already. Poor Mr. Dey and his wife. And the sheriff's deputy, she had a family. Even Harpoon Harry's got all shot up and won't open for days." He blew smoke from his nose and talked to the sky.

I wanted to ask him how he knew about Carl Dey, but Tita took my hand and led me toward the stairway. "Let's go upstairs, I think we have a few things to talk about and this seems like a good time."

FIFTY-SIX

Tita's wanting to go upstairs surprised me. Being a man, of course, I thought her "we've got a few things to talk about" meant sex. Our relationship hadn't progressed to where we had pet names or expressions for each other. We hadn't reached, or maybe we had bypassed, the cooing of a personal love language. I thought her hurry to get upstairs under false pretenses was a ploy to be romantic. As happened too often with Tita, I was wrong in thinking I understood her. Any man that thought he had figured out women was a fool, at the minimum. Mel, who I wasn't thinking about as we climbed the stairs, once told me proof of women's superiority over men was that they allowed us to believe women were the weaker sex. I should have surrendered then.

Johnny was lying on the bed in the first room. His eyes were closed but he said, "I needed to lie down. If I knew it was going to hurt this much I would've shot you, Mick." His words came out slow and dreary.

"You did shoot me," I said.

"Not in the head," he sighed. He never opened his eyes.

"Thanks," I added sarcastically, and Tita pulled me toward the end room.

She closed the door and sat on the bed.

"I should look at your side." She patted the bed.

I sat down and removed my shirt. The bandage was damp and showed small hints of blood. Tita got up and found the

249

package Doctor Jack had given me at the hospital. With a smile, she yanked the bandage off.

"We need to talk about what's going to happen tonight," she said, as she walked into the bathroom.

She came back with a towel and wet facecloth. My side was red, but not bleeding. The gash looked awfully raw to me. Tita gently cleaned it with the hot facecloth, without saying anything. She patted the area dry, applied ointment and put on a new bandage. The pain was worth the feel of her gentle touch. She finally took a pill from her purse and gave me a tepid bottle of water. I swallowed the pill.

"For pain?" I handed her back the bottle.

"It isn't Viagra," she said, laughing. "Listen to me, okay? Seriously."

"Yeah." I leaned back in the bed, bringing my feet up.

"This whole thing is like a drug." She stayed standing. As an attorney, maybe standing made her comfortable. "I keep catching myself getting excited about the . . . I don't know, what do I call it?" She paused. "The action? This is beginning to turn into a Bruce Willis movie. But the reality of it is, Mick, it also scares the bejesus out of me. This thing on the boat, what is it? And I want the truth."

"Two things, Tita." I stretched out and looked up at her. "First, you heard Norm, Jim is in charge now. Whether that means this whole thing is official and out of Norm's hands, I don't know. What it does mean is, we have no say in what's going to happen. And I've been kept out of the planning, so I am not sure what's going to happen. From what Jim and Norm have said, they're doing surveillance on the drop at Cay Sal and then they'll turn the cocaine smugglers over to the Coast Guard."

"But the Coast Guard is going to be waiting somewhere else, so they don't know about Cay Sal." Her words would have been a question, except for the underlying excitement in them.

"Yeah, that leaves me thinking R.L. and the *paco* are not part of the official job. Because of me, Norm wants to oversee that."

"You believe that?" She paced in short steps.

"Catch the seaplane and charter boats at Cay Sal," I said. "There's a reason they aren't doing that and I have to equate it to Norm."

"And I called him." She sighed. "Where would this be right now if I hadn't?"

I laughed, because the answer scared me. "Johnny or someone would have killed me."

"That's what I thought." She frowned. "If you intend to go on the boat, I want to go, too." She said it firmly and I had no doubt she wasn't asking permission.

I blew out a deep breath while shaking my head. "Tita, your presence on the boat would put everyone in jeopardy."

"And yours wouldn't?" She held her ground.

"I have some experience, and you have none," I tried to explain. "Bottom line is: if the shit hit the fan, everyone's attention would be on your safety and not on what was happening. And that could get people killed. Shooting an M1 up in the hills of Puerto Rico doesn't prepare you for what trouble these guys are likely to get into."

"I am not asking for special treatment!"

"No, but you're on a government boat, you're a civilian and if something happened, there would be hell to pay for Jim." I looked into her angry green eyes. "For that reason, I am not sure they'll let me go."

"Norm's involved," she growled.

"Just proves what I've said all along: Norm works for a government agency and JIATF is a group of agencies, so it's feasible that his agency is part of it."

"When I think about this and how evil, to quote Padre

251

Thomas, all this is and R.L. is, I get angry." She paced a little more and then sat on the bed. "I am excited about being a part of stopping this and seeing justice served, but then I think of what could go wrong and it frightens me. I remember Jay's body, and think of Rebecca dead in an elevator shaft, and I get sick to my stomach. But when I think of you out in that boat, in the middle of the ocean and who knows what's going to happen, I can't bear it."

"And your being there would do what?" I reached for her, but she kept her distance.

"You couldn't die, if I was there. I wouldn't let you."

The thought was nice and it was probably her way of saying she loved me. And that only added to my concern. It was the right time to tell her about Mel, and how badly I screwed that up, but I didn't. Sometimes, you have to keep your nightmares to yourself, until they've beaten you with all they have and you're still standing. Kind of like a boxer in the ring, it's you and the nightmare, one-on-one, and each night is another round. But unlike boxing, the match often goes beyond fifteen rounds. It goes on until you win or lose. When you've won, if you do, you get to share.

I laughed softly, to keep from yelling and crying. "Tita, it's a beautiful thought, but when the bullets start flying, you or I don't have much say in who lives or dies, unless we're the only ones shooting."

"Sitting here waiting would be worse," she moaned.

"It's a moot point right now." I reached out to her, but she didn't come to me. "I honestly doubt they'll want me onboard."

"Yeah, maybe," she mumbled, "but you want to go."

"If I thought it was only a surveillance trip, yeah."

"If it's only surveillance, I wouldn't be in anyone's way."

I laughed, but held back because my side began to hurt. "We'll talk to Norm." I wondered if she knew I was lying.

"Promise?" Her green eyes stared hard at me.

God loves drunks, fools and Irishmen, and I was batting a thousand, because before I could answer, my cell rang. The screen showed Richard's cell number.

"Yes," I said as I put the phone to my ear. Maybe she thought I was answering her.

"Jesus, Mick, I thought they'd never leave me alone," he huffed into the phone. "Can you talk?"

"Yeah, can you?" I looked at Tita and she nodded her understanding.

"Do you know what's happening?" Spoken with frustration, maybe anger.

"I think so. Can you get away and meet me?"

"When and where?"

"One-thirty, Kyushu's back room."

"I can."

"Alone?"

"Yeah, alone. Are you all right?"

"Tita and I will meet you, but you have to be alone. Give me your word. I don't need a lot of cops bustin' in."

Fifty-Seven

I don't know if Johnny was sleeping, but his eyes were closed and his breathing was light and slow, so we passed quietly. He must have taken something strong for the pain, if it overrode the shot of doctor-feel-good Jim had given him. I was still wide awake, and we'd gotten the shots at the same time.

"R.L. turn his phone on?" I asked as Tita and I walked into the living room and found the three men busy at their computers.

"No, sir," Matt Pierce said. "Could mean he's at the warehouse and using a landline."

"Wouldn't they have called you?"

"Paul or Bryan would have called Captain Ashe, not us."

"Would you call me, when you find out where he is?" I wrote my cell number down and gave it to Pierce.

"You going somewhere?" Jerry Blankenship looked up from the computer.

"That's what I came to tell you," I said. "The police chief is meeting us at Kyushu at one-thirty."

"Give us a couple of minutes," Dan Arthur said from across the room. "We'll meet you outside."

I called Norm from the porch, but he didn't answer, so I left a message and told him when and where we were meeting Richard.

The afternoon sun hung high in the ocean-blue, cloudless sky. A soft breeze crept across the porch, barely rippling the

254

foliage, and did little to help with the humidity. Traffic moved along Southard and Simonton streets, and Sarabeth's restaurant was busy with a lunch crowd.

"I'll get the Jeep." Arthur carried a green duffel bag onto the porch.

We nodded our agreement as Blankenship came from the inn.

"We'll leave you by the back door," he said, and walked toward the parking lot. "And we'll have both entrances covered."

Tita and I followed. Her look, a quick smile and widening of her eyes, indicated she was impressed with their thoroughness; maybe she was even surprised. The Jeep's back door was open, its engine running, as we came into the parking lot.

Arthur made a quick left onto Simonton and then the next left onto Angela. He drove through the narrow streets of Old Town, dodging around cars and pickup trucks parked half on the sidewalks, turning right onto Windsor Lane at the Key West Cemetery, left on Olivia, following along the outer rim of the cemetery, and then right onto Packer Street and into the back parking lot of Kyushu.

A sheriff's car, a white pickup truck and an old Ford were in the small lot.

"Any of those the cop's car?" Blankenship got out and hung the duffel bag over his shoulder.

"No. But the sheriff's car belongs to a woman who eats here a couple of times a week," I said.

He walked into the back of the restaurant and returned a few moments later.

"No one in the back rooms." Blankenship opened the door for us to get out. "There are five people in the restaurant, plus the sushi guy and a waitress."

"Tuesday, the waitress would be Elena." Tita and I got out.

Blankenship laughed quietly, the first time I saw anything but

255

seriousness on his face. "A Japanese restaurant with a Russian waitress, go figure." He closed the door. "You want me to wait inside with you until the cop gets here?"

Arthur turned the Jeep around in the parking lot so it faced out, and parked. He stayed inside.

"We'll be okay," I said. "But if this screws up and the chief has me arrested, you just walk away. Right?"

The last thing I wanted was a shoot-out between these guys and Richard's cops inside the restaurant. It would mean Richard lied, and even if that was the case, I didn't want any local blood on my hands.

"Yeah, but if it's not the cops and either of you look like you're struggling, we put a stop to it," he said coldly.

I believed him.

Tita and I pushed through the beaded curtain and walked over the koi-pond bridge that led to the interior of the restaurant. Off to our right were private dining rooms and from the left we could hear activity in the kitchen. Elena saw us; I pointed to the right and we walked into the first room.

The lights were dim and I lowered the bamboo curtain to keep our whereabouts private. Tita sat across from me.

"You want to eat in here?" Elena asked from the doorway. "I'm by myself."

"We're meeting some friends and want a little privacy," I answered.

She nodded and left, returning with menus and a sushi list. "I'll be back with the iced teas."

The table was set for six. It was lower than the restaurant's regular tables, and thick pillows rested on a bench for patrons to sit on. I peeked out from the curtained window, but didn't see Richard or Norm.

"Do you really think this will be over tomorrow?" Tita checked off items on the sushi list.

"They'll make arrests tomorrow." I took my Glock and put it on the bench next to me. "Cleaning up the mess will probably take days, if not longer."

"What does that mean?"

"Well, do they arrest R.L. and Cluny? Maybe some Colombians? The Colombians are dangerous and that means a possible shoot-out. Will R.L. surrender or fight?" I ran a list through my head of what could happen. "The DEA will have Chance close the road north, to keep suspects from escaping."

Tita sighed. "So the answer is no."

"What was the question?" Richard asked from the door.

I had foolishly concentrated on Tita's question and missed his approach.

"We were wondering if this would be over by tomorrow afternoon."

Richard moved into the room and sat next to Tita. She looked small and fragile, next to him, and he didn't look comfortable on the low bench.

"I'd be happy if someone could tell me what's going on," he said in a tired voice.

"This was your operation," I reminded him.

"*Was* is the operative word, Mick," he complained. "What the hell happened at Harpoon Harry's?"

"What happened to my house?" Tita said harshly. "Can I go home?"

"Is it all related?" He gave me a puzzled look.

"Do you know the local involved?"

"If I did, he'd be in jail," Richard grumbled.

"R. L." I said it like two words.

Richard looked at me hard. In his head, he must have calculated what I said and then he frowned.

"No way." He shook his head. "You know this for sure?"

"You know Johnny Dey?"

"The guy who shot you?"

"I never said that."

"Let's cut the bullshit!"

I began the story. "Johnny is undercover DEA. He was tied to a chair in Tita's house because he didn't kill me, like he was supposed to. The house was rigged to blow when we walked in. He was there when R.L. and a Brit mercenary named Cluny killed Jay and Rebecca. R.L. recognized Rebecca and panicked."

He sighed. "Reed never said anything about Johnny."

"Because he doesn't know."

"How do you know?" He sat back on the bench and let out a deep breath.

I brought him up to date on everything that had happened to me since our meeting at Hotel Key West on Saturday. When Elena came in with the iced teas and our chopsticks, I stopped and Tita gave her our sushi list. I finished with the update before the sushi arrived.

"What makes you think you have a dirty cop in the department?"

"Reed says there's one in his agency and told me to consider the possibility there's one in mine."

"Does he think it's Joel?"

"How the hell do you know that?"

"You can't underestimate Norm."

Elena brought our soup and salads and a pitcher of iced tea.

"And I'm supposed to arrest R.L. tomorrow morning?" Richard drank his miso soup.

"We thought you'd want the honors," Tita said, between bites of salad.

Richard wiped his mouth with a napkin and laughed softly as he shook his head. "Damn it, Mick, I'll need legal advice before I do it. You don't fuck with R.L. in this town."

"Maybe those days are gone," Norm said from the doorway.

He came in and sat down next to me, after shaking Richard's hand. Norm didn't look any more comfortable than Richard, sitting so close to the floor.

"You know something I don't?" Richard picked at his salad.

"If this goes right, you're going to arrest him holding the dope." Norm used his fingers to pick a piece of salad from my plate. "The DEA and Coast Guard will back you up."

"When is someone officially going to let me know this?" Richard began to eat.

Elena brought Norm's soup and salad. "A few more minutes for the sushi," she said and rushed out.

"The Coast Guard's in charge right now." Norm lifted his miso soup and drank. "When they've tracked the boats to marinas they'll notify the DEA, who will put you into the loop."

"Mick said this *paco* shit is coming separate from the coke."

"It's coming on the same plane, but we'll be following it into Key West."

"And *we* are who?" Richard stared at me.

"What I tell you isn't official." Norm finished his miso soup as he waited for Richard's answer.

"If you know about a dirty cop, I have to act on it."

"I have no information about your department."

"But you know about a dirty DEA agent."

"Yeah," Norm smiled coolly. "From another DEA agent."

"Johnny Dey?"

Norm nodded as he began to eat his salad.

"How do you know he's not lying his ass off?"

"A couple of years ago, I helped train him."

The small room became quiet as a cemetery at midnight. The comment surprised me, probably more than the others. Norm also knew Coco Joe, something he'd kept to himself until it became too obvious. There were two too many coincidences for me.

FIFTY-EIGHT

Norm told Richard how JIATF's intelligence led to the discovery of the drug shipment and, eventually, to R.L. and the *paco* scheme. He lied better than I did, twisting the facts to create the story he wanted to tell; he even used the lie of omission. I noticed that Tita had a hard time hiding her surprise while Norm explained the situation, but she kept quiet. I wondered if maybe he had used the same technique in our friendship.

"Do you think it could be Reed?" Richard sat back, looked uncomfortable, and sighed.

"The other guy." Norm snapped his fingers, "Joel. . . ."

"Joel Martin," Richard mumbled. "They both seem like good cops."

"The Miami DEA office is watching them," Norm said. "But that's not your problem."

"Hell it ain't." Richard sat up. "They have access to my building and computers."

"You need to control what goes in and out of the computers."

"And how do I control my men, who have been working closely with them?"

"Let's begin with a short list of officers you trust."

"Why?"

"Because you'll only need a few to bust R.L."

Richard nodded and picked at his salad.

Elena came in with a large tray of sushi. "Is there anything else?" She smiled and waited for our answer.

"More iced tea, please," Tita said.

Elena left and returned with another pitcher of tea. "I'll check back in a little while."

"I've heard all kinds of rumors on R.L., but never any involving drugs." Richard put a couple of pieces of sushi on his plate.

We mixed soy sauce and wasabi mustard together in small bowls and then chose pieces of sushi from the tray. Tita had selected rolls and an assortment of other sushi for our meal. I grabbed a couple of pieces of sliced tuna and sections from the spicy tuna roll.

"I still need to talk to legal," Richard said between bites. "What about FDLE?"

The Florida Department of Law Enforcement is the equivalent of a state FBI. It has labs and officers available to small communities when the local cops can't cope with a crime, like murder or Colombian drug smugglers, or didn't have the money for their own expensive lab equipment. Richard wanting to consult with them wasn't unusual.

"Richard, I can turn the whole operation over to the DEA and be on my way." Norm chewed a piece of salmon and then took a drink of iced tea. "This guy's responsible for killing a cop. . . ."

"A deputy sheriff," Richard corrected him. "I've got to talk with Chance. Rebecca worked for him."

"County sheriff," I explained for Norm.

"We've got twelve or so hours ahead of us, before the plane even unloads the drugs," Norm complained. "The more people involved, the more chances of a leak. When we know the drugs are on their way, and the *paco* is headed here, call Chance. Hell, get his damn SWAT team to help, but for right now, work on the short list."

Richard ate another piece of sushi before taking a pen from

261

his pocket and writing on a napkin. Then he began reading the names.

"Scott, Alfredo, Donny, Robert, Lee, Jim and Woody," he said.

"You know who he's talking about?" Norm stared at me as he dipped a piece of sushi in the wasabi sauce and ate it.

"Yeah, I know 'em." I finished my sushi and went for another piece.

"Anyone you think should be off the list?" Norm continued to stare at me and ignored Richard. "Think about it." Then he turned to Tita. "Counselor, you have anything to say about these cops?"

Tita shook her head. "I know a couple of them socially."

"You have any reason not to trust them?"

"No," she said, and ate a piece of spider roll.

"Why do you care about my officers?" Richard sounded as much piqued as curious.

"A leak might put these bad guys on the run, or keep them away so we can't prove anything, kind of like what happened at the hotel." Norm turned his stare toward Richard. "I'm not fighting you; I'm the new guy, an outsider, looking with fresh eyes at something that needs fixing. Somewhere there was a major fuckup that cost two people their lives; I'm trying to see it doesn't happen again."

There was no animosity or challenge in Norm's tone and from the look on Richard's face, I had a feeling he wasn't disagreeing.

"You know how hard it is for me to agree with you?" Richard responded with a mumble that turned into a frown. "I want it to be anyone but one of my officers." He chose a piece of sushi, dipped it into the sauce and ate it. "Mick knows how the department has cleaned up." He nodded toward me. "I've got kids that grew up here and retired New York City cops on staff, and

I'd bet my life they're all honest."

"You're betting a lot of people's lives," Norm said. "We cut your team down to a small nucleus, for a temporary operation, and it's safer for all of us."

Richard nodded his understanding while he pulled a piece of salad out of the dish and ate it. "These are good cops," he said. "Where will R.L. be?"

"Don't know." Norm looked over the remaining sushi, before choosing a piece of tuna roll. "We think he'll be at his warehouse on Stock Island." Norm dipped the tuna in the sauce and ate it. "If he's overly concerned, he may show up at the dock. He has to know we're circling in."

"He's cocky," Richard said. "He might even think he can fix things. Maybe nothing has to change."

"Can he do that?" Norm asked harshly.

"I wouldn't think so, not with the Feds involved." Richard stretched and drank tea. "But that doesn't mean he feels that way."

"We have a source who thinks he'll run." I had finished all the sushi I wanted.

"To where?"

"He has property in Costa Rica and Colombia." I looked to Norm for confirmation.

"Never heard that, either." Richard drained his iced tea, and the frown returned to his face. "I need to involve Chance."

"At the last minute."

"You don't trust the sheriff?"

"If I had my choice, I wouldn't trust you," Norm said casually. "I would do this with a small group of my people and be over with it."

"And who are *your people?*"

"Don't get mad, Chief." Norm held his hands up, as if he were surrendering. "I usually work with a small cadre and we are swift and final."

"Well, Norm," Richard leaned back and sighed, "some of us have to work within the Constitution and obey all the laws."

"And some of us don't," Norm said with an unpleasant smile.

FIFTY-NINE

"My job takes me outside the States." Norm played with his chopsticks as he eyed what sushi remained. "Where I go, there are no Constitutional rights. Might makes right is the rule, and the people I'm after *are* the bad guys—there's no doubts about it. No second-guessing, by the time I'm involved." His speech was slow and flat, and his timbre told me he believed what he said.

"What there are, are leaders and cartel czars who are corrupt because the financial rewards exceed everyone's expectations." He leaned back and stretched out his long legs as best he could on the low bench. He still wore old cowboy boots.

I'd never heard Norm explain himself before, to anyone. I was a captive audience, but felt this was not the impulsive, off-the-top-of-his-head explanation I knew him capable of.

"My job is impossible." He frowned. "With everything I do, with everything others like me do, we stop maybe ten or fifteen percent of the drugs coming in. And you know why that is?" He picked up the last piece of spicy tuna roll, dipped it into the sauce and ate it. He didn't expect an answer.

The ice in our teas had melted, leaving the drinks tepid.

"Because of the money involved," he continued, after drinking tea. "It buys power and people. We take down a cartel kingpin, and three fight for the job; we take out a junta officer, and a junior officer moves in like that." He snapped his fingers. "The amount of money is obscene, so much so that people risk

265

death or prison for a chance to get their hands on it. Then there's the power. You have no idea of how powerful men dictate; how they rule and make laws, break laws. Do you know why?"

We sat quietly at the table, listening. Tita stared, wide-eyed.

"Because they can," he said with a snide smile. "Washington keeps us in line, because if they allowed us to go in and clean up the mess there'd be a lot of killing."

"Would it stop the drugs?" Tita sat up and waited for an answer. "Would all the killing put an end to the drugs?"

Norm laughed at the irony and then said, "No." He put his chopsticks down. "There's such a demand for cocaine that people will always believe the risk is worth the reward." He pulled aside the bamboo curtain and looked into the restaurant's center.

"Not to take anything away from the chief, but there's no crime in Key West," he said quietly. "What's a bust get you? A few rocks, a baggie of grass?"

"There's more here," Richard said, "but that's all they carry on the street, because they know it affects the sentencing. They sell what they carry and go back for more."

Norm laughed again. "Chief, in LA the drug dealers don't worry about sentences. They carry automatic weapons that help them outgun the cops." He sighed. "It reminds me of the killing fields of Central America. But I'm not here to justify my actions. I'm here because my friend, here, Mad Mick Murphy, appropriately named, I might add," he said with a chuckle, "went and got himself shot." He pointed at me and smiled.

"He's my friend, too," Richard answered. "But he's brought a shitload of trouble on himself."

"Wait a minute," I protested. "This was all in motion long before I was aware of it."

"I think you are overlooking something more important than

266

your egos." Tita got our attention. "R.L. made a deal with these smugglers to bring in something he knows will kill its users. He's no better than the cartel bosses, and how many others has he corrupted over the years? How many cops?" Tita turned to Richard. "I called Norm after Mick was shot," she said, taking responsibility for his being there. "I wasn't sure it was the right thing to do, but I knew it was what Mick would want." She pursed her lips. "From what I've seen in the past two nights, *especially at my house*," her voice rose, "I think the only way to deal with these men is Norm's way. My life has been dedicated to the law, but it's obvious that there's a point where one side manipulates the law until it has no meaning." She hesitated. Maybe she wanted to be sure that we were listening. We were.

"I may personally buy that, Tita." Richard sighed and pushed himself up in the low seat. "But I have to follow the law." He looked at Norm. "I've sworn to uphold the Constitution and it still applies in Key West, as far as I'm concerned. The DEA needs help arresting R.L., I'm there, but *you* haven't any authority to do so."

"Chief, you know more about what's going down than the local DEA and there's a reason for that." Norm stretched his arms behind his head and locked his fingers. "Give me 'til morning, and you and the DEA will be arresting R.L."

"And what about the dead Colombians outside Harpoon Harry's?" Richard's stare focused on Norm. "Who put the bomb in Tita's house and"—he glanced briefly toward me—"who shot Mick and how's all this connected?"

"When it's over, everything will be explained and there won't be any loose ends."

That was a lot for Norm to promise. I had my deal with Carl Dey and I wasn't about to give up Johnny. What could Norm give to guarantee no loose ends? I wondered. Tita surprised me most of all. I knew the law had been her life, but when violence hits home, it has the ability to manipulate people's emotions and beliefs. I thought how quickly, as a nation, we gave our rights away after September 11, and to a bill so ineptly named the Patriot Act. It was wrapped in the flag, but there was nothing patriotic about it.

"I consider everything you've told me to be speculation, since you haven't produced evidence to support the accusations," Richard said. He forced a smile. "If, and when, you or any agency produces warrants or evidence, then my department will react. Unfortunately, I believe you because it adds names to what we were doing at Hotel Key West. And, for your information, Norm, I like that our drug sales are small and low key. I also think it's good police work that keeps crime down and away from Key West."

"No argument from me, Chief." Norm stood.

"I am concerned about the killings at Harpoon's."

Norm stood still.

"I know where you and Mick were, what you were doing and I'd probably call it self-defense if you had killed them, but someone in a car smashed into the perps and then shot the driver, up close and personal." Richard put money on the table, even though the bill hadn't arrived. "I'm concerned that someone is in Key West who has the ability to step into the gunfight and take out the three perps."

"A person came to our defense," Norm said. "If he hadn't, we'd be dead."

"Should I classify it as a loose end to be cleared up by morning?"

"Yes." Norm placed bills on the table.

"Can I assume that by morning there won't be heavily armed men on my island?"

"I think they're probably already making plans to leave."

Richard gave me a cold stare. "Let me make this clear to all of you." He sat against the low table and checked his wristwatch. "You have twenty-four hours to put this all together, clear it up to my satisfaction and get off the island." He glanced at Tita, but he was obviously talking to Norm. "At five P.M. tomorrow there will be an arrest warrant out for you, Norm, and a John Doe warrant for anyone hanging around you. The Constitution allows me to do that, because I have the evidence." Richard stood and walked to the exit. "Good luck." He smiled and walked out.

Sixty

"Jesus." Norm laughed as we watched Richard leave the restaurant. "The sheriff's given me twenty-four hours to get out of Dodge. My life's turned into a western."

I didn't bother reminding him that Richard was the chief of police, not the sheriff.

"Usually the bad guy doesn't leave and there's a gun fight," Tita said seriously.

"Fortunately, I'm not the bad guy." Norm smirked, and led us out the back of Kyushu and into the waiting four-door Jeep. "We have to make a stop."

Dan Arthur was driving and Jerry Blankenship rode shotgun with an M4 on his lap and the duffel bag at his feet. The Jeep turned left onto Packer Street, a narrow road that had room for only one vehicle to move at a time and, when there were parked cars on the street, you had to drive on the nonexistent sidewalk or the neighbor's lawn. He turned right on Olivia, the cemetery to our left, old shotgun cottages on the right. The next left put us on Frances Street, and we drove past Tita's house. She stared out the tinted window and saw the police car parked on the corner.

"What are they doing?" She turned and watched until we were past Southard Street.

"Waiting for you," Norm answered.

"But Richard knows I'm not coming back today."

"I don't think Richard's sharing a lot of information about

270

the case right now," he said. "We're meeting Jim at Fairvilla."

Fairvilla is an adult-themed store on Front Street, in Old Town, and I think both Tita and I were caught by surprise at the location.

"JIATF shop there often?" Tita joked.

"Ah," Norm laughed, "so you've been there, too."

"Everyone goes there, especially for Fantasy Fest," she answered him with a smile. "What were you doing there?"

"Shopping." He laughed loudly and so did Arthur and Blankenship.

I knew Tita and I missed something in the conversation, it had to be an inside joke, but I had no doubt we were in for a surprise at Fairvilla. She looked at me for an answer, and I hunched my shoulders and sat back in the seat.

Arthur parked in the loading zone and we followed Blankenship into Fairvilla. The store's entrance is up four steps and you walk into an open area full of clothing and jewelry. To the right is a stairway to the office and we followed Blankenship in that direction.

"See anything you like?" Norm asked Tita.

"Yes." She smiled vampishly. "I hope we have time for me to try some things on."

Blankenship knocked softly on the door, gave his name and the door opened. Jim and a couple of men I hadn't met stood around the large office. The door locked upon closing.

"How was lunch?" Jim perched on the edge of a desk.

"Good sushi," Norm said and nodded to the men. "You want to fill us in?"

"Tita, Mick, this is Tom McGee." Jim pointed to a clean-cut guy with a military haircut, a shade under six feet, and he nodded to us. "This is Charlie Thompson." He pointed to the man standing straight as a rod, as if he was at attention, who smiled at us. His curly hair was longer than Tom's, but well within

271

military guidelines.

"Charlie is in charge of our supplies," Jim said. "We need to make sure your vests fit."

Tita looked at me and I wasn't sure what to say, so I smiled back.

"Vests?" I finally mumbled. "What's going on?"

Jim looked at his wristwatch. "We have to be on the water before midnight. You want to come with us, don't you?" He looked at Norm. "You said. . . ."

For a moment, I thought they were talking about life vests, but I was wrong.

"Yes," Tita answered. "We want to go."

I turned and looked at her. She was smiling. She was caught up in this, and the image of Mel and her enthusiasm flashed in my head.

"Where is it we're going?" I forced out slowly.

Jim began to explain, in more detail, what Norm had told us at lunch. The Coast Guard and DEA were waiting for the Albatross seaplane close to the main Bahamian islands. Jim's two boats would be mixed in with the commercial and private dive boats at Cay Sal and follow whoever took the *paco* to Key West. As Jim's *Eduardoños* tailed the smugglers' secondary boat, Jim would call in the true location of the seaplane's landing. The plan called for DEA, Coast Guard and Key West Police to be at the docks as the fishing boats with packaged cocaine arrived. The Coast Guard would track them from the air while we followed the *paco*.

"Who's going to arrest R.L.?" I pulled a chair out for Tita and she sat down.

Jim looked at Norm again and shook his head. "We don't have the authority to do any of that in the States. We can make a last-minute call to the cops and hope they get there in time."

"Richard already told us he wouldn't arrest R.L. on Norm's

say-so," Tita said. "Shouldn't we let him in on this now?"

"The DEA rep in JIATF thinks there's a leak in the Key West office." Jim stood up. "We have to figure there's one in the PD too, because everything they did at Hotel Key West went to shit once the sheriff's undercover person got there."

"So, what happens to R.L. when he gets the drugs?" Tita continued with her questions.

Again, Jim looked toward Norm. Was there something Norm was supposed to tell us, that he hadn't?

"Tita, we expect R.L. will have Cluny and some of his cowboys at the pickup," Norm said, and leaned against the wall. "If Richard won't help us, like he said at lunch, we have to take care of it."

"And that means what? Kill them?" Her tone wasn't challenging and it surprised me.

He sighed. "We expect they'll put up a fight."

Tita looked at me with a scared expression and I thought of the shoot-out earlier at Harpoon Harry's.

"Mick and I are out of that, right?" She directed her question to Norm.

"You can leave now," he said.

She looked at me with a confused expression etched on her face. "I don't want to leave, Norm. I want to know what is expected of us."

Norm raised his arm, still leaning against the wall, and pointed to Jim. "It's your show."

"Tom is in charge of our marine division." Jim sat back on the desktop. "We have a third boat that will be in the mangroves off Key West waiting to spot the smugglers. The other two boats will be following from Cay Sal. You'll be on the third boat."

"With Mick?"

"No, with three other men."

"Where's Mick?" She looked at me and couldn't make up

273

her mind if this was a game to separate us or not.

"In one of the other two boats," Jim answered matter-of-factly. "Is there a problem?"

"I would like to be with Mick," she said quietly.

"This isn't about what you want," Jim answered coarsely as he turned to Norm. "I have an operation here that is very sensitive, thanks to Norm. I can't have civilians involved, so I'm already going out of my way with you."

"He's a civilian." Tita pointed to me.

"He's also a journalist and it's a card I can play if I need to." Jim folded his hands and waited for Tita's reply. The room went quiet and the sounds of traffic along Front Street wafted in.

Sixty-One

"What kind of protection will Mick have?" Tita moved around in her chair and gave me a thin smile. She was determined to keep me alive.

She was also flip-flopping on what she wanted. The excitement around us brought an adrenaline rush that is hard to describe—feeling invincible comes to mind—and to say drugs, illegal or prescribed, can't come close to it isn't stretching the truth too much. I understood, because I'd been caught up in it before, but that afternoon in Tijuana, when Mel died, my rush crashed real hard and I didn't want that happening again. I had thought the feeling was a thing of the past. I was wrong.

"Nothing special for him or you." Jim stood up. "We'll be wearing vests."

"Bulletproof vests," Norm said from across the room.

"We have type-three vests." Jim pointed toward Charlie. "They're the best available. Let's see if we have one that fits you."

Charlie opened a wood crate and brought out an uncomfortable-looking vest with large Velcro straps in the front, and handed it to Jim. It was flat, unlike the bulky orange life vest required along near shore waters by the Coast Guard. It was designed to hug your body.

Tita stood up, took the vest from Jim and put it on.

"That's the smallest we have."

She pulled the straps tight and wiggled around, made a fist

275

and hit her stomach. "This will deflect a bullet?" She looked uncomfortable.

"No." Jim smiled. "It'll catch a bullet and spread its impact force. If you're hit, you'll go down and it *will* hurt, but the bullet will be stopped."

"And that's a good thing, right?" Tita smiled back at him and turned to me. "Have you worn one of these?"

"Years ago, the old Kevlar." I took a vest from Jim and put it on. "This is a lot lighter."

It was also something I was sure wasn't in Fairvilla's regular inventory.

The new vests were better protection than the old Kevlar flack jackets popular in the mid-1970s. The type-three vest is top-of-the-line and a little overkill for our operation, or so I thought. It can stop a 7.62-millimeter, nine-millimeter, and Magnum slug. I hadn't heard how it worked against armor-piercing bullets.

"I suppose you had something to do with it?" Tita looked at Norm as she loosened the Velcro and removed her vest.

"I'm always lookin' out for him," Norm said with a teasing smile. "If he needed a vest, Tita, he got himself in trouble, but I probably had to pull his stuck ass out," he drawled and kept the impish grin for her.

"This fits well." I pulled the bottom down and it fit snugly around my chest and back. "Tita's looked a little loose." I removed the vest and handed it back to Charlie.

"I have sweaters for the boat," he said taking the vest. "If you wear one and then put the vest on, it will fit better," he said to Tita. "There'll be foul-weather gear, too."

"Thank you," she answered. "What is the schedule?" She moved next to me and squeezed my hand briefly.

She might have been looking for my support or trying to show me she had confidence in her decision, but underneath she had to be scared to death. If I had to go into court and interpret the law, I would've been facing a major anxiety attack right about then. Here Tita was, on the threshold of a lifestyle she refused to believe existed, that went against everything she believed in—because individuals were judge, jury, and executioner—and she was ready to cross over and be part of it. I wondered, when it was over, would she have issues with her decision? This would change her. It already had.

Jim's cell chirped. He answered it and walked away from us for privacy.

"You okay?" I took the opportunity to whisper to Tita.

She nodded her reply and gave me a forced smile. "I'm angry, Mick," she whispered. "But I've made my decision. I'm not happy about us being separated." She looked up at me with suspicious green eyes.

"I'm fine with walking away right now," I said and took her hand. "We go back to the Mango Tree Inn and wait with Padre Thomas and Johnny. They don't need us to do this."

She smiled. "At least we'd get a good night's sleep."

"And we wouldn't need vests or foul-weather gear. Get some takeout from the Hog Fish."

"Picnic by the pool." She almost laughed. "Who are you trying to fool, me or yourself?" She never lost her know-it-all leer.

"I'm thinking about you," I mumbled. "I don't like you being close to any of this."

"Thank you." She smiled brightly and hugged me. "I signed on to share your life and for some damn reason you get in these messes, it's what you do, so it's what I do, now."

"I can walk away," I said and meant it, as she ended the hug. "We should."

Tita looked up at me, her eyes searching for what truth I was hiding. "If we left, right now, it would be because of me and that's not fair. I couldn't go on being with you, because you chose me. I don't want to change your life"—she stared me down—"I want to be part of it. And I don't want you trying to change me. We stay or we go our separate ways."

Jim closed his cell and came back to the center of the office with a puzzled expression on his face. "Hell of a coincidence."

It was said as a rhetorical statement, so we waited.

"I just got a call from Pierce at the inn." He sat back on the edge of the desk and took time to look at each of us, before he went on. "Fat Albert is down." His tone of voice did little to hide his concern.

"Routine maintenance," Tom said. "They only have the one since Hurricane Wilma, so it requires more maintenance."

Jim smirked. "I'd love to believe that."

Fat Albert is the nickname given the government's tethered surveillance blimp that flies high above the Lower Keys and, when working, tracks air and sea traffic around Cuba, the Gulf of Mexico and parts of the Caribbean. There were two large blimps before Hurricane Wilma flooded the Lower Keys and ruined one.

"Who has that information?" Tom asked.

"It would be in our briefing tonight, but the maintenance schedule has to be top secret and that's what concerns me."

"So the smugglers know there's no surveillance," Norm said. "Why's that important? It might make them a little less cautious, thinking we aren't tracking 'em."

"That's true, Norm," Jim said, "but since the maintenance schedule is considered top secret, if the timing was passed on to the cartel, it means someone high up is a bad guy."

"And that would mean all our operations are jeopardized, including our operatives," McGee griped from across the room. "It could cost lives."

"We know about Cay Sal and the *paco* because of you." Jim paced in the crowded office. "Someone knew we'd be waiting by the main islands, so the smugglers feel safe—as Norm said—by getting our intel from that someone and rescheduling their drop location."

"We've got two problems here." Norm moved away from the wall and walked to the crate of vests. "One problem is R.L. and the *paco* and how we're gonna handle it. The second problem is your leak. It's too late to stop the leak, but we can use it to our advantage." Norm, always the pragmatist, has been successful in turning bad situations to his advantage in the past. "Our advantage is that the smugglers aren't expecting us at Cay Sal. Their false sense of security will make our tailing 'em easier and safer."

"Unless we're being too smug about it." Jim frowned and stopped pacing. "We can't assume we're outsmarting them and then let our guard down. We also have to consider that the DEA or PD leak may have compromised us."

"Richard told us at lunch. . . ."

"Trust no one outside our group." Jim cut me off. "That includes Richard. It's almost certain there's a DEA agent involved, and he may be local and we have to assume it goes up the chain of command." Jim paced again, stopped at the window and checked his wristwatch. "You and Norm trust Richard, but we don't know who he trusts and that's the weak link in the chain."

Sixty-Two

There wasn't an argument against Jim Ashe's comments. Norm had said the same at lunch, when he asked Richard for the short list of officers he trusted. These men didn't tolerate weak links, because weak links cost lives. As honest as Richard may have been, he carried with him the questioning doubt about his cops, even if it was only one, and that was reason enough to exclude him.

The room went quiet, because the boss had spoken and these links were strong, maybe because of chain of command, or maybe because of trust. When he wasn't asking for input, no one second-guessed Jim. He and Norm shared many of the same character traits, and I thought it admirable of Norm to keep his personality out of this and let Jim run it. I was seeing a new side of him, or so he had me believing.

There must have been some silent command I didn't see to end the meeting. Jerry Blankenship opened the door and we followed Jim down the steps and through the busy store. Tita didn't get a chance to shop, even though Norm pointed out displays of lingerie with a roguish smile.

We exited into an alley, where Jim and Norm got into a Jeep. Charlie Thompson and Tom McGee put the box of vests in the back of a small white pickup truck and followed Jim's vehicle out of the alley. We were between Fairvilla and Pat Croce's Pirate Soul Museum.

The alley fed onto Simonton Street, after it passed by Croce's

Rum Barrel Restaurant. Blankenship stopped at the back door of the restaurant's kitchen.

"Wait here," he said and walked to Simonton.

"A little overprotective?" Tita frowned.

"They're just being careful."

She shook her head and then stopped. Her grin vanished. "Jesus, Mick, I forget what's really going on." She took my hand and squeezed it as Blankenship came back.

"Why the precautions?" I asked.

"Dan saw three scooters circling the block, with Latin males," he began to explain.

"That's profiling," Tita said in a tone she usually saved for the courtroom.

"Yes, ma'am." Blankenship smiled. "It is also what Colombian hit men ride for street assassinations. These guys are on scooters and there's plenty of parking, so why circle?"

Tita looked at me, hoping for an explanation.

"It's a precaution, Tita," I finally mumbled as we stood there.

Dan Arthur backed the Jeep into the alley and we followed Blankenship.

"Do you really think the scooter riders are Colombians?" Tita asked as we got into the Jeep.

"It fits their profile," Blankenship answered. He had the M4 on his lap.

Arthur drove onto Simonton and stopped at the Greene Street intersection stop sign.

"And sometimes profiling works." Blankenship checked the mirror on his side and whispered, "Shit."

The heavily tinted windows allowed me to turn without being noticed by the scooter drivers behind us. "That them?"

"Yeah." Blankenship cycled the bolt on his M4.

"Where is the third one?" Tita looked out the back window.

"Behind them somewhere," he said harshly. "Their backup."

Arthur pulled away slowly from the intersection. Oncoming traffic was heavy, so the two scooters ran the stop sign and continued to follow us. I put my Glock on the seat beside me. Tita took hold of my hand, but said nothing.

Blankenship handed me Arthur's M4. "It's locked and loaded. They'll come at us on both sides," he said, keeping his eyes on the side mirror, "as soon as we slow down and have to stop." He rolled down his window and raised his M4.

I rolled the window down, put the Glock back in my waistband, and lifted the uncomfortable M4.

"What if you're wrong?" Tita almost shouted.

"If they split and come on either side of us, I'm not wrong," Blankenship answered in a controlled voice. "Put your seatbelt on," he said without looking at Tita.

I nodded my agreement. She let go of my hand and buckled up.

Arthur caught a green light at Eaton Street and turned left, cutting off an approaching car. It gave us a minute's lead on the scooters, but it was probably done as a check, to see if there were assassins chasing us.

The two scooters dodged between vehicles and hurried to catch up. Eaton Street traffic moved slowly and the road was wider than Simonton, leaving room for them to attack.

"I don't see any weapons," I said, staring at the approaching scooters.

"They'll have Uzi pistols, and that's enough firepower," Blankenship said, still glued to the side mirror.

The Israeli Uzi pistol is a small nine-millimeter semiautomatic with a thirty-two-round magazine. At close range, its spray pattern would be deadly.

The next stoplight was at Grinnell, a half block from Finnegan's Wake. I could see the red light from where we were, at Elizabeth. I pulled Tita closer and smiled at her. She smiled back, hiding her concerns. Traffic continued to move slowly, with sporadic vehicles in the oncoming lane.

The scooters were less than a car length away and not slowing down.

"They're right behind us," I said, trying not to sound too anxious. My hands were sweating. I raised the M4 to the window.

We were passing William Street when Arthur drove the Jeep onto the sidewalk and raced toward Margaret Street, knocking newspaper racks over and banging against a concrete power pole. A small cube van, parked half on Eaton and half on the sidewalk, unloading furniture near Margaret, blocked the way.

"Oh, shit." He slammed on the brakes and turned sharply to get back onto Eaton, cutting off an electric car full of tourists and barely missing an old VW bug as the Jeep fishtailed onto the street.

The scooters zipped between traffic, one going into the oncoming lane. The light at Grinnell was still red and Arthur swerved the Jeep into the oncoming lane, forcing the scooter into the curb. The driver and scooter slid across the sidewalk, hitting a fence before they stopped.

I watched in surprise as the driver picked up the scooter, started it and got back into the chase. He had to be hurting.

Vehicles on our right beeped their horns angrily as we sped past. A car turned into the lane from Grinnell, saw us, and moved onto the sidewalk seconds before we would have collided.

Arthur kept the Jeep hugging the yellow centerline as close as he could without hitting the stalled traffic on the right.

"Three lengths back," Blankenship said. "Plan?"

"Right at the light." Arthur sped the Jeep the last few yards as the light turned green. He kept the Jeep's horn blaring as he made a sharp right turn in front of traffic, and almost skidded

283

into the fence at the Cuban sandwich shop on the corner.

Our sudden turn kept the scooters from crossing over Grinnell and following. I could see them waiting as traffic moved through the congested intersection. Arthur slowed at the red light at Fleming Street, checked for vehicles and drove on through.

"Cemetery ahead," he said, taking a breath. "We turn on Angela, and you get out."

"Yeah," Blankenship answered. "They're coming."

I turned and looked back. The two scooters caught the green light at Fleming and sped toward us.

Arthur decelerated at Southard, checked the one-way street for cross traffic and then shot through. I stared at the lighted entrance to the Five Brothers convenience store. If this had been morning, the street corner would have been full of city and county workers getting their morning *con leches.*

The streetlights, dim and few, didn't help our visibility. The large wrought-iron fence of the cemetery loomed in the darkness in front of us as Arthur slowed. The scooters were lost in the shadows, but we could hear the tinny drone of their engines.

"Keep your head down and you'll be okay," Blankenship calmly told Tita as he undid his seatbelt.

Tita grabbed my arm, and her frightened look asked me what I was doing.

"I have to help," I said and forced a quick grin as the Jeep swerved left and slowed even more.

Blankenship opened the front door and jumped out. I lost my balance as I got out of the moving Jeep. I quickly stood up and hoisted the M4 into the air, showing I was okay. With hand signals, Blankenship told me to move into the overgrown bushes, while he leaned against the cemetery fence, half hidden behind a concrete power pole. I moved into the shrubbery and saw dim light from a home's window highlighting a small porch.

The scooters' lights shone onto the street and I heard the small engines whine as they tried to slow down where Grinnell ended. Both skidded through the stop sign and quickly turned in our direction.

Arthur kept the Jeep slowly moving toward the darkness of Frances Street. The scooters hurried in our direction. Blankenship stepped out and shot off three bursts from his M4, shattering the quiet of the neighborhood as one scooter driver careened into the fence.

I stepped out, fired a long burst from my weapon, and watched as the scooter driver tried to zigzag to safety. Blankenship and I both fired as the scooter sped closer.

The driver fell off, the scooter shot forward and then scraped across the pavement on its side. Porch lights along the narrow street went on quickly and then I turned, surprised to see someone from Frances Street shooting toward the Jeep.

Arthur was returning fire as he backed up.

Sixty-Three

Jerry Blankenship pointed toward the two downed shooters, indicating I should make sure they were dead. I nodded my understanding as he turned and ran toward the third shooter at Frances Street. Dan Arthur continued to fire randomly from the window, keeping the shooter jumping around, as he backed up the Jeep.

I thought of Tita in the backseat, but ran up to the closest downed shooter. I kicked the Uzi pistol away from him. His eyes were open and I saw his chest move slowly, blood pumping from a half dozen holes. I turned around, thinking of Tita, and moved to the next scooter assassin.

The first shooter Blankenship had shot lay against the cemetery fence and lacked most of his face. His scooter's engine was still revving.

The street went silent, and off in the distance I heard sirens. I turned and saw Blankenship at the side of the Jeep, talking with Arthur. The intersection was in darkness, but I guessed the third shooter lay there somewhere. Blankenship, still holding his M4, waved me forward. I ran. Neighbors were peeking out windows and porch lights snapped on. A spider web of cracks from bullets had spread across the rear window of the Jeep.

The windshield was pockmarked with bullet holes. Blankenship held open the back door; it was lined with a string of bullet holes, too. I tossed the M4 to the floor and grabbed Tita. Blood caked below her right shoulder.

"Tita's shot!" I yelled and pulled her up next to me.

The shooter's bullets had punctured the lower section of the Jeep's door and windshield, ricocheted and hit her. I felt a warm, wet stickiness on her back. I leaned her against the seat.

Blankenship turned. "Why isn't she wearing her vest?"

"They took ours to the boat," I said and held her head.

"Shit," he mumbled. "Tita can you hear me?" he called out.

She didn't answer.

"Tita!" He yelled.

She opened her eyes.

"You're going to be okay," he said calmly. "Just hang in there until we're at the inn. It's not serious."

His words were meant to calm her. He had no way of knowing the seriousness of the wound.

She nodded her head slowly and winced. "I'm shot," she said softly and smirked at me. "You okay?" she murmured.

"I'm fine and you're gonna be fine too." I tried to sound confident. "Shouldn't we go to the hospital?" I whispered to Blankenship.

He gave me a hard-assed look in return, indicating I should know better than to ask.

"We have everything she'll need at the inn," he lied and turned.

"There's no doctor," I said and grabbed his shoulder.

"Between us, we've handled more gunshot wounds than all the doctors in Key West," he answered coarsely. "The bleeding has stopped," he went on, pointing at Tita. "She's going to be fine."

Blood was hardening on her T-shirt. She looked at me and tried a weak smile, but I didn't buy it. Arthur turned left on Frances and then onto Southard Street. The Mango Tree Inn was only a few blocks away.

"I'm okay," she whispered. She ran her hand across my face

287

and offered a shallow smile.

Streetlights flashed overhead as the Jeep rushed along the dark residential street. Blankenship talked on his cell.

"Jim and Norm are going to meet us," he said as the Jeep sped along Southard Street.

Matt Pierce and Padre Thomas were in the small parking lot as we pulled in. Pierce opened the door, and Padre Thomas reached for Tita, but Blankenship moved him aside and picked her up. Padre Thomas looked hurt.

"I'm going back to the base," Arthur said and handed me the duffel bag of weapons. "She's in good hands." He hesitated before getting into the Jeep. "We thought you had vests." He shot me a sad smile and said, "You did good back there."

His shirt was torn where bullets had hit his protective vest, and for the first time I saw blood trickle along his left arm. He sped down Southard and crossed Simonton on a green light.

I rushed up the outdoor stairway, passing Padre Thomas. When I reached the top, I saw Jim and Norm enter the parking lot.

The door to the end room was open. Johnny Dey was standing in the doorway of the first room. "Tita?"

I nodded, put the duffel bag on the floor and kept going.

Tita sat against a stack of pillows, the right shoulder section of her T-shirt cut away, exposing a small black hole caked with blood. Blankenship was gently cleaning blood off her back with a wet towel. I heard Norm calling my name, but ignored him. The white towel had brownish red stains on it when Blankenship tossed it to the floor.

"Hi," Tita mumbled.

"Hi," Norm said, and pushed me aside and went to her.

I thought she was talking to me. I'm sure she was.

He looked at the small wound and then moved her gently forward and examined her back.

"She needs a doctor," Norm told Blankenship.

"It's through and through," he said. "We can take care of it."

I moved up to the bed, and Norm stared at me. I could see pain stamped on Tita's face as she gazed up and listened.

"If Norm says she needs a doctor, we take her to the hospital," I blurted out.

"I said doctor, not hospital," Norm corrected me. "The bleeding has stopped, but I don't like her back."

"We can get a doctor." Jim walked in with a hypodermic. "This is for the pain, Tita." He swabbed her shoulder and gave her the injection.

"Thank you." Tears welled up in her eyes. "Doctor Jack," she said, and fought back the tears.

"Doctor Jack is our friend."

"Christ," Jim moaned. "Not another outsider. We can get a doctor we trust."

"She trusts Jack. Right now, that's important."

"We can pick him up and keep him here until the morning," Norm suggested and received Jim's dirty look. "Right?" He looked at me.

"I can call his cell. His office is two blocks from here, so the meds are close."

"Norm." Jim shook his head. "You know all of this goes against procedure. Two civilians, the journalist. Now you want to add a doctor."

"What's one more?" Norm smirked, ignoring looks from Jim and Blankenship. "We're controlling the situation and that's what procedure calls for when procedure can't be followed."

"You do it," Jim mumbled and walked out with Blankenship.

Tita had a more relaxed expression on her face as I called Jack's cell. The pain shot was helping. Tuesday night, Jack might be at the hospital, but he shouldn't be out partying.

He was finishing dinner with a friend when I called. I

explained, briefly, that Tita needed him. That she'd been shot and we couldn't take her to the hospital. He asked some questions and I gave the phone to Norm, who talked medical jargon. He gave the phone back.

"First you, now Tita?"

"There must be a full moon. Someone will meet you at the office. Okay?"

"It's almost nine, Mick," he grumbled. "Hold on."

I heard his muffled voice and then a woman's afterward.

"Thirty minutes, my office, and I'm bringing the dinner bill." He hung up.

"The Jeeps are gone. Can I walk to his office?" Norm put two fingers against Tita's throat, checking her pulse.

"Where are the Jeeps?" My attention went from Norm to Tita.

"They know what we're driving. No reason to advertise where we are," he said. "She's sleeping."

"That's good, right?"

"That's good. Two blocks from here?"

"I know where it is," Padre Thomas spoke up from the doorway. "I can show you."

Norm and Padre Thomas walked away. Johnny Dey stood in the hallway and frowned. I sat on the bed and ran my fingers through her hair, fear growling in my stomach.

"These guys are good, Mick. They'll take care of her." Johnny walked slowly into the room. He was still hurting. "I'm sorry."

"It's not your fault." I looked at the small, dark, blood-caked hole in her chest and wondered how bad the wound in back was. I didn't want to look, because I knew bullets went in small, but usually left gaping holes when they exited. It was enough to concern Norm and that scared me. "How are you doing?"

"I guess some ribs are broken." He lifted his shirt and showed me his wrapped chest. "I won't be on the boat tonight, but you can bet your ass, I'll be at the dock for the bust," he said softly.

"Tita wanted to be on one of the boats."

"She won't be thinking of boats for a while."

"Yeah," I moaned. "I'm having second thoughts about all of this, too."

"There are things you're needed for, Mick," Johnny said seriously. "You gotta crucify R.L. Don't allow him one damn break and I will give you everything I know."

"You may not be allowed to."

"Bullshit, I am out of this, once it goes down." He smiled. "I'm going to the police academy at the community college."

"A cop, huh?"

"It's what I've been doing for the past two years, DEA."

"Norm told me. So, why the police academy?"

"Need the technical stuff."

"That will make your grandfather happy."

"I wonder if it will make up for the two years of hell I've put him through?"

"Knowing you were a good guy at Hotel Key West will do that."

"He knows I was involved?"

"Oh, yeah."

"You know what else you need to do?" Johnny sighed. He looked very tired, especially for someone who'd slept most of the afternoon. "You need to expose this *paco* drug. I've seen what it's capable of in South America. It's cheap and it kills."

"So I'm told."

"You think you can do it?"

"I think we can talk about it tomorrow."

"Your word on it?"

"My word, Johnny."

"See you at the docks." He smiled and walked away slowly.

Tita moaned as she slid down a little in the bed. A red streak stained the pillows behind her and a knife turned in my stomach.

"Honey, I didn't mean for this to happen," I said quietly and stroked her hair. "I would've walked away, for you. No damn story is worth getting you hurt."

I knew if I went to sleep now my nightmares would include Tita. Maybe she would replace the image of Mel in the drug dealer's car as it exploded.

I heard Dr. Jack's voice and got up to greet him. "Honey, Jack's here," I whispered and kissed her forehead.

SIXTY-FOUR

Dr. Jack greeted me with a frown, handed me a credit card receipt from the Bagatelle restaurant and sat next to Tita. He wore a dark-blue guayabera shirt, white linen pants and boat shoes without socks. Even his normally unruly hair looked combed. The date must have been important for him to dress up.

Norm and Padre Thomas, holding Jack's medical satchel, stood in the doorway. Jim Ashe, Jerry Blankenship and Johnny Dey stood behind them in the hallway.

"What's she on?" Dr. Jack checked Tita's eyes.

"Demerol." Jim pushed into the room. "It's all I had available."

Dr. Jack moved Tita away from the pillows and looked at her back. His expression remained indifferent, something they must teach in medical school. He gently laid her back against the pillows.

Tita opened her eyes. "Can I still wear a bikini?" She smiled and yawned.

"The only thing that worries me, Tita, is you're catching Mick's sick sense of humor." Jack smiled back. "I'm going to clean up the hole in your back and you'll be fine."

She replied with a grin and closed her eyes.

"Okay, admiral, grab my bag," Dr. Jack said to Jim. "We need to wash up, and the rest of you, out. That includes you, Mick."

Before I could say anything, Norm gripped my shoulder and

293

walked me out of the room, as Jim took the satchel from Padre Thomas. The door closed behind us. I knocked Norm's hand off my shoulder and stopped in the hall.

"You need to know when you're in the way, Mick," Norm scolded. "There's nothing you could do in there."

"I could be there," I said angrily. "That's what I could do."

"And to what purpose?" He challenged me. "Tita won't know you're there and you haven't any medical background. Tita trusts this doctor, why don't you?"

"You know why I have to be in there." I stared at him as the words spat out.

"This ain't Tijuana, Mick," he said calmly. "Tita's not going to die and we've got to get ready to go." He looked at his wristwatch. "If your head's fucked up, you should stay here. There's no place on the boat for someone that's gonna second-guess the situation." He returned my stare with a lot more callousness and a thin smirk.

"You know she's okay?" I mumbled and lost my stare.

"This guy's going to clean the wound, keep infection away and give her some meds to help her sleep," he said. "Infection was the only thing that concerned me."

He spoke calmly, to help minimize my anxiety about Tita's condition, and it did to a certain extent. I believed Norm, he knew my instincts would tell me to, but somewhere in my unconscious mind I was conjuring up her death and my responsibility for it. The thoughts themselves were enough to torment me. I don't know if he was aware of that.

"I got two things." I tried to rub the weariness from my eyes. "Why'd he call Jim admiral?"

"I don't know, maybe he figured these guys were military. Everything about 'em is military, so it wouldn't be too hard to guess. Is he that smart?"

"Yeah." I continued to rub my eyes.

294

"What's the second thing?"

I looked up at him, and a soft laugh burped out. "I need a vitamin shot, if I'm going to be up all night."

"I could use one, too."

We walked to the first room, where Johnny lay in the bed talking with Blankenship.

"What's the latest?" Norm asked.

"Two boats waiting for us," Blankenship said. "Is he okay?" He was talking about me.

"Mick?" Norm turned to me.

"Yeah," I sighed. "What's the schedule? I'd like to talk to the doc."

"Can't leave without Captain Ashe." Blankenship smiled. "Vehicles are downstairs, waiting."

"Vitamins?" Norm asked.

"In the blue bag." Blankenship pointed at the chest.

Norm opened the bag and removed two throwaway hypodermic needles, both filled with a clear liquid—doctor-feel-good juice. He lowered the corner of his pants and injected himself.

"Next," he grinned, buckling his belt.

I lowered the corner of my pants and he injected me with the amphetamine-based vitamin shot in my exposed rump. It has kept presidents running, and hopefully this would be the last time I would need it.

"Where are we boarding?" Norm asked.

"At the Truman Annex boat ramp."

"With civilians?"

"The boat ramp is outside base security."

Norm chuckled. "So much for Homeland Security."

"We're in and out of the gate all day long," Blankenship said. "We still have to show ID."

Jim walked into the room and yawned. He took a needle from the blue bag and injected himself. "You?" he asked Norm.

295

"We're both done."

"That was quick," I said nervously.

"Cleaned up her back, nothing we couldn't have done," he griped as he stared at Norm. "We have the journalist coming back here. Carpino and Papaccioli drove him to get his laptop."

"The doc okay with staying here?"

"Not like he has a choice, but, yeah, he understands," Jim said. "He has some military intelligence background."

"Can I see Tita before we leave?" I wasn't sure what I'd do if he said no.

"Five minutes." Jim looked at his wristwatch. "The doc is still with her."

I walked out of the room, though I wanted to run. Jack was putting items back into his satchel.

"Interesting friends you have," he said without looking up. "She's a lucky girl."

"Yeah, I know."

"No, you don't," he said harshly. "A hair one way or another and the bullet would have punctured a major artery and she would have bled to death. What were you thinking, taking Tita with you?" He turned to me.

"What do you know about all this?" I sat down and wiped hair out of her eyes.

"Nothing," he sighed. "Because I don't want to. If I don't report this, I could lose my license to practice. You know that, right?"

"Yeah, Jack, but she wanted you."

"I'm stuck here for the night," he mumbled. "I understand that. I don't like it, but I understand it. There's another guy down the hall that needs looking at?"

"Yeah, Johnny Dey, Carl Dey's grandson."

He whistled at hearing Carl's name. "Not shot?"

"Beaten real bad."

Jack stood up and walked to the door. "Mick, she's going to be fine, but let me tell you something." His words came out insistently. "Don't ever put me in this position again." He walked out of the room.

"Sounds upset," Tita said. Her lips barely moved.

"Don't blame him," I said between deep breaths.

"You going with them?"

I had to move closer to hear her. "Yes." I held her cold hand.

"Don't get yourself shot again." She opened her eyes and tried to smile. "Jack will kill you."

"I think you're right," I laughed. "This is only observation."

"Hey." She tried to keep her smile. "Come here."

I moved closer to her.

"Did I hear you call me honey?"

"Yeah," I admitted with a soft grin.

"Well, just 'cause you called me honey, don't expect me to start calling you sweetie." She forced the words out slowly and lost her smile. "When I wake up, you'd better be back."

"First thing in the morning."

"Come here first and let me know you're okay."

"Right off the boat." I kissed her forehead. She was already asleep.

Jack was examining Johnny when I got to the door of the room. Only Norm was there. He nodded toward the hallway and walked me out of the room.

"Pierce is staying here with them," Norm said as we got onto the outdoor stairs. "From here on, you listen to me."

"We doing more than observing?" We walked down the stairs to the waiting cars.

"What do you think?" he grumbled and led me across the parking lot.

297

Sixty-Five

Tita was on my mind as I walked with Norm to the parking lot. I almost bumped into Paul Carpino, Bryan Papaccioli and Kram Rocket, carrying a heavy shoulder bag, as doctor-feel-good rushed through me. All three looked tired. Kram stared as Norm pushed me toward the waiting car, but kept his large know-it-all grin.

"Showtime?" Kram almost laughed, gesturing with his arms.

"We told you it could be over in the morning," Norm answered.

"I expect it all," Kram yelled, and Norm nodded.

Jerry Blankenship drove the car down Southard Street toward the Truman Annex waterfront. Duval Street was crowded and when the light turned green, Blankenship drove slowly, so he wouldn't hit the jaywalkers. A half block further, music escaped the large open windows of the Green Parrot Bar and patrons overflowed onto the sidewalk of the Meteor Barbecue restaurant. Not even midnight and the island was busy celebrating something.

My left side hurt. I touched it, but my hand came away dry, so I knew I wasn't bleeding. My thoughts wandered. I wanted to think about anything but Tita.

Southard Street takes you through Truman Annex and to the waterfront, which leads to the military base, the state beach and property the city owned and hoped to turn into a park and marina. Most of the open area had public access, but dark SUVs blocked the road and armed men were ready to enforce the closure. Blankenship showed his ID, and Norm and I showed our licenses. After checking to see we were on the list, we were allowed to pass into the security zone.

"We're part of the program?" Norm put his license away.

"Everything by the book," Blankenship answered and drove toward the fenced boat ramp.

Overhead lighting lit up the area, and two Colombian-built *Eduardoño* go-fast boats floated at the base of the concrete ramp.

"Thirty-foot?" I stared at the two open boats.

"Thirty-two," Blankenship said. "We've got a few, thanks to the Coasties."

The boats appeared sleek, with two engines angled out of the water.

"Fast?" I hated fast boats. People that drove them loved to ride the waves, which forced the boat to go airborne briefly, then violently crash back into the water. The fools did this repeatedly, thinking it was fun. It hurt my back.

Blankenship pulled into a dirt lot and we got out. Some men wore military uniforms, while others were in civvies, but judging from haircuts, they were all military and heavily armed. I felt for my Glock and realized how under-armed I was.

"You expecting this?" I asked Norm.

He laughed softly. "I thought this was a secret."

Realizing Norm had known Johnny Dey and Coco Joe, and avoided mentioning it, I wondered how much of a surprise all this was to him. He even tried to locate Johnny's government file while we were at Tita's, but couldn't, and made a big thing of it. He never mentioned he knew Johnny Dey or knew what was in the file.

Jim Ashe met us at the fence. I could see Tom McGee and Charlie Thompson on the *Eduardoño,* loading small boxes. I also recognized Dan Arthur.

"We ready to go?" Jim spoke to Blankenship.

"Yes, sir."

"You good with leaving her there?" Jim stared at me. "We don't need you on this mission." He stressed *need* and kept his cold stare.

"He is okay." Norm spoke up. "I've run the whole thing by him and he's good to go."

"Welcome to the team." Jim shook my hand, but stared at Norm. "What's it look like out there? Weather good for the seaplane to land?"

"Yes, sir," Blankenship said. "A weak cold front has stalled north of the Straits, near the Keys. The forecast is for light westerly winds, with a slight chance of showers during the morning, as the front washes out. In the morning, the wind will shift to east and high pressure builds."

"Is that a good forecast?" Norm said, looking at Jim.

"Westerly winds help hold down the Gulf Stream, so it will be a good ride over, but coming back will be choppy. The seaplane won't have any problem landing, which was my concern."

Norm looked around the secured area. "We have a change of plans?"

"No." Jim smiled. "The whole operation was planned before you came to me, so it's continuing. We're an observation team. If the plane was going to drop somewhere else in the Bahamas, it would pass over us and we'd call it in."

"When it lands at Cay Sal?"

"We'll see what happens." Jim smiled wider. "If the whole shipment goes as Dey said, we report it and let the team do its job. If the *paco* shit goes separately, as expected, we tail it and put an end to this, get the city commissioner and the Limey."

"Why the security?"

It was a question I wanted to ask, and when Norm asked, it

made me think maybe he didn't know what was going on.

"Admiral Bolter is a cautious individual," Jim said quietly. "In his briefings he's heard what's going on in town, from the DEA."

"He thought they'd attack here?" Norm seemed surprised, which surprised me.

"There is that possibility."

"Which means he knows there's a leak."

"I think we all know that." Jim sounded irritated. He turned and walked toward the boat ramp.

"What am I missing?" I walked along side Norm and kept my voice low.

"Whatever it is, I'm missing it, too," Norm said.

He walked away from me, caught Jim by the elbow, and pulled him into the shadows.

Sixty-Six

I watched them in the shadows. Norm pointed toward the armed men. Jim Ashe pointed in my direction. Norm became animated and then Jim pushed him, something I had never seen anyone do. I honestly thought Norm would pull his gun and knew it would be the last thing he ever did. He must have too, because he turned and walked away.

"What was that about?" I caught up with him at the top of the boat ramp.

Norm looked at me and shook his head. I didn't know the meaning of it, but held my ground.

"It involves me, I deserve to know." I moved in closer, so my words wouldn't carry on the water.

"It's not about you," he huffed. "Well, in a way it is, but it's more about me. We're dealing with government bureaucracy."

"Tell me something I don't know."

Jim and Jerry Blankenship walked past us.

"My agency, the one I don't work for"—he fought a grin—"has someone assigned to the mission and they're with the team in the Bahamas, so I am an odd cog. Jim doesn't like that, and the fact I brought you in, the doctor, the journalist and Tita, well, it isn't going down well."

"Without us they wouldn't know where the drop is." I tried to keep my tone neutral, but couldn't. "We saved Johnny Dey, and his information is what got us here."

"You're singing to the choir, hoss." He slapped my right

302

shoulder. "Don't take it personal. If this was my operation, you'd be back with Tita."

We walked down the boat ramp and were the last two to get on the go-fast. I followed Norm and we boarded with Jim and Blankenship. Tom McGee was piloting the boat, and Charlie Thompson handed us armored vests. Dan Arthur stood quietly off to the side.

"Wear your shirt over them," Thompson said.

It fit snugly and bulked up my loose Tommy Bahama shirt. I wondered if, when the boat recoiled on the choppy water, the vest would aggravate my wound.

Thompson gave us each a deflated flotation vest that fit loosely around our necks. It opened to full size when you pulled a string that set off a miniature gas canister. We put them on, like everyone else.

"Where are the weapons?" I asked.

"Forward."

The deck of the boat was open around the center console, and the transom held two two-fifty outboard engines. There was no cabin. The boat had been used for smuggling, and a cabin was wasted space. McGee hydraulically lowered the engines and then started them. They hummed, spitting water. Someone on the ramp cast off the lines, and both boats moved quietly into the blackness of Key West Harbor.

"Shit, Norm," I mumbled, trying to get my balance. "He's gonna open this fucker up as soon as we're out of the harbor."

Norm laughed. "Maybe before."

"You might as well take a seat," Thompson said, and pointed to the many boxes on the deck. "It may get chilly. If you need it, we have foul-weather gear."

The second *Eduardoño* came along next to us and then shot off to the right and was soon lost in the darkness. Radio noise squawked from forward, and the night swallowed the boat.

"We're not in a rush," Jim said and sat on the box next to Norm. "The first boat will get there in a couple of hours. He'll radio back what's there."

"No satellite photos?" Norm said.

"Plenty of 'em. Boats have come and gone all day." Jim seemed relaxed. "Some from the Carolinas and northern Florida are there for five days of diving. Others run over from the Bahamian mainland and the Keys."

"Fishing boats?" I asked.

"A couple."

"For the drug pickup?"

"Hard to tell," Jim said. "Radar shows a few anchored offshore a ways and they could be leaving now, like us. That's why we're there to observe." He got up and walked forward.

"What do you think?" I sat on the watertight box as the boat sped along, bouncing off the small waves and banging down repeatedly, sending a saltwater spray across the bow.

The last time I sailed the Florida Straits at night, there was an easterly wind and five-to-eight-foot waves in the Gulf Stream, but the *Fenian Bastard* cut through them quietly, her rail almost in the water. Phosphorescent sea life twinkled near the surface, and flying fish hit the sail and slid down into the cockpit. In the morning, we had dolphins crisscrossing the bow and sea turtles lazily floating on the surface, unafraid of us.

I stood up, waiting for Norm's reply. My sailboat has an eight-knot hull speed. The go-fast sped along, probably at a steady twenty to twenty-five knots. I held onto the rail and looked at black water, catching a glimpse of the twinkling sea life.

Above, the sky held millions of stars that sparkled on their own, and the lights from Key West cast only a haze in the distance behind us. Dim instrument lights from the control panel shone around the center console, leaving most of the boat in darkness. In less than an hour, the water and horizon would meet and be undistinguishable. While the two engines were not as noisy as I expected, the banging of the bow against the waves made me uncomfortable. A sailboat is quiet and you hear the water rush against the hull and feel the motion of the sea as she slices through the waves. I love that feeling.

Norm stood next to me.

"Not like the sail we had from California to Panama." He stared toward Key West.

"I hate these boats."

"I know," he said. "I don't blame you, but we need the speed."

A small white light burned at the stern and bow. A red light on the right and a green light on the left reflected off the water. These running lights were required by law, but smugglers often ran without them.

"Running lights are on." I pointed to the stern light.

"You see the dive tanks all tied off?" He pointed forward.

"Yeah."

"The way I see it, we're a dive boat, so we're doing everything legally." He didn't sound convincing.

"Two DEA agents and one of them is a bad guy, and we're supposed to get away with being a dive boat."

"Why not both of them?" he said about the DEA agents. "I think you're right, though, and our cover is blown."

"You think?"

"As Jim said, we can't trust anyone outside our group." The wind made listening difficult, so Norm spoke almost into my ear. "Too much at stake to do otherwise."

"But no one in Richard's group knows about this."

"Look at it this way. JIATF has representatives from federal law enforcement agencies, some foreign agencies. They all work hand-in-hand and work well together, but there's a bad guy in the mix and there's no way of judging what he knows."

"So assume he knows everything?"

"I would and Jim's gotta, too. Maybe we're the decoy and the other boat is the secret."

SIXTY-SEVEN

The night turned us invisible as the go-fast disappeared into the mass blackness of the Atlantic. The stars and moon reflected off the slick, dark water, only to be lost in the swirl of foamy wake as Tom McGee steered the boat on its course to Cay Sal Banks, in the Bahamas.

The boat created its own wind that rushed over our heads and made talking difficult. Norm stood and joined me, and we watched over the side of the bulkhead as the wake broke up the twinkling phosphorescent life.

"You've been here, before?" He spoke close, keeping his face out of the wind.

"Flew once." I tried not to yell. I turned into the wind, to face him, and had to turn away because I couldn't breathe. "Seaplane. We were diving, spear fishing."

Norm shook my shoulder and indicated we should sit. I pulled a watertight box next to the bulkhead and sat, protected from the wind. Norm did the same. The air noisily rushed above us as the go-fast sped forward, banging its way on the choppy sea, the vibrations traveling through the boat.

"Flew there once with friends to go diving and spear fishing," I said again. "Problem was, they were into diving underwater caves."

He looked at me, wide-eyed, because he knew my phobias.

"Yeah." I almost laughed at his expression. "I got a few feet

307

into one cave, and my claustrophobia took over. I couldn't do it."

"Chicken-shit," he mumbled, shaking his head.

"I decided it was like jumping out of a perfectly good airplane, not something I wanted to do."

"You're missin' out on life, hoss, letting your fears control you."

"I can live without those two things." I looked up and, as always when on the ocean, I stared in amazement at the number of stars—billions, I'd bet—that crowned the heavens. How could anyone think we were alone, when there was so much potential out there?

Norm shook his head and let it go, because we'd been over the subject of overcoming fears before. We agreed to disagree and left it at that.

"What's it like?" He changed the subject. "Are we gonna stand out?"

"Cay Sal is a sandy, uninhabited island." I pulled my stare away from the heavens and spoke between the banging of the bow against the waves and the vibrations. "Boaters barbecue their catch, picnic, whatever on the beach. Play beach bum. But the Banks are a collection of small, deserted islands with some pretty tough landscape, steep walls coming out of the water. They're worth exploring, when you're waterlogged. Mid-week, there could be dive boats there for a few days of diving and spear fishing."

"Uninhabited. All the islands?"

"Yeah. There used to be coconut plantations, but the people are gone, and the coconut palms are still there. No fresh water on the islands, that's the problem. Some derelict buildings, an old lighthouse and no authorities. Rumor is that one of the islands used to be a CIA training camp."

"Training for what?"

I laughed into the wind. "I thought you'd tell me."

"No idea," he said and leaned back. "Only CIA guys I knew were in Central America."

It might have been a lie, or maybe the truth, but at that moment, it didn't matter. We were along for the ride and only had a slight idea of what the ride was taking us to. Though Norm didn't say it, I think we both felt Jim Ashe hadn't told us the whole truth about the mission. We were supposed to look like a dive boat, and we did, but we were heavily armed and wearing bulletproof vests. We were also riding in a Colombian *Eduardoño* go-fast the smugglers would recognize from miles away. Even from the air, my guess was, the seaplane pilot would recognize the two boats. And there was the fact that a DEA agent had turned to the dark side.

I told Norm what I was wondering about.

"The boats are popular with other folks than smugglers," he said. "You can go on the Internet and buy one, have it made to your specifics."

I'd never heard of the boat builder until a few days ago.

Our conversation stopped when Jim sat down. "Just got an update on the plane from Pierce."

"Anything change?" Norm leaned against the bulkhead.

"Communications from command indicates its spotters are following the plane, Fat Albert not being available, and it already passed the western tip of Cuba."

"Spotters, in Cuba?"

"Probably using local radar from south Lou'siana, Alabama. Fat Albert isn't our only resource." Jim's pronouncing of Louisiana indicated his Southern background, something I hadn't picked up in his earlier speech.

"Good to know." I spoke above the rushing wind and banging bow. "Won't they know when it lands in Cay Sal?"

"As soon as it lands, we'll communicate with the CO." He

309

kept his smile. "My guess is the first reply will be for us to continue our observation while they scramble the Coasties. Probably planes from Miami."

"Observation only?"

"We're not prepared to intercept. At least, command doesn't know we are." He stretched his legs. "Boats and choppers from Key West will be able to intercept, probably on the water."

"What happened to the plan of following them to the marinas?" Norm asked.

"A point I'll bring up to the CO when I make the call, but we can't count on his agreement. The Coasties are the pros at high-sea chases, and it eliminates chances of casualties on US soil."

"And the *paco?*" I leaned forward so I could see Jim's reaction.

He grinned. "If it's loaded on a separate boat, we follow it into Key West like we planned."

"You can't make the arrests." I looked at Norm. "Everyone is chasing the fishing boats, what do we do?"

"I'm depending on our friendly neighborhood cops." He stood up. "A last-minute call to Richard, who calls Chance, and the cops and sheriffs make the bust."

"They'll be outgunned."

"That's why they have SWAT teams."

"And maybe some black-ops people," Norm said so we could hear him over the wind.

"There's coffee forward." Jim looked at his wristwatch, ignoring Norm's words. "We're less than an hour out."

He walked to the center console and spoke with Dan Arthur, who had headphones on, an M16 hanging off his shoulder, and seemed to be talking to himself.

We walked forward, and Jim poured hot black coffee into Styrofoam cups for us. Sugar was already added.

The GPS showed our route, and Jim pointed toward a cluster of dots. "Cay Sal Banks," he said. "About an hour?" He turned to Tom McGee.

"About, we'll slow down before getting close." McGee kept his eyes on the invisible horizon.

The knot meter indicated the boat was moving along at twenty-five knots, which would mean we'd traveled a little more than seventy-five miles since leaving Key West. Saltwater spray carried as far back as the console each time the bow crashed down.

I looked at my wristwatch and figured we would be in the Banks around four A.M. A false dawn would begin to lighten the sky soon after.

"What time do you expect the seaplane?" I sipped my coffee.

"It should make a pass before six," Jim said without looking at me. "If their spotter-boats don't turn them away, they'll wait for the boat crew to drop glow sticks in the water."

"To mark the landing area?"

"Yeah." Jim turned to us. "The idea is to get everything unloaded and be back in the air before sunrise."

"How many on the plane?" My curiosity was getting the best of me and I made mental notes of what he said.

"Probably two, the pilot and kicker."

"Kicker?"

"A cargo guy, his job is to kick the bundles out into the water. When he's done, the plane goes airborne and gets the hell out."

"Being still dark, they may not spot us from the air."

"Probably not." Jim stretched, bent over and touched his toes. "I'm not worried about the plane. It's what they got in the water I'm concerned about. The fishing boats won't do recon, there'll be at least two go-fasts, and their job is to protect the plane and then, maybe, get the *paco* to Key West."

311

Sixty-Eight

"Do you expect trouble?" I looked around and didn't see any weapons but the one Dan Arthur had. The only items on deck not in the watertight boxes were related to diving.

"M16s are forward, in the boxes," Jim Ashe said between sips of coffee, and nodded toward the bow. "Hopefully, we won't need 'em until the plane is landing."

"Worst case." I turned to Norm and saw a blank expression.

"They have a couple of go-fasts and we have to protect ourselves." The words came without emotion. It could happen or it couldn't and it didn't matter to him, was what his tone said to me.

"Best case."

"Everything goes as planned." Jim smiled, as if he knew his words were lies.

I wanted to tell him not to try to shit a shitter, but said nothing because, if I were in his place, I would defend my lie.

"More likely, something in between," Norm added.

Jim turned his stare toward Norm. "You begin the missions with the best plans you can, and you hope for the best intel." He sighed. "It never goes as good or as bad as you expect. Intel is wrong, things change, human error, and sometimes luck is on your side. Being prepared is what saves lives."

"Yeah," Norm agreed with a sour expression. "Sometimes things go better than planned, but sometimes they go to shit."

312

"And once in a while, they go as planned." Jim finished his coffee.

Charlie Thompson came forward in wet, yellow foul-weather gear and poured himself a cup of coffee.

"The damn spray is cold." He warmed his hands around the cup and sipped. "The water temp is in the high seventies, so why's the spray cold?" His soft laugh was almost lost in the noise of the boat. "Weapons and ammo are dry." He spoke to Jim and nodded at us.

Tom McGee kept the boat at twenty-five knots and his eyes forward. Dan Arthur watched off to the south and Jerry Blankenship looked toward a non-existing northern horizon. When I sail, especially at night, everyone takes a turn at the "watch." The Florida Straits is a shipping channel from the Atlantic to the Gulf of Mexico, and the *Fenian Bastard* would not be picked up on a large ship's radar. A ship probably wouldn't even realize it hit a sailboat. But ships are lit up, and out in the open seas you look for moving lights off toward the horizon, even when it blends in with the night sky. That's the "watch." All these concerns applied to the Colombian go-fast we were in.

Norm and I walked back to where we had been and sat down.

"Is he expecting trouble?" The banging of the bow was finally beginning to make my side hurt.

"It's a question without an answer," Norm said and leaned back. "I think he's being cautious. I'd do things differently."

"Like what?"

"He's a team player and I'm not exactly a person who works with a team."

He was trying to skirt around my question.

"Meaning?"

"I would've taken this R.L. out on his boat. I don't arrest people." He rubbed his hands together and let out a deep breath. "I'd've let the Coasties blow the boats and plane out of

313

the water and been on my way before they began."

"Did you talk to him about this?"

"Back at Finnegan's." He turned to me. "Mick, he has restrictions on him I don't have on me, because I don't work in the States. JIATF has men that work outside and men that work within the States. Out here"—he pointed toward the bow—"he's legal. Once we're in US waters, his authority is gone."

"Meaning what?"

"If he's gonna fight, it will be at Cay Sal." Norm stretched his legs. "If we have to chase the *paco* to Key West, he needs Richard to make the bust. This won't be a neighborhood drug bust that the local cops and sheriffs are used to. These men with R.L. are well armed and fight to the death. Unless there are some Iraqi vets on the force, the locals are going to take casualties, maybe a lot, and Jim's thinking of that, too."

"Will he let the *paco* go?"

"No," he muttered. "He'll get R.L. and maybe Cluny. Whatever it takes, but if it comes to that, he might as well kiss his career good-bye."

It was the most Norm had ever opened up to me in conversation, but I knew enough to leave questions unasked. He was thinking aloud, as if I wasn't there, and if I tried to drag more conversation out of him, he'd laugh and deny he had ever said anything. It was a game he played and I always joined in.

I sat back against the bulkhead and tried to ignore my throbbing side by looking toward the star-filled sky. There are so many things I love about sailing, but the one that always captivates me is the night sky. I am not much into science, but the heavens have always filled my mind with unanswerable questions.

When I see the Hubble Telescope mentioned in the newspapers or on TV news, I am drawn to it. Billions of stars and millions of galaxies out there and most people stubbornly stick to the idea we are the only intelligent life there is. I guess realizing how insignificant we are is too much for them to deal with.

Since I was a kid, I always thought there had to be other life in the universe, and that's when I thought we were the center of it all. I don't have the faith Tita thinks I do, or the faith Padre Thomas displays, but as I learn more of how unbelievably enormous the heavens are I kind of understand why God sometimes seems to forsake us. We are probably a pitiful, failed experiment that He comes back to occasionally, only to be disappointed again. I sometimes wonder if He's given up on us, and if not, why not?

If I had met the angels, instead of Padre Thomas, would it have increased my faith or filled me with more questions?

"Cay Sal," McGee yelled over the wind.

I came out of my reverie when McGee yelled and Norm tapped my shoulder. We walked to the center console. I looked at the GPS. A few miles ahead of the blinking arrow that indicated where we were was a flashing X, showing our destination.

"How far?" Jim asked.

"About two miles." McGee slowed the boat down. "Grizzle called in the coordinates for where we should anchor."

Ahead of us, white anchor lights twinkled like stars. International boating rules require anchored boats to have a white anchor light on all night. It's a safety issue, like the red/green running lights.

"What do we have out there?" Norm asked before I could.

"Fishing boats, dive boats." Jim turned to Norm. "About a half dozen go-fasts, too."

315

Sixty-Nine

Tom McGee maneuvered us between anchored boats very slowly, so the wake was minimal. Charlie Thompson stood on the bow, ready to drop anchor. McGee's eyes darted between the shadowy outlines of boats and the flickering X on the GPS. His nod to Jim Ashe got Jim's closed-fisted hand to shoot into the air, and Thompson dropped the anchor, while McGee shut the engines down. There was a gentle jerk of the boat as the anchor hit bottom and held.

Our eyes had adjusted to the night and with the dim glow from the anchor lights, some on high masts of sailboats, others on the stern of power boats, we were able to see the shadowy outline of cliffs on the closest island.

When Jim had poured the last cup of coffee, the large thermos was empty. Now that the engines were off, the faded sounds off anchored boats carried on the water. Halyards slapped against masts, sending out a pinging sound; the current pulled tight on anchor lines, straining them on cleats. Soft music drifted from somewhere, barely recognizable. The beat echoed into the night, but the words, in whatever language, were lost.

"I know you can't see out there." Jim spoke above a whisper and pointed toward the darkness to our south. "We're less than a mile from open water and that's where we expect the plane to land."

"Where's the other boat?" Norm looked back toward the anchor lights.

316

"Hell if I know," Jim laughed. "But Grizzle gave us this location, so he's keeping an eye on us."

To the east, the black of night was turning dark gray, and by inches the gray turned lighter as the rising sun chased the darkness away. Even with the cacophony of sounds carried on the water, we were surrounded by a unique-to-the-water stillness.

As the dark skyline lightened before sunrise, boaters would awaken. While music floated from opened hatches, the smell of coffee and sizzling bacon would eddy through the anchorage, and soon men and women in varying stages of disarray would be outside, yelling greetings and orders, ready to begin the day.

"This is the beginning of the Cay Sal Banks." Jim pointed to the north. "I think that's Elbow Key, with the old lighthouse."

I turned to look, but it was too dark to see anything other than the outline of the large cliff.

"Hurry up and wait?" I turned to Jim.

He waved Dan Arthur over to the console. "Does Pierce have anything for us?"

"Cell-phone activity," Arthur answered, almost standing at attention. "The guy is moving, stopping and going. Made and received about a half dozen calls, but Pierce doesn't have the equipment to eavesdrop."

"We get the numbers?"

"They're being identified."

"Let me know when we have more." Jim turned to McGee. "Anything from command?"

"Mexicans have busted the group in Chetumal. No big shots."

"Now you know what I know," he said to me. "The plane will approach without lights, so we listen for it. When the pilot sees the glow sticks in the water, lights come on, he lands, kicks off the booty and leaves."

We now knew what Jim had been told, but we didn't know what his plans were for his team when the plane landed and

317

that's what worried me.

"Will he know the Mexican base is compromised?"

"If he doesn't, he will before he gets back. He'll have an alterative landing spot, probably in Belize."

McGee and Arthur kept their headphones on. Arthur's was mobile, so he could move about, while McGee's was plugged into the console. I walked forward to the bow, my cup of coffee cooling, and stared at the gray eastern horizon. The boat swayed rhythmically with the current.

"Are you nervous?" Norm came up beside me.

"Should I be?" I finished my sweet coffee.

"Sometimes it's a good thing, keeps you on your toes."

"And other times?"

"It's a waste of energy." Norm took our empty cups and tossed them in a small trash bag hanging off the rail by the center console. "Listen for the engines of a go-fast to start," Norm said as he came back. "That will tell us someone has been in contact with the plane. They'll ride the landing area and then drop the glow sticks. Maybe one or two boats."

"What should we expect?" I turned to look behind us and was surprised to see more gray than darkness.

"Knowing these assholes, large-caliber weapons." Norm turned to me and ran his hands through his unwashed hair. "If Dey's right, it's a big shipment and Cluny's job is to see it gets to Miami. In the Bahamas there'd be a seasoned organization meeting it. . . ."

"And R.L. doesn't have a seasoned gang," Jim interrupted, stressing the word *seasoned*. "Jesus, Norm, seasoned? You got a way with words."

"What would you call them?" Norm's words came with a challenge.

"Experienced thugs would've come to mind. Ruthless." Jim chuckled. "Cubans and Bahamians have used these islands for smuggling, probably since before recorded time. During Prohibition for liquor, then for marijuana, coke and human cargo smuggling, these days."

"Have you been to the discarded campsites, seen the skeletons of old boats?"

"Oh, yeah," Jim said with a frown. "You've been here before?"

"One diving trip, by seaplane. From my charts, I'd say it's a good layover to the Keys from the Bahamas and Cuba."

"The Coasties patrol the area more than the Bahamians." Jim looked out toward the south. "Migrant smugglers and drug runners, what a mix."

We looked off into the early dawn without speaking. My side throbbed. Doctor-feel-good was dwindling, and I knew that in a couple of hours I would be able to fall asleep in the middle of a Cat-5 hurricane.

The coughing sound of a cold engine trying to start drew all our attention toward the eastern anchorage. It took two attempts and then the engines begin to purr. Sound carries on the water and plays tricks as it runs around, so we stared east and then looked toward the island, and then turned our stares south. No one spoke. The engine noise bounced all around.

Jerry Blankenship tapped Jim's shoulder and pointed behind us. We turned to see a boat's running lights headed in our direction. Thompson quickly went to the deck, opened a box and handed Blankenship two M16s at a time. He gave the first one to Jim, then Norm, and went back and got mine and one for himself. Thompson came by and handed us all two extra magazines.

"It's like the M4, only with a longer barrel," Jim began to explain.

"I'm familiar with it," I said.

"Keep 'em below the rail." He nodded to me. "It could be a guy headed home, or it's our spotter."

"If he watched us come in, he might be giving us the once-over," Blankenship said.

He and Arthur went to the dive tanks and pretended to check them, as McGee focused a low-wattage light onto the work deck.

The suspicious boat passed two lengths away. It was a large go-fast, painted yellow, red and blue. It would be noticeable on the open water. Even in the false dawn, the colorful boat stood out. With its powerful inboard engine, the go-fast would outrun us easily.

Jim whistled. "I bet that one races out of Miami."

McGee laughed. "Or was stolen from Miami."

"Good point," Jim said. "The other boat is looking for us."

"How do you know there's another one?" I kept my voice low.

"A couple of things. It's a big shipment, so they have back up and we know there's a bad guy in the DEA, so whatever he knows about us, these guys know."

"How concerned should we be?"

"Look, these guys might not be the pick of the litter"—Jim chuckled at his choice of words—"but they are in contact with Cluny and he's right out of the British Special Forces. They'll do what he says, without question, and he hasn't survived this long by being a fool."

We watched the boat move quietly south, our weapons held low.

"Grizzle's having breakfast on a fishing boat," Arthur said as he walked toward us, his headset and mike on. "The captain's telling him they weigh anchor at sunrise and head back to Key West. This Captain Andy Griffiths told Dave five fishing boats came in yesterday afternoon from Key West. He knows only two of the captains."

Grizzle was miked for sound, so Arthur was able to listen to the breakfast conversation.

"Dave's going back to the boat." Arthur repeated what he was hearing.

"At least two of those five boats are waiting for the same plane we are." Jim stretched his arms high and then bent over and touched his toes.

I assumed he was doing the stretching because he was losing the effects of doctor-feel-good, too. I stretched against the bulkhead until my side told me to stop.

Blankenship and Arthur kept scanning the mooring field, looking for another go-fast, while Jim kept his eyes on the running lights of the go-fast that had passed us.

I walked back toward the stern with Norm and slipped the two extra magazines next to my Glock in the crook of my back.

"You see the sight on Arthur's weapon?" he said, when we were away from the others.

"That small hump?" I had noticed a small bulge above the barrel.

"He's the sniper," Norm said. "It's a holographic sight that has great night-vision capabilities." The flatness of his words concerned me.

"Which means what?"

"He could take out the engine of the plane from here; make it impossible to take off."

"Could he shoot it while it's landing? Make it crash?" I didn't like the picture in my head.

"He could."

The coughing sound of an engine trying to start cut our conversation short. It sounded like more than one boat was getting ready, but the water can play tricks with sound, so we kept scanning the mooring field, looking for running lights. Norm tapped his ear and pointed toward the island.

321

SEVENTY

The eastern sky turned from gray to reddish purple as the sun began to ease its way out of the Atlantic. The engines we heard could have been from boats ready to go fishing, or begin the long journey home. We expected the worst, so we scanned the anchorage and walked forward, following the sound.

Jim Ashe kept watching the go-fast as it moved, focusing on its small running lights as it crisscrossed the open water, almost impossible to see from where we were. He pointed in the boat's direction, and Norm nodded that he saw it. Jim put his fists together and made a breaking motion, as if he held the glow sticks. Norm shook his head *no,* and Jim hunched his shoulders but never pulled his stare away.

"No binoculars?" I whispered.

"Bad guys are checking the perimeter and we don't need to draw their attention."

The clouds to the east began to reflect the sunrise's colorful highlights, while a yellow haze grew on the horizon, promising the sun would show itself. A light breeze carried the moist scents of seaweed and salt as the boat gently rocked in the current.

Tom McGee banged on the wheel to get our attention. Jim didn't turn. McGee pointed his clenched right fist with one finger raised into the air, and made a circling motion, telling us the seaplane was close.

"Lock and load, hoss," Norm whispered, and clicked the safety off his M16.

322

I did the same, and got a strange, quick look from Jim. Then he turned back to the go-fast.

The sounds of the mooring field coming to life reverberated, but we stood quietly still. Jim followed the go-fast, while Norm and I scanned the sky.

"Glow sticks in the water," Jim said with some relief in his tone. "It's close."

Norm tapped my shoulder and pointed to the east. I didn't see anything.

"No winds," he whispered. "He'll approach with the sun behind him."

There was no sun but I understood what Norm meant.

Jim referred to the plane as it, while Norm said "him." To Jim, I assumed this was another job, one of many and when it was done, there would be another, or maybe three, waiting. To Norm, what he did was more personal, and whatever the job, there was a name involved because he had to stop a man and, once in a while, a woman. I think Jim's impersonal way handled the stress better.

The loud cough and rumble of inboard engines intruded on the natural noises of the mooring field. Pieces of shouted commands could be heard, but not understood.

"Getting busy." I shook Norm's shoulder to take his stare from the eastern sky.

Norm nodded and pointed high above the horizon. "Lights," he said.

Jim turned to follow Norm's direction. "Could be it."

The second go-fast moved carefully through the anchored boats and finally met up with the boat that had laid out the glow-stick-lighted landing area.

"Once this plane lands, everything happens quickly," Jim said to me. "It's estimated there'll be a thousand kilos of coke coming off, and the pilot doesn't want to be on the water one second longer than necessary."

A kilo is a bit more than two pounds, so the load would weight more than two thousand pounds—a ton of coke. Add to that the one hundred kilos of *paco* we expected, and the weight would increase by another couple of hundred pounds. How long, I wondered, would it take one man to unload all that? Even if it was only throwing it off a plane, I thought it would be time consuming.

"They really just toss it into the water?" I had read stories of packaged cocaine found floating off a beach or picked up by a boater in the Gulf Stream.

"It's in waterproof packages," Jim said. "It floats and the boats have crews for retrieving it."

"Ten o'clock high," Jerry Blankenship called.

Off to the east the Albatross seaplane took shape against the gray sky. Wing lights flashed and its pontoons seemed to hang unattached below the tips of its long wingspan.

"It may make one more pass," Dan Arthur said, his earphones still on.

I watched as the large, bulky twin-engine seaplane began to grow.

"Trying to patch in to its frequency," Tom McGee said.

The plane looked like a large bird floating on the wind current as it moved toward us.

"Damn, how big is it?" I watched, amazed at the size of the Albatross.

"Sixty feet," Jim answered. "A wing span of ninety feet."

"It's an old seahorse," Norm said with respect in his voice. "It's gotta be sixty years old, and there ain't nothin' like it, today."

"It would be a shame to shoot it down."

Norm and I turned to Jim.

"Are those your orders?" Norm asked.

"If we have the chance," Jim answered, staring at Norm. "You know who's flying it?"

Norm shook his head. "Someone we know?"

"You may know him, but we want him." Jim kept watch as the plane approached.

"Crazy Paul?" Norm almost shouted.

Paul Clarin was an old smuggler and had as many arrest warrants with his name on them as there are DEA agents in Miami. He was a legend when it came to flying illegal cargos and escaping detection. Because locations where he landed and took off were often considered impossible for a sane pilot, he got nicknamed Crazy Paul by the DEA. His usual sidekick was another American named Declan Bruns. Rumor had it that once, the Bahamian police shot Crazy Paul's plane so many times in an attempt to keep him from taking off, that they emptied the clips from their M16s into it. Bruns was shot twice and Crazy Paul flew him to Key West for medical treatment. He got Bruns the care that saved his life and flew back to Mexico before the DEA knew he was in Florida.

It is smugglers' legend, and only Crazy Paul and Bruns know if it's true.

"If you shoot it down, we lose the *paco*," I blurted out.

"It could be shot down during takeoff, too." He turned to Norm. "We want him alive."

Norm grinned. "So, shooting him out of the air would be too dangerous."

"Once we know the *paco* is unloaded, I begin to follow the JIATF game plan," Jim said. "I promised you the *paco*, but afterward Crazy Paul is our target."

Norm and I nodded our understanding.

The twin engines of the Albatross roared off in the distance as it passed over the two go-fasts. The plane rocked its wings back and forth twice and then turned. It was painted gray, the same color as the early morning sky, making it almost invisible to the naked eye, and it lacked tail markings.

"He's landing and wants to know where the other boats are," McGee called. They had plugged into the smuggler's radio frequency.

The plane banked and began its descent. I had flown in much smaller seaplanes and wondered why the Albatross seemed to be making a long descent, especially since the water offered a large, open landing area.

"He's probably overweight," Norm explained. "When he takes off, he'll use a lot less space." He turned toward Jim, who continued to watch the plane.

"Safety is not an issue," Jim muttered. "He's got a thousand kilos; he adds another hundred or two, to make an extra few bucks."

"Crazy Paul likes his money," Norm agreed. "Is Declan with him?"

"Declan's his good-luck charm, of course he's with him."

"Why's he care about the other boats?" I watched the large plane slowly lower itself toward the water.

"He'll keep going if too many boats approach," Jim said. "That's why the go-fast lays out a landing area away from the mooring field. If Crazy Paul even thinks a boat that isn't supposed to be there is getting too close, he'll take off."

"What about the drugs?"

"It comes out the hatch as he climbs." Jim exhaled with a sigh. "I've seen him do it."

The large Albatross slid across the water, its spinning propellers forcing water over its wings and fuselage. For a brief second it looked as if it might have been sinking, but as the engines slowed, the flow of water subsided and the plane's pontoons settled and kept it afloat. The two go-fasts sped to it.

"Three o'clock," Blankenship called.

Off the starboard side, we saw a fishing boat slowly making its way through the mooring field, heading toward the seaplane. A second boat followed close behind.

Seventy-One

I don't know how the Albatross stopped from skidding across the bay. It didn't have brakes for use on the water, but even if it had, brakes don't stop boats—and now that it had landed in the Atlantic, the pontoons keeping its long wings afloat while the fuselage settled down, the Albatross was more boat than aircraft. Maybe its engines went into reverse, but it stopped quicker than I expected.

"Blankenship, Arthur, you're on watch," Jim Ashe ordered. "McGee, what are they saying?"

Charlie Thompson handed out binoculars. Jerry Blankenship from the bow and Dan Arthur at the stern were responsible for our safety as they scanned our perimeter, M16s at the ready hung from their shoulders. Keeping the weapons out of sight was no longer a priority; our safety was.

"Dive one reports two go-fasts moving this way from between islands, port side," Tom McGee reported.

"Watch the perimeter," Jim repeated. "What's Crazy Paul saying?"

"Telling the boats to hurry up, he wants to get back into the air."

Jim looked at his wristwatch. "He's nervous."

"How do you know?" I watched the hatch of the Albatross open.

"Less than a minute and he's talking about leaving."

"He knows something's wrong," Norm said.

328

"You know him, what do you think?"

"He's not afraid of us." Norm scanned the Albatross. "He's scared of the Coasties and he knows they're at the main islands."

"So, what's he concerned about?"

"Does he know we're here?" I watched the first package of cocaine fall into the water. The go-fast crew ignored it.

"The DEA bad guy had to give the cartel a heads-up about us, and they aren't about to lose a thousand kilos of product." Jim watched the unloading of the cocaine. "Fishing boats?"

"Two minutes away," Blankenship answered, without taking his eyes from the binoculars. "Starboard side, two of 'em."

Someone I couldn't see, not even with the binoculars, kept pushing black bundles from the hatch. They splashed into the water and floated, but some were starting to move with the tide.

"Why aren't the go-fasts picking them up?"

"Not their job," Jim said. "What we're watching for are the packages the kicker hands off to the go-fasts. That would be your *paco.*"

"Do you think he knows we're here?" I asked again.

Jim laughed. "He knows someone's here. We're going to have to move closer, I can't let him take off."

"What's the plan?" Norm moved next to Jim.

"McGee, once the trawlers begin to load, be ready to move," Jim ordered. "Watch the perimeter."

"Go-fasts still approaching," Blankenship said.

"Toward us?"

"No, sir."

"Let me know if that changes." Jim turned to Norm. "The plan is simple: don't let the plane take off."

"We're a little outnumbered, aren't we?"

The two forty-foot fishing trawlers moved into the view of my binoculars. Each had two men on deck and one on the fly bridge steering. One go-fast moved toward the front of the

329

plane, making room for a trawler by the open hatch, half hidden by the wing pontoon and engine propeller. The second trawler went with the current and headed off the packages of cocaine before they floated away. The crews had the pickup routine down to an art, hooking the floating packages and pulling them onboard. As I watched them work, I could almost hear classical music in my head; strings playing smoothly as the hooks approached the water, horns blaring as the cocaine was caught, and an intertwining of the instruments as the packages were lifted out of the water and into the boat. It was strange.

"Approaching go-fasts have stopped," Blankenship reported.

"How far?" Jim asked.

"Fifty yards, max," came the reply.

"Watch for the pass off," he said to Norm and then moved his binoculars toward the two approaching go-fasts. "Observation boat, bad guys," Jim yelled. "I think they've found us. Start the engines."

Thompson began winching in the anchor, while McGee lowered the engines into the water and started them.

I turned away from the Albatross and scanned where Jim looked, and saw one of the go-fasts. It was similar to the one we were in and had a crew of four that I could see. They were watching us with binoculars, too.

As our anchor came up, one of the bad guys' go-fasts shot forward and we felt the wake from its large engines as our boat rocked. It went into open water, moving toward the Albatross, then turned away from the fishing trawlers, faced our direction, and stopped.

"That's not good." Norm watched forward.

"Is Grizzle saying anything?" Jim yelled to McGee.

"Watching the port boat, sir," McGee answered. "He doesn't think they've spotted him as one of us."

330

"What's it doing, Norm?" Jim kept his binoculars on the port side.

"Watching us. Talking among themselves, maybe communicating with the plane." Norm kept his binoculars on the forward go-fast.

"McGee, any communications with Crazy Paul?"

"No, sir, not on the frequency we're monitoring."

I turned my binoculars back to the Albatross and watched as one of the go-fasts moved toward the forward boat that concerned everyone. I scanned the trawlers; they were busy picking up the cocaine. Declan Bruns, if that was him, kept booting bundles from the hatch. I told Norm about the boat's move, pointing it out to him.

"They're meeting," he called to Jim.

Norm and I watched as the two go-fasts pulled close against each other. The crews seemed to be talking and pointing between the Albatross and us.

McGee began to move us forward, carefully maneuvering between moored boats.

"The second boat backing us up?" Norm turned to Jim.

"He's going to keep the other go-fast from sneaking up on us." Jim turned his binoculars toward the two go-fasts forward of us. "Has the *paco* come off?"

"Everything's gone into the water," I said. "Are the trawlers' crews armed?"

"Probably, but the other boats are security. They're our main concern."

"You're still planning to keep Crazy Paul from taking off?" Norm scanned the mooring field, looking for what, I don't know.

"Go-fast moving toward the plane." I watched as the trawler made room for the smaller boat.

The man in the plane tossed four black-wrapped packages into the go-fast and then waved the boat off. It moved away, not stopping by the plane's tail this time.

"The go-fast has packages," I said.

"That's your *paco.*" Jim watched the moving go-fast for a minute and then brought his binoculars back to the two forward go-fasts.

"Are we a little outnumbered?" Norm wanted to know Jim's plan for keeping the Albatross from taking off.

"Grizzle's supposed to shoot out the engines, call in the landing, while we follow the *paco.*" Jim watched the two go-fasts. "I think we need to improvise.'

Norm laughed out loud. "They'll want us to chase them."

"Yeah, and when we don't they'll fight, to give the plane a chance to take off."

"And your plan is?"

"Forward!" Arthur yelled from the bow.

We all focused on the two forward go-fasts.

"Oh, shit," Jim cussed. "Get us out of this mooring field, now," he yelled. "McGee, RPG, tell Grizzle. Let's move."

McGee turned the boat and moved it as quickly as it was safe to do, to get us away from the moored boats. We left a hefty wake behind us, rocking the anchored boats, tossing about most anyone that had been sleeping.

"Grenade launcher?" I turned to Norm and hung on as the boat continued to pick up speed.

"Probably Russian." He held his binoculars in one hand and tried to keep watch on the boat with the RPG launcher, while balancing himself with our boat's quirky motion.

"What's its distance?" I had given up trying to use the binoculars and held on.

"We're an easy target, we can't zigzag. No way we can avoid it."

Everyone but McGee was looking behind us. Our M16s were useless. While the engines growled, I heard the explosion that

332

ignited the rocket-propelled grenade. As far away as we were in the early morning dimness, I saw the back-flash as the grenade shot out of the tube and flew toward us.

"Incoming!"

I don't know who said it. I looked to Norm. He smiled, dropped his M16, and with the swiftness of a much younger man, grabbed me under my arms and tossed me overboard; binoculars and M16 came along.

I hit the warm water and sank like a rock. I got rid of the binoculars and rifle, but the bulletproof vest and my sneakers made it impossible for me to swim toward the surface. I looked up and saw our boat explode into pieces; I even heard the explosion, muffled by the water barrier. I remembered my life vest and pulled the cord that inflated it, and stopped sinking. As the boat broke up, I saw Norm fall into the water. Blood filled the area around him. His soggy cowboy boots helped him sink. My lungs hurt from holding my breath, but I swam in his direction as I forced myself toward the surface. I saw others in the water, even watched a section of the boat sink, but focused on Norm as I swam. I needed air, but I couldn't let Norm drown.

Seventy-Two

I only had a few seconds before I'd pass out and drown when I pushed Norm from the back, trying to force him toward the surface. He turned and looked at me, surprised, and then gave a thin smile. As I swam next to him and pulled the line that made his life vest inflate, he grabbed onto me and I thought for a second he would hold me there. I needed to breathe, to stop the burning in my lungs, but it was my turn to be surprised when he pushed me toward the surface, helping save me for the second time in minutes.

My head came out of the water and I coughed and choked as I tried to take deep breaths; my throat had closed in expectation of swallowing water. Amazing how the brain works on its own sometimes. I gagged, then relaxed, floating on the surface, and was able to suck in small breaths. Norm surfaced a couple of yards from me. I wanted to swim to him, see where he was bleeding from, but I needed to get more air into my aching lungs, so I floated with the help of the life vest, taking more short breaths, and looked at my surroundings.

Boats were moving toward us with people hanging over the sides, prepared to pull the injured from the water. Boaters, as a group, react automatically when there is a disaster on the water. It's a natural response to help, usually before thinking of the possible consequences to themselves. No one could have realized what caused our boat to explode, but the boaters came anyway.

Pieces of the *Eduardoño* floated in the water, but any recognizable portions were gone. I paddled over to Norm, trying to disregard the pain in my arms, but I couldn't ignore how blood colored the water around him.

"Where you hurt?" I forced out the words between shallow breaths while I fought nausea.

"Something in my shoulder." He winced, but forced a smile. "Shrapnel from the RPG. I'm okay."

"The boat. . . ." I couldn't finish the sentence.

"You noticed that, huh?" He looked toward a small launch headed our way. "Do you see the plane?"

I wasn't sure what way I was facing. I circled in the water, saw the island, and turned away from it. The two fishing boats were gone, and off in the distance I saw the gray outline of the large Albatross in the sky.

"Gone. Do you see anyone else?"

"Arthur and McGee stayed with the boat."

I wanted to hold out hope for them, but his tone told me not to.

The launch came up next to Norm.

"He's hurt; be careful lifting him," I shouted and the two men nodded. They said something I couldn't hear and then lifted Norm from under his arms. His expression was what I'd expect from a person having a root canal as the Novocain wore off. I paddled and kicked my way over and they helped me onboard.

When they lifted me, a pain shot through my left side and stopped at my shoulder. I slumped on the deck next to Norm and reached under my life vest, shirt and bulletproof vest to touch my gunshot wound. My hand came away without any blood on it.

"Get the water out of my boots, will ya, hoss?" Norm mumbled.

335

Blood dripped from a few places along his shoulder and neck. The vest had protected his vital areas.

One man, tall, with a shaved head and sunburned brown, stood over us as I pulled Norm's boots off and emptied them of water.

"Coast Guard wants us to take everyone we pull out to the island," he said slowly, gazing at us and trying to figure out if we were the good guys or the bad guys. "You okay with that?"

"Yeah." I handed Norm his boots. "He needs some medical attention."

"There's a nurse on the island. She's from one of the boats out of Raleigh."

I looked at my wristwatch. Not ten minutes had passed since we'd noticed the RPG, and somehow a nurse was waiting for us.

"Things came together real fast," I mumbled between breaths.

"Accident happens on the water, you ain't got a lot of time," the bald man drawled as he rubbed his sunburned nose. "She's a nurse, she's doing nurse's things. We're boaters. . . ."

"Pulling people from the water," Norm said with a smile. "All this done over the radio?"

"Yeah." The man grinned back. "Weren't no time to form committees and assign responsibilities."

He said it as if he had done such things once and used his poor English to disguise that. Or maybe he was just water-smart after years of making a living on his boat. The launch was headed to the island.

"What did the Coasties say?" I asked, taking in deeper breaths.

"Told 'em what we saw, a lot of radio squawk after the first explosion."

"More than one explosion?" I had only heard one while I was sinking.

"Oh, yeah." He grinned. "Your boat got hit twice. And a boat at the other side of the mooring field got hit twice, too, and there are a lot of other boats damaged." He rubbed at his sunburned nose again. "Have something to do with that big seaplane?" His voice lowered as he spoke. "It was bringin' in drugs, weren't it?"

"What did the Coasties say to you?" Norm ignored his question.

The man chuckled. "Sometimes no answer is the answer. Back in the sixties, if you were over here, you were up to no good. Still that way for some, today."

"You here a lot in the sixties?" Norm held one boot upside down, trying to drip water from it.

"And seventies."

"You go away?" He meant, had he been caught.

"Nope." He smiled at us. "When guys showed up carrying more weapons than they needed, I knew things was gonna get bad and I didn't need bad."

"Charter business?" Norm turned the other boot upside down.

"I knew the waters, why not?"

"This ain't your charter boat?"

"Nope." He laughed. "My charter boat is a yacht for rich, pampered Yankees, who sometimes don't have enough sense to use lotion when they're in the sun. Got a dive master and we bring 'em here to dive the caves."

"Pretty good business?"

"Not as lucrative as some." He laughed again. "But I know I won't be going away because I'm doin' it. You boys gonna be able to walk when we get to the island?"

The helmsman was pulling the launch onto a sandy beach, where people had gathered.

337

SEVENTY-THREE

The sun began to rise, a beautiful, large yellow-orange orb as it emerged from the cold Atlantic. A salty morning breeze fought a losing battle with humidity as we got off the skiff and thanked the two men. Norm had his boots on by the time I helped him out of the boat. Other small boats littered the shoreline, some with the wounded and others with the curious. The RPGs had destroyed more than our two boats; there seemed to be a lot of collateral damage.

"Over there, under the palms." A man pointed to where a group of people gathered in the morning shade. "There's medical help."

Norm and I nodded our thanks as the man moved on.

"I'm okay," Norm said, and pushed my hand away. To prove it, he walked quickly toward the palms.

"Remove your shirt," the anxious, middle-aged nurse said after giving Norm's shoulder and neck a quick inspection.

She wore shorts and a damp bloodstained T-shirt. To keep her sun-bleached, dirty-blonde hair out of her eyes, she had it pulled into a small ponytail. She didn't wear latex gloves or any type of protection you find today with paramedics, and blood smeared sections of her bare arms and legs. Her expression as she talked to the injured was blank; it did not reveal any sense of urgency, but when she finished and smiled, you knew she was good at what she did.

One young man, her assistant for the moment, drew the

nurse's attention back to Norm as he removed his damaged shirt to reveal the bulletproof vest. He dropped the vest next to the shirt as the nurse returned. Her blank expression was replaced with anger.

"Who are you?" she demanded. "Keep checking the wounded," she said to the young man and then turned back to Norm.

"I'm with the government," he answered quietly.

"And you've got ID?" She was shorter than Norm, but invaded his space without care.

"No."

She looked down at the vest. "You were prepared for this," she said and then glanced at his bleeding shoulder again. She took disinfectant from her medical bag, cleaned the wound, and then wiped the small cuts on his neck.

"Yes."

"The gun in your pocket didn't help you much, did it?" She wiped the area again and then applied an adhesive bandage.

"No."

"The Coast Guard will be here soon to take the wounded back to Key West." She spread the bandage, making sure it stuck to him. "You will go on that chopper, won't you?"

"Do you think my injury requires that?" He looked down at her and smiled. "I'm feeling fine."

"Not my decision." She wiped at a bloodstain on her arm. "Medical evacuation first, for all injured."

"I'd like to look for some friends, is that okay?" he asked, still keeping his words soft.

"Who are they?" She stepped back and looked up at him.

"Friends from JIATF."

She almost lost the angry look. "You're looking for them with the gun in your pocket?"

"No, I'm with them." He removed the Glock and offered it to her.

She ignored his offer. "They have guns too."

"I know, we came together." He put the Glock back in his pocket.

"Their guns didn't do any better than yours."

"No, ma'am, they didn't. I've learned there's always someone with a bigger gun."

"Yes, there is." She smiled and stepped aside. "But boys need their toys, don't they."

"Too often, yes, ma'am."

"Halfway down the shoreline." She pointed toward the east.

"How are they doing?"

"The living or the dead?" She lost her smile.

"Thank you," he said, as she walked away. "Shit," he mumbled as he picked up his shirt and vest, "I didn't expect this kind of firepower." He put the shirt on.

"Did Jim lie?" I shuffled along next to him, the sun beginning to dry my clothes. The bulletproof vest was uncomfortable, but I decided to leave it on because I didn't need to draw attention to myself.

"No one really expected RPGs."

"I didn't think you bought their observation story."

"Me," he huffed a laugh, "not believe someone?"

"Yeah, unbelievable, ain't it."

"Mick, these guys work outside the States, that's their charter. In Key West they had restrictions, here there ain't so many. So, yeah, I expected them to do something." He slowed and scanned the beach. "And when Jim said they were going to keep Crazy Paul's seaplane from taking off, I thought that was it."

Jim Ashe and Jerry Blankenship were sitting on the beach, looking out at the water.

"How many did we lose?" Norm sat on his vest.

"McGee and Arthur for sure." Jim sighed. "You two okay?'

"Shrapnel in the shoulder." Norm rubbed the bandage. "I'm told I've got to go back with the Coasties."

"Command wants us all back and they want to know how all this came down here and not where they expected," Jim grumbled, and stared up at me. "You okay?"

"A little waterlogged."

"Norm, you'll be checked out at the clinic on South Roosevelt," Jim said. "Mick, you'll come with us, but I think I can get you out of the debriefing."

"What went wrong?"

"They were expecting us." Jim stretched his legs and got up. "It's gotta be the DEA agent. He knew more than we thought he did."

"That was a lot of firepower to stop two go-fasts." Norm got back up.

"I agree." Jim nodded. "They didn't want to stop us, they wanted to kill us."

Most everyone on the beach looked east as the rotor noise from four white-and-orange Coast Guard helicopters began to vibrate across the island.

SEVENTY-FOUR

Four Coast Guard Jayhawk helicopters approached, their whirling rotors churning the water and tossing anything loose across the island. They touched off a swirling sandstorm as they landed, causing everyone to turn away to protect their eyes.

"Are you sure we're on the same side?" Norm coughed the words out with a thin smile.

"With what's happened, I'm surprised they landed." Jim Ashe looked toward the water. "There could be a sleeper out there."

Norm and I turned to look at the moored boats. We wouldn't have heard the whoosh of an RPG if it had been launched, because of the rotor noise.

"Do you know these guys?" Norm scratched at his bandaged shoulder.

Jerry Blankenship stood and wiped sand from his damp legs. We watched as the side doors opened and members of the Coast Guard's Tactical Law Enforcement Team jumped out, prepared for a fight. TACLET's primary mission is counter-drug law enforcement, especially in the Caribbean.

"I'll introduce myself," Jim said. "You all wait here." He walked toward the armed men.

"Does he know 'em?" Norm turned to Blankenship.

"If they're from Miami or the Keys, he could."

"Do you know where anyone else is?"

"It doesn't look like Arthur or McGee made it. They were still trying to get the boat out of the mooring field when we jumped." Blankenship wiped at sand on his leg. "I dragged Charlie Thompson onto the beach. He had a stomach wound, so we took him to the nurse."

"How bad?"

"Not good, but I stayed with the captain, helping others come ashore."

An armed man standing out in front of the TACLET team greeted Jim. No one saluted. Jim turned and pointed toward us, the mooring field, and then toward where the wounded were in the shade. Orders were given, but we couldn't hear them, and some of the men headed for the crude triage carrying small bags of medical supplies while others followed with their weapons.

The sixty-five-foot Jayhawks dwarfed the men. The main rotors, fifty-four feet in diameter, whirled slowly overhead and their noise carried across the island. From the mooring field, boaters watched using binoculars.

Jim and the man from TACLET shook hands, and then Jim walked back to us.

"I know the lieutenant," he said and stopped. "The admiral's pissed."

"Why?" Norm scratched at his bandage.

"Because his intel was bad." Jim smiled. "These TACLET guys will take 'em down in the Keys, but it's not a plan admin likes."

"No local cops, then?" I thought of how Richard would like all this to go away.

"I can't see this going down without the pretense of local co-operation."

"What about us?"

"You come with us." Jim pointed at me. "Norm, you need to go with the medevacs, but your cover is intact and the lieutenant will keep your name off the list."

"Why can't I fly with you?"

"Procedure," Jim sighed. "All wounded to be evaced to the clinic on South Roosevelt, and it's too late to cover you up."

"I don't like it," Norm grumbled.

"Well, no one cares, so let's go." Jim turned and we followed him to the helicopters.

Norm and I agreed to meet back at the inn and wait for news. He suggested I give Richard a heads-up on the situation.

Civilians, shaken up but not injured, were put in one helicopter. In another, the three of us joined Dave Grizzle and two men I didn't recognize. We took off, the six of us pushed together with the crew. While flying, we noticed at least a dozen fishing boats headed in the direction of Key West. What two were the drug smugglers' boats? We moved by them quickly and in less than an hour, we landed at the Coast Guard base.

I wasn't introduced to the lieutenant, but he nodded as I followed Jim out of the Jayhawk and onto a grassy knoll. The large parking lot was full. The dockside, where the Coast Guard cutters berthed, was empty.

"You're done." Jim shook my hand. "My men at the inn will pack up and be gone within an hour. Tita will be all right with Dr. Jack's care."

"What about Johnny?"

"We'll let the DEA know where he is and they'll come for him."

"I'd like to know how this comes down."

The Jayhawk took off, headed back, I supposed, to help track the fishing boats.

"Read the paper," Jim yelled above the noise.

"I'd like to know what really happened," I said, trying to be heard over the helicopters.

"Well, my guess is your friend Norm will know everything." Jim smiled as the noise faded. "I have a feeling he doesn't walk away leaving business unfinished."

A horn beeped and when I turned, I saw DEA Agent Reed Fitcher standing outside his government sedan in the base parking lot.

"What's he doing here?" I waved at Fitcher.

"DEA is part of our team." Jim frowned. "I guess every agency knows what happened to us, all the way to command on the mainland."

"Is he here for me?"

I liked Fitcher, the little I'd dealt with him, but he was on the list of possible bad guys, as was local agent Joel Martin.

"He's a ride back to the inn," Jim said. "We've got a debrief here, so unless you want to stick around for a few hours, I'd take the ride."

"I'd like to buy you a drink, after all this plays out." We shook hands. "I need to give you back the vest."

"I don't know, from what I've seen, hanging around you can be dangerous. Maybe you should keep it." He laughed and slapped my back. "I know how to reach you."

Jim walked toward the main building and I headed toward Fitcher.

"You look beat up." He held the car door open for me. "Where can I take you?"

"Mango Tree Inn," I said, and he closed the door.

"You were down the street from my office all this time?" He started the car and we slowly drove from the Coast Guard base through the Navy's Trumbo Annex and out into Old Town Key West. "And we've been looking all over for you."

"How'd you know I was here?"

"JIATF agent contacted our office from the Bahamas," he said, as he turned onto Eaton Street and then took the first left onto White Street. "I'm picking you up, and Joel's picking up your friend Norm at the clinic. Seems," he laughed, "the military

345

wants you off their bases as quick as possible."

"It didn't go well," I mumbled as we turned onto Southard Street. "Has anyone found R.L.?"

"He's not home, we know that." Fitcher stopped the car in the driveway of the inn. "His boat and warehouse are staked out," he grumbled. "I think there's too much involved for him to run, but you never know."

"And the Limey?"

"Three dead Colombians on Caroline Street." He chuckled grimly. "Three more dead in the cemetery. I don't think Cluny can afford to lose another man."

"So?"

"So, he's focusing on the drug shipment and getting it to Miami, would be my guess."

"JIATF is pulling out of here," I said and noticed there were no security men in the parking lot. "Everyone must think the same thing."

"Only makes sense. You don't mind if I come back later so you can tell me the whole story, do you?"

"I expect Richard will want to know, too."

"I'll have him meet us here. His office is too official."

"Okay." I got out of the car and saw Paul Carpino on the porch. "Maybe tomorrow?"

Fitcher nodded and drove off, turning right onto Simonton Street.

"No security?" I stood at the foot of the steps leading upstairs.

"Bryan." He pointed to the wooded yard across the street. Bryan Papaccioli was barely visible.

"How long have you two been here?"

He smiled. "Forever."

I was so tired, and it finally hit me as I walked up the stairs. When had I last slept? I couldn't remember, but I certainly knew that Norm's doctor-feel-good meds were out of my system and I looked forward to the soft bed that waited for me.

Padre Thomas greeted me when I reached the top of the stairs.

"You look horrible," he said softly.

"I feel worse," I said and hoped there was a smile on my face. "Tita?"

"She's fine. Dr. Jack said there's nothing to worry about, but wants to see her in his office tomorrow."

"I think he wanted to see me there today."

"They told us we could go." He lit a cigarette. "Kram left right away."

"Yeah, it's almost over, so I guess he wants to write his story."

"Almost?" He blew smoke from his nose. He looked at his wristwatch. "Norm said in the morning."

"Padre, I need to see Tita, check with Johnny and get some sleep," I yawned and realized again how tired I was. "I don't think you can expect the fishing boats in before noon. They'll come in with the morning charters or after five, with the all-day charters."

"But it's over?" He stomped out his cigarette butt and I saw a small pile of them on the wood deck.

"All but the shooting, Padre." I squeezed his bony shoulder and walked into the hallway.

The door was open to Johnny Dey's room. He sat in a chair, two M16s lay on the bed, and Dr. Jack walked out of the bathroom.

"Back and safe," Dr. Jack greeted me.

"Tell us what happened," Johnny yelled from his seat. "Do they know where R.L. and Cluny are?"

Tita put one arm around my waist and kissed my ear. "You smell."

I squeezed her hand and turned to face her. She had her left arm in a sling, but had color back in her face.

347

"You also look like hell." She grinned, but her eyes showed concern.

"All I am is tired."

"So, tell us what happened," Coco Joe said from the hallway.

"You're back," I said. "Everything okay?"

"In a manner of speaking." He smiled and leaned against the doorframe. "What happened?"

Before I could answer, an explosion on the first floor rocked the building. Tita grabbed onto me, but before she could speak, another explosion sent items tumbling off the walls.

We could hear small-arms fire outside, but couldn't tell if it was incoming or the JIATF men shooting back. It could have been Papaccioli, shooting from across the street. Smoke billowed up along the outdoor stairway. Coco Joe ran, looked outside, and then closed the door.

"We've got to get you down the back stairway," he ordered, looking at Tita. "Johnny, you too."

"No fuckin' way!" Johnny yelled as he helped move us toward the back entrance, an M16 in one hand. "How many of them?"

The fire department was a block away, on Simonton and Angela streets, and we could already hear the sirens.

SEVENTY-FIVE

Coco Joe pulled the back door open and had us wait while he stood on the small deck, M16 raised, and scanned the yards and street below. Johnny Dey walked past and went outside, talked to Joe and then moved down the steps with more flexibility than someone recently beaten should have, his M16 ready.

Sirens wailed off in the distance and I assumed they belonged to the police, because I saw the flashing red lights of fire engines reflected in the windows below. Whiffs of smoke blew past the backyard, and the small-arms fire had stopped.

Coco Joe motioned us outside and we followed him down the narrow stairway to the alley behind the Mango Tree Inn. Tita held tightly to my hand and forced a smile when I turned to her; Padre Thomas and Dr. Jack were close behind. A fire truck pulled up, and firefighters prepared to hose down the backside of the inn. The smoke was thinning, but the odor of burnt wood was strong.

Johnny said something to one of the firefighters, and we were motioned forward as Coco Joe ran back upstairs.

"I'll call you when Norm gets here." Johnny looked toward the corner.

"We can go to my office," Dr. Jack bellowed over the noise of the firefighters and the approaching sirens.

"I thought this was over," Padre Thomas moaned.

"Everyone did, Padre." I sighed. "Maybe this was their last hurrah?"

"You armed?" Johnny scanned the hectic movements of everyone on the street.

"Yeah." I touched the grip of my Glock. Carrying it tucked into my back, under the bulletproof vest and my shirt, was feeling natural and I didn't like that. "You okay?"

"Never felt better," he lied with a grin.

Reed Fitcher stopped his sedan across from us, its blue lights flashing, and beeped the horn.

"What the hell happened?" he yelled as his window lowered.

"Who is he?" Johnny stared toward the car.

"DEA."

"I don't know him." There was concern in his voice.

"From Miami, and he's been working with Richard on this."

"There's a DEA leak."

"I know."

"Be careful," he warned and went upstairs.

We crossed the street, and Tita and I stopped at the passenger side of Fitcher's car, while Padre Thomas and Dr. Jack waited on the sidewalk.

"Jesus," Fitcher cried as he lowered the passenger window. "I heard the blasts, but that's not why I came back."

"RPGs," I said. I didn't have to see them to know.

Tita looked at me. "How do you know that?"

"It's what they blew up our boats with," I muttered. "I know the sound up close and personal."

"Are you okay?" Fitcher noticed Tita's arm in a sling.

"Yeah." She almost laughed and I saw it in her eyes. "You hang around this guy long enough, you expect to get shot."

"God almighty," he barked, "who shot you?"

"You'll get the whole story tomorrow," I reminded him.

"I might get it sooner than that." He smiled. "As I was pulling into the parking lot, I got a call and decided to come back for you."

"R.L.?"

"He's at the warehouse on Stock Island." Fitcher's grin showed a perfect set of straight white teeth. "I thought you'd want to be there."

"Damn right," I yelled. "Have they got him?"

"No," he said, a little angst in his tone. "They're sure he's inside with the drugs, but they don't know if he's alone. We'd better hurry."

I looked at Tita and she nodded her head. I walked her to Dr. Jack.

"Where's Padre Thomas?" I hadn't seen him leave.

"He said he had to go and headed down Simonton Street," Dr. Jack answered.

I promised to call Tita as soon as anything happened. If she wasn't at Dr. Jack's office, she'd be at hers, she said. I kissed her good-bye and got into Fitcher's car.

"Seat belt," he ordered and moved slowly through the closed street.

As we passed the inn, I turned and saw firefighters on the front porch, but they weren't rushing around, so I knew the fire was out. But where were the JIATF men? And Coco Joe and Johnny Dey? Fire trucks, thick water hoses spread across the street, and arriving police cars clogged the road.

Fitcher shut off the flashing lights as we passed Key West City Hall. He picked up speed as he hurried down Simonton to United Street, where he turned left.

"I don't know what to expect." Fitcher let out a deep breath. "This whole operation has gone to hell in a handbasket."

"You said the drugs are here?" It had to be the *paco* that came on the go-fasts.

"That's what my caller said."

He turned right onto White Street, then left on Flagler Avenue and after passing Bertha Street, he put on the flashing

351

lights and punched the gas pedal as the avenue became a four-lane road. Key West High School was a blur as we passed.

"How did they find us?" I wondered aloud.

"Could have followed me from the base." Fitcher sighed. "Probably my fault."

"The JIATF guys thought they'd be protecting the drugs."

"I did too." He kept his eyes on the road. "Damn Colombians, you can't depend on them."

"Who's watching the warehouse?" I wanted to get back to R.L.

We were passing Kennedy Drive. The light was red, so he hit the siren, slowed down a little, and then picked up speed again after the intersection.

"DEA," he said, keeping his eyes on the road. "Richard is supposed to be coming with the sheriff's SWAT team."

"Wouldn't it be nice if they were all there?" I thought after everything that had happened, maybe I was going to run into some good luck. I was mistaken.

"Put an end to the whole mess, which would be nice." He slowed down, blasted the siren again, ran the red light and turned left onto South Roosevelt Boulevard, and then turned right over the Cow Key Channel Bridge, and we were on US-1 on Stock Island.

He knew his way around the neighborhood, because he didn't slow down when he turned right on Cross Street, and we flew by the working-class trailers that fill Stock Island. He blasted through the stop sign at Fifth Avenue, made a screeching left, ran the stop sign at Fifth Street and swerved right onto Shrimp Road.

Fitcher slowed the car to twenty mph and shut off the flashing lights. "Are you armed?"

"Yes."

He pulled into the empty parking lot of the old shrimp-boat

docks. The long-forgotten icehouse showed its age and hung out over the murky black water of Safe Harbor Channel, one of the deepest ports in the Lower Keys.

"I didn't know his warehouse was off Safe Harbor." I scanned for any sign of activity.

"I followed the directions as they gave 'em." He shut off the car's engine and checked his handgun. "Something's wrong. If it were over with, there'd be crime-scene tape. Hell, there'd still be evidence people here."

"We wait?" I pulled my Glock.

"I check it out." He got out of the car, leaving the keys in the ignition.

I looked across the water and heard the breakfast crowd at the Hog Fish Bar and Restaurant. I could smell the aroma of frying eggs and greasy beacon and sausage. I was almost as hungry as I was tired, and the aromas were a reminder I hadn't eaten in a while.

"It's gotta be the wrong warehouse." I got out of the car.

"I suppose I could've misunderstood," he mumbled. "Looks deserted. You wait here."

"I've been in the place before." I remembered the times I'd bought fresh shrimp at the small indoor retail store. "See the ramp?"

I pointed to the weathered ramp that ran the length of the rickety warehouse. The metal loading doors were rolled down. "That small door at the water end leads into the icehouse offices."

"How many offices?" He walked slowly, his gun hanging down by his side.

"A small retail store to the right, then three doors on the left to offices. They look over the shrimp docks."

"Are there any windows we can look through?"

"Nothing on the land side."

353

"I guess we try the door." He stifled a laugh and walked up the ramp.

I stayed close, my Glock at my side. This part of Safe Harbor was quiet, and the breeze blowing across the water carried hints of old fish. The shrimp boats were out, so the harbor was empty and clean. The marina on the other side of the Hog Fish held houseboats, but you couldn't see them from where we were. The sky was a bright morning blue and cloudless.

Fitcher stopped outside the door and turned to me. "Precautions save lives," he almost whispered. "You stay here."

"I know the layout."

"I don't need you shooting a homeless person," he grumbled quietly.

"I won't shoot first."

He shook his head, as if telling me I was a fool. Then he turned the doorknob, and the door opened inward. Fitcher waited. He raised his handgun and inched slowly into the dim hallway.

I followed. He stopped at the first door and listened. The faint sound of classical music played from somewhere in the old building. Fitcher tapped his ear and I nodded.

He pointed to the door and shook his head, telling me he didn't think it came from there. He walked to the second door and listened and used hand signals to tell me to stay where I was.

I didn't move. I tried to listen, to see if the music came from the icehouse's main room. It could have, I wasn't sure.

Fitcher reached for the doorknob, turned it, raised his handgun and pushed the door inward. Light spilled out. I raised my Glock and moved toward the block of light, only to discover it spilled across the room from a large window. The room was empty. Fitcher raised one finger, indicating the next door. I nodded.

He followed me out into the hallway. We could still hear the music.

"Has to be coming from in there," he whispered.

I nodded my agreement.

"If anyone is going to shoot, it will be me, understand?" Even his whispers were orders.

I nodded again.

Fitcher turned the doorknob gently and then pushed the door open. It banged against the wall and came back to hit him on the shoulder. He stood there for a moment and then walked in. Bright light spilled out into the hallway and classical music came with it.

"Good morning," he said.

I walked to the doorway, my Glock raised. R.L. Beaumont sat at a table on the outdoor deck, drinking a *café con leche,* and the room smelled of the strong coffee. He had a silly grin on his face. There were no weapons on the table or in his hands. He pushed his chair back but didn't stand, and drank coffee.

"Murphy, you fucked up a perfectly good plan," he said with a smile. "You and your boat bum friends have cost me a lot."

I turned to Fitcher, who hunched his shoulders. I walked into the room.

"Sorry, R.L., but it's over." I stood less than twenty feet from the man who had been trying to kill me.

I heard him laugh, and then felt the first bullet hit me in the back before I heard the retort. The impact forced me forward. I almost lost my balance, and then I heard and felt the second shot. I stumbled and dropped my gun. The third shot put me down.

355

Seventy-Six

I hurt so bad I couldn't move. I thought of the times in Central America when my legs cramped from all-night jungle marches during guerrilla wars I covered, or when tropical bugs whose names I couldn't even pronounce bit me and I swelled up or itched insanely, and the time I fell down a muddy Nicaraguan hillside, clutching my camera bag while sliding over rocks and shrubs, bruising myself black and blue, and now I realized none of that was pain. Discomfort, yes, but pain was what I was feeling while I lay helpless on the icehouse floor.

I was face down and tasted blood, not a good sign. The pain kept me from moving my arms or legs and then I remembered the cause. I had been shot. Three times in the back. My eyes were open, but my vision was blurry. I tried to blink it away. I remembered I was wearing the bulletproof vest Charlie Thompson had given me on the boat, and I was elated because I knew the bullets had not torn into me. I wasn't going to bleed to death, paralyzed on the floor. The pain would lessen and eventually go away, while death from gunshots never got better.

I heard muffled sounds, people talking. No, they weren't talking. They were arguing. My whole upper body ached when I tried to breathe normally, so I took shallow breaths. I tried to focus on the argument. When I realized it was R.L. and Reed Fitcher, my elation about the vest vanished. I suddenly understood how a manic-depressive felt.

What were they arguing about? Where was my Glock? It had

to be behind me, since I seemed to be in the middle of the room and I remembered falling forward as I came through the door. More bad news. As I focused on the argument, the words became clear. Getting my hearing back was a good thing, I told myself.

Were they arguing over who was going to shoot me? Helpless as I felt, I wasn't ready to give up and die without a fight. Of course, I couldn't move, the pain was so bad, and that pretty much eliminated my making a mad dash through the opened patio door and into the water to escape.

The louder R.L. and Fitcher argued, the more I was able to understand. It had to do with money and why R.L. had moved it. Someone banged down on what sounded like a wooden table or desk; it must have been Fitcher, because R.L. laughed.

"It's done, Reed." R.L. was unsympathetic. "And there's no way I can undo it."

"God damn it, R.L., we were supposed to be a team," Fitcher shouted. "You shouldn't have done it without talking to me. How can you expect me to leave my family behind?"

"That's what we agreed to back in college," R.L. shrieked.

"Forty years ago, damn you." Fitcher was agitated. "Things change. I have kids and grandkids. I could've retired and no one would've known."

"You know as well as I do, after this fiasco they would have found the offshore account and confiscated it and connected it to you. Then we would have had nothing. Is that what you want?"

"If you had talked to me, there had to be something I could've done."

"They can't find the account now. It's in Panama, and soon it will be in Brazil. Come on vacation," R.L. said, taking control of his emotions. "We can set up your new account then."

Fitcher sighed. "Jesus, I am tired of this, R.L. You ever wonder about it?"

"Do you?"

"Sometimes," Fitcher mumbled.

"Your cut is ten million. Not a bad retirement package," R.L. said. "Think about that instead of your fuckin' bleeding heart. You can't go back, so get over it."

"You're right," Fitcher muttered. "This was our last deal, and it failed."

"This is our only failure, as far as I'm concerned," R.L. huffed, anger in his words.

"I guess we've had setbacks before."

"Yeah, and after a few years of the good life in Brazil, we'll consider this a setback, too."

"I hope you're right," Fitcher sighed.

"What's wrong, now?"

Fitcher didn't answer right away. "Isabel and the kids," he finally mumbled, and it was hard for me to hear him. "When all this comes out, what are they going to think of me?"

"Who gives a good goddamn?" R.L. said. "You've got ten million reasons not to fuckin' care."

"But I do, R.L.," Fitcher whimpered. "I didn't know how much until now."

R.L. laughed, and it was so sardonic, it frightened me. "What am I going to do with you, old friend?"

Fitcher didn't reply, or if he did, it was a whisper, because I didn't hear it.

"Can I show you something that might help?" R.L. said calmly, and that was as scary as his laugh.

"I don't think there's anything you can say or do that will change the way I feel," Fitcher said.

"I know there is," R.L. assured him.

I heard a drawer open. Then a gunshot exploded and I

couldn't control my body's spasms. A second shot followed, and the smell of cordite was strong. I forced my legs to bend and my arms to straighten and made myself sit up. The pain stayed in my back, but my legs worked and my vision cleared. Fear can be a great incentive.

"Where the hell do you think you're going, Murphy?" R.L. laughed in a scary, heartless tone.

I turned away from the opened patio door, my only escape route. Fitcher lay on his back, blood pooling around his large body. R.L. stood about ten feet away, maybe fifteen from me. Even I could hit something that close, and he held the menacing revolver, while my Glock was at the hallway door.

Fitcher gave a soft cry and squirmed on the floor. He was still alive. R.L. moved closer and looked down at his old friend. He raised the revolver and shot Fitcher in the head. I closed my eyes as I saw his finger tighten on the trigger. Because I knew it was coming, the retort sounded louder than the first two.

"Did you hear me try to get him to change his mind?" R.L. said calmly.

I opened my eyes. The top of Fitcher's head was gone. Splattered brain and blood filled the area around him. Even with the stink of cordite, I could smell the coagulating blood's sick sweetness.

"Did you, Murphy?" he bellowed.

I flinched, and it embarrassed me that he saw my fear.

"I heard you," I mumbled, half in surrender. "Why kill him? You could have just left him here."

R.L. walked to the patio door and closed it. So much for my mad dash to the water.

"He was my friend," he said, as if it was supposed to make sense to me, and leaned against the glass door. "This whole mess is your fault." He looked at Fitcher's body. "We were going to get rich on this deal, and both of us were going to retire."

I didn't reply, but moved my legs and arms a little, to make sure they would work in case I had the opportunity to rush him.

"If I'd left him here, they would have discovered his connection to me," he mumbled, more to himself than me, "eventually. We went to FIU together and that would've come out."

"Why care?" I tried to straighten my back, but the pain was too much. "You would've been in Brazil with his ten million."

"Ah," he smiled cruelly, "you did hear." He moved away from the glass door. "He wouldn't have done well in prison."

"So you killed him?"

"You wouldn't understand," he said, smirking. "Why aren't you dead?" He walked over, his revolver pointed at my head.

He stared at me, more than an arm's length away, and kept the cruel smile. Then he circled around, careful to avoid Fitcher's blood. He stopped at the wooden desk.

"Take the shirt off," he ordered with a laugh.

I hesitated and he raised the revolver.

"I'm a good shot," he said.

I unbuttoned my shirt, my arms aching and my back screaming as I removed it.

R.L. laughed at seeing the bulletproof vest. "Dumb luck, Murphy, you should've bought a Lotto ticket this morning. Take it off."

I hesitated, but knew it was only for my pride. I undid the Velcro wraps, fighting tears from the pain in my back. I didn't want him to think he was frightening me that much. I stretched my left arm, pulled the vest down, and stopped halfway because I caught a glimpse of Padre Thomas at the hallway door.

"Off," R.L. shouted.

I turned toward R.L., to keep him focused on me. I didn't want to get Padre Thomas shot, too.

"I don't think it will fit you," I said as the vest came off. I tossed it to my right.

"I don't need it." He smirked. "I have the gun."

"Now what?" I wanted him looking at me. I secretly prayed Padre Thomas wasn't alone, or at least that he'd made a cell-phone call for help.

"I'm going to kill you," he laughed scornfully. He checked his wristwatch. "But I don't know how. You've fucked up my life, so I should do the same to yours."

I thought to myself that killing me would certainly do that. What more could he want?

"How do you expect to get away, with everyone looking for you?" I said, trying to keep control of my nervousness. I saw Padre Thomas hunkered down outside at the doorway.

"My plane is fueled and ready," he said. "Didn't know I flew, did you? No one does and that's why I'll get away."

"You'll walk away from your family? Everything here?" God, I prayed silently, have Padre Thomas call for help.

"Not hard, Murphy, because my whole life here has been for convenience." He sat on the desktop. "The people are sheep," he said. "I gave 'em a little as a city commissioner, keep their taxes low, and after that they'd kiss my ass looking for a little more. They'd do anything I wanted. I wanted something from the cops, I'd get it because they couldn't see past me." He spoke with a grin so wide I realized he was enjoying himself, and I hoped it bought me time. "I wanted something passed on the agenda, I'd get it. I've fooled the fools for years."

"Until now," I said. "They know, now."

"Too little, too late," he scoffed. "By sunset I will be in Mexico, tomorrow Panama."

"And you'll be rich. That include Fitcher's money?" I hoped it would keep him talking.

"What do you think I should do with his share? Maybe send it to his family? Feed the hungry of Key West?" He laughed.

"Fuck you, Murphy, I am going to spend every penny and enjoy doing it."

As he spoke, I caught a glimpse of Padre Thomas picking up my Glock. What the hell was he going to do with it? The last person I wanted to see with a gun in his hands was Padre Thomas.

Seventy-Seven

"How am I going to do you, Murphy?" R.L. stood away from the desk as he thought about my fate.

"Well," I said, hoping to keep his attention away from the doorway, "since you shoot your friends, maybe you should let your enemies go."

"No brass ring." He mocked my attempt at gallows humor. "You know, I may give you the opportunity to live."

"I'd appreciate that." I forced myself up and I thought the pain would kill me as it ricocheted through my back.

"And what do you think you're doing now?" he shouted.

"I'm not a dog on your floor, I'm standing up." I almost lost my balance and stumbled back, stopping at the locked patio door. "Not an easy task, thanks to your friend."

I glanced over at the office doorway. My gun was gone and so was Padre Thomas. I must have smiled, because R.L. responded.

"And you think that's funny?" He raised his hand with the gun.

"I didn't know it showed."

"You think the cavalry is coming?" He looked from me to the open doorway.

"No," I said quickly, then, "Yes, I expect people to show up because they know everything about you, so this warehouse can't be too big a secret."

He gave a sardonic cackle and I knew he was going to kill me, and there seemed little I could do about it.

"Murphy, Murphy, Murphy," he repeated scornfully and sat on the desktop. "No one knows about this warehouse or my plane. So no one is coming to save you."

"We'll see, because I think you're wrong," I mumbled.

"You think you've got the time to wait and see?" This was funny to him. It was buying me time. "You don't, and there's no cavalry, so you can stop looking for help to come through that door." He got up and walked toward it.

"Okay, so no one's coming," I yelled and hoped he would stop.

R.L. turned to show me the revolver, but kept walking. He got to the door, turned and grinned at me as he walked into the hallway. The moment of silence was torturous. I was sure he'd shoot Padre Thomas on sight.

He laughed as he came back into the room. "No Yankee blue coats." His face got serious as he scanned the floor.

"Where's your gun?" He wasn't laughing now, he was concerned.

I looked at the floor and hunched my shoulders. "Your good friend must have fallen on it."

He thought about that, without moving. "You didn't have time to pick it up. You couldn't move that quickly," he said more to himself than to me. "Okay." He accepted that Fitcher had fallen on it.

"As I was saying, I am going to give you an opportunity to live," he said with a smile. "I've seen Cluny and his Colombians do this. Want to know what it is?"

"If it gives me a chance to live, yeah." I looked over his shoulder and saw Padre Thomas in the doorway holding my Glock. I moved a little to my right, placing myself by the center of the patio door.

"First, I'm gonna shoot you in each knee. Know why?"

"To keep me from getting away," I said coldly, because I

didn't want him to turn away.

"Good." He smiled. "Then I shoot you in each elbow and then in both shoulders. Know why?"

"Because you're a cruel bastard?"

"Yeah, well, there is that, but no." He kept the silly smile and I knew he was enjoying himself. "Then I gut shoot you. You're still alive, trust me on that, I've seen it done."

"It won't insult you too much if I don't trust you, will it?"

"No insult taken." He walked to about ten feet from me. "You are going to bleed to death, Murphy, slowly, and while you're dying, I want you to remember why."

"Because I didn't want drugs killing the kids of Key West?" It was my turn to smile and somehow I managed to, because I saw the anger on his face.

"No, you asshole, because you messed with me," he yelled.

"Where's my opportunity to get out of this alive, if I'm bleeding to death on the floor?" I wanted Padre Thomas to hear this and run. He didn't run.

"The cavalry, Murphy, that you are so sure will swoop in at the last minute and save your sorry ass. If you're right, you could live. I think you'll bleed to death before anyone finds you."

"I don't think so." I stood as straight as I could. "Padre, you have to shoot him." I watched as Padre Thomas moved a few feet closer to R.L. If he didn't shoot him, and I didn't think he would, R.L. would hear him and then we'd both be dead.

"The old priest?" he snickered. "That the best you can do? And as I turn to find no one there, you do what, Murphy? You charge me, wrestle my gun away?"

"Padre," I pleaded, "if you don't shoot him, he's gonna kill us both. Just pull the trigger."

R.L. laughed. Shaking his head, he turned, and I wish I could have seen the expression on his face when he saw Padre Thomas.

"You old fool," R.L. yelled and stepped toward him.

I began to move, hoping I could at least tackle R.L. before he could shoot, but stopped in mid-motion when I heard a shot. I had every bad thought possible in less than a second, and then a tear opened on R.L.'s back and blood oozed out.

I looked past R.L., and the pain I saw on Padre Thomas's face was a million times worse than what I felt. He dropped my Glock and I swear I saw tears in his eyes.

"Pray for me, Mick," he sobbed, and his thin body trembled. He turned and walked away.

"Padre, don't go," I yelled, but it did no good. He was gone.

R.L. turned, still holding his revolver in one hand. With the other hand, he tried to stop the blood from trickling out his stomach.

"No . . . no . . . no," he repeated as he pulled his bloody hand away and looked at it. He took two steps and went down next to Fitcher, but he caught himself and ended in a sitting position in his friend's blood, holding his revolver. Blood brothers to the end, I thought.

He looked up at me with an enraged glare, his eyes bulging, and made me realize how close I was to evil. Padre Thomas had been right: there had been an evil in Key West.

The outside door banged opened and I expected to see Padre Thomas leading sheriff's deputies into the room.

"Mick!" I heard Norm call my name.

"In here," I yelled. "The third door."

Norm, followed quickly by Richard, entered the room, guns in hand. Richard's short list of officers pushed them forward and soon the room was full.

"You okay?" Norm asked.

One of the Key West Police officers bent down and took R.L.'s pulse.

"Weak but there," he said and used his radio to call for

paramedics. He looked at Fitcher's head and didn't bother to search for a pulse.

"I'm fine," I sighed. "Where's Padre Thomas?"

"Was he with you?" Norm looked around the room.

"No, no," I mumbled. "I mean, he was here. He shot R.L."

Norm and Richard looked strangely at me.

"Mick," Richard said, smiling, "we were at the ramp door when we heard the shot. The priest didn't come out and he wasn't in the hallway. No one was."

"It can't be," I sighed. "He just dropped the gun and walked away."

Sirens filled the parking lot. Sheriff Chance Wagner walked through the door, followed by two paramedics.

"You shoot the commissioner?" He looked down at Fitcher. "That the DEA guy?"

The paramedic checked R.L. and shook his head, telling us he was dead.

"Take him to the hospital anyway," Chance ordered. "This is still my jurisdiction, right?" He looked at Richard.

Richard smiled. "Don't be an ass."

"Have you made up a story yet? Another fairy tale? I'm all ears." Chance opened the sliding glass door and beckoned Richard to join him.

Norm came along with me. I leaned against the railing and began with Fitcher picking me up at the Mango Tree Inn, and ended with Padre Thomas shooting R.L., dropping the gun and walking away.

"But no one saw the priest?" Chance's quizzical expression said it all. He didn't believe me, either.

Richard shook his head.

"He could've been in one of the other rooms; we didn't check them," Norm said, with a look that suggested he was trying to help me.

"It's not a problem." Chance smiled. "FDLE can pull prints from your gun and we'll know who fired it. My crime-scene people will swab your hands, make sure it wasn't you."

If I had fired it, they would find gunpowder residue on my hands. I knew they wouldn't.

"Chance," Richard chided him with his tone. "This isn't murder."

Chance looked as the paramedic stood over R.L., who was now in a body bag. Other paramedics came in and studied Fitcher. Crime-scene people from the sheriff's office waited for instructions.

"Yeah, well, I got a dead city commissioner and DEA agent and one live, black-hearted journalist," he sighed. "I'm going to have officials from Key West and Miami demanding answers, and I want to make sure I have them."

One of Richard's officers brought in the bulletproof vest and handed it to him.

"Three shots in the back." Richard held the vest up for Chance to examine.

"You want to go to the hospital to get checked out?" Chance asked. "I need to take you in for questioning."

"I want my attorney." I looked at Norm, hoping Tita was okay.

Chance smiled. "I wouldn't expect anything less from you, Murphy."

We walked out of the icehouse to the full parking lot. At least I wasn't wearing handcuffs.

SEVENTY-EIGHT

The seagulls squawked as they dove into the water for breakfast scraps boaters tossed overboard, while pelicans splashed into the bight for mangrove snappers that also fed off the scraps. Otherwise, Garrison Bight was quiet, because the charter boats were out and everyone with a job had left the marina. US-1 Radio played from the cabin of the *Fenian Bastard,* because Tita and I wanted to hear what newsman Bill Becker had to say about R.L. and Fitcher during his noon report. We sat on deck drinking *café con leches* delivered earlier from Sandy's Café on White Street. We had ordered breakfast, too, but ate it quickly.

"I feel like a rainy day," Tita said between sips, and watched the dark clouds move in off the Atlantic. "Don't you?" She was talking about herself, not the coming weather.

Sheriff Chance Wagner's detectives questioned me for an hour before Tita arrived yesterday, wearing her arm in a sling and looking like someone's old laundry. She still looked beautiful to me. Two hours later, we were headed to Garrison Bight. It would be weeks before her house was habitable, so my sailboat was going to be home for a while.

Chance had kept Richard out of my interrogation, for spite. He wouldn't even consider allowing Norm into the sheriff's offices. But that was yesterday, and it was over. Well, kind of over.

"I would've slept longer, if it had been raining." My *con leche* was gone.

We had both slept more than twelve hours and were still

369

tired, at least mentally.

Norm and Richard hailed us from the dock. They carried care packages of *con leches* and egg sandwiches on Cuban bread.

"You expecting company?" Tita took one bag and cup carrier from Richard.

"I guess we both had the same thought," Richard said and climbed on deck.

"Thought you'd be hungry." Norm left his cowboy boots on the dock and climbed on board, balancing his bag of sandwiches and tray of hot drinks.

"We come bearing gifts and news." Richard smiled. "You're not hungry?"

"We ate." I reached for a *con leche*. "Two sugars?"

Richard nodded. "I've been up since the wee hours with DEA agents from Washington and Miami." He took a long drink from the coffee. "There will be a press conference in Miami"—he looked at his wristwatch—"at four today."

"Why Miami and not here?" Tita mixed her fresh *con leche* in the cup she was drinking from.

"Media coverage was the reason the DEA gave." Richard sat down. "But they are gonna put this all on R.L., and they didn't want to be in Key West when they do."

"Am I going to like this?" I sat up, and my back reminded me why I was lounging around the cockpit of my boat.

"Probably not, hoss." Norm bit into an egg sandwich.

"Chance called in some favors from FDLE for the fingerprint check," Richard sighed between sips and talking. "Your prints were the only ones on the Glock."

"No residue on my hands." I stretched my right hand toward him, as if it proved something.

"No Padre Thomas, either. No fingerprints, anywhere. I had a tech dust the hallway, the door handles, everything, Mick." Richard tried to smile as he spoke.

"What's the offer?" Tita spoke in her attorney's voice.

"Chance and I will be at the press conference," Richard said and stood up. "The DEA will announce that with our cooperation their agents broke up a drug distribution ring in Key West. During the apprehension of local and Colombian suspects, a DEA agent was killed by a city commission member and suspect, who in turn was killed by an investigative journalist."

I almost choked on my drink. "You're shittin' me, right?"

"Fitcher had more than twenty years, they're protecting him." Richard leaned against the wheel. "His wife will get his pension."

"It's done, Mick." Norm hunched his shoulders. "They protect their own. Hell, I cover the ass of my people. And when your friends stole Tom's ashes, you covered for them."

Richard shook his head, not wanting to hear more.

"The son of a bitch shot me three times in the back," I yelled. "He's going out a hero?"

They didn't reply.

"And I've gotta live with the rep of the guy who killed R.L.?" My back hurt.

"Mick, the evidence is there. It was your gun, and Chance figures you had on gloves when you shot it."

"Do you think that, Richard?"

"I am only glad that I don't have to evaluate the evidence, Mick," he said. "If there was anything reliable that indicated someone else pulled the trigger, I'd pounce on it."

"Charges against Mick?" Tita was protecting me.

Richard smiled. "None."

"No chances in the future?"

"They don't want to put him in the spotlight. But"—Richard hesitated—"he can't repeat the Padre Thomas story to anyone.

You shot him after he shot Fitcher, and you need to stick to that."

"What was he doing there?" She was always looking after me.

"What he does best, getting in the way so he could get a story." Richard was paying more attention to Tita than me. "I have to run, there's a plane taking us to Miami." He turned to me. "We good with this?"

I looked at Tita. "Are we?"

"What if we aren't?" She stared at Richard.

"Then Mick's a suspect in the murder of a popular city commissioner and veteran DEA agent, not to mention what happened at Harpoon Harry's and the cemetery," Richard recited. "JIATF won't come to your rescue, so forget that. They don't know who you are. I already talked to Admiral Bolter. With Norm's background, I'm not sure how he'd hold up on the stand in Miami, if he'd even take the stand. So, Tita, that leaves Mick's word against the evidence and as those CSI TV shows have proven, evidence doesn't lie."

"Mick, let it go," she advised with a sad stare. "I couldn't help you. You'd need Nathan."

"It's bullshit, you know that," I screeched.

They said nothing, again.

"Let it go, Mick," Norm finally said. "The dead are dead, and you did a good thing. You set out to stop R.L. and he's as stopped as he can be."

"Half the island is gonna hate me," I mumbled, defeated.

"Yeah, but the other half is going to love you," Richard laughed. "I'm good to go?"

"Did you find his airplane?" I needed some good news.

"DEA found it." Richard smiled. "He had a million dollars in cash, bank books from a Panamanian bank and other records."

"Like accomplices?" It was my turn to smile.

"We know the plane is registered to Fernando Paz. The Feds

are investigating this and have already brought Fernando and some others in for questioning."

Paz was a longtime city director, who had worked his way up to city manager. I whistled. "There's gotta be a long line between R.L. and Fernando."

"Yeah." Richard smiled wider. "Expect the headlines to use 'Bubba bust.' "

"Try not to mention my name too often this afternoon." I stood and we shook hands.

Richard said his good-byes and left. Norm watched him walk up the dock and then used his cell phone.

"Come on down," he said and closed the phone. "I spent most of the night trying to find your Padre Thomas." Norm finished his sandwich and went for a second *con leche*. "Jim Ashe was some help, and you might not like what we found, either."

Seventy-Nine

"I didn't shoot Padre Thomas, too, did I?" I reached for another *con leche* and winced a little.

Jim Ashe walked down the dock and greeted us as he climbed aboard. He looked at Norm, who nodded, and Jim sat down.

"I heard," he said, "about the DEA decision. Sorry I can't help you."

"I understand," I lied. I guess I did understand, but I didn't like it. "Hey, we accomplished what we set out to do and I ain't going to jail."

Even Tita faked a laugh and we all shared an uncomfortable minute.

"Did the Coasties get the drugs?"

"No," Jim mumbled. "They either made it in without us noticing them, or, as some figure, they headed to the Bahamas after the fiasco at Cay Sal. I'm thinking the Bahamas."

That was disappointing news I could've done without. At least the *paco* was found in R.L.'s warehouse and it would not be on local streets.

"Jim never dealt with Padre Thomas," Norm began, and I didn't see this leading in a direction of my liking, "so he was impartial."

Tita and I were quiet.

"You know what I tell you is off the record?" Jim looked between Tita and me. "Most of the information I found doesn't exist, you understand what I'm saying?"

374

Tita and I nodded.

"I'm reciting from memory, so I'm ninety-nine-percent sure I've got it right and Norm can correct me if he needs to," Jim said. "Father Thomas Collins is, or was, a Jesuit missionary in Guatemala. Twelve years ago next month, he disappeared. No notes, no word to his superiors in Guatemala City or Washington. He was replaced about six months later and that missionary also disappeared. Government death squads were thought to be responsible, but there was no proof. After peace between the government and rebels was established, the Jesuits sent another missionary, who still works in the area."

Jim bit into a cold egg sandwich. "Norm?" he said between bites.

"Go on."

"Last year, an OAS team of archeologists, working with the Guatemalan government to unearth possible mass graves, found one outside the village where Collins's mission had been. They unearthed a couple of dozen bodies. One was wearing the remnants of a priest's collar and had rosary beads in his hand. The Jesuits believe the body is that of Collins."

"Why not the other priest?" I knew Padre Thomas was alive.

"Dental records are being checked, but the priest was beaten around the head and most of his teeth were gone." Jim looked toward Norm and then went on. "The age of the victim fits Collins and that's what the Jesuits are going on."

"You met him." I looked to Norm. "Coco Joe, one of your guys, knew him in Guatemala and he recognized him here."

"I called a contact," Norm mumbled and hesitated. "He knew some of the Guatemalan death squads and got back to me a little while ago."

It seemed even the seagulls and pelicans waited for Norm to go on because it became very quiet.

"The head of the death squads hated the priest because he

had embarrassed his men a week or so prior, and he personally shot him in the head. His written report stated that the priest's rosary beads couldn't save him this time. Sounds like the story Joe told you, doesn't it?" Norm sat down and looked tired.

"They have written reports?" I don't know why that surprised me.

"No," Norm lied. "There are no written reports."

"Okay," Tita interrupted, "let's, for argument's sake, say what you have is fact. Who is our Padre Thomas and how'd he fool Coco Joe?"

"Somehow, he stole the dead priest's identity," Norm said.

"Why?" I asked.

"He could have a criminal background and figured a priest was a good cover, and down here in this hellhole, it worked. Maybe it got him out of Guatemala and he decided to keep the con going."

"What about his angels?" I said. "You and I have seen him do unexplainable things." How could anyone explain what he knew about Tijuana? I would have to ask Norm when we were alone.

"A good con. Mick, identity theft is a major problem these days."

"I've known Padre Thomas ten years. He's always had his angels, and what about the stipend he gets from the Jesuits?"

"They deny it," Jim said. "I have friends in Washington with relationships at the highest level of the order. Mick, understand that this was done quickly and there's certainly room for error, but to be totally wrong about the priest is unlikely. On the other hand, we're beating a dead horse, here. You'll be the pride of the media for a couple of days, and then this will go away. Your friend Kram got what he needs about R.L., and most of it will support your protecting yourself when you shot him."

"It doesn't explain what I saw or how Padre Thomas fooled Coco Joe." I stood up and looked toward the stern. "It doesn't explain the things I learned from him during the past ten years."

"It's the best I can do, Mick." Jim shook my hand. "Maybe he hid in the warehouse until this was all over. Maybe he'll show up today or tomorrow and have all the answers."

"Where is he now?" Norm asked. "No one has seen him since he left the inn yesterday morning. And for Joe, it's been years since they met. The similarities were there, and it fooled him. He wanted Thomas to be alive after all these years."

"I've seen him." I reminded them. "I know he was there and shot R.L."

"You know what I know, now," Jim said, ignoring my comment. "I look forward to that drink when you're up and about." He smiled. "And bring Tita, she's better company than you."

"I have a question for you," he said as he was about to jump to the dock. "You know an old salt named Robert Murdock?"

"Doesn't ring a bell. Why?"

"Would you know a Captain Maybe?" he laughed.

"Yeah, that's Murdock?"

"He got towed into Havana yesterday. Some people are going to want to talk to him when he gets back. You should let him know." Jim walked up the dock to the parking lot.

I didn't bother telling him Captain Maybe wouldn't be back.

"How long are you staying?" I sat back down.

"I'm at the Pier House through the weekend."

"Suite?"

"Same one as last time." He smiled. "Lonely in there."

"We're comfortable here," Tita said.

"You feel like a good dinner tonight?"

"Not too late." I was tired. "Clint Bullard is filling in, since Coco Joe's band is gone, and he's offstage at nine."

"Nine at the Ocean Key House, Hot Tin Roof restaurant?"

Tita nodded her approval.

"We'll see you there."

377

Norm kissed Tita on the cheek, which surprised me, and then climbed down to the dock.

"There's another explanation about Padre Thomas you are not considering," he grunted as he pulled his boots on.

"What's that?"

"You believe in the angels?"

I nodded. "Sometimes it's the logical answer."

"Well, if Padre Thomas is Padre Thomas and if he was murdered in Guatemala, maybe he's your guardian angel." He spoke seriously, but Tita couldn't hear him. "God knows, during the last few years he has kept your ass out of the fire." He laughed to himself. "Think about it, hoss."

He swaggered up the dock as the first raindrops began to fall.

Tita hugged me as I watched Norm walk away. The sky was dark and it was going to be a heavy rain.

"What's he laughing about?" She kept her arms wrapped around me.

"He thinks Padre Thomas is my guardian angel." I returned her hug. "Think we have enough sense to get in out of the rain?"

"It feels good," she giggled. She sat down and turned her head toward the clouds, letting the rain soak her. "We could see him, and he said the living couldn't see angels," she said, seriously considering Norm's comments.

Lightning flashed off in the distance. A few seconds later, thunder boomed, and I wondered about Padre Thomas and the angels.

"I don't think Padre Thomas is dead," I said while the rain beat down on us. "I saw his expression after he shot R.L. It was pure terror. He saved my life, but lost a part of his."

The wind picked up and a patch of blue sky showed off over the Gulf of Mexico, even though the wind was blowing the rain clouds in that direction.

"I think he's in seclusion somewhere, maybe a church," I said.

"I can almost hear him laughing about all this." Tita smiled, still looking skyward.

"I can hear him too," I said. And when the next thunder boom cracked the air, I heard him crying, but didn't tell Tita.

ABOUT THE AUTHOR

Michael Haskins lives in the Florida Keys. He has worked as the business editor/writer for the daily *Key West Citizen* and for the City of Key West as its public information officer. He freelances for Reuters News Service and other local papers and is almost finished with his third book in this series, *Car Wash Blues*. When the hurricane season is over, he often sails on his thirty-six-foot sloop, *Mustard Seed*. Visit his Web site at www .michaelhaskins.net.